RUTH MOHRMAN

# Gold of Pleasure

*A novel of Christina of Markyate*

 **Cadoc Publishing**

*For Andrew, without whom this novel would never have been written*

# Contents

# Preface

## Hours of the Divine Office

*Matins:* During the night, around 2am

*Lauds:* Dawn Prayer, around 5am, earlier in summer, later in winter

*Prime:* Early morning prayer, First Hour, around 6am

*Terce:* Mid-morning prayer, Third Hour, around 9am

*Sext:* Midday prayer, Sixth Hour, around 12 noon

*None:* Mid-afternoon prayer, Ninth Hour, around 3pm

*Vespers:* Evening prayer, around 6pm

*Compline:* Night prayer, around 7pm

# Acknowledgement

Thank you to all those who have played a part in the genesis of this novel.

To Roger Ellis, PhD supervisor and friend, who fostered my interest in all things medieval.

To the members of Edgeworks writers group whose close reading and helpful criticisms of early drafts of the novel were invaluable: Norman Schwenk, Deborah Kay Davies, Jane Blank and Claire Syder.

I especially want to thank those who generously agreed to read the completed novel and offer their comments: Liz Porter, Anne Griffith, Ruth Evans and Marion Glasscoe.

Last but not least I want to thank my husband, Andrew, for his patience and unfailing encouragement in what has been a long journey.

# Chapter 1

*Hermitage de bosco*

*Seventh day of November, AD 1143*

My coming has disturbed a wood pigeon and it flies up and away, with a great clatter of wings. I lean back against the log to rest my aching hip and watch as one leaf, then another, drifts down to join its fellows on the woodland floor. The air is still here, under the canopy of beeches. Morning sunlight filters through half denuded branches, striking the carpet of russet leaves in shafts. The only sound is the rippling of the stream. I feel my breath settling after the walk, my heart beat slowing.

But now comes the crack of twigs and the crunching of leaves underfoot. I turn to see Matilda, picking her way deftly towards me through the trees. Can I not be left alone, even for a moment?

'The Abbot of St Albans is here.'

'Take him to my parlour, Matty, and send to the kitchen for some apple wine. Tell him I will come to him soon.'

1

The younger woman does not move, her composed features not quite able to mask her discomfort.

'I beg your pardon, Mistress, but Abbot Geoffrey can't stay. There are knights with him.'

We hurry back together through the beech wood. As we come out into the light of the clearing, the bell begins to sound for Terce. I turn to Matilda.

'Go to the chapel with the others. I will join you when I can.'

She curtseys, then glides away, and I cross to the kitchen block. Behind it, close by the stabling, stands Abbot Geoffrey, holding the reins of his palfrey. Three knights on coursers wait further back, their mounts circling, impatient to be off. Steam is rising from the necks of the horses.

I am shocked at how much more grey his hair has become, even in the time since I saw him last. I step forward to greet him.

'Benedicite.'

'Dominus te benedicat.' He rushes through the customary blessing, clearly agitated, his raven eyes darting from my face to the hermitage buildings, then back. 'The King has summoned me to court – I am on my way there now. He has given no reason.'

I peer pointedly behind him to the men on horseback, sheathed swords hanging from their belts, an axe blade glinting in the sun. The Abbot and I know each other so well that I do not have to spell out my question.

'I fear Stephen's fickleness,' he says in answer. 'There are those close to him who speak against me.'

'But the King held his court with you at the Abbey – just now, at Michaelmas. You have given him your support.'

2

Geoffrey shakes his head in derision. 'That's no protection. It didn't stop him from arresting Geoffrey de Mandeville and demanding his castles.'

The Abbot's face is pinched with anxiety.

'Is there more to this? Do you think Stephen suspects you of something?'

'This revolt in the fenland – it has made him angry. As soon as de Mandeville was released, he joined forces with Bishop Nigel against the King and now he has taken Ramsey Abbey.'

'But what has that to do with you?'

Geoffrey pulls his horse away from a patch of nettle. I see the frank fear in his eyes.

'Nothing.' He pauses. 'But when de Mandeville was taken, I petitioned the King on his behalf. What else could I do? It was a violation - to arrest one of his barons in the precincts of my Abbey – and while he was a guest at court.'

'How did he respond?'

'There's been no word yet. But some of Stephen's men rode into St Albans last week and demanded money. They threatened to torch the town.'

The Abbot calls for the stable boy to come and help him mount.

'Lady Christina, I beg you to pray for me, you and your maidens. The King's mind is not stable when he is roused. He sees disloyalty all around him.'

The boy stands waiting, but Geoffrey ignores him. Instead he moves closer.

'What does your spirit tell you?' His voice is strained. 'I would ride easier if you have assurance of my safe return.'

I take a deep breath and look behind me, past the stone building the Abbot built for us, to the circle of cells where my maidens sleep and on towards the curved wall of the chapel. The faintest sound of singing reaches us on the morning air. Turning back, my gaze is drawn away, beyond the Abbot and his knights, to the beech trees, swaying gently now in the breeze. They seem alive to me, quick souls relishing the rays of God's sun. The sky above stretches away: infinite, blue as the Virgin's robes, redolent with hope. In the mysterious way that I have learned to trust, a certainty is forming in me that the Abbot has nothing to fear.

Geoffrey's eyes are fixed on my face, his sharp Norman features warped by dread.

'I see nothing that need disturb you. Go, with the Almighty as your protection.'

The Abbot signs himself with the cross but still I feel fear issuing from him like sweat. I take him inwardly into the deep place of calm in my soul and hold him there. There is no danger. How can I reassure him?

'Go in peace. Today is Sunday. By Thursday, you will be back here, with good news of your audience with the King.'

He looks at me intently and now I see the strain in his face begin to ease.

'I pray you are right, Christina, as always.'

Geoffrey reaches for the horn of the saddle and the boy grasps his leg and heaves him up into place. He signals peremptorily to his men and they turn their horses towards the track that will take them back to the old Roman road. I watch him ride away. For all his commanding demeanour, I see in the Abbot the old man he will soon become. A tremor of unease passes across my own mind.

4

*Hermitage de bosco*

*Eleventh day of November, AD 1143*

'So why did the King summon you?'

Geoffrey is standing in my parlour, his back to the fire. I have offered him the chair bequeathed to me by the hermit Roger, but he is too animated to sit.

'Oh, it was nothing - nothing of consequence. Just a charter for the Bishop of Lincoln that I must witness.'

'And he was warm towards you? He harbours no suspicion about your loyalty?'

'There is no reason why he should,' he answers airily. 'I have given him no cause these whole two years - not since it became clear that the Empress's claim to the throne will come to nothing.'

I think of how fearful Geoffrey was, just a few days since, and keep my silence. His pride will not suffer a reminder of that. But it seems he is grateful to me, nonetheless.

'Christina, I came to thank you for your intercession. On the road, a course of action has been taking shape in my mind.'

The Abbot's mind is always full of schemes that will benefit the Abbey or those he needs to please. He picks up the hearth stool, brings it across, and sits down in front of me. His eyes are shining.

'I shall have an account of your life written! How you escaped your husband and the world. And it will detail all your visions. Father Thomas can do it – when he comes here to say Mass. I will instruct him to sit with you and take down everything you say.'

What is he saying? His words have sent my thoughts scattering, like a startled flock of sheep.

'I always listen to you, Christina - now you will listen to me, for once. God shares the secrets of his heart with you. He grants you to see what is in the hearts of others. Shouldn't your visions be written down for the edification of all God's people?'

'An account of my life? But it is only the saints whose lives are recorded,' I manage to say.

'Well?' Geoffrey's eyebrows are raised and a smile spreads across his face, revealing his closely-set teeth. They are discoloured now but still as good as when I first set eyes on him, nearly twenty years ago.

I stare, spellbound, as his meaning becomes clear to me. When I was a girl I loved to read saints' lives - the Life of Frideswide, of Cecilia. I remember reading her Life to Burthred and I feel my cheeks become hot.

'And besides,' he says, straightening his back, 'if we are to make your little hermitage into a Priory, we will need plenty of grants. The circulation of a Life would do our cause no harm.'

There is a knock at the door and my sister walks in, carrying a tray with cups and a jug of wine. She places it on the small table and makes as if to leave. To my consternation, Geoffrey stops her.

'I have put a course of action to your Mistress,' he says. 'If anyone can convince her, it will be you.'

Margaret looks at him, puzzled.

'I am commissioning an account of your sister's life. Do you not think it is time for her fame to spread further afield?'

I watch Margaret's eyes open wide. They switch from me

6

to Geoffrey and back again. She says nothing, only makes a gesture that might be a curtsey.

'Father Abbot,' she murmurs, turning towards the door.

I know what her silence means. She has been giving me that look of humble reproach since we were girls together in Huntingdon, in our father's house. A bubble of anger rises up inside me.

'Wait, Margaret,' I intervene. 'Have you nothing to say in answer to Abbot Geoffrey?'

She turns and regards me with those grey-blue eyes, looking more and more like our mother as the years go by. She inclines her head in Geoffrey's direction.

'If this account be the will of God, Father, it will surely be written.'

'And why should it not?' I cannot help myself. 'You know I am shown what is hidden from others. You have witnessed it many times.'

The blood is rising to my sister's face. 'I have – it's true.' She seems flustered. 'And perhaps that is enough …'

Geoffrey is on his feet now, wrapping his riding cloak around him.

'You will both see. Many will come here, and to the Abbey - drawn by your sanctity, Christina.' He smiles at Margaret. 'And that of all your community.'

My sister blushes even more at this.

'We will have to start work on a new church before long,' he says. 'The old chapel is too small.'

He wishes us both farewell and then turns to me.

'Father Thomas can come tomorrow or Saturday and begin to take down your recollections.'

He blesses us and takes his leave. No sooner is he gone

than I turn to Margaret. What did she mean: *perhaps that is enough*?

But she forestalls me, moving nimbly towards the door, the tray in her hands.

'I must take this to the kitchen. They will ring the bell for None any time now.'

The last prayers of the day are over and I send the others to their supper.

'Will you not come and eat something?' Margaret asks me. She is being especially solicitous.

'No. I will stay here and pray for a while.'

She pauses a moment but then goes to the door and opens it. It is dark outside and a keen wind slices into the chapel. The latch closes and I am left alone, the guttering candle flames throwing uneven shadows onto the rough stone walls. My predecessor, Roger, built this oratory with his own hands. He told me once that its circular shape was to remind him of the love of God, which has no beginning and no end. Thinking of this, tears start to prick at the corners of my eyes.

I sit on the bench by the wall and give myself up to the sweet sadness of my memories. It was here that the wise old man and I spent so many hours, caught up together in the chaste fire of God's love. Here that he taught me to rest in Oneness. Where he nurtured the small flame of my seeing and protected it. What I would not give to be back there with him: a pure young woman, innocent and unsullied, surrounded by friends.

The tears are falling in earnest now and I wipe them away with my fingers. It pains me to think that the Abbot will tear this chapel down and build a church, no doubt in the Norman style. Roger's simple hermitage is to become a Priory, under

Benedict's Rule and the authority of the Bishop, dependent on grants which must be sought and carefully cultivated – everything that Roger despised and tried to leave behind. And all this has happened while I have been Mistress here. How could Roger have been so wrong as to leave the hermitage to me?

My throat aches, thinking of the morning when I found him, slumped here against this very bench. And all that happened afterwards, that does not bear thinking of. And yet now, it seems, I must think of it and bring to mind all the sufferings of my youth too, and speak of them to Father Thomas.

I take a deep breath and try to compose my thoughts. *The Life of Christina of Huntingdon.* For an unworthy moment I allow myself to thrill to the notion and how it would teach my father a lesson. He would be sorry then for casting me out. But to have my life written, as if I were a saint … when that is so far from the truth. What can I tell Father Thomas? The thought makes me faint and sick. Surely the only path open now is to confess everything.

I lean back against the wall, my thoughts a tumult. But even as I consider refusing the Abbot in this matter of the book and making a true confession at last, I know in the depths of my heart that I will not do it. That, for good or ill, my fortunes are tied inextricably to Geoffrey and his belief in my purity. Undo this knot and the whole work will unravel. No. I must sit with Father Thomas and depict my life for him, from the beginning, so that he can make a tapestry of it, to be gazed on by others. I must be judicious and keep a tight rein on my mouth. I must tell enough but never all.

# Chapter 2

*Huntingdon*

*Twenty-seventh day of July, AD 1110*

The broiderer's house is by the marketplace, close to St Mary's. Like a choice nut to be squirrelled away, I save my visit there till last. There is no market today but the air is full of noise and dust, where the masons are at work on the new stone church. The walls are growing high and now they make the old wooden church look squat and mean beside them. The shopkeepers complain about the disruption but Father says it will be good for trade in the end.

The bell tinkles as I open the door and step down into Leofa's shop. She looks up from her work and greets me, wisps of dark hair escaping from under her hood. I love to come here and watch her a while. Her needle has a life of its own, flashing up and down through the cloth, so sure and fast. Today she is only working white stitches on a man's shirt but sometimes she has her coloured silk threads laid out on the trestle - mulberry and madder and indigo and silver gilt - and pearls too, for decoration. Putting the shirt down, she crosses over to the shelf, lifts down a box and places it on her worktable. She pulls off the linen covering to display the headbands inside.

I draw in my breath. The bands are of varying colours and materials, each one broidered with a different design. There are butterflies and lilies, pansies and robins, all outlined in the neatest split stitch.

'I thought you would like this,' Leofa says. She picks out a velvet one of peacock blue, with trailing morning glory worked in rich russet thread. 'This one would become you,' she says, wrapping it round my forehead and holding it there.

She leads me to the wall, to look in her mirror. Leofa keeps the copper well-burnished and I can see clearly how beautiful it looks. My braids hang down from under the headband, the thread matching the colour of my hair exactly. There is no question; I must have it. I hand the headband to Leofa and tell her I will be back before dinner to buy it.

I run out into the sunshine and across the cobbles to find my mother at the butcher's with my sister, buying a hand of pork.

'And I want you to kill me two capons,' she tells Thomas, the butcher's boy. She is fumbling for coins in her purse and takes no notice of me.

'Mother, can I have a penny?'

She looks up at me. 'What for?' she asks, her eyes narrow slits of suspicion. 'Take some of the weight from your sister.'

She thrusts a basket in my direction. Loaves, still warm from the oven, are threatening to topple out of it. 'Wyn is sick and Meg had to take the bread to be baked on her own. Where were you?'

'I've been to Leofa's. She made me this perfect headband but she wants three pennies for it and I only have two.'

My mother, Beatrix, catches my sister's eye and shakes her head, as if to lament my vanity.

'I can't spare you a penny today,' says my mother, although I can see she has plenty in her purse.

Beckoning to Margaret, she starts to walk away, but then turns back to me.

'If I had your hair, I wouldn't want to draw attention to it.'

I am smarting at her words. Just because her precious Margaret has gleaming hair the colour of butter, like hers used to be before it faded.

'I'm going to find Father,' I call out to her disappearing back but she just continues picking her way along the cobbles, keeping clear of the foul gulley.

I head for home but then remember the messenger who came last night from King's Lynn. My father's boat put into Wisbech and now it will be on its way up the Ouse to us; Father will be waiting at the wharf. I take the dyers' street down towards the river, brooding on my mother's spitefulness. There won't be time to find Father and get back to Leofa before she closes her shop for dinner.

The street is busy and a poor woman peddling plums clutches at my sleeve but I shake her off. It is a warm day and the tannery stinks to high heaven but my mood starts to lift as I come to the river. Up to my right, the castle squats on its low hill, looking down on the rows of vines in full leaf. They will be harvesting the grapes soon for the Earl's wine.

The bridgeman at the tollhouse knows me and he waves me through. I love to cross the river and look at the town from the other side. As if I were a traveller passing through on the way to London, or even a pilgrim bound for Rome or Jerusalem. Mother does not like me to walk here, especially since I have started to have my flowers every month. She fusses but I am quite safe. The men who work on the wharf would not dare to harm the daughter of Auti. Father holds more land than anyone in Huntingdon and everyone knows that, come the Feast of St James, he will be Master of the Merchant Guild.

From the bridge, I catch sight of Father on the wharf. He is standing alongside his boat, talking to the portmaster. I call and he looks up, the surprise showing on his face. The portmaster goes aboard but Father waits for me.

'What are you doing here, Dora? Did your brother not come with you?'

'Gregory? I don't know where he is.' My brother is probably out sporting with his friends, glad to be free for a day from working in the shop.

My father pretends to be cross that I have come alone, but he kisses the top of my head. I scrub at the bristly red hair on his cheek with my fingers.

'When is the barber coming again? You need a shave.'

I stand back to survey the boat. The portmaster and the ship's governor are drawing back the palling, to reveal the bales of cloth in their wrappings.

'Is it more burel?' I ask. 'Or serge for capes?'

There is always a demand for the woollen cloth my father imports from the Low Countries. But this time, it is something much more exciting.

'It's silk, all the way from Byzantium.' Father beams down at me. 'This cloth has travelled a long way. To Marseilles and Montpellier, up the River Rhone and across the sea to

Wisbech, then up the Old Wellenhee and at last along our own Ouse. What do you think of that?'

'You are a very clever man – that's what you want me to say, isn't it?' I grab him by the arm and pull him towards the landing stage. 'Can I see it? Please?'

'All right, you shall see your spangly silk. It might be the last for a while. Bruges is so silted up that soon nothing will get through.'

The sun is high as I follow him aboard. He pulls back the wrapping on a bolt of taffeta of a rich purple. The beauty almost takes my breath away. I rub my finger over its smooth surface, wondering at the glossy weight of it. He moves on, showing me a poppy red ciclaton, with coin-shaped circles of green and, best of all, a length of gleaming golden orfreis.

'Who will buy this?' I breathe.

'Most of the silk is sold already,' Father explains. 'And the rest I will sell on to the merchants in St Ives. It's all written in my orders, if you have a mind to see it.'

He is making fun of me, but I would truly like to understand how the trade works. 'Will you show me tonight, Father?'

He steps back to look at me, swaying with the movement of the boat, then shakes his head and laughs. 'You have more of a head for business than your mother, or Gregory, for that matter.'

His mention of Mother reminds me why I came. 'I wanted to buy a headband from Leofa but Mother wouldn't give me a penny for it.'

Father grins at my complaint. 'Never mind your mother. I married her because she was tight with money.' The bell of St Mary's rings for Sext as he feels in his coin pocket and hands me the penny. 'Come. It's time to go home for dinner.'

14

Father leaves Alric, his apprentice, to oversee the unloading of the boat and we walk back across the narrow bridge together. It is crowded with people and laden packhorses, but all along the way people step back to let us pass.

Father takes me up through the Jewry, where I never go on my own. He leaves me to stand and wait in the street while he goes in to see Isaac about his loan. A young boy passes, wearing the Jew's hat, but I'm not afraid of him; they say it's the women who cast spells, not the men.

The house is quiet when we get back home. 'Maybe they're already upstairs in the hall,' I say.

'The salle, not the hall.'

Father likes us to use the new French words, instead of our English ones. He pushes the door to the pantry open and starts to wash his hands.

I am right. When we climb the stairs, there they all are, at table: Gregory and Margaret, my little sister Matilda and my mother, of course. I sit on the bench next to Matilda and she screws up her nose at me and grins, while Father goes to his high-backed chair. Mother says nothing, just starts carving the capon, but I can tell she is put out that they have had to wait for us. If she is angry, why doesn't she complain to my father? I tear off some bread and dip it in the garlic sauce. I will never be like my mother or my sister Margaret, who think only of the household chores and meekly creep back into the shadows when the men come in.

Father doesn't seem to notice that the food is cold. He shares a bowl with Gregory and they discuss how much tax he will have to pay on the shipment of cloth. Mother likes to share with Margaret, so I am left to cut up Matilda's chicken and break the bread for her.

'Don't forget that Canon Sueno is coming after None,' says Mother irritably, passing the wine cup to me. 'You were so late for dinner, there will not be time for a proper rest before he comes.'

Why does she blame me? It's not my fault that Father had to stop at the moneylender's house.

It is agreeable to lie here on the bed in my inner chamber, which opens off from Mother's workroom. I can hear Margaret and Matilda whispering together next door. Beginning to be drowsy, I picture myself wearing a gown made from golden orfreis, perhaps with red velvet lining to the sleeves. That picture fades and I am back in my favourite daydream, standing in the market in Byzantium that Father has described to me so many times. It is morning, the sky is cornflower blue and the onion domes shine golden in the sun. Peddlers are calling out in their strange speech to the passers-by, all dressed in embroidered silks, the men's shoes pointed, their beards long and curled. There is no-one with red hair like mine or fair hair like my sister. Instead, they are all tall and shapely, with olive skin and black hair. Before me is a stall covered with length upon length of different silks, in every colour of the rainbow. I choose first one, then another, till my arms are full.

The bell for None wakes me and I get up from the bed, yawning. Our teacher from the Priory will be here. He is old and sometimes his breath is bad, but I still look forward to his weekly visit. Margaret may be Mother's favourite but she is not so quick at learning her Latin. Canon Sueno likes me better.

I hear him at the town door and run down to open it. The

Canon follows me up to the salle. My sisters are already there at the table and soon, Gregory joins us. He reads as well as my father, better maybe, but Sueno still gives him exercises to do, changing prose to verse, or composing letters for business.

Breathing heavily, the old man settles into my father's chair, then sets us our tasks. While we work, he closes his eyes, sipping at the herbed wine my mother has left ready for him. I finish copying out the passage he has given me but Sueno is busy helping Matilda. I rest my head on the table, on top of my arms, and start to feel sleepy again. There is something soft rubbing against my leg and I reach down to find that our tomcat, Acwel, has found his way upstairs. I stroke his thick grey fur and remember the velvet headband, waiting for me in Leofa's workshop. There may just be time, after the lesson, to get there before she bolts her door for the day.

'Very neat, Theodora.' Sueno is standing beside me, casting his eye over the dense writing on my wax. He always uses my full name.

I sit up with a start.

'Your thoughts were a long way off. What were you dreaming of?'

'My new headband,' I answer, before I've had time to think better of it. 'It goes beautifully with my hair.'

'A woman's true beauty is in her character,' he says, 'not in her dress or her baubles.'

The old man is smiling, but still I feel a tug of regret. I don't want him to be disappointed in me.

# Chapter 3

*Feast of St Leonard, sixth day of November, AD 1111*

I didn't want to come, but Father insisted that we all make pilgrimage to the Abbey of the Martyr. And now that we are on the road, I find I am curious to see the wondrous new church of Alban, after all.

'Dora! Come and look at this.'

My brother has ridden on ahead and he steadies his horse to wait, while I catch up with him. Father thinks we will not meet anyone we know out here in the wilderness so he has let me ride like a man, without a side saddle.

Beside the road, a mottled cow is lying on its side in the ditch, a filthy discharge running from its eyes and nose. Before dinner we passed two carts, piled high with dead cattle, but this one is still alive; I can see its ribs heaving.

'Murrain,' Gregory says. 'God forbid it comes to us.'

I walk Samson closer and the cow seems to stare up at me, her brown eyes full of pain. 'Can't we do anything?'

Gregory smiles but when I go to dismount, his voice sharpens.

'What are you doing? Come away, Dora.'

'Why? Can a horse catch the pest?'

I think of Samson lying dead in a ditch and move away quickly, but I fancy the eyes of the cow are following me. Despite the autumn sunshine, the day seems darker than it did before.

Gregory is walking his horse beside mine. 'What's wrong?' he asks. 'You've been in a mope ever since we set off yesterday. I thought you'd be glad to leave home for a while.'

I shrug my shoulders. 'I want to see the Abbey, but...'

'But what?' Gregory looks across at me, surprised. 'Don't you want the protection of Alban? He's a powerful saint.'

I stroke Samson's neck and listen to the clatter of his hooves on the stone. Gregory thinks in the old way, like my parents do.

'But we don't need a saint to intercede for us. We can pray to the Mother of God and to the Lord himself.'

Gregory chuckles. 'That sounds like old Sueno speaking. Did he tell you there was no need to travel to St Albans? That's because he is a canon and has no great love for the black monks.'

I shake my head. Why must Gregory spoil everything precious? He sees baseness everywhere.

'Anyway,' he goes on, 'you should be grateful. It's for your sake that Father is making us go.'

'For my sake?'

'Your birthday. Now that you are fifteen, he is looking to arrange your marriage. He wants Alban's protection for you when you are brought to bed with a child.'

My chest tightens, making it difficult to breathe. I stare across at Gregory. 'Did Father say that to you?'

'Just last night,' Gregory says. 'They are making plans.'

Mother talked about marriage in the summer but I just thought she wanted to be rid of me.

Gregory sees the anguish in my face.

'Don't be miserable. You can't stay at home forever.'

My brother does not understand anything. 'I am never going to be married.'

'What do you mean?' he asks. Then he bursts out laughing so suddenly that Samson shies away and I have to pull him back. 'It's Sueno again, isn't it? He's been filling your head with talk about holy virginity.'

Gregory no longer has instruction with Canon Sueno, but I see him every week, sometimes more than once. During the summer, we often walked outside, and he would talk to me about the shining crown that the Blessed Virgin gives to those who keep themselves chaste.

I turn on my brother. 'I have made up my mind,' I say, cool as silk, 'and nothing you say can stop me.'

He resorts to being coarse. 'I wondered why Sueno was always at our house. Holy virginity? I've seen the way he looks at you. How do you know what is going on under that habit of his?'

I dig my heel in Samson's flank. I will not listen to this. Canon Sueno is a holy man.

After a while, Gregory catches up with me and comes alongside, reaching out to touch my arm.

'I'm sure he means you no harm. But you should know how hard it is for a man to be chaste. Most men would fuck any woman they could get their hands on, even if she was a leper.'

Gregory means me no ill-will. In his own way he is trying to help me, but he is walking in darkness nonetheless. I look up at him.

'It's not too late to amend your own life.'

I nudge Samson to a faster pace. When I turn back, Gregory is staring at me but I can't read what is in his face.

Now that the horses are stabled in the town and we are on foot, I find an opportunity to walk with Father alone. I grab his arm and make him stop and look at me.

'Is it true?'

'What, Dora?'

'Gregory says you are looking for a husband for me.'

Father shakes me off impatiently but I know when he is uncomfortable.

'Look, Dora! Have you ever seen such a sight?'

I look up the hill towards the great Abbey of Alban. Father knows very well that I have never set eyes on anything like it. I can't deny it has a kind of beauty, but to me it seems to tower arrogantly over the houses and fields: a cruel, foreign presence.

'I don't care about the Abbey. Is it true?'

He sighs. 'Dora, you are fifteen years old. I cannot keep you at home much longer.'

He speaks gently but he could not have hurt me more if he had struck me with his hand.

'But who will help you with the accounts?'

'Gregory will have to do it,' he replies. 'He needs to learn.'

My feet are still carrying me towards the Abbey as if nothing had happened, but inside my life is crumbling down around me. I think of all the times I have pored over the

21

fabrics in the workshop, discussing them with Father.

He is looking at me, puzzled. 'What is it, poppet? I will find you a fine husband, who will treat you well. Don't you want to be married?'

Every word is like a fresh slap. After all, he seems to think I am only like my mother or Margaret. I need to make him understand but the words that come from my mouth sound feeble, as if I am talking of some cheap bauble rather than the pearl of great price.

'But, Father, I have decided to live chaste and win the Virgin's crown.'

He is clearly taken aback. We walk on in silence and now he turns to me.

'The life of purity is a wonderful thing, Dora.' He gives me his best smile. 'But it is not your path. Perhaps Margaret or Matilda may take the veil,' he says, 'but not you.'

'Why, Father? Why not me?'

'You are the prettiest. You are …' He is searching for words, then he grins as if I were being coquettish. 'You know what you are. You will marry well and help to bring our family back up. We need to tread a clever path under these Normans.'

I always thought he loved me better than either of my sisters. But now I see how things are, how they have always been. He is resolved. I pull a little apart from him, my heart bleeding; from now on, I will have to walk alone.

Mother is waiting for us at the great gate of the Abbey, with Margaret and Matilda. She looks at us curiously. Father takes me aside one more time.

'I will speak to your mother and we will wait a little longer but in the meanwhile you must be less with me and more with her, learning how to manage the house.'

Father squeezes my hand as if he has given me a reprieve, instead of a death sentence.

It is growing dark as we enter by the great west door. The towering height of the church and the echoing of my feet on the stone floor do nothing to lighten my heart. There are people scattered in groups throughout the nave, talking in hushed voices. A boy is making his way along the side wall, lighting the candles with a taper fixed into a long pole. As my eyes adjust to the gloom, I realize that the lower part of the wall is hung with tapestries. I move closer and in the candle light the colours begin to reveal themselves to me. I lose my sadness in the beauty, the richness of the silk thread, the gold couching. Mother has always been proud of the hanging of Jonah and the whale in our salle at home, but now I realize how rough the needlework is. I move along in a trance. The next tapestry is a village scene: green hills all around, houses and figures, each one beautifully worked. There is a young woman in a blue gown. A man is serving red wine but from a water barrel. Our Lord stands beside him, with his hand raised. It's the wedding at Cana.

I hear Gregory's voice whispering my name. 'Come on. They're clearing the chapel for us.'

For a moment, I had forgotten all about the Saint and why we have come. I follow my brother to the side chapel where the relics are housed. It is true; the other pilgrims have been turned out, leaving only my mother and father, my brother, my sisters and me. I can tell by the obsequious way the monk is behaving that my father has made a big offering. With the others, I kneel at the rail below the reliquary, hardly aware of what is being said. The vow to Alban means nothing to me. All I can think of are Father's words as we climbed the hill.

23

The air fills suddenly with sound; the ringing of the bell for Vespers from high in the tower. We are being ushered out of the chapel and through the nave. It is time for the monks to sing the hour and it seems that the pilgrims and the townsfolk must withdraw and have their service apart, in another place. Father sees a side door and goes to open it, but a monk pulls him back.

'Not that way,' he says. 'That's the door used by the brides of Christ, as they come from the almonry.'

I feel a tingling, running from the top of my head and down my spine. *The brides of Christ.* As he finishes speaking, the door is opened from the far side and there on the threshold stands a young woman in a black nun's habit, her hair tucked beneath a veil, a candle held in front of her bosom. Her skin is smooth, her eyes shining in the reflected light. She looks straight ahead as if she does not see us: the wife, not of a workman, nor a merchant or a knight, nor even of a lord, but of Christ himself. She will never stand in the shadows, serving a man, or be brought to bed in fear with the pains of childbirth. Behind her, there are more nuns waiting in line. They follow her, gliding gracefully across the nave - a train of black swans, silent and oblivious to the gaggle of townspeople moving towards the west door of the church. I watch them till the last has taken her place in the choir.

Once Vespers is over, I slip out quickly before the others have noticed, making my way through the congregation and out into the night air. I hardly heard the singing of the psalms amid the smarting pain. How could my father betray me like that?

My mind is made up. I cross to the great west door of the Abbey church. If Father wants me married, then I shall be married. There are no wedding notices pinned up on the intricately carved surround, as there are in our church at home. No matter. My betrothal will be a secret one, but it should have a sign nonetheless. I stand in the shadows beside the door, people passing by me, and begin to scratch in the soft wood with my fingernail - the sign of the holy cross. I hear Mother's voice calling my name and gouge harder, deeper. At last it is done and, spinning round quickly, someone bumps into me hard. It is one of the monks of the Abbey, walking purposefully down the steps. He is not so very tall but broad and hard-bodied. He stops for a moment to beg my pardon before moving on and, though his hood is up, I can tell by his voice that he is young and a Norman.

Mother has seen me now. 'Why must you always be the one to get lost?' she mutters, taking my arm in the throng.

We find the others in what the townspeople here call Romeland, outside the great gate of the Abbey. As we set off for our lodging, I hug the secret vow close to my heart and barely notice Mother's fingers, grasping me tight. It will be a sennight before the marks will fade from my arm.

# Chapter 4

*The house of Richard and Alveva in Huntingdon*

*Twenty-first day of April, AD 1114*

On the apple trees behind my aunt's house, the pink-white blossom dances in the breeze, thick this year and luscious. The kitchen is bustling. What could be better? It is always like this when the Bishop visits, on his way down from Durham to London: a house full of relatives, an abundance of special dishes, excitement everywhere. Such a far cry from this last winter at home, with Mother ill and the heaviness that always descends on the house when she and Father are at odds.

'How many knives do we have?'

My aunt Alveva is rummaging through a box of silver and now she brings out several tiny dishes, fashioned in the shape of ships.

'I had forgotten these,' she says and calls for someone to bring salt to fill them.

Though she works fast, everything seems to be accomplished with a kind of ease and pleasure. I have often wondered how two sisters can be so different. If my mother were obliged to entertain the Bishop of Durham, she would be sour and tetchy.

Mother is sitting beside the fire, unmoving amid all the activity. It is sunny today but in her weakened state she still feels the winter's cold. Now she remembers something.

'The silver winecup! We forgot to bring it with us.'

My aunt turns around and I see the disappointment pass across her face. Mother always lends her the winecup for Bishop Ranulf to use when he visits. It was passed down by their mother and is better than anything Alveva has.

'No matter, sister,' she says. My aunt is not one to fuss. 'He can use Richard's best cup.'

I have not seen my grey, stooping uncle, as yet today. He is probably at the mews, keeping company with his hawks till the preparations are over.

Mother is insistent. She seeks me out with her eyes.

'Theodora, go back home and get the cup.'

Everything in me longs to stay in this busy, happy house, close to my aunt.

'There's no need to trouble yourself,' Alveva says. 'Richard's best one will do.'

I look at my mother. Surely she can see that my aunt does not want the cup.

'Theodora, do as you are asked, will you?'

A bitter reply is forming on my lips but before it has time to burst out, my sister Margaret pipes up from somewhere.

'I'll go and get it.' She appears from behind me, holding out her hand.

I unhook the key to the silver chest from my belt and pass it over, but Mother is not finished.

27

'I don't know why your father gave you the keys when I was confined to bed. He would have been better to give them to your sister.'

'Oh, but Dora is the eldest daughter,' my aunt says and Mother has to acknowledge that, even though it pains her.

I catch Aunt Alveva's eye and smile at her - she always takes my part. But still the day has lost something of its glow. I run outside after Margaret and catch her by the arm.

'I'll save you the best place at table.'

Margaret looks at me steadily for a moment. She thanks me civilly enough but still I am left feeling somehow in the wrong.

Extra trestles have been put up so that we can all be at table together. My cousins are here and all my family, even my half-brother Simon and his wife. Uncle Richard sits with the knights from the Bishop's retinue and I have secured a place high up, next to my aunt, where we have a good view of the Bishop on the dais.

Alveva notices that his cup is empty and goes to refill it, leaning over his shoulder to pour the wine. It interests me to watch her and the Bishop together. He is my father's age or even older and not so tall, yet still his face is well-shaped and handsome. There is something compelling about his quick, sure movements, his teasing wit. Ranulf the Torch Bearer, they call him, and the name seems just right, though some of them mean it for an insult.

When Aunt Alveva sits down again beside me, I notice that her cheeks are flushed. It is many years now since she was Ranulf's mistress and shared his bed. All that came to an end when I was too young to remember, when he became Bishop of Durham and married her off to my uncle Richard.

My uncle must have been quite an old man, even then. It was a long time ago, but she still seems more animated when Ranulf visits. Perhaps it is just that he brings news of the sons she bore him.

'Is the Bishop on his way to London?' I ask. Ranulf arrived yesterday with his chamberlain and his knights. No doubt they will stay a few days.

'He is summoned by the King to Windsor, with the other bishops,' my aunt replies. She seems to take pride in his high position.

Bishop Ranulf is one of the highest in the kingdom and much hated in this part of the country but it is hard to remember it, when I see him at my aunt's house. He has risen from low stock and always treats my family with the greatest respect. He is my father's friend.

'Does he have news of Elias and Ralf?' I ask.

My cousins are young men now and long ago left my aunt's household to be educated elsewhere.

'Elias is to be made prebend of Lincoln.' My aunt's eyes are shining. 'At Christmas, he says.'

As the meal wears on and the sweet dishes are brought, I notice that the Bishop's eyes often stray in our direction, to my aunt. I catch him looking once again before he turns to talk to my father. He might be a man of the Church but he clearly can't forget the pleasure he knew with Alveva. I wonder whether she is troubled by the memory of it too. Better by far, as Canon Sueno says, to live the life of chastity.

The Bishop gets up from the bench and calls Alveva over.

'He wishes to be excused,' she tells me when she returns. 'He has some accounts to look over.'

The fruit is brought in, and more wine, but something has

altered with Ranulf's absence, as if the sun has gone behind a cloud.

It is not long before William, the Bishop's chamberlain, appears at the door of the hall. He is a portly man, still quite young. He makes his way between the benches towards us with small, mincing steps, as if he were a woman. I have to swallow back my laughter. Instead of addressing my aunt, he turns to me.

'The Bishop would be pleased if you would attend him,' he says.

I stare at him. Ranulf used to bring presents for me and my sisters when we were children and he would sometimes play games with us, but I have never conversed with him alone. I turn to my aunt and catch a dark look on her face.

My father's voice sounds from the top table, thick with drink.

'Don't keep him waiting, Dora. I have told the Bishop how quick you are at reckoning. Perhaps he needs your help.'

I look around for my brother. 'May not Gregory go?'

Alveva only shakes her head and tells me to hurry.

My aunt and uncle must be sleeping in the hall because they have given the Bishop their bedchamber. I have rested here in the day many times and I love this room. When I was small, I used to lie on the great bed and look at the hanging - the one with the cherry tree in blossom and the meadow full of gillyflower and daisies. Now, as William ushers me into the room, it seems strange to see the Bishop and another of his servants here. My aunt has put a writing chair and desk for him under the window, but he is not working there. Instead, he sits on a long stool beside the fireplace. I hesitate in the doorway.

'Theodora - come in.' He stands to greet me, his tone offhand, as if we had spent many easy hours together. 'Would you like to play a game?'

I walk over to the fireplace and see that a board sits on the stool, laid out for Nine Men's Morris.

'Do you want to play black or white?' the Bishop asks.

I am good at this game and often beat Gregory at it, sometimes even my father.

'I will take white.'

He smiles and draws forward another stool for me. I notice how good his teeth are. He looks younger when he smiles.

We take it in turns to lay down our pieces. It is important to spread my white men out around the board, not to be impatient and try for a mill too soon. Ranulf sees what I am doing and looks up at me, with a wry smile.

'I see you have a knowledge of this game,' he says, and I am pleased.

When the moves begin in earnest, I find that he is a clever player but I can match him. He breaks my first mill but, before long, I have put him in jeopardy and returned the favour. Looking up from the board, I see that William and the other servant are busying themselves with the Bishop's clothing, muddied from being on the road.

'Is it a long journey here from Durham?' I ask Ranulf.

'It is,' he replies. 'Eight days' ride and another three to Windsor. I pray the rain will keep off for my masons back at home. They are building me a wall around the castle, to strengthen the town.'

Eight days' ride. I try to imagine Durham and what it is like there. The Bishop must be from home a lot, when he travels to London to the King. I can't think what would happen to his business if my father was away so much as that.

'Who is in command of the building, while you are away?'

The Bishop looks up at me and laughs.

'Pinceon, my steward, is to be trusted with the building of a wall, I think.'

He begins to regard me closely. 'Your father tells me that you have an interest in many things. Perhaps one day I will show you my new wall. And my church, of course.'

It feels as if he is making fun of me. I take refuge in the pieces on the board, but the Bishop seems to have lost interest in the game.

'You are your father's favourite, I think,' he says, and when I look up, I find his quick blue eyes resting on me. 'Your hair is red like his but today I see how much you are like your aunt.'

I feel a blush bloom up from my neck, into my face. My heart starts to beat faster, but I find that I am not frightened of this man. He is not so different from my father and yet again he is different, in a way that pleases me. He returns to the game and we play for a while longer but my attention is scattered now and, at last, there are only three of my white men left on the board. I move one of them a double space to escape danger and he complains, laughing.

'But my men can fly now that you have reduced me to three!' I insist. 'Don't you play to this rule?'

'I will play to any rule you choose.' He is no longer laughing and somehow his words leave a tingling imprint on my body.

Ranulf is sitting back on the stool, watching me, a smile creasing the skin around his eyes. He moves forward and takes my hand in his. At his touch, something stirs, deep inside my belly and low down.

'Your father tells me you wish to take the veil.' His voice is languid, like a stream in summer.

I take my hand away and look down, uncertain how to answer. What has Father said to him? I risk a nod of the head in answer.

'That is an intention much to be praised,' he says.

I look up but Ranulf's face is grave; he does not seem to be mocking me now. He is a man of God after all – a bishop. Maybe he can dissuade Father from making me marry.

'Ever since I was young, I have longed to wear the virgin's crown.'

He nods in approval and I take courage to continue. 'And I have made a vow to Christ, to be his bride alone. Canon Sueno from the Priory has confirmed it.'

'A bride of Christ,' he repeats.

I want him to understand but now he is looking past me to the corner of the chamber where William and the servant are at work. He makes the smallest movement of his head, barely anything, but soon the door opens and the chamberlain and his boy leave the room.

'Now tell me, Theodora,' he goes on, 'what is the debt a bride must pay to her husband?'

I am confused. Something in the Bishop's tone begins to frighten me. He is not going to help me, after all. His voice is gentle but perhaps he means me ill.

'It would be wrong for a woman as beautiful and as spirited as you not to play bride to a man,' he says, calmly, as if we were deliberating over the chance of rain.

'But I have sworn before God...'

'The estate of marriage is no shame. Many women are called to it and know the sensations of the flesh.' He smiles at me. 'As you do, Theodora.'

My heart is pounding and I begin to feel sick.

'Come now, you cannot deny what you felt when I took your hand in mine,' Ranulf says.

I cannot move or think, like a calf that has been stunned for the slaughter, aware only of the truth of what he says. But then the words of Jesus in the gospel come into my mind. *Be wise as serpents and harmless as doves.* Sueno quotes these words often, reminding me that my vow will be tested.

'Come and lie down with me,' he is saying.

He stands up and pulls me gently to my feet. But instead of walking towards the bed, he places my hand below his belly, over the top of his tunic.

'See what you have done, with all your talk of being a bride,' he whispers in my ear. His breath smells sweet with fennel but, this close, I see that the skin on his face is pock-marked. 'Come now and give me relief.'

I am frightened but, at the same time, rage is welling up inside me. Are all men, then, ruled by their members, as Gregory said? Suddenly, my mind is sharp and clear. The Bishop may not be young but he is still strong and able to compel me. I open my mouth to cry out but who would hear, only the Bishop's servants? It comes to me with a sickening clarity that my father knows of Ranulf's interest in me and is not displeased by it.

I allow myself to be led towards the bed and, in his haste, Ranulf knocks over the Nine Men's Morris. The men scatter onto the floor, becoming lost among the rushes. An idea is forming in my mind, though I let nothing show on my face. Strength of purpose flows through my body like quicksilver, heavy and bright.

I do not wait for Ranulf to act but, instead, I help him onto my aunt's bed and lift up his coat and the green silk tunic he wears underneath. The material feels heavy and expensive under my fingers. He smiles down at me, his eyebrows arched as if he is delighted by my acquiescence.

'Don't be frightened, Dora,' he says, his breath coming quickly now. I am incensed that he should use my pet name. 'You and your family will not suffer.'

I suppose he wants me to touch him. I force myself to start unloosing his braies but then stop, as if I have just remembered something.

'Should I bolt the door?'

He has taken my hand, ready to guide it, but he pauses.

'My aunt might come in or one of our servants,' I say. 'I will go and bolt it.'

Now he props himself up on the bolster and looks down at me. I see one thought after another cross his face. The teasing look returns to his eyes and I sense his urgency begin to fall away.

'If I let you go, do you swear that you will come back to me?' he asks and now I am not sure whether he is laughing at me again.

'I swear.'

I climb off the bed and am at the door before he can get up to follow me. I open it, the heavy oak creaking, slip out and close it behind me, bolting the door on the outside. I listen but there is no sound of footsteps from within the chamber. My legs are shaking but I run along the gallery to the door and down the outside stairway. It is beginning to be dark and the air is fragrant with the scent of blossom. I hurry through the streets, back to our house.

## Eighth day of May, AD 1114

The May sun is warmer each day and, resting after dinner in my chamber, I no longer need the heavy coverlet. The first thing I know is Mother flinging open the door. She runs over to the bed, her eyes alight with excitement.

'Get up, Theodora! He's here. He wants to see you.'

My head is still wreathed in sleep. 'Who? Who's here?'

'The Bishop,' she cries. 'And he has brought presents. Silks and other things. Be quick!'

My heart gives a sick lurch, as if it will drop into my belly. I sit up in bed and stare at Mother. I have not seen her look so glad in a long time. My thoughts are a swirling tangle but one thing is clear to me.

'I won't come. I won't see him, not even if you beat me.'

Mother is truly taken aback. I wait for the angry tirade but what I see in her eyes is more like terror. She moves towards me, her hand outstretched, then seems to change her mind and turns for the door.

'I'll fetch your father,' she says, over her shoulder.

I wait on the bed, growing more fearful, every part of me tingling now with wakefulness. Surely Father will not force me to receive the bishop and his bribes. I do not have to wait long.

'Dora.' Father is at my bedside now, Mother and Margaret waiting at the door. 'Enough of this. What do you mean, to refuse him? The Bishop took no offence from your rebuff before - this is welcome news, Dora. He has brought you the most exquisite Turkish silk. Now get up and ready yourself.'

I lunge towards him and grab both his hands. 'I won't see

him. Please, Father. Don't make me.'

He tries to shake me off. 'If this is more of your nonsense … Don't you know that it's an honour for a man like Ranulf to favour you?'

The tears are coming now and perhaps they will help my cause.

'But he is an old man - and he incited me to a lewd act. I wonder you are not ashamed to ask this of me.'

Father looks away for a moment and I can see that the arrow has hit its mark, but he is torn. Ranulf's liaison with my Aunt Alveva has brought preferment and riches to our whole family and he fears their loss. He takes hold of my face in his hands and peers into my eyes and I don't know if he is going to slap me or kiss me. In the end, he does neither but just lets me go. He walks to the door without another word.

I burrow down into the bed and cover myself, blanking out the world and all its ugliness. Truly, as the psalmist said, I am alone. Even my mother and my father have abandoned me.

After a time, I creep to the door and peer around it, but Mother's workroom is empty. I walk through to the landing on tip-toe. There are voices coming from the salle. The door is not quite closed and through the crack I can see the leg of Father's chair by the hearth and a dusty riding boot, a spur jutting out from the ankle. I hear Father's voice, quick and nervous, but I can't make out the words. Then comes a laugh – Ranulf's. The boot moves out of my view. The Bishop's voice is loud.

'No offence is taken, my friend. She is a fine girl, much like Alveva was. God knows, I am no longer a young buck.'

My father says something more, then the voice of Ranulf again:

'No, no. Let her keep the silk and the combs. They can be for her wedding.' I hear them moving about in the room. 'I shall prove my goodwill by speaking to young Burthred on your account, before I leave for Durham. The marriage will advance your family. I have given his father reason to fear me, and love me too. I doubt the son will object.'

Suddenly the door is flung open and I am caught there, before them. My father looks horrified but Ranulf only explodes in a laugh.

'You see her spirit?' he says to my father. 'Burthred is to be envied, I think.'

Mortified, I turn and run down the stairs.

'I advise you to rein your daughter in, Auti,' I hear him say. 'Let nothing prevent this marriage.'

# Chapter 5

*Huntingdon*

*Seventeenth day of December, AD 1115*

Helisen comes to the street door herself, all smiles. The door to the workshop is open and I catch a glimpse of her new husband, leaning across a pile of furs on his counter, bargaining with a customer.

A quick glance is all it takes to see that there have been changes since my last visit. There is now a length of heavy green wool at the window and a gleaming new chest, bound with iron. Helisen catches hold of my hand and pulls me towards the stairs.

'The hanging has arrived - come and see!'

She remembers herself and calls for the servant. The girl appears from the scullery and Helisen instructs her with just the right degree of hauteur.

'Take Mistress Theodora's cloak, and fetch us some warm wine.'

I look hard at her, but there is nothing in my friend's face to show that she remembers all those hours we talked together. About how we would not follow our mothers but embrace the gospel and live chaste, like the virgin martyrs of old. It pains me to see how she has thrown herself headlong into being the mistress of a household. Surely, she can't have forgotten what we said? But then Helisen always was like warm wax in my hand. Left to herself, it seems she assumes a different shape altogether.

I follow her up to the chamber where she sleeps beside the furrier, William. The bed has been raised up from the floor on a frame and takes up most of the space in the room. I don't care to think of what they do there in the dark, behind the curtains.

Helisen is excited. 'See, Dora? You were right about the roses.'

I stand back to get a good view of the hanging, which covers the wall at the foot of the bed. We went to the broiderer together and it was my idea that she should work fine strands of crimson in among the pale yellow, with just a hint of green. And it's true; the roses stand out like pearls amid the tangled foliage - a shell pink.

I can feel a sharp knot of bitterness forming itself inside me. Murmuring something about being needed by my mother at home, I turn towards the door. Helisen is behind me on the stairs.

'What is it, Dora? Don't you like it?'

'It's beautiful. But the blue ground is a little dark, don't you think?'

She looks crestfallen and a base part of me is glad. All I want is to be gone from her, gone from this house. In the hallway, she takes my hand again.

40

'Leofa can make you a better one, Dora. You're lucky - Burthred's family are very wealthy. You'll have a much bigger house than this one.'

I am incensed. Does she think I envy her? All those afternoons we walked together on the meadow by the river, when we became too old to play. I used to pretend we were twin sisters and my Aunt Alveva was our mother. Now I see that she is a stranger to me.

'Helisen, you know I cannot marry.' Her uncomprehending look is the last straw and the scathing words come tumbling out. 'Not all of us are so easily turned away from the vows we have made.'

Wyn is waiting for me at the door of Helisen's house. It has begun to snow a little and her nose is red with cold. Without saying a word, I wrap my cloak around me and start off for home, the girl following a few steps behind. I don't need a servant to accompany me everywhere I go; I promised Father that I would not go against his wishes and visit Canon Sueno. *Just agree to the marriage and you can go to the Priory all you wish*, Father says, again and again. Tears gather in my eyes. Just now, I would like nothing better than to sit beside my old teacher and hear him talk of the glory of living chaste. Of being chosen by the Blessed Virgin.

The sky is grey: a soft, sodden mattress, with feathers of snow dropping lazily onto my shoulders. There are not many people abroad, the street sounds are dulled, and soon the pain in my heart seems to lose its edge. When I come to think of it, Father has not pressed me so much, these last weeks. Perhaps he has thought better of trying to make me wed this man, Burthred. In a week it will be the Nativity of Our Lord. Surely, in the days of feasting, he will give me leave to visit

Sueno.

Now I regret offending Helisen about the wall hanging. The blue ground is not so very dark. At the town door of our house, I turn and wait for Wyn to catch me up. I smile at her - she is only doing what Mother bids her, after all.

The snow may have brought quiet to the streets, but the house is in uproar. Matilda is half way up the stairs but when she sees me, she comes running back down.

'Dora! You are to go up to the salle. Father wants to speak to you.'

My little sister loves it when there is some excitement, some happening.

'Why? Where's Mother?'

'Up there - with him.'

When I go in, Mother is speaking. She still has her cloak on and I see that, like mine, it is wet with snow.

'... the eve of Christmas or even the day before, my sister said.'

'So soon?' Father hears me come in and he turns, all the lines of his face sharpened by fear.

'Theodora. Your mother has news, from Alveva. The Bishop is even now travelling south, to Alban's abbey for the consecration. He is to break his journey at your aunt's - he will be here for the Nativity.'

I stare at him stupidly. I never want to set eyes on Bishop Ranulf again. Perhaps I might take sick and keep to my bed while he is in the town.

Father is standing by the window, his hands crossed behind his back, clasping and unclasping. He takes a deep breath and turns to face me.

'Dora, the plans for your marriage must be hastened. I have

already met with Burthred and the dowry is settled.'

A sound, like the bleating of a lamb, escapes from my mother's mouth. 'There is so much to be arranged,' she says. 'And there can be no betrothal during the fast.'

Fear lends a new edge of harshness to Father's voice. 'It must be done, as soon as the fast is over - on Christmas morning. Yes - the Bishop may see with his own eyes that we have followed his wishes. I will ride over myself to Burthred's father - damn this snow!'

The truth is trickling into my mind - pooling, gathering an awful weight. I run towards him with my hand outstretched but his face is set like iron and I know that the time for pleading is past.

'I do not consent to it - you cannot make me marry!'

Mother makes a hissing sound. 'Why do you let her speak to you like that?' She turns on me. 'Your duty is to obey your father.'

I ignore her. It's Father who matters, not her - surely he won't force me. 'You can put me to the torture, but I will never consent to marry.' My voice is breaking. 'Father, I have made a vow.'

But he only rounds on me with an unfamiliar rage that turns my blood to ice. 'Would you ruin me with this foolish notion? Would you see your family brought to nothing through wilfulness?'

'What about your precious Aunt Alveva?' Mother chips in. 'If we cross the Bishop, he will never let her see her sons again.'

I turn and run from the room, across the landing and through Mother's workroom, where Margaret sits sewing, as if nothing had happened. She looks up but I run into my inner chamber and slam the door, throwing myself on the mattress.

## Christmas Day, AD 1115

The snow has cleared and now the channel that runs through the street is overflowing with all the waste of the last days. We are obliged to walk in single file, keeping close to the houses, on our way to church. The stink is dreadful but I am glad that I do not to have to speak to anyone. I woke before dawn, my heart heavy and cold as lead, even though it is the morning of the Saviour's birth. I lay a long time on my bed, gathering courage. Did St Catherine feel as fearful as this before she was brought before the emperor and his council? The others made much of breaking their fast - the first meat of the Christmas season - but I could eat nothing. Matilda tried to coax me. *It's Christmas and it's your wedding day, Dora. Aren't you happy?* She doesn't understand.

The spire of the church of St Mary passes in and out of sight, behind the houses. I clench my fists tights and will myself to be strong. I can see it all with the eye of my imagination. The priest calls me to the church door for the handfasting. Instead, I turn to face the crowd and speak out boldly. *I am already betrothed to Christ. I can be the wife of no man.* Father starts to object but the priest forestalls him. *Has your vow been confirmed, Child?* he asks. *Yes, by Canon Sueno of the Austin Priory.* A gasp goes up and the priest stands between me and the man they have chosen. *There will be no wedding*, he pronounces. Just thinking of it, a tingling warmth seems to take root and rise up through my breast, my neck, my face.

Father is waiting in the market square and now he falls into step beside me. I catch a look between him and my brother Gregory, as if they are frightened I will run away. Why would I run away when this is the test I've been preparing for? People are gathering outside the church.

'He's here, Theodora, with all his kin.'

Father points out a young man in a fur-trimmed cloak, talking to a short, stout woman who might be his mother. He is not tall either and slight, I would guess, under that bulky cloak. Father looks about the square and back along the street behind us.

'Your aunt and uncle are not here yet,' he says, but I know that it's really the Bishop he is looking for so anxiously.

We cross to the church, my feet reluctant, as if I were bidding them walk to the gallows. My hands start to tremble: so many strange faces. This man they have chosen is not from the town but from out beyond Wennington. His kin must be even wealthier than us, they are dressed so richly. Mother has on her best fox-fur but still she looks plain beside them. I am suddenly glad that she made me wear my new plum-coloured cloak. Father had the cloth from Genoa and it is the latest weave - pile on pile.

The townspeople wish us joy of the season as they pass on their way into church. If only this were just a Christmas morning, like any other. Father is talking with the priest and with the man they wish me to wed. Burthred pulls back his hood and, despite everything, I am eager to see what he is like. I was right. He is small, with pale sandy hair and sharp features that make me think of a weasel.

Mother pushes me towards them, but then comes a commotion. The crowd is splitting apart to make way for Bishop Ranulf Flambard who is striding across the square towards us. My Aunt Alveva follows on behind, supporting my uncle Richard on her arm. The Bishop raises his hand to acknowledge the bows of the assembly, then embraces my father.

'I am glad to be here with you all to witness this happy day,' he proclaims to the crowd. 'It gratifies me to see these two families joined in marriage.' Then he bends over me, his mouth close to my ear. The fennel on his breath carries me straight back to that night, in Aunt Alveva's chamber. I shrink away from him.

'I hope you take pleasure in your husband, Theodora. Did I choose well for you?' The mirth of his smile is tinged with malice.

I open my mouth to answer but my tongue feels like a piece of wood. The priest steps forward. He turns to my father and to the weasel, Burthred.

'Is the dowry agreed?'

They murmur assent and an old man with Burthred's flaxen hair steps forward.

'My son has agreed to build a house in the town, near to Auti's. When it's finished, he and Theodora will live there as man and wife.'

I did not know that a new house was to be built for me. Hearing them talk, this false marriage suddenly seems to take on form, as if it were really going to happen.

The priest bids me approach the door of the church and the families draw back. The chattering dies down and all eyes are on me. Now is the time to speak out and I cry in silence to the Virgin to help me yet still I am mute, my feet carrying

46

me forward against my will.

'You have the ring?' the priest asks. Burthred takes it from his belt and holds it up. 'Then say the words.'

He steps towards me and I am close enough now to see how the hairs of his beard are mixed: some fair, some the rusty brown of bracken in autumn. In the cold morning air, his breath escapes from his mouth as a mist. His eyes, the colour of burnt umber, are on me but he does not have the look of a forceful man. I take heart - perhaps I could defy him. When he speaks, his voice surprises me - it is deeper and more manly than I thought.

'I promise to take you as my wife.'

I gasp for breath. They are all watching and waiting - Father and Mother, my brother, my sisters. And so many unfamiliar faces, those of Burthred's wealthy kin. My Aunt Alveva is standing beside the Bishop, imploring me with her eyes not to cause trouble.

As if it were being spoken by another, I hear the oath come from my own mouth. 'I promise to take you as my husband.'

Burthred reaches across to take my right hand. His hands are shaking as he slides the ring first onto my thumb, then onto my forefinger, then onto its neighbour.

'In the name of the Father, and of the Son, and of the Holy Spirit.'

I am trembling now. The world has lurched out of its course and I am left with no ground to stand on. Burthred's eyes are on me as the priest and all our kin repeat the Amen.

# Chapter 6

*Huntingdon*

*Twelfth day of February, AD 1116*

In my dream, I am lying dead in a chapel. The shroud they have placed over me keeps falling away and I have to stretch out my cold hand and pull it back over my head, again and again. I wake to the sharp air in my chamber and my fingers grasping at the coverlet.

At once the dream falls away and I remember that it's the morning of the Guild Merchant feast. There is a jagged rim of ice around the edge of my bowl and I quickly splash water on my face, then pull down the purple gown from the pole above my bed. Last night, I watched Mother hang it there, and wondered at her forbearance. I thought she would be jealous. If it comes to that, why has Father asked me to be cup-bearer instead of her? It makes no sense, after all his ill temper with me.

I can hear him again now, standing in my doorway, shouting, his face ruddy with rage. *If you will not see your own husband, you will not see anyone.* I cannot make him out. First, he keeps me solitary, a prisoner in the house. Now he bids me go abroad in the town and serve wine to the noble guests in the Guild Hall.

When I open my door, Mother is there, ready to pounce.

'We must make you ready, Theodora.'

She leads me to the mirror in her room and begins to braid my hair. It is a long time since my mother did that.

'Now, you know what your duties are, Child?'

I twist my head, where the comb is pulling. Of course I know. Haven't I watched her a hundred times when we have guests at home?

'Your father will bless the cup first and make the welcome speech, then you must offer the wine. Remember, each guest will speak a few words.'

'I know what to do, Mother.'

She finishes my hair and then turns me to one side and starts to gather up the folds of my gown and wrap them tight against me.

I push her away. 'What are you doing?'

She desists. 'We can leave it for now, I suppose, but you will have to tuck it up later, because of the spills. Don't forget. When the nobles return the cup to you, it is gracious to take a sip of wine. And you must be seen to taste the beer too, and the ale, every time the cup is refilled.'

Mother has not made such a speech to me for months and suddenly I see what is in their minds. They want me to be immoderate with the wine and make a fool of myself. I look her in the eye and she reddens and turns away. Is it not enough for them that they stop me going to hear service at the Priory?

She stands back to examine me, nods her satisfaction and turns to go. Then she seems to change her mind and inches closer.

'You are clean, Dora?' she murmurs. 'Your flowers have not come during the night?'

I shake my head. Why does she want to know that?

We take the back way along Cobblers Lane, coming out just opposite the Priory of the Blessed Mother of God. To be so close, to be able to touch its familiar walls, trace the latch of the door with my finger, and yet be forbidden to enter! Inside the church, the canons will be singing None. Two boys are running along the street, late for school, and I watch them disappear in through the gate behind the church, my heart aching.

Father is steering me across the alley to the Guild Hall. The guests are beginning to gather outside in the frosty air. I recognize many of the merchants: Father's friends, most of them, though there are strangers too. Some have brought their wives. Even Thomas de Vere from the castle is here and I marvel at the soft vair lining of his crimson mantle, blue-grey mottled with white.

Inside, the trestles are up and the fires already ablaze. Mother takes me to the kitchens behind. We stand there in the broiling heat, amid the hiss of roasting boar and the shouting of the cooks, and I allow her to draw together the folds of my gown with tapes and fasten up my sleeves to keep them clean.

As we walked through town, I kept wondering why Mother should ask about my bleeding. But now, all at once, it comes to me – what they are plotting. Why didn't I see it before? They plan to make me tippled with drink and have Burthred come to the feast, to take advantage. The air in the kitchen is hot and steamy. The savoury smell of the meat is pungent with cinnamon and cloves and galingale, but now I hardly notice it. Let them lay their traps. I will serve the wine as they bid me and be on show for all the guests to ogle at. I will smile and make them proud, but not one drop of liquor will pass my lips and I will never let my husband, nor any other man, bring me to bed. They cannot compel me to break my vow.

Mother seems to sense my resolve and now she reverts to her usual spiteful self.

'Canon Sueno came to the house yesterday,' she says.

My heart jumps. 'He came to see me?'

'He didn't even ask after you. I have heard he speaks ill of you to all the neighbourhood - ever since the betrothal.'

I can only stare at her but then the horn sounds and it is time to wash our hands and make our way into the great hall. Father and the other officers of the Guild are standing by the high table, talking, but I am numb with distress. *He speaks ill of you*. Mother is lying. Or worse - my friend thinks I have wantonly broken my vow - but that's not how it was. They pressed me so hard, what could I do? And words alone don't make me the wife of any man - even the priests say that.

All through the welcome speech, I keep watch on the guests filing in past the door-wardens. There is no sign of Burthred but still I don't trust them anymore, not even Father. In the side pantry, a servant is waiting with the Guild Cup. It is two-thirds full of wine and heavy; the silver feels cold, the tracery delicate under my fingers. One hand at the base and the other at the lip, I carry it carefully back to Father for the blessing. The noise in the hall subsides as, all eyes following me, I take the cup to the highest guest, the Earl's steward.

'Will it please you to drink, my lord?'

Father looks gratified that I have spoken clearly and with confidence. Thomas de Vere smiles at me and makes a little bow with his head.

'I have great pleasure in receiving the cup from such a graceful bearer,' he replies. He turns to Father and the other officers of the Guild. 'And I am honoured to be invited to this, your annual feast. I am entrusted with greetings from Earl David and his lady, Maud. The merchants of Huntingdon bring great wealth and standing to our borough.'

He drinks from the cup and I move on to Cenric who imports wine from Rouen, then to a short man with silver hair, whom I saw once in my father's workroom, then on and on till each one at the high table has spoken. Now I can sit and take a breath while servants run to pour wine for the lower tables. A horn is sounded and the doors from the kitchen are thrown open. The rich, sweet smell of boar wafts into the hall but before that comes the civet of hare.

Above us, in the gallery, the harpist strikes up and I take some comfort in the sweetness of his playing. When the day is older and the wine casks emptier, the noise in the hall will drown out the music. The hare is good and succulent but I only toy with my food. How can I contrive to speak to Sueno alone?

Father is beckoning me; it's time for the next round of drinks. A servant brings a bowl of beer and he ladles it into the cup, then waits. Mother is leaning forward, watching me. I take a sip but hold it in my mouth and, turning away, I spit it out onto the floor without her knowing.

The guests are merrier now and at his turn, Cenric offers

me the cup after he has drunk.

'Will you not sup with me?'

I smile. 'You do me honour, my lord, but myrtle beer is not to my taste.' I move on quickly.

The boar is served, with dish after dish of salads, and then comes the eel I saw them cutting in the kitchen. There is no respite for me. Again and again I have to serve the guests at the high table: beer, then more wine, then mead to drink with the honey custards and the preserved pears. They are drinking deep now and the cup needs refilling before I have served them all. I step down from the dais and battle my way between the benches towards the kitchen, amid a sea of jesting and laughter. Don't they know how coarse they sound? I can barely hear the flutes above the din, the insistent beat of the drums. I slide on something sticky on the floor and a hand reaches out to steady me, but then slips from my arm and onto my buttock. Glaring down, I see that the hand belongs to Helisen's husband, the furrier. Everyone knows that he is a lecher. He leers at me but then I see recognition crawl out from behind the drink and spread across his face, and he drops his hand. The heat in the hall is intense. A side door has been opened to let in air and, across the alley, I catch sight of one of the Priory windows and feel a catch in my throat.

Back at the high table, Father draws me towards him as I pass. His face is red and there are beads of sweat on his forehead. He is drunk but happy.

'You are the most beautiful daughter a father could have, Dora.'

It reminds me of the old times, before this wretched marriage and all the quarrelling. I feel tears pricking behind my eyes. Burthred has not come to the feast after all. Was I wrong to think that Father could plan to harm me?

It begins to grow dark outside and there are no more dishes to come from the kitchen. The tables are littered: dirty knives and gravy-soaked trenchers, the bones of meat and fish, the shells of nuts, but still the guests drink and the musicians play. Now comes a commotion at the door.

'Ah good - the scop has come!' I hear Father call out and I smile. If he were sober, he would never use the old Saxon word, not here, before the top crust of Huntingdon.

While the story-teller is conferring with the musicians, Father orders me to take the cup round once more. The noble guests are sotted with drink already but they do not refuse it. I come to the Earl's man, Thomas de Vere, and he shakes his head. But when I go to pass on, he takes my hand and leans back, as if to study me at his leisure. He may hold high office but he is still a young man, and I cannot help but notice how closely his bliaut fits to his chest. He does not speak but his eyes travel slowly up from my feet to my face, pausing to take in my bare arms and throat. I blush under his scrutiny but it gives me pleasure nonetheless. Snatching my hand back, I turn away and offer the mead to old Godwine, but his head is lolling on his chest and he is snoring. I drop the cup onto the table, spilling the drink, and run down the steps at the end of the dais and along the side of the hall. The guests have drunk enough.

At the side door, I look back. Father has not noticed me go and Mother is nowhere to be seen. Stepping out into the alley, the chill evening air is welcome on my burning face. I pull down my sleeves and loosen the folds in my tunic, breathing in the blessed quiet. Very faint, from inside the

Priory Church, comes the sound of voices - the canons are singing Vespers. *Hail Mary, full of grace, the Lord is with thee, blessed art thou among women.* It is as if the Mother of God herself is commending me.

It's late and we retired to bed a long while ago, but still I am not ready to undress and go to sleep. My body is wasted with tiredness but my soul is on fire. All the day I have been among lewd men, drinking and boasting, but the Virgin has kept me safe. I take up my book of saints' Lives and find the account of the chaste Saint Cecilia and her husband, Valerian. I have read it many times but tonight, amidst the shadows thrown by my sputtering candle, the story impresses itself on me in a new way. I am not alone. St Cecilia was forced into marriage, yet she was able to guard her virginity.

*And the angel had two crowns of roses and of lilies which he held in his hands, of which he gave one to Cecilia and that other to Valerian, saying: Keep these crowns with an undefouled and clean body, for I have brought them to you from Paradise, and they shall never fade, nor wither, nor lose their savour, neither may they be seen but of them to whom chastity pleases.*

I read on, enthralled, as the saint and her husband preach to the pagans and they are converted. But before I have reached the part that always thrills me, the part where they are martyred, there comes a noise from the workroom next door. Perhaps Margaret cannot sleep either. The latch clicks up and the door slowly opens.

'Meg?'

Whoever it is carries no candle and it's very dark there in the corner. I gasp. It is not my sister, but a man. Father? I get to my feet and, raising my candle to get a better look, I let out a small cry. Burthred is standing there, his face almost obscured by a dark hood.

'Meg! Mother!'

'Don't call out, I beg you,' he says, but there is no alarm in his voice.

He pulls back his hood. He seems surprised, uncertain, even frightened. Thoughts are tumbling through my mind. How did he get in to the outer chamber? Where is Margaret? I listen but the house is quiet and it comes to me with a dull, sick certainty that it's no use calling my parents; it's they who have let him in.

Burthred has gathered himself. Did he expect me to be in my bed, asleep? He throws off his cloak and crosses the room, pulling at the belt around his tunic.

'Theodora,' he whispers. 'Blow out your candle and get undressed.'

He unbuttons his tunic and starts to take it off, revealing his shirt and braies. I can smell his lean body - a sharp tang of sweat that is not unpleasant. He is breathing quickly. I back away from him, horror giving me a voice.

'No! Keep your clothes on, I beg you.'

He stops and looks at me and in that moment I know something. However much he complains, he will not force me.

'You are my wife,' he says. One arm in and one arm out of his tunic, he lunges towards me, pushing me down onto the bed, but I twist away from him.

He looks shaken. 'Why won't you embrace me?' There is something of the sulky boy about him.

My hand touches something on the coverlet – the book I was reading. All at once I see the beauty of what has been ordained. What my parents intended for evil, God has intended for good, just like Joseph, thrown into the pit by his brothers.

I jump up, out of his reach.

'Providence has brought you here to me tonight, Burthred. I have just been reading about Saint Cecilia and her husband.'

He is not coming after me. I take heart.

'You remember – when they came together - how she told him about her vow of chastity?'

Burthred doesn't answer. He is sitting on the bed, his back to me. I pick up the book, find the place and begin to read.

' "*I have an angel that loves me.*" See how she speaks to him? "*Which ever keeps my body whether I sleep or wake and if he may find that you touch my body by villainy or by foul and polluted love, certainly he shall anon slay you and so should you lose the flower of your youth.*" '

He turns round to face me.

'Are you saying that there is an angel who protects your purity?'

He is unnerved and I am thankful for it - fear will keep him from touching me. But now a sourness creeps into his voice.

'Is it my fate to have married a saint, like Cecilia?'

He sounds bitter but his anger is the kind that smoulders rather than burns and I sense that he is tractable.

'Who knows if there may not be an angel watching over me?' I answer him. 'I made a vow. It was confirmed by a priest – a canon of the House of the Blessed Virgin.'

He says nothing and, hoping against hope to make him understand, I read to the end of the saint's Life. He does not try to touch me again. I go on - telling him all that Sueno taught me about the crown of chastity and the glory of this way of life. He listens in awe, his eyes not straying from my face. After a time, I fancy I can see tears in his eyes. We sit together on the bed, like brother and sister, till the candle has burnt down and all the while I find I can open my heart to him. He does not contend with me.

'I like listening to you talk, Theodora,' he says, when the night is quite old. 'My mother and my father are always at loggerheads and I had not dared to hope we could be comfortable together.'

I smile with relief at his words.

'The house will be finished by Easter,' he goes on. 'It's time for you to choose the furniture.'

I nod my assent. 'When the house is ready, I will go home with you.' I feel warm towards him. 'I beg you – don't be offended, as if I had spurned you. You needn't be humiliated before your family and your friends - we can live like husband and wife in the eyes of the world.'

'What do you mean?' Burthred asks.

'No-one need know that we are living chaste. Then, after a time, we can each take the habit and offer ourselves to a religious house – God will make it clear.'

He looks down at the coverlet. He has taken a fold of it in his fingers and is rubbing it to and fro. I feel the battle waging within his soul and breathe a prayer to the Virgin.

'Many of the saints kept a chaste marriage,' I urge him, 'and many more are following in their footsteps these days. Haven't you heard this?'

His hair, glinting golden in the candlelight, falls across the side of his face.

'Give me your hand, Burthred, and we will make a compact before God, never to touch one another, or even to look at each other with lust.'

He remains silent but at last he looks up at me and I see the consent in his eyes. He gives me his hand.

# Chapter 7

*Huntingdon*

*Hock Monday, third day of April, AD 1116*

All through Lent, Burthred was overseeing the building of the new house, close to ours in Merchants Row. Father still keeps me from the Priory but he lets me go to see the new house as often as I want. It is finished now and the furnishings are all in place. With Holy Week came a sickness. Each day I woke, still fatigued, with a scratchy throat and a dull ache in my head, glad to share just a little in the Saviour's sorrows. When the Resurrection dawned at last, just yesterday, I could not feel the same joy as usual. The house was in uproar, not for Easter, but with preparations for my wedding banquet. Mother has called in Aunt Alveva to help her oversee the cooking but still she is running about, her face blotchy with worry that the family of Burthred will not think us generous enough, or refined enough.

Now the day has come. First the wedding feast, then a procession around the market square to show off to the town.

It will end at the new house, where Father is to hand me over to my husband. But this morning, I woke with a pain in my head that made me cry out. My body was first burning, then shivering with cold. After a while, even Margaret believed that I was ill and went to fetch Mother. She stomped up the stairs and came in. Strands of hair had escaped from her wimple and were hanging, dark with sweat, over her eyes. She looked as if she might shake me but then composed herself and took a deep breath. *Stay in bed and rest till the guests arrive*, was all she said. Why must she stare at me as if I were an enemy? And on the day when I am to obey their wishes.

She has sent up bread and whey but I cannot eat anything and lie back, trying to find a place on the pillow that eases my throbbing head. At last, sleep takes me.

The latch on the door clicks and I look up to see Burthred in the doorway. He comes into my room and Mother is there too and Father and Bishop Ranulf, and there are other people but I don't know who they are. The Bishop is smiling, brandishing a stout stick. Burthred is taking off his clothes and I see that his member is stiff inside his braies. He lurches towards me and now they are all calling out – inciting him with filthy words. I try to move but my body will not obey me. *Don't touch me. Don't touch me.*

I wake, to find Mother by the bed again. She is hushing me, her hand like ice on my hot forehead.

'Is she very sick?'

It is Burthred's voice, from the doorway. He sounds anxious. Father is with him and my half-brother, Simon, come for the banquet.

Mother turns to them. 'She's more terrified of what's to

61

come, by the sound of her.'

I twist my head away from them, towards the wall, and close my eyes but I can still hear their low talk, like the chirping of evil frogs.

'What's she frightened of? Haven't you swived her yet, Burthred?' asks Simon. 'The handfasting was at Christmas.'

Mother cuts in. 'We've tried everything, believe me, but we can't do it for him - he must bed her himself.'

Now I hear Father's laugh. 'You know what a silver tongue your sister has. She even tried to talk him into living chaste. He was on her bed once, half the night, and did not touch her.'

At last, Burthred's voice, eager to silence them. 'I'll not live chaste and neither will she. Just wait till tomorrow morning. I'll show you the sheet myself.'

A wave of cold passes over my body, prickling my skin. There is a dull ache in all my bones. Father lowers his voice still further, but I have good ears.

'Maybe it's best that she thinks she has persuaded you.'

Now comes muffled laughter and Simon's voice again. 'If you have any trouble with her tonight, we'll come and hold her down.'

They leave me alone and despair closes in around me. After a while I cannot bear to lie still any longer but when I sit up, the chamber spins around and suddenly I heave and spew, soiling the coverlet and my pillow and the floor too. Margaret comes in and calls for Mother and now everything becomes a nightmare that seems as if it will never end. There is calling and the noise of feet on the stairs and Wyn is here with a pail and a cloth. Someone is holding a cup to my lips with cold water. I am so thirsty. Then it is gone and there is a physicker in the room, talking to Mother. I sleep a little and feel easier but then I am burning hot again and they help me down the stairs to the scullery and dunk me, head first, into a great pan of cold water. An unbearable smell of roasting goose wafts from the kitchen. Matilda is crying.

I don't remember climbing the stairs but we are back in my chamber and Wyn is holding one of my arms and Margaret the other. Mother comes in and she has something in her hand - a poker from the kitchen range, its tip glowing red. I struggle but the girls have me tight, holding my arms fast to the bed. Mother marches towards the bed and I let out a long, high scream. Quickly, she lays the poker across the flesh of my inner arm, in the crease – one arm, then the other. Father is standing in the doorway, his face turned away. When it is over, he tiptoes closer. My arms are on fire. From my elbows to my fingertips there is only pain.

'Hush now, Dora,' he says, in between my screams. 'Hush. The blistering will help to draw off the humour and break the fever.'

His face fades away and then I am calling for water and they give me something cold and bitter and perhaps I sleep. Some time passes and the pain is not so fierce and now Mother is examining the blisters which crawl like fat, pink caterpillars across my arms. She looks satisfied.

'Your face is a better colour. Try to get up now and dress.'

Father is there, watching, as I sit up and slowly swivel my legs around, across the damp coverlet; for all their scrubbing, there is still a sour smell coming off it. Mother takes my arm but as soon as I try to stand on my feet, the room is swimming again and I reach for the bowl on the bed and retch into it. Father helps me back onto the mattress.

63

'It's no good,' Mother says, her voice low. 'You will have to send to say she is sick. We cannot have the town see her like this.'

Father frowns. 'I suppose there is nothing more to be done?'

Mother's face creases up in an alarming way. I have never seen her cry before. 'After all that expense. What will we do with the food?'

She turns on me. 'You have never given me anything but trouble.' Her voice rises and every word is a fresh blow on my pounding head. 'I wouldn't wonder if you brought this sickness on yourself, to spite us.'

What can I do? Pain roars through my body, flaring out along my arms. The tears are streaming down my face and I look to Father but there is no comfort there.

'This is not the end, Theodora. We will delay the wedding feast for now but mark my words, it will take place and you will go to live with your husband.'

They leave me with my agony. I lie in a damp bed, listening to the sound of wooden shoes going up and down the stairs to the salle, and cry till I have no more tears left. I have never felt so alone. *Many are they that rise up against me. I have looked for some to take pity but there was none, and for comforters, but I found none.*

*Priory of St Mary, Huntingdon*

## *Twenty-first day of April, AD 1116*

Only half a year ago, it would have filled me with wonder to be given leave to stand here, in the quiet of the canons' cloister, but now there is nothing for me in this place, only fear and censure. For all his wealth and high position, even Father seems a little awed. He looks up as a figure in white turns the corner of the cloister. He walks towards us, his nut-brown beard long and tangled.

'Turn away, and keep your head down,' Father whispers. 'By rights, women should not be in this place.'

The canon passes, without speaking a word to us. We have been asked to wait for the Father Prior, but there is no sign of him. Perhaps it is only the weakness after my fever but I long to lean against Father and rest my head on his shoulder, even though he is the one who has brought me here for judgement.

The hearing is to take place in the chapter house and the whole community, including Sueno, will be present. I imagine his eyes on me while they debate my marriage, and begin to tremble more violently.

*I will obey you and go to live as Burthred's wife.* Would it be so hard just to say the words to Father? Yet it's not the words that are hard, it is the living of them. To be a common or garden wife like my mother, brought to bed with birth pains, hanging on my husband's word. When I have been chosen to be a Bride of Christ, serene and implacable, like the virgin martyrs. I see now that I can't trust Burthred to abide by my wishes and live chaste. He is a weakling and bends wherever the wind blows him.

A stout old woman is struggling with a heavy basket in the

kitchen alley and I am surprised when she ventures into the cloister. Father glances away from her in disdain and moves on ahead. When she passes me, I catch her low whisper.

'I have a message, from Sueno.'

I stare after her. Suddenly the weakness is gone and my thoughts are running fast like a stream in winter.

'Father.'

He turns and walks back. 'Come along, Theodora.'

'Wait - I have to piss. Let me ask that woman.'

He looks at me, his eyes narrowing.

'Father, I need to ...'

He calls and the woman turns. Father takes my arm and approaches her.

'My daughter needs to relieve herself. Show her where, if you please.' He takes out a coin and hands it to her. 'Be quick and do not allow anyone to speak to her. Bring her straight back here. She is to appear with me before the Prior.'

I follow the woman back along the alley, which opens to the garth on one side. The sun is shining and a spring wind is up, blowing white clouds, like dandelion puffs, across the sky. As soon as we are out of sight of the cloister, I clutch at the woman's gown sleeve.

'What is the message? Tell me.'

'Canon Sueno wrote it down. Come with me, Mistress.'

The serving woman heaves the basket of barley onto her hip and leads me to the brewhouse, where she lowers it to the floor. A young boy looks up with interest from stirring the contents of a barrel, but the woman ignores him. She reaches up to a shelf and feels under some cloths, then hands the wax to me. Sueno has written in Latin.

*The truth of your marriage and your suffering has been told to*

66

*me. Can you forgive me for doubting you?*

I hold the wax to my face and my eyes fill with tears. My teacher has touched this, he has scratched these words with his own stylus – I am not abandoned. The ale-wife is peering at me. She grins, showing more gum than teeth.

'Quick - fetch me a pen. I must write a reply to him.' The woman looks around the brewhouse blankly.

'You must have something I can write with.'

The boy has been listening and now he puts down his ladle. 'I'll run to the kitchen for a goose feather.'

'Yes - yes, but be quick,' I urge him.

I am still thinking of what to write when there is the sound of boots at the door and my father is in the doorway. I hide the wax behind my back.

'Theodora! Where have you been? The Prior is waiting.'

With a nod to the woman, Father grabs my arm and hustles me out into the spring morning. The woman may not know her letters but she is cunning. She slips behind me and takes the wax from my hand.

The canons are gathering at the door of the chapter house. My heart is like a young colt in my chest as Fredebert, the Prior, acknowledges me with a bow of the head. I scan the faces of the fathers as they enter through the vestibule. There is no sign of Sueno. Now a stooped figure joins the line and at once I recognize the shoulders, the greying beard, of my friend. With an effort, I keep from crying out.

The Chapter House is in silence, the canons seated all around us on benches built into the curving wall, the Prior in his own carved chair. Father and I are left to stand but the relief of having Sueno's approval has swept away my nervousness. The Prior is saying some opening words, but

I only have eyes for my teacher. He sits not far from me, his head in his hands. It seems to me that his shoulders are trembling.

Father begins to speak, his voice unfamiliar in this bare, echoing space. He speaks with confidence, sure of his case.

'Reverend Prior, my fathers, I beseech you to counsel my daughter to marry in the Lord, as she has promised.'

I barely hear what he is saying. There is something glistening in the candle light. Perhaps I am mistaken, but I fancy that there are tears running down the back of Sueno's hand, forming a grey wet patch on his white habit.

Courage seems to flow into my body and I turn towards the Prior. He is a tall man who sits erect, his beard the more striking by dint of his baldness. There is no malice in his look but I sense that the canons do not like to cross him. Father is in full flow, and now he turns towards me.

'I know, and I acknowledge to my daughter, that she has consented to this marriage against her wishes. But, however that may be, she has given her consent. And now, as an obedient daughter, it is her duty not to oppose her parents and to make us a mockery and derision before our neighbours.' He appeals to Prior Fredebert. 'Tell her this. If she only abides with our wishes, she will have all that we possess. She will not dare to oppose your authority.'

The Prior has been listening, his hands folded in his lap.

'I have heard you, Auti. Now, leave us if you will, while I address myself to your daughter.'

As Father turns to leave, there is a spring in his step, a hint of triumph in the way he lifts his eyebrow. The canons shift a little on their benches and murmur. Once the door has closed behind him, quiet descends again.

'News of your obstinacy in this matter has reached us before today, Theodora,' the Prior begins. 'And we are puzzled at what is tantamount to madness. Each of us here is a priest and we have been assured that your betrothal was conducted according to ecclesiastical custom. As you know, the sacrament of marriage cannot be revoked.'

Standing alone before so many men of God and hearing words like these, I begin to tremble again and put out a hand to steady myself on one of the pillars that rise to the vaulted ceiling.

'You are a woman and are not familiar with the scriptures, so I will bring these words to your notice. The Apostle Paul states: "Unto the married I command, yet not I, but the Lord, let not the wife depart from the husband and let not the husband put away his wife." '

The Prior speaks clearly and patiently, a man who finds satisfaction in doing his duty fairly.

'You are more familiar, perhaps, with the commandment that children should obey their parents and show them respect. Both commandments are great, but you should know that the bond of marriage takes precedence over even the authority of parents.'

He leans forward in his chair.

'Theodora, if your parents were to command you to break off this marriage, you would not be free to do so. But, as it is, they are commanding you to do something which we know, on divine authority, to be more important than obedience itself. If you persist in refusing to live with your husband as his wife, you are doubly at fault.'

My palms have become sticky and the walls of the chapter house seem to buckle and shift, closing in on me. Prior

69

Fredebert's face softens and he permits himself a smile.

'Theodora, you must not think that salvation is reserved only for the chaste woman - many mothers of families, too, are lauded for their virtue.' He gets to his feet and composes himself. 'Nothing remains but that you accept our teaching and advice and submit yourself to the lawful embraces of your husband, Burthred.'

He is so learned and his words proceed so exactly, thought building upon thought, principle upon principle, that they seem to make an impregnable fortress. But what about love, the vow between the soul and her heavenly husband? I stand facing the Prior but the image of my teacher's hand, wet with tears, gives me strength.

'My parents bear me witness, Father Prior, that since childhood I have never thought to be a wife but have chosen the way of purity.' I glance towards Sueno. 'I have vowed this before one of your own fathers.'

My voice sounds meagre, lost in the lofty space of the Chapter House, but still there is a kind of solace in speaking out. I feel a new vigour flowing through my body and the words come to me.

'But even if Canon Sueno were not present, God himself would be witness to my conscience. As far as I have been allowed, I have tried to abide by my vow. If my parents order me to enter a marriage I never wanted and to break the vow to Christ which they know I made, I leave you to judge how wicked a thing that is. And as for married women, no doubt what you say is true, but does the Church not teach that a virgin may more easily attain heaven?'

There is a sound of tutting behind me. Some of the canons are staring, others are looking down into their laps. Prior

Fredebert seems at a loss. Taking his seat, he makes the shape of a steeple with his hands, his fingertips touching his lips. At last, he leans forward and speaks, quite differently now, as if we are family, at table together.

'But how do I know that you are doing this for the love of Christ? Perhaps you are merely hoping for a more wealthy match?'

'A more wealthy match: yes, I am. Who could be richer than Christ himself?'

The words seem to come easily now, for all the world as if I were trading wit with Father or with my brother, Gregory. But Prior Fredebert does not like my answer.

'I am not jesting, but treating with you seriously.' His voice becomes precise. 'If you wish us to believe you, take an oath in our presence that, were you betrothed to him, as you have been to Burthred, you would not marry even the king's son, William Atheling.'

I look up to the vaulted ceiling, painted blue and gold for the heavens, and a passion of courage flows through my body. The crown of chastity is almost in my grasp.

'I will not only take an oath - you can put me to the ordeal. I will prove it by carrying red-hot iron in these, my bare hands.' I hold out my hands before them. I have borne blistering once and I can bear it again. 'I can only say what I have said many times before. I have made a vow to the son of the Eternal King and by his grace I must keep it.'

Silence. I take a breath and seek out Sueno's face; his eyes are wide with awe.

Prior Fredebert is discomfited. 'What is the point of bringing suffering on yourself, to no purpose?' he asks quietly.

He does not seem to require an answer and calls for Father to be admitted again to the room.

'We have tried our best to bend your daughter to your will,' he says, 'but we have made no headway.'

Father looks appalled.

'We know, however, that our bishop, Robert, will be coming soon to his vill at Buckden. Reason demands that the whole question be laid before him. Let the case be put into his hands and let her take the verdict of the Bishop, if of no other.'

Is he saying, after all, that he does not consider my vow to Christ binding? The disappointment is so great that I think I might fall to the floor. But he has not finished yet. He takes in the circle of canons with his gaze, then turns back to Father and pronounces in a firm voice.

'We respect the high resolution of this maiden as founded on impregnable virtue. And I have little doubt that Bishop Robert will be of the same mind.'

There is nothing more to be said and we are dismissed. I walk back through the town with Father, my steps light on the cobbles, my heart joining in the dance of the clouds through the blue sky. It is spring, the sun is shining, and the Prior has spoken on my behalf. Father walks ahead, silent and sulky, till we are almost home. It is not till we are in sight of the house that he speaks to me.

'Well, you are made mistress over me today. The Prior has praised you to the skies and exalted you above us all. If the Bishop is of the same mind, then I suppose you must live your life as you please. But don't expect any help or comfort from me.'

He walks on alone while I stare at his back, trying to take in what he said. Has he given me leave to keep my vow to

Christ? Despite everything, I want to run after him and plead with him and burrow my head in his shoulder as I used to do.

# Chapter 8

*Huntingdon*

*Twenty-fourth day of April, AD 1116*

At last I hear a door opening upstairs and the sound of Father's voice, bidding farewell to his chaplain. I put down my work and yawn, for Margaret's benefit.

'I need some air. I think I'll go and see the hens.'

At the bottom of the stairs, I look around but there is no-one in sight. I slip into the scullery and wait. Now comes the ring of boots on the stairs and the door of the scullery opens slowly. I take Wulfstan by the sleeve and pull him in.

'What news do you have for me, Father?'

The canon darts a glance behind me, along the passage that leads out to the kitchen. He is right to be cautious. The servants would be curious if they saw me whispering with my father's chaplain in the scullery.

'Good news, Mistress Theodora.'

He wastes no time, keeping his voice low and quick, and I am suddenly humbled by his courage. Heaven knows what would happen if Father found out he was helping me.

'I went with Sueno to your husband. He says that he is prepared to release you from your marriage.'

I cannot believe what he is saying. 'Did you tell him what Bishop Robert said to the Dean?'

'Yes. I think that is why he has softened. He seems certain that the Bishop will support you on Thursday in his court.'

I can feel the tears forming in my eyes. Father Wulfstan stretches out his plump, freckled hand, but he does not dare to touch me.

'And we gave him our assurance that you would marry no other, but only take the veil.' When he grins, as he does now, his cheeks are like two red apples. 'There is more. Burthred says he will make a grant of land to the monastery of your choice, so that you may enter.'

I let him go, back to the Priory, before anyone should discover us. But first I thank him from the bottom of my heart. 'And please greet Father Sueno for me.'

I skip back up the stairs to the dayroom and only just remember to stop outside the door and compose my face.


*Bishop of Lincoln's court, Buckden*

*Twenty-seventh day of April, AD 1116*


Father rides ahead of me all the way along the great north road, without turning his head once. The Bishop's house at Buckden is imposing. As we are being shown into the vestibule, I reach out to touch Father's arm. He pats my hand but will not look me in the face; perhaps he already knows in his heart what Robert Bloet will say. Coming out of the spring sunshine, my eyes take time to grow accustomed to the dim light. There are men of quality and clerks in small groups, dotting the spacious hallway and villeins too, from the Bishop's manor. A few stop their talk to turn and stare at me, the only woman in the room. Burthred and his father are already there, together with the priest who was present at the betrothal. Father goes over to join them, leaving me to stand alone.

Every so often, the door to the great hall opens and the murmur of talk dies away. Names are called out by a steward, some people enter, then the door is closed again. There seems nothing to do but wait. Warm from the ride, I take off my cloak but no-one comes to relieve me of it. There is a bench running the length of one wall and in crossing over to it, I make sure to pass close to Father and the others, trying to catch Burthred's eye. He must have seen me. Why doesn't he make a sign?

No-one else is sitting but, after a time, I perch on the edge of the bench. I am uneasy. Then it comes to me that Burthred is a coward and he has probably not told his father that he intends to release me. His father is laughing at something, head back, eyes to the ceiling. Father turns and I see that he is laughing too. No matter. We shall hear Bishop Robert's judgment soon enough and then the smiles will be wiped from their faces.

The morning wears on and my belly begins to rumble. I should have had a second piece of bread at breakfast. The door opens again and the steward reads from his list.

'Burthred of Wennington.'

76

My heart starts to beat faster as we are ushered into the great hall, with its high vaulted roof. The gallery has a screen intricately carved from oak and even from here I can see that the hangings are very fine. Everyone knows that the Bishop of Lincoln is a rich man. There is a clerk at a desk to one side but the Bishop is seated in the centre of the dais, a thin, pinched man, quite old. Father says he was clerk to the first King William, long before I was born. The usher indicates where we should stand but when I go to follow the others, he puts up his hand.

'This way, Mistress.' He points to the other side of the room.' The defendant's place is to the left.'

My knees begin to shake under my gown but I try to look as if I were at ease. I will not let them see how hard my heart is beating. To still its frenzy, I think of my friends at the Priory and of what Bishop Robert was heard to say when the Dean brought up the matter of my marriage over dinner. *No-one can be forced to marry against their consent.*

Robert Bloet is looking at me with curiosity. He has dark, protruding eyes and a beaked nose. Now he turns his attention to the other side of the hall and makes a sign. Burthred steps forward from the others and starts to speak, his voice higher than usual and tighter, as if someone were grasping his throat.

'My lord Bishop, on the day of the Nativity last, Theodora, daughter of Auti of Huntingdon, consented to be my wife, at the door of the Church of the Blessed Virgin and in the presence of many witnesses, including Ranulf, my lord Bishop of Durham.'

Clearly, he has prepared this speech. Burthred's father moves closer to mine and whispers something. I become aware that the Bishop's eyes are resting on me as often as on Burthred. He holds up his hand and Burthred's voice falters and halts. The Bishop turns to me.

'Theodora, why do you stand alone? Do you not wish to take counsel?'

Confused, I look down to the floor, then up again. Should I have contrived to have a message sent to Canon Sueno? I shake my head and the Bishop turns back to Burthred.

'Continue.'

When he has finished, the priest speaks on Burthred's behalf, confirming all that he has said and praising his character. In the mouth of the priest, refusing to share my husband's house and his bed sounds like a wilful act of malice on my part.

Bishop Robert leans forward in his chair. 'Theodora, you have refused to comply with the will of your parents and that of the man to whom you are betrothed. What do you have to say?'

Now is the time to speak out but this is not the Priory of St Mary and Canon Sueno is not seated close by, praying for me. The clerk looks up from his desk, his hand poised above the wax.

'My lord...' My mouth is dry. The words struggle to form themselves in my mind. 'I made a vow, years since, when I was a child...'

'A vow?'

'A vow of chastity.'

'So you do not consent to this marriage?' I see now that the Bishop is trying to help me and my voice grows stronger and steadier.

'No, my lord. I do not consent. I have been pressed into

this marriage against my will - my father admitted it to the Prior in Huntingdon.'

The Bishop glances at Burthred and then back at me. 'The case that has been made against you is strong. You should take counsel.'

Why does he keep saying that? 'Whose counsel can be better for me than God's and yours, most holy father?'

'That is a good answer,' the Bishop replies. He leans back in his chair, appearing to consider the case. At last, he gives his judgment.

'I find in favour of the plaintiff, Burthred of Wennington.'

I have not seen Mother so happy in a long time, perhaps never. She did not complain even when Father invited all of Burthred's family to ride over from Wennington to sup with us. It is like a feast day. Of course, I am to sit beside Burthred at table and share the bowl with him. He is eating hungrily, fowl grease on his lips and in amongst the hairs of his beard. When he offers me the bread and the greens I turn my head away.

Father is all smiles too, jesting with Burthred's father and his uncle. He is drinking freely. Now he gets up and makes his way to where I am sitting.

'Now, now, Dora.' He is pawing at my shoulder, speaking far too loud. 'It is for the best, poppet, you'll see.'

When he is back in his place, Burthred leans in close to me. It seems that his tongue, too, has been loosened by drink.

'See - now I have bettered you before two of the most powerful bishops in the land - Durham and Lincoln.'

I stare at him in contempt. 'It is you who has been bettered, time and again. My father has always been able to bend you to his will, like a wet reed. And not only my father, if you care to remember. '

Burthred's face reddens but he is not to be silenced yet.

'You thought the Bishop would find in your favour, I know it.' He grins and I can see there is a piece of green stuck between his front teeth. 'But you did not reckon on Robert Bloet's greed. How do you think he came by the office of Chancellor?'

All at once, I see how things are: why Burthred's father was so unconcerned at court.

'You think you have succeeded?' I am hissing at him now. 'Where is your success? I have never been yours and with God's help, I never will be, bribe or no. I would rather be cut to pieces.'

He is staring at me as if I were crazed. 'But you cannot mean to go against the judgment of Robert Bloet. He will have you excommunicated.'

I bite my lip. His words have hit their mark.

'Burthred, you truly believe that we are husband and wife in the eyes of God?'

'Yes.' He thinks I have softened and takes my face in his hands, as if I were a child. I can smell the ale on his breath. 'And in the eyes of the Church. Bishop Robert has confirmed it.'

'Tell me then, as you hope God may have mercy on you, what would you do if another were to come and take me away from you and marry me?'

I see suspicion begin to creep across his face like a shadow. He gets to his feet.

'I would never allow it, as long as I lived.' He is clenching his fists. 'I would slay him with my own hands, if there was no other way of keeping you.'

I fix my eyes on his face. 'Beware then, Burthred, of taking to yourself the spouse of Christ. What might He do to you in His anger?'

Burthred's wits may be dulled by drink but my meaning does not escape him. He stares at me, uncertain, and then fearful. I get up to leave and he lets out something like a growl and makes a grab for me. But I am too fast for him and slip out behind the extra benches, across the landing and the dayroom, to the safety of my own chamber.

The evening air at the window is chill but I don't want to block out the last of the day's light with the shutters. I can hear them still at table in the salle, raucous in drink. The musicians have started up. I feel darkness all around me. I walk around the foot of my bed and back, again and again, as if walking might keep it at bay, but now comes shouting from the far side of the house, and the sound of a bench being knocked over. The darkness gathers strength and I begin to tremble. There are heavy footsteps in the dayroom and then my door bursts open. It is Father, his cheeks ruddy with drink and rage, his hair flying in all directions.

'Get out of my house,' he yells. 'You will leave - tonight.'

'Father...' My whole body starts to shake.

'Enough! You call me Father but you dare to defy me. And your husband, and now the Bishop of Lincoln himself.'

He strides towards me and I back away and up, onto the bed, wrapping the curtain around me. He tears back the drape and plants himself before me, holding out his hand.

'Give me the keys to my chest, girl. You are no daughter of mine.' His breathing is heavy and fast.

I fumble with the knot in my girdle but my fingers will not do as they are told. The tears are streaming down my face.

He grabs the girdle and drags me to the edge of the bed by it, tearing at the knot till it gives and the keys drop to the floor. He stoops to pick them up.

'Now your pendant and your rings.'

I take them off and hand them to him but there seems no end to his rage. He looks at my gown.

'That silk cost me dear. Take it off. You were born into this house with nothing and you shall leave it with nothing.'

'Father, please…'

'Not one word. I have indulged you for too long.'

It is hard to catch my breath between the sobs. When I hesitate, he lunges towards me as if he means to undress me himself and so I hasten to take off my tunic. There are noises at the door. I turn to see the burgundy velvet of Mother's best gown.

'Mother, talk to him, please,' I beg.

'It is no use pleading with your mother. We have both had our fill of you.' He drags me off the bed and pushes me, dressed only in my shift, towards the door. 'You wish to turn your back on your family, then go, but you will take nothing with you.'

Through my tears, I see my half-brother, Simon, standing in the doorway.

He looks past me. 'Father, calm yourself. She cannot leave now. It's late.'

'Don't gainsay me in my own house,' Father says, but I can feel that the fire of his anger has passed its peak and must start to die down. His first-born son has always had a way with him.

Simon walks over to Father and lays a hand on his shoulder. 'Think of what the Guildsmen would say to a daughter of yours wandering undressed in the street at night,' he says, his voice soft and cool as butter. 'You are master in your own house. There will be time enough tomorrow to plan a course of action.'

Father just stands, clutching the keys to his chest. Suddenly, his shoulders drop and he lets out a groan. 'Dora, what have you brought me to?'

Simon puts an arm around his shoulder and steers him towards the door. As they pass, my brother whispers to me. 'Go to bed. Keep out of sight.'

It is dark now and I fasten the shutters and kneel beside my bed to pray, but no words will come. It is as if the blood has been drained from my body and with it, all feeling. I cannot sense in my soul the love of Christ or his mother. Only two things seem clear to me. The first is that Father will repent his anger in the morning. The second is that I must find a way to leave this house and this life.

# Chapter 9

*First day of May, AD 1116*

It is the first truly warm day of this cool spring and the men seated at table in our salle are drinking more ale than wine with their roasted pork. Father has brought the most powerful of the Guildsmen together to discuss what can be done about the problem of St Ives. Since the Abbot of Ramsey was granted an annual Easter fair some six years ago, trade in Huntingdon has suffered. How can the King's taxes be found for his wars in France?

I notice that Cenric the winemerchant's cup is empty. The ale jug is getting low and I am glad to have a reason to escape, at least for a few moments. Why did Father insist that I serve his guests? I suppose that by honouring me, Father thinks to make up for his terrible display of temper, but all it does is rile my mother even more.

The kitchen is full of steam and the stench of boiling cabbage. Mother is there, by the range, watching old Alice as she stirs the frumenty.

I hold the jug out to her. 'The ale is running out.'

'So? Go and get some more.' Her mouth is working strangely and now she almost spits at me. 'You think to take my place - I know it. He has always cared for you more than for me.'

She turns her back and I make my way through the kitchen and into the brewhouse. It is cooler in here. I go to the next cask in line, hoping it is the right one, and tease out the bung. A faint whiff of costmary reassures me that it is ale, though a darker batch than the last. I watch it frothing into the jug and think of Mother and how she seems more crazed with every passing day. She has taken to inviting strangers - old crones - into the house and whispering with them. I saw a woman with her in the back yard at Prime this morning, younger this one than the others, short and dark-skinned. Her dove grey cloak seemed to be of fine stuff. As I passed, I heard her talking quickly in French, though God knows how much Mother would understand of that.

When the jug is full I replace the peg, screwing it in tight, and suddenly I remember where I have seen the woman in grey before - in the street of the Jews. The jug is heavy and I look around for someone to carry it up for me but Alice is busy, spooning the frumenty into serving bowls. There is no sign of Mother. I start carefully back up the steps by the pantry.

Suddenly comes the sound of running feet behind me. I feel a painful thud in my back and the jug slips from my hand and smashes against the edge of the step, cracking into two. The drink splashes up onto my tunic, then surges outwards in a foamy flood, pouring in rivulets down the steps.

'Look what you've done!' I yell, turning to see who is responsible.

But it is not Wyn or John or Alice. It is Mother and she has a rolling pin in her hand. Before I can think to protect myself, she is flying at me and beating me on my arms, my shoulders, wherever she can reach. I scream for help and try to cover my face but now she catches me a blow on my elbow and the tingling pain is unbearable.

'Mistress!' Alice is here now, pulling onto Mother's sleeve, but Mother is beside herself and pushes her away roughly. Bent double and clutching my arm, I try to back away from her.

'See?' She manages to land another blow, this time on the side of my head. I cry out at the pain. I have never seen Mother like this before. Surely someone must come. Her face looms towards mine, bulging with spite, and now she drops the pin on the floor and grabs hold of a handful of my hair. 'Where are the angels now?' She tugs hard, jerking my head down right to my shoulder, stretching my neck. A trickle of spit is escaping from her mouth. 'The Jewess was wrong. I can do whatever I want with you.'

My scalp is on fire and now, at last, help comes in the shape of my sister, running along the kitchen passage.

'Margaret! Stop her!'

She is still a moment, taking in the scene.

'Look, Mother.' Margaret speaks calmly. 'The ale jug is broken. Shall I fill another for upstairs?'

I feel the grip on my hair loosen. Mother is looking down at the jagged pieces of earthenware, the sodden rushes underfoot, as if seeing them for the first time. She nods and now, at last, it seems that the fight is going out of her. When

I prise her fingers open to free myself, she makes no move to stop me. She looks down at the strands of hair in her hand, surprised.

Now, as if nothing out of the ordinary has happened, she sends Alice to fetch a trug and sets about picking up the pieces from the floor. Margaret runs back towards the brewhouse, leaving me shaking with shock. To escape, I must pass Mother. She seems intent on her task but there is no knowing what she might do; the rolling pin is still within her reach. I reach up gingerly to touch my temple and find a bump swelling. There is blood on my fingers. I begin to cry but Mother takes no notice.

Margaret returns with a new jug of ale. 'I'll take it up to them. They'll be waiting,' she says, her voice even.

'No.' My mother sounds like herself again now. 'Your sister will take it.'

'But …' Margaret hesitates. 'They'll see her face.'

Mother looks at me and I see that her violent hatred is not spent after all, but has only sunk back down, gleaming dangerously in her eyes. 'She will take the ale. Let your father's guests see her as she is - a disgrace to us all.'

I climb the two flights of stairs, trying to hold the jug steady but my right arm is weak from the blow to my elbow. At the salle door, I put the ale down on the floor and wipe away a trickle of blood from my face. How can I go in, looking like this? There are footsteps behind me on the stairs and I jump in fear but it's only Margaret. She looks at me in her quiet way.

'Quick! Go to your chamber before Mother sees,' she whispers. 'I will make some excuse and serve for you.'

'Oh, Meg.' The tears well up afresh at this unexpected

kindness.

My sister picks up the jug.

'Wait,' I say, remembering Mother's strange words. 'What did she mean - about the Jewess?'

Margaret's eyes drop from my face, then she looks back up at me. 'You'd better go.'

'No - wait.' I can tell she knows something. 'What was that about angels?'

Her resolve weakens. 'Don't tell her I told you, Dora. She brought in a wise woman to make a potion for you.'

'A potion? What for?'

My sister's face colours. 'To make you immoderate in your desires. All she can talk of now is that some man - any man - should despoil you. But the Jewess told her to leave you alone. She said she saw figures in white, protecting you. Now go, I beg you, in case Mother comes up.'

Back in my chamber, I find the tom, Acwel, asleep on my bed. Somehow I manage to drag my small chest in front of the door, then stand before the mirror on trembling legs and peer at my face. The bleeding has stopped but the swelling on my temple is the size of a bantam's egg. A bruise is beginning to spread around my collar bone and my neck pains me whichever way I turn my head. All at once, I feel terribly tired and climb up on the bed next to Acwel. I curl myself around his furry warmth and fall asleep.

In my dream, I am standing in a church, its walls covered with the most exquisite paintings. A priest stands at the altar in a green and gold chasuble, ready to celebrate Mass. He turns and beckons to me. When I approach, he hands me a branch of white lilac, the fragrant blooms drooping heavily from the stem.

'Take it, Child,' he says, 'and offer it to the lady.'

I look up and there, on a dais close to the altar, sits a great lady, like an empress. Her gown is of sky blue and she wears a crown that twinkles and glimmers in the candlelight. I climb the steps and curtsey, offering her the branch. She accepts it but then breaks off a twig bearing one of the tapering white blooms, and hands it back to me.

The lady's eyes are a soft grey and she looks into mine deeply. 'How is it with you?' she asks.

'Ill, my lady,' I say. 'They ridicule me and they are cruel. They keep me locked up.'

'Don't be afraid,' the lady replies. 'I will deliver you from their hands and bring you to the brightness of day.' She seems to know that I long to stay here forever. When she speaks again, her voice is as gentle as a dove's. 'Go now.'

My heart is breaking. I turn and step down from the dais only to find Burthred, dressed in a black cloak, prostrate on the floor of the church. He reaches out to grab the flowing fabric of my white gown but I pull my skirts close and slip along by the wall of the church, out of his reach. He lifts his head and follows me with staring eyes, groaning horribly.

Now appears ahead of me a twisted flight of steps leading to an upper chamber. Somehow I know that if only I can reach that chamber, I will be safe forever. The steps are narrow and jagged and there is no rope to cling to. I hear footsteps behind - it is the lady herself, the queen. We climb together to the upper room, hung sumptuously with scarlet. There are logs burning in the grate. A delightful piping sound comes from a golden cage by the window, where two wrens sit upon a perch. Opposite the fireplace is a polished oak bench, running the length of the wall, piled high with feather cushions. I sink down into the velvet softness and now the lady returns. Without a word, she lays herself down beside me and places her head in my lap. I feel tears pricking my eyes and now they fall silently, on and on, as if they will never be spent. There is only one things that spoils my happiness; I cannot see her face.

She turns her head. 'You may look now,' she says. 'And afterwards, when I bring you and your sister into my chamber, you may gaze to your heart's content. You do well to gaze upon me. Do you know that I am able to touch the highest point in heaven? Be assured that I have chosen you from your father's house, and not only you, but your brother Gregory also.'

I wake and find my pillow sodden with tears.

# Chapter 10

*Huntingdon*

*Fifth day of May, AD 1116*

Wyn follows a few paces behind me as I wander through the kitchen and out into the back, beside the brewhouse. It has been such a hard winter that the quince is not yet in blossom and even the pears are only starting to bud. I pass the pigpen and then walk slowly among the fruit trees, as if taking my leisure.

'Stay here, within sight of the house,' I tell Wyn,' and keep watch.'

She was reluctant to help me against my parents, but her father is sick and must pay the physicker so she has great need of the pouch of coins I have given her.

The fading light has sent the hens to bed and soft roosting sounds are coming from the henhouse. Here, close to the fence, it is growing dark and the air is chill. I shiver a little, with no cloak around me, but I could not bring it with me from the house for fear of questions.

I stand on tiptoe to look over the pales of the fence and along the alley. It's deserted, though I can hear a dog barking from one of the yards further along. Will he come, this Eadwin? I told Wyn to give my message into the hands of the hermit himself but whether she did I cannot be sure. It's a good thing that her father lives out in the fenland or Mother would have wondered at her going that way.

A tall figure is striding along the alley, the hood of his cloak pulled up over his head. Is this the hermit? Sueno always spoke of Eadwin with respect – a holy man with many friends amongst those who live as recluses. Surely he will help me escape and find someone to shelter me.

The man is slowing his pace and looking about him. I whisper a prayer to the Queen of heaven, then call softly to him. He comes quickly to the fence and, glancing both ways to see that there is no-one watching, he pushes the hood back from his face. He is not an old man; his dark eyes are bright and alert, his face weathered, his black hair unkempt.

'You are Theodora? The daughter of Auti the nobleman?'

He uses no customary title, only my name, but I am not offended. I know that men like him live simply, as the apostles did, with no regard for wealth or position.

'Master Eadwin? Thank you for coming.' I can hardly get my breath, now that it comes to the point. 'I have been praying for succour. Can you help me? I must leave this house.' Tears are beginning to form in my eyes. 'I have vowed to be a bride of Christ but they seek to make me marry.'

'I know your situation. I have spoken with Canon Sueno at the Priory.' He seems unmoved by my distress but my heart leaps to hear that he has spoken to Sueno. Somehow I feel that he will help me.

'I cannot house you myself out at Higney, it's too close - this whole country is full of your relatives. But I have sent to my cousin, Roger, to ask what can be done.'

'Roger? The recluse in the woods near Caddington?'

'The same. He has influence, even with the Bishop of Lincoln perhaps.'

I dare to hope a little. Roger is well-known in the whole of this eastern country - consulted by the highest in the land.

Eadwin hears someone coming and covers his head quickly. He must leave, before he is seen. There are plenty in this town who would take information to Mother or Father if they thought there would be a reward in it.

'Wait! How will I know when you have news for me?' I whisper.

'Are you not able to leave the house?'

'No - only with my family or a keeper.'

Eadwin drops down out of view for a moment then reappears. 'See this gap between the pales, near the ground. When I know something of use to you, I will write it in a letter and bury it under the earth on your side. Now, farewell and may Christ keep you.'

He is gone, his figure lost in the shadows. I hurry back to Wyn. She looks relieved but asks nothing. I think if she had her way she would know nothing at all of this. It is completely dark as we come in by the kitchen door. I stop a moment and look out into the night, giving thanks. But there is fear tangled up with this new hope. What if Eadwin is discovered in helping me? What if he can find no-one willing to take in a betrothed wife?

*Priory of the Blessed Virgin, Huntingdon*

*Feast of Pentecost, twenty-first day of May, AD 1116*

We are at Mass and the body of the Lord is still on my tongue, his blood stinging the back of my throat, when I turn and see him - Eadwin - standing by the pillar. Christ has indeed become flesh and now he comes to me in the form of his servant! I can feel the blood rushing to my face. Keeping my head down, I walk to my place.

He is back, then, from Canterbury. I have been counting the days since I saw disturbed earth by the back fence and found his buried message. When I read it first, I was cast down. Roger had refused to help a runaway wife – that's how he deems me. But Eadwin wrote that he would ask the Archbishop for help. Ralph d'Escures supports all those who wish to live in the new way of holiness.

Through the antiphon and the priest's blessing, one thought after another tumbles across my mind. My palms are sticky. Gregory is standing next to me and he looks down as if he can see what is in my head, but of course he can't. My brother lives a godless life, but still I will be sorry to leave him.

I steal a glance across the church, to the back of Eadwin's head. To be so close and yet to have no conversation is too much to bear – I long to know what the Archbishop said. Yet how can I approach him here, in front of my parents?

The service is over. Because of Pentecost, the church is full of townspeople. I crane my neck to keep Eadwin in sight across the heads of the congregation. Father and the others start to wend their way towards the door and I contrive to follow very slowly, trying to open up a distance between us. I feel a hand on my elbow. It's John, Father's steward, steering me out of the church.

'Hasten, Mistress. Your father doesn't want you to tarry here. Or perhaps, there is someone you wish to speak to?' He smirks at me. 'Your husband is here, with his mother.'

My hand itches to strike him across the face, but I say nothing. If John were not a faithful dog, devoted to my father, I might offer him money. God knows that I would give enough gold to fill this whole church in exchange for news of my fate. But what can I do?

Back at the house, I offer to see to the hens and slip out, but the earth beside the fence is just as it was yesterday; there is no new message. When dinner is called, I find that guests have been invited for the Feast, so for once Mother and Father do not berate me at table. I leave before the fruit is served and take my needlework upstairs to my chamber. I bar the door, fearful these days of what Mother might do if she were to catch me alone.

I lie on the bed as it gets dark, listening for Matilda's tread. When I hear her moving beyond the wall, I pull the chest from in front of my door and open it. My little sister is getting ready for bed and I watch her undressing; she is no longer a child. I think of all the games I played with her when she was small, all the times I have fed her the choice tidbits from our plate.

'Tilda, will you do something for me?'

She stands in her shift, looking at me. 'What?'

'In the morning, will you carry a message for me, to Higney?'

Matilda doesn't even stop to think. 'No.' She starts to

unbraid her hair. It is darker than mine, the colour of chestnuts. 'Mother says I am not to help you. You are bringing our family to shame.'

I wince at her words. Margaret has always been close with Mother but I thought Matilda loved me. I go back into my chamber and open the chest, taking out the headband of morning glory that Leofa made for me. Matilda has always admired it. I hand it to her.

'You can have this if you take the message.'

She ties it around her forehead and goes to view herself in the mirror, then looks at me coolly. 'All right. I will go for you.'


*The river meadows, Huntingdon*

*Fourteenth day of June, AD 1116*


I breathe a prayer of thanks for this glorious morning. The sunshine broke through the mist early and seems to have gladdened Mother's heart. She was agreeable when I said I wanted to take a walk by the river, even though it meant losing Wyn's help in the house. *You are not to cross the river. Stay on the town side*, she warned.

We turn off the road just before the bridge, but not before I notice the bridgeman staring at me and whispering to his boy. I hold my head higher. They all talk about me and my marriage, I know that.

The willows at the water's edge are drooping gracefully, sunlight filtering through the yellow-green curtain of leaves.

The lambs have had the first grass and now that they are shut out from the meadow, wild flowers are shooting up among the lush new growth: daisies and buttercups and hay rattle. But this morning, I barely notice them. Every few yards, I stop and peer towards the bridge, shielding my eyes from the sun, searching for a tall figure with dark hair. I turn and wait for Wyn to catch me up.

'Keep back if a man joins us. I must speak with him.'

Fear passes across her face. 'But Mistress - your mother would not allow it.'

I look her straight in the eye. 'Wyn, you will not tell my mother or my father anything of what passes here, if you fear God. My parents would have me break a sacred vow.'

She bites her bottom lip.

I steel myself. 'Wyn, if you blab to them about this meeting, I will tell them that you took a message to Eadwin before, for money.'

She gasps, understanding my meaning, but I'm still not certain that I can rely on her silence.

There are foot passengers crossing the bridge into town but Eadwin is not one of them. Two women with a basket on each arm pay their toll and pass on, headed for market. A short, squat youth with a thatch of yellow hair crosses the bridge, then turns aside onto the meadows, walking quickly. He looks rough so I move away, towards the river.

Turning back, I see that he has stopped. My heart starts to beat faster. I call out to Wyn but the youth thinks I am calling to him and he comes towards me, as bold as anything.

'Stop there,' I call out. 'What do you want with me?'

He ignores me, coming closer with every stride and now I see that though he is young he is stocky and strong looking.

'Mistress Theodora?'

'How do you know my name?' I have never seen him in the town.

'My master Eadwin sent me.'

Wyn has come running but I gesture to her to keep back. The youth looks like a villein and speaks in the old language but he seems sober.

'I went to Canterbury with my master. He has sent me with news of those who can help you.'

I am astounded. Why did the hermit not come himself? How dare he send a boy? I am disappointed and angry. And yet it seems that Eadwin must trust this servant, so I have no choice but to do the same.

'Did your master tell you what the Archbishop said?'

'He is a friend to all the hermits and recluses, Mistress. He said that it is your mother and father who are at fault, in making you marry against your vow.'

It is disturbing to hear this stranger, a servant boy, speak of my marriage. But is it true, what he says?

'We stopped at all the hermitages on the journey home. My master explained how things stand with you and what the Archbishop said.'

The more the boy speaks, the more I see that he doesn't lack wit.

'I am to tell you the anchorites who have offered you refuge and you are to choose which you will.' He takes a breath, preparing himself to remember the message. 'There are two holy women who dwell in the woods behind the Mill at Stotfold - they will take you in and hide you. And the anchorite in the cell at St Mary the Virgin in Cheshunt. And Alfwen at Flamstead – she will take you.'

My thoughts are racing. I have never been to Stotfold, though I have heard Father speak of it. If he does business there, perhaps I should go elsewhere. Cheshunt is very far off.

'This Alfwen, she is at Flamstead?'

'Yes. Not far from Roger's hermitage in the woods. The hermit oversees her life. She will hide you from your enemies.'

Roger. He refused to help me. Yet somehow I feel drawn to be near this man – everyone speaks of him with such awe.

'I will go to Alfwen at Flamstead, if she will have me.'

The youth nods. He looks to left and right along the river, but there is no-one in sight. Wyn is looking miserable.

'Mistress,' she calls. 'We must walk on.'

'Wait. I will not be long.'

I turn back to Eadwin's servant. 'How will your master arrange to take me to my new home?'

The boy looks out, across the bridge to the flat fields on the far side of the river, then back to the town. He is frowning.

'If you can contrive to meet me outside the town boundary…'

I feel the heat gathering in my cheeks. Is this rough youth, then, to take me to Flamstead? What if we were seen together on the open road?

Now, when it comes to it, I see just how difficult it will be to get away. I cannot leave the house with Wyn, as I did today. How could she go back without me? They would flog her at the least. Suddenly, a thought comes to me. On the Feast of St John the Baptist Mother and Father will be making their yearly journey to holy Guido, to beg his prayers. They never miss - not since that first year of King Henry's reign when

Father's ship was lost in a storm. Yesterday I heard them talk of how they will leave me with my aunt, Alveva.

'What is your name?' I ask the young man. A new certainty is taking hold of me; the Feast of St John will be the day of my deliverance.

'Loric, Mistress.'

'Go then, Loric, and tell your master to prepare two horses, one for you and one for me, for Saturday week.' I point across the river to the field on the far side. 'Wait for me over there with the horses, at dawn. I will come across the bridge to you somehow.'

How can it be done? I must wear a disguise.

'Wait for me and don't go up to anyone else. You may not recognize me - I will be wearing my hood up. When I am about to cross the bridge, I will make a sign - like this.' I point to my forehead with my right forefinger. 'When you see that, rein the horses in ready, for we must ride as soon as I get to you.'

The youth seems to have understood the instructions. 'I will tell my master and do as you say, Mistress. Dawn on the Feast of St John.'

'And, Loric, I may have to wait for the right moment. If I do not come exactly at dawn, be patient. Wait for me.'

# Chapter 11

*Huntingdon*

*Feast of St John the Baptist, twenty-fourth day of June,*
*AD 1116*

Father dismounts and knocks on my aunt's street door. Even
as we wait for an answer, the darkness of night here between
the houses seems to loosen and lift. The horses are impatient
to be off, their hooves scraping against the cobbles. I look up
at the clear sky. One by one, like candles, the stars are being
snuffed out. Thinking about what this new day holds, my
heart quickens.

Aunt Alveva is at the door. She smiles at my parents. 'It
looks to be good weather for your journey,' she says. 'Give
Guido my greetings and ask his prayers for Richard. That
cough of his is no better.'

Mother reaches down from her horse to push me forward.

'Keep a close eye on her, sister,' she says. 'This one is not to
be trusted.'

'We will be back before dark tonight,' Father says. 'After

the hermit has prayed with us, we will dine with him, then ride straight home.'

He frowns at me then climbs back onto the horse, turns his head, and they are gone, clattering down the street.

Alveva pulls me into the house with a smile and asks if I have breakfasted.

'Yes,' I reply, glancing back anxiously toward the street door. It is lighter with every breath. How long before the sun will be visible, above the river meadow?

'I see you have brought your embroidery,' she says, indicating the bag slung over my shoulder. She leads me up into the salle and sits down beside me.

'So, Theodora,' she says. 'What news of your marriage? Your mother says that the house is finished.'

'There is still some furniture to be got, I think.'

I am very afraid that she wants to talk and I will have no chance to get away.

'I am sorry to hear about Uncle Richard. If he needs you with him, don't worry about me.'

Aunt Alveva looks at me closely. She knows me well and it's not easy to keep things from her. At last she takes my hand.

'Theodora,' she says. 'It's going to be a fine day, by the look of it. I shan't keep you tied down, like my sister does. They should be ashamed of themselves. What harm can you get up to, out and about in the town or walking down by the river?'

I am unable to believe my fortune and kiss her on the cheek. 'God bless you, Aunt! I think I shall go out now - I like to walk first thing, when the day is fresh.'

Wrapping my cloak around me against the early morning chill, I hurry down the stairs and out of the street door. People are beginning to stir and I narrowly miss being soaked on Silver Street as a woman empties her night pot from one of the upper windows. Down by the river, I peer across to the meadow on the far side, straining my eyes, but there is no-one in sight. The sun will soon be up. Where is Loric?

The Priory bell is ringing for Prime. It seems to me that, while I wait, I might go there one last time. It would be fitting to wish Sueno goodbye and leave with his blessing. But when I open the heavy door of the Priory church, I find he is not amongst the brothers singing the Hour. I kneel at the back and pray that Eadwin's servant will come soon. We must get away safely to Flamstead before my parents return.

I cannot stay when, even this moment, Loric may be riding across the meadow. What if he were to come and find me not there? I run from the church, along the street and down to the river's edge. It will be a warm day; there is no cloud and precious little breeze. The first of the day's passengers are paying toll to cross the bridge into town but the meadow across the river is empty. I walk to and fro a little and when the bridgeman waves to me, I wave back, as if it were a day like any other. I try not to keep looking but my eyes are drawn back, again and again, to the meadow. Still no-one there. Fearful that the bridgeman will suspect something, I walk back to my aunt's. Alveva has been tending my Uncle Richard and now she joins me again in the salle.

'Sit down and have some wine with me,' she says. 'Why don't you take off your cloak and rest? You are like a cat on a hot bakestone today.'

Amid all the anxiety, my aunt's kindness is too much to bear and I burst into tears. It comes to me all at once how much I love her and this house and how I will never see them

103

again, after today. Alveva puts her arm around me.

'What is it, Dora? Don't cry now. Tell me what's the matter.'

I struggle to master myself. My aunt mustn't know of the escape – that way she cannot be blamed. Already, I fear my parents will be angry that she let me wander the town alone.

'It's nothing. I'm being foolish, that's all,' I answer, in between the tears.

'Is it your marriage, Dora? It's not so bad, is it, to be Burthred's wife?'

I let her talk on, so that she thinks her words are soothing me, and soon I am calm again. She brings me a glass of warm wine and I drink it down quickly.

'I have a mind to go to church, Aunt.'

'Go then and make the most of your freedom, before your mother and father return.'

Setting off once again from the house, I make straight for the river, hoping against hope to see Loric and the horses on the far side. When I find that there is no-one in sight, the disappointment is like a leaden weight, almost robbing me of breath. The sun has been up some time and Loric has not come. Guido's hermitage is only out at Graveley. What if Father decides to return and dine at home after all?

Wandering back into town with no real purpose, I come across Geoffrey the Reeve parading the streets with some of the better citizens, dressed in their finery. Of course - it is the Feast of St John. The Reeve is a great friend of my Father and I stand aside to let them pass, but Geoffrey has seen me. The June sunshine seems to have made him merry.

'Good day, Mistress,' he calls. 'You are out alone today.' He glances toward the man beside him and winks. 'What would your father say to that, Theodora? Are you planning to run away?'

I cannot believe my ears but, quick as lightning, a reply comes to me. I smile. 'Yes, sir.'

Geoffrey laughs out loud and turns back to his companion. 'You hear that? And when is this escape to take place?' he asks.

'Today, sir,' I say, with another broad smile and, making a small bow, I pass on, the laughter of the citizens following me down the street.

Shaking, I turn off at the Priory and enter into the cool of the church. There is no-one inside. Falling to my knees, I cry out to God.

'Why have you forsaken me? Why hasn't the boy come?'

There is no movement of air in the church; the candles on the altar burn steadily. The silence, too, is unbroken and seems almost audible now, a low, tense hum. A terrible certainty comes to me, that I am being punished. My enemies have been right all along. I suddenly see myself as they do: a disobedient wife, resisting the will of God, full of pride and arrogance.

With a heavy heart, I get to my feet and leave the church. One more time I make for the river, the cloth bag with the few belongings I have packed strung across my shoulder, mocking me for a fool. The streets are busier now and I spy my friend Helisen, walking with the farrier, her belly swollen with a child. I turn off into an alley before she sees me. Why is her way so smooth, when mine is beset by thorns?

Down by the river, of course there is no Loric waiting with horses in the far meadow, only a girl driving her geese towards the bridge. I turn back along Bridge Street and make for our house on Merchants Row. I don't have the heart to go to my aunt's and pretend to be merry around the Midsummer table.

I wander aimlessly to the kitchen. Alice stops stirring the pot and looks at me curiously.

'I thought you were at your aunt's.'

Wyn appears from the brewhouse passage. I know what is on her mind. Will my parents expect her to guard me if I am not under Alveva's roof? Overcome with lassitude, I settle myself by the range, staring into the fire.

Perhaps I slip into sleep for a while but then I am roused by something, a change, as it were a fluttering, deep inside. Hope and joy are stirring gently within me, like baby birds in a nest, and now they seem to take flight, and fledge from my mouth in the shape of words. *Get up, Theodora. Loric is waiting.*

Trembling, I look around, but Alice is still picking over her greens and John gives me no glance as he passes with a heavy bucket. They heard nothing, yet the words ring in my ears, warm and redolent with truth. All my dark thoughts are dispelled, phantoms in the dawning light of day. I jump up, pull open the drawstring of my bag and snatch out a few of the things I have packed. Alice stares at me but there is no time to lose. I pull my riding cloak around me, and run along the kitchen passage, through the house, almost bumping into Matilda coming down the stairs, and out into the street.

Pulling the hood up over my head, I make for Bridge Street but then I hear my sister calling. She is following me.

'Are you going to Aunt Alveva's? Can I come with you? I am bored at home.' She looks up at me, her pert face framed by curls.

I could cry with vexation at the delay. Then it comes to me

- there is one place Matilda will not follow me.

'I'm going to the Priory first, sweetheart. You go back home.'

As I hoped, she falters. But in my fluster, I loosen my grip on the man's tunic I have brought with me to ride in and one of the sleeves starts to drag on the ground.

'What's that, Dora?' Matilda asks.

I stop and turn round to face her. 'Oh it's nothing, just a tunic of Gregory's I was planning to mend at Aunt Alveva's.'

All at once, a longing to be free and unencumbered takes hold of me like a madness. 'Look, why don't you take this back home? It's only getting in my way.'

I hand my sister the tunic and a veil and some other things I have brought with me and then, suddenly, I remember Father's keys. Unhooking them from my belt, I give them to Matilda.

'Father might return home while I'm gone and need something from his chest,' I say. Now she will have to stop following me.

When I see her heading back to our door, I set off in the direction of the Priory, then rejoin Bridge Street. I am running now, sweating under the heat of the sun and my cloak. By the riverside, I make out the figure of a youth on horseback in the far meadow. Yes! He is holding the reins of a second horse and peering across the water towards me. I make our secret sign, glance around me in every direction, then walk towards the bridge, keeping my head down. There is no toll to leave the town but I still have to pass the bridgeman at the far end. Thanks be to God – he is busy taking coins from a carter and I slip through beside the cart, unnoticed.

Loric is no real distance away across the meadow, but every step is an agony. I force myself to walk in a leisurely way when I long to run, expecting any moment to hear someone I know calling out to me. I want to take Loric to task for being so late but there is no time to lose. Without the man's tunic, there is nothing for it but to mount the horse in my own clothes and trust to the providence of God. The horse is more skittish than my Samson and harder to handle. I turn him around in an attempt to control him.

'Follow me at a distance,' I say to Loric. 'If we are caught, I am frightened they will take you to prison.'

I dig my heels into the horse's flanks and now we are flying across the meadow and towards the track that will take us south to St Neot's. From there we must go on to Shefford and Shillington and at last to Flamstead.

# Chapter 12

*The road to Flamstead*

*Feast of St John the Baptist, twenty-fourth day of June,*
*AD 1116*

It is long past noon and we have been riding full pelt under a hot sun. My buttocks are aching and the insides of my knees chafe painfully against the horse's sweaty flanks. We stopped only once to eat and drink and to water the horses, but soon Loric was urging me to mount again. He seems anxious, although whenever I look over my shoulder, there is no-one following.

We are on a track through beech woods now and I fix my eyes on Loric's tow-coloured hair, trying not to fall behind. The shade here is welcome and Eadwin's servant has slackened his pace a little. Since coming under the trees, we have encountered no-one, travelling either way. The woods begin to thin out and passing in and out of sight between the pale new leaves, I catch sight of a chapel ahead. Loric pulls on his reins, and the mare slows to a trot. Soon I have caught up with him.

'Why are you stopping?'

'Flamstead is a little further on, Mistress. But Alfwen's anchorhold is here, up against the church.'

I stare at the chapel. It is no more than that - an English church, built of timber, no great size. How can the recluse live here? We walk the horses on and now I see that there is a small lean-to structure built up against the chancel on the far side. It is surely only big enough for one room. The door is hidden behind tall fence pales that enclose an outside yard. Tarred palling has been stretched across the pales to provide some shelter for the yard.

Loric calls out to let the recluse know of our arrival and now a servant in a rough tunic emerges through a low opening in the fence. As she stands upright, I see that one side of her face is completely disfigured; a purple-red scar billows across her cheek. I turn away in distaste to find Loric waiting to help me dismount.

'Greetings, Alfwen,' I hear him say.

*Alfwen?* This is the venerable anchoress? I look at her more closely. She is small but wiry and strong, a woman perhaps of my mother's age. She hurries towards me, smiling, but her face only looks more monstrous, with one half of her mouth pulled down by the scar.

'You are right welcome, Theodora.' Her accent tells me that she is from the north country.

She says no more but makes a cradle with her arms so that Loric can remount his mare. She hands him the reins of my horse. Suddenly I am frightened.

'Don't go yet.'

But he is already turning his mare's head back towards the

110

track. He waves to us in farewell.

'Greet your master for me,' Alfwen calls, and he is gone. 'Come,' she says to me, 'it's not safe out here. You may be seen.'

The little woman bends to pass under the fence, sharp and bird-like, full of purpose. I follow her. The yard is small but the dirt has been well brushed and there is a barrel half full of water and, in the middle, a fire for cooking. A young girl kneels beside it, stirring the contents of a pot. When she sees me, she gets to her feet and makes a curtsey, her movements as slow and ponderous as her mistress's are quick. She is tall, with a wide moon face and frizzy brown hair.

'This is Johanna,' Alfwen says. 'She's a good girl.'

Alfwen leads me in through the open door of her an-chorhold. As I guessed, it is not a large room, and barely furnished. Here, too, the floor is of earth, but with a thin covering of stale rushes. There is a bed and I notice two stools and what looks like a bench leaning up against the wall that might serve as a table.

'It's not what you're used to,' Alfwen says. I look at her closely and see that she is not excusing the roughness of the place. Instead she seems proud.

The main feature of the room seems to be a tiny square window, cut into the church wall. There is a low prie Dieu beneath it and she invites me to kneel. When I obey, I find the window has been positioned so that the kneeler has a narrow view of the altar.

'This is where I pray,' Alfwen says. 'And now you will pray here too.'

I gaze at the altar in awe and imagine the priest beside it, holding up the Host. On a shelf beside the prayer stool,

I see what looks like a psalter. There is a box of candles beside it. Somehow, the sight of these objects seems to change everything. The strangeness of this place and my fear drop away and I forget the aches and pains of riding. It comes to me in a rush of understanding. At last, I am free to live the life I have dreamed of. And this holy woman, in her humble dress, with her disfigured face, will be my guide. I get to my feet, all at once sickened by my expensive clothes.

'Alfwen, I do not wish to wear these things any more. I want to live as a bride of Christ.'

She nods approvingly. 'It's all in hand, pet. Johanna's mother has made you something suitable.'

Alfwen turns to a doorway that I had not noticed before and I follow her. There is a storage space off the main room, just big enough for the mattress of straw laid on the floor.

'This is Johanna's bed, but now it can be yours. The girl will sleep at her mother's house in the village from now on.'

She picks up a blue woollen tunic and hands it to me. There and then, I take off my cloak and Alfwen helps to unlace my gown. Even the linen of my shift seems too fine, but Alfwen has thought of this. She hands me a hemp undergarment. The material is stiff but it still does little to protect me from the itching of the wool tunic, which is large and without shape. It has no sleeves and has been made simply from a folded piece of cloth, with a hole cut for the neck. The edges have not been hemmed properly and I take a grim delight in this coarseness. Father says that I am vain and love beautiful things too much. What would he say if he could see me now?

Alfwen folds my old clothes and calls for Johanna. 'Give these to your mother to sell. And mind she gets the best price for them.'

The girl takes the pile and strokes my cloak with the tip of her finger, her eyes wide. When she leaves, carrying my plum-coloured gown, my white shift, the grey velvet cloak, it is as if all colour, all richness has left the room.

To my dismay, Alfwen notices my quiver of pain. 'There will be two mouths to feed here now,' she says, tartly. 'The money from the clothes will help.'

I feel the heat rising up my neck. Why didn't I think of this before? It's clear that Alfwen lives on a pittance. A few sacks hang from hooks on the ceiling, but there is no other food that I can see.

'I can ask for money,' I blurt out but then find that tears are forming behind my eyes. What am I saying? I shall never see my parents again. They do not know where I am.

Alfwen sits me down on one of the stools. 'Come now, Child,' she says, more gently. 'God will provide. My lord Ralph of Tosny brings me two sacks of grain every quarter and enough candles to last me. And Roger sends salad and greens from his garden, and eggs too. And the people of the village are generous.'

She calls to Johanna to bring some ale. 'You must be thirsty and hungry,' she says to me. 'There are beans cooking.'

The drink is thin, not like the ale we drink at home, but it is welcome nonetheless. I begin to feel how tired I am, and how empty my belly is. Alfwen busies herself out in the yard for a little, then comes back. She sits herself down on the other stool, the purple scar turned to me, and it is all I can do not to look away.

'How long have you lived here?' I ask.

'It will be eight years, come Michaelmas.'

'You are not from here.'

113

'No, Lord love you. I was born north of Torksey. My mother and father fled south when the Norman armies came to sack our country.'

'How did you come to be an anchoress?'

'It was Blessed Roger.' She makes the sign of the cross.

At the sound of the hermit's name, I begin to feel anxious again. Does he know I am here, with Alfwen?

She continues the story. 'Roger helped my mother time and again, when my father died. A crannock of peas, a silver penny, whatever he could spare. I vowed then that one day I would live religious, like him.' Alfwen is staring at the wall, remembering. 'The pledges were got and the anchorhold was built. It was mizzling, the day they put me in here, but it was the most blessed day of my life.'

Alfwen turns to me, her eyes shining. The livid skin on her face is ridged and furrowed and does not move as it should. She sees me staring.

'Ah - you mustn't mind this,' she says, touching her cheek, and I wonder at her quick eyes. For all her simple speech, it's clear that nothing passes Alfwen by.

'I fell into the fire,' she goes on, 'when I was a young bairn. It doesn't pain me anymore.'

'Is it far to the village?' I ask, eager to talk of something else.

She eyes me sharply. 'Our life is here, not in Flamstead. When they closed me in this hold, and the priest prayed, it was the committal prayers he said. I will never leave this place. It has become paradise on earth to me. And you...'

'I wish to live as you do, Mother, as a bride of Christ.'

'One step at a time, Child. One step. First we have to keep you hidden – there are those who would take you back, aren't

114

there? You mustn't go outside - not even into the yard, except at night time. No-one knows you're here - only those we can trust.'

'And you will teach me to pray as you do, and fast, and live as a bride of Christ?'

'I will teach you. It will not be easy, mind, after the life you have led, with your frills and your furs.' She fixes her beady eyes on me. 'I wonder if you are ready to leave that old life.'

'I am ready,' I insist. 'I do not care a fig for my old life or my home.'

A thought has been taking shape in my mind all day on the road.

'Alfwen, I have decided to take a new name for my new life. I wish to take the name of my husband in heaven and be known as Christina.'

Alfwen says nothing but she gets up from her stool, calling for Johanna. I follow her to the doorway. 'Don't you think it fitting that I take this name?'

She turns to me. 'Christina,' she repeats, as if trying out the sound of it. Then she reaches up to the shelf and brings down a crock with a half-eaten loaf of dark bread inside it. 'It's time to eat,' she says.

We have scarcely finished our beans and bread when I hear noises outside. I freeze in fear. *Someone followed us after all. My father has come to take me.*

'Don't fret. It's only the first of the villagers come for Vespers. The church will be full tonight for St John.'

She tells me to hide in the cubbyhole till the service has begun, then I may come out and steal a look at the priest. I sit on the mattress that will serve as my bed. The straw pokes through the rough sacking and what with this and the itchy

115

clothing, I am driven almost mad by the need to scratch. But Christ was born in a manger, of poor parents. If the King of Kings was content to live like this, how much more should I give up all comfort for him? I lie down on my side and the itching relents a little.

I am drifting down into sleep when I see Alfwen in the doorway, beckoning to me. She has me peer through the squint into the chancel, but the priest is out of sight. Neither can I see the villagers in the nave, but I hear coughing and the crying of an infant, as the priest intones the kyrie eleison. On the other side of that wall, just a few feet from me, stand strangers whose faces I will never see. Alfwen kneels after me and crosses herself as the priest begins the paternoster.

At the first words of the dismissal, I am bundled back to my mattress and the cupboard door is closed. I listen carefully to the sound of feet, the calling of voices, as the villagers leave the church. In a while, I hear a man speaking very close by, then Alfwen's voice as she replies. She does not sound alarmed. I edge open the door of the cubbyhole, just enough to see my mentor standing by the open window that looks out on the churchyard. She is conversing with a red-faced man outside, his hair cut like a priest's. They are speaking in the old language and I realize for the first time that I have heard no French since I left Huntingdon. He passes something through the window, then takes his leave.

When I venture back into the room, Johanna is clutching a jug of milk and Alfwen is counting out the coins that lie in her palm.

'God be praised!' she exclaims. 'Because of the Feast, people have put more than usual in the box for us.'

A thought comes to me. 'Does the priest know that you are

hiding me here?'

'I shall tell him when the time is right.' Alfwen smiles. 'Don't fret yourself over Osbert. He is a good man - one of the people. He won't give you away.'

I lie on my mattress, thinking of dawn this morning, when Mother and Father left me at my aunt's house. It seems so long ago, so far away. When I wake it is barely light and there are more voices coming from the anchorhold – a man's voice again, a different one. I am surprised – I had imagined that my new life would be one of silent prayer and devotion. Alfwen opens the door.

'Get up, Theodora. Ulfwine is here, from the hermitage.'

'Christina, not Theodora,' I remind her.

I stand up, brushing the straw from my tunic. Ulfwine is tall, his brown hair growing thin over his forehead, though he is still a young man. He dresses like a peasant, but I am learning that among the brotherhood of hermits and recluses, this means nothing. He nods his head to me in greeting.

'Roger has sent him with news,' says Alfwen. She laughs. 'It seems that a bride has run away from her husband.'

I stare at them both as her meaning dawns on me. But now the smile leaves Alfwen's face.

'They say she has a young man with her, her lover,' says Ulfwine. 'The father and the husband are even now searching for him, to take their revenge.'

I begin to tremble.

'As you see, Ulfwine, she is here with me,' says Alfwen. 'Ride back and tell Roger that things are not what they seem. Christina has vowed herself to Christ and she has come to learn godliness. She is one of us now.'

'But what of the Bishop of Lincoln?' Ulfwine has the voice

of a learned man. He turns to me. 'I hear that he pronounced against you in support of your husband and your parents.'

I blush, uncertain of how to answer, but Alfwen speaks for me.

'That's as may be but Eadwin went to the Archbishop himself. He says the vow of chastity came first and that is binding. And you can tell Roger that she is sincere – I see it in her heart.'

Ulfwine seems to accept this. 'I will go and tell him.' He puts out his hand to me and, for the first time, he smiles. 'You are welcome. May you grow in God's grace under the care of our sister here.'

He turns to go and I am grateful for his warm welcome. But it is Alfwen's words about me that sing in my heart.

# Chapter 13

*Alfwen's anchorhold, Flamstead*

*Tenth day of July, AD 1116*

*Iste pauper clamavit et Dominus exaudivit eum; et de omnibus tribulationibus eius salvavit eum. Vallabit angelus Domini in circuitu timentium eum et eripiet eos.*

The evening is sticky and we sit with the door thrown wide, the psalter open on my lap; there is just enough light filtering through the yard fence for me to make out the words. With no book to read from, Alfwen recites the thirty-third psalm with me, word for word, and once again I marvel at her knowledge of the scriptures.

'It comforts me to think of the angel of the Lord camped in the woods, keeping us safe from our enemies,' I say, when we have finished. 'Surely no-one will find me here.'

Alfwen says nothing in reply, just regards me suspiciously, her head cocked to one side. I wonder if I have offended her in some way.

'Imagination is the enemy of the soul, Christina,' she

answers at last, with that way she has of signalling that there is no more to be said.

'But I am not imagining – it's what the psalmist says!'

I am stung by her rebuke but then a new thought occurs to me and I don't have the sense to keep it to myself.

'You understand the meaning of the Latin, don't you, Mother?'

She looks down at her hands, then back up at me. 'I am a simple woman. I don't have your learning.' She gets up from her stool. 'But it's not for us to pass comment on the scripture. It's time to pray.'

By rights Alfwen should take the prayer stool by the squint but instead she prostrates herself on the sour smelling floor, among the crawlers, leaving me to feel guilty that she has taken the lowlier place. Kneeling down by the little window, I take out my beads and begin the first *Ave*, mouthing the words silently so as not to disturb her. I try to think of the Blessed Virgin, but my belly is crying out for food. Yesterday was a fast and the bread we ate earlier did not satisfy me. Later, Johanna will boil us some eggs. I imagine the rich, yellow yolk on my tongue.

Whenever we come to pray, fear jumps out from the shadows where it has been lying in wait and assails me. What would happen if Father and Burthred find me here? Sometimes I fancy I can hear the sound of hooves thundering through the trees, the shouts of the Bishop's men.

My finger slips onto the paternoster knot so I must have completed ten *Aves*. I begin the Our Father, forming the words silently, but my thoughts dart away like the fish in our pond at home. I think of Alfwen, reciting the psalms day after day, without understanding. How can she teach me the ways of God when she is so ignorant? I steal a glance behind me. She is lying, arms outstretched, her face in the dirt. She may not be learned but perhaps her humility makes her the best example to me. With a pang of sadness, I remember walking under the fruit trees with my old teacher, Sueno, the apple boughs clustered with blossom, the air fragrant. He is explaining the meaning of the words we have just read together. I stumble over some roots and he reaches out to steady me, his hand on the sleeve of my best peacock blue gown, the one with the fleur de lis edging worked in gold.

A clicking noise wakes me from my reverie and I know myself once more in the anchorhold, in my shapeless rough tunic. There are tears trickling down my cheeks. I bend to pick up my beads from the floor and start my prayers again.

*Next morning*

When I wake and get up from my bed, it seems that the weather has broken. Even with the door open, the anchorhold is dark and there is rain dripping though the roof, but nothing can dampen my elation.

'Alfwen!'

My companion comes in from helping the girl and stands in the doorway, scratching her neck. The lice crawl on me too and Alfwen says I must welcome them as they will cure me of my pride.

'Listen to my dream, Mother. It's still with me – the comfort of it.'

'Tell me then, before you forget it.'

121

'I dreamt of Eadwin's servant, the one who brought me here. He spoke to me - I remember everything, every word.'

'What did he say?'

'He said *Have no fear, Christina. You are safe from those who are seeking you. They will not find you. Put your trust in the Lord.* Do you think it's a true dream, Alfwen? Is it a message from God?'

Alfwen sits down on a stool.

'You dreamt of Loric?'

'Yes, the boy who brought me here.'

'I know who he is,' she replies, sharply. 'And he called you Christina, your new name?'

I think back. 'Yes, I'm sure that's what he called me. We were together in a glade and the sun was shining right onto his face.'

Alfwen gets up and steps towards me. 'His face was golden?' Her voice sounds tight.

'Yes - it was the sunlight.'

She says no more but goes to the prayer stool and kneels down. There is smoke blowing in from the yard outside, where Johanna is having trouble with the fire. 'Go and help her,' she orders me.

'Do you think the dream is from God?'

'We shall see,' she answers, but there is no joy in her face.

Johanna and I get the fire going at last but Alfwen will not take anything to eat or drink, not even the mess of oats with which we break our fast. It seems that she will spend the whole day in prayer so I am left to myself. The rain doesn't let up and the joy of the dream begins to fade a little but still, at my prayers, there is a new peace. *They will not find you. Put your trust in the Lord.*

Only a handful come from the village for Mass at midday and when they have gone, Osbert the priest passes the body and blood of Christ to us, through our little window. He knows now that I am hidden here but he is a simple man, with a wife and children, and would not risk drawing the Bishop's attention to himself. Hearing the sound of hooves later, I think it must be Osbert riding back to the village but I am wrong.

'Ulfwine has come, Mistress,' says Johanna.

Alfwen gets up from her prayers at once. 'Pour him some ale, Johanna,' she says.

The rain is less now but Ulfwine is soaked to the skin from the dripping trees. He strides in, his height filling the space, and takes no time to greet us.

'I come with news - Loric is dead. Eadwin says he died a truly Christian death.'

A cold thrill passes through my body. Was it the boy's spirit, then, that appeared to me in the night?

'He came to me in a dream,' I say to Ulfwine. 'Only this last night. And he said that I will be safe here.'

Slowly I become aware that Alfwen is frowning at me. Ulfwine, too, keeps his silence. Now Alfwen crosses herself and bows her head.

'How did he die?' she asks at last.

'In the Bishop of Lincoln's house,' Ulfwine replies, and I catch the look that flies between them.

'Why was he there?' I blurt out, already frightened that I know the answer.

Ulfwine turns to me, his voice low. 'Your parents found witnesses who saw him with you in the wilderness. Robert Bloet's men brought him there to question him.'

123

I look to Alfwen and then back to Ulfwine. 'It's on my account that he is dead?'

Ulfwine takes my hand. 'Do not distress yourself. He was glad to be of service to his master. And to all who wish to live like Christ in these evil days.'

I think of the boy, riding ahead of me across the fields, flaxen hair streaming behind him in the wind, and I feel sick. Then an even more troubling thought occurs to me.

'The Bishop's men – what if he revealed to them where I am?'

Alfwen sniffs loudly and turns to walk out into the yard, leaving Ulfwine to answer me.

'Loric died ten days ago,' he says, his voice gentle. 'You may rest assured that if he had told them anything, your father would have been battering down the door before now.'

Ulfwine is persuaded to take some ale and I go to my mattress while he and Alfwen sit talking in low voices, mostly about people and places unfamiliar to me. My thoughts wander, again and again, to the boy Loric. Though he was only a servant I cannot bear to think of him put to pain. Instead, I remember him on the morning of my escape, waiting in the river meadow with the horses. It seems so long ago. And now, because of me, he is dead.

After Ulfwine has gone, a woman from the village comes to consult with Alfwen through the churchyard window. I close myself in so that she will not see me and lie on my mattress, trembling all over. I can't stop. Are the Bishop's men riding this very moment through the woods towards us?

The low drone of Alfwen's voice comes to me through the door. In a while the trembling stills and I find myself drowsy. I am not asleep, I could swear it, but neither am I any longer in Alfwen's anchorhold. Before me spreads a meadow, as it may be the river meadow at Huntingdon, but this one is swampy, the grass green with patches of reed and hidden pools of water. I look down at my feet, safely planted on firm ground. The field is full of black bulls with menacing horns, shaking their heads in rage. With all their fearsome strength, they strain to come after me, but the swampy ground holds their hooves fast and they are powerless. A voice speaks, not audibly but in my head. *Do not move from where you are and you will be safe. If you retreat one step, you will fall into their power.*

I must have cried out in fear because Alfwen throws open the door.

'What is it, Christina?'

The vision, if that is what it is, folds back at once and is gone. What is happening to me?

The village woman has left and I spill everything out to Alfwen. Surely the black bulls must signify those who are searching for me, to take me back to my husband.

'What does it mean?' I ask. 'Is my chastity the firm ground I am to stand on?'

Alfwen seems angry. 'It is clear what this means. Now reach down that sack for me.' She points to a canvas bag of dried peas hanging from the roof, but I make no move to obey.

'Tell me – if you see the meaning,' I plead.

'All I know,' says Alfwen, 'is obedience, and loving my Master.'

'Yes - but you said the meaning of the vision is clear to you.'

She draws herself up, though I am still a head taller than her. 'All I will say is this. If a fence pole is to stand straight and strong against the wind, it must first be driven deep into the mud.'

I stare at her. Perhaps her mind has begun to wander.

'You have a lot to learn,' she says, her eyes holding mine. 'I wonder you are not ashamed. When Ulfwine came and told us about Loric, I was ashamed on your behalf. That young man who helped you was tortured to death and all you could talk about was your own safety.'

She walks over to the prayer stool and kneels to pray. Johanna is standing in the doorway, listening, her eyes wide. My face is burning and all I want to do is run to my bed and close the door, but Alfwen has one more thing to say.

'The voice told you to stay where you are. So stay here with me. Stay and learn humility.'

# Chapter 14

*Seventh day of May, AD 1118*

When I hear the thudding of hooves along the track, I am not surprised. At prayer this morning, the face of Ulfwine came into my thoughts and I am learning to trust this seeing. I run out into the yard just as his tall form emerges through the gap in the fence and unfolds itself. Alfwen is behind me, at the door of the anchorhold.

'Greetings, Brother,' she says.

I offer to take his cloak, eager that he should stay and eat with us, but he says he cannot stop for long.

'I have just now ridden from St Paul's and must get back to the hermitage. I've only come to collect the linen.'

Alfwen goes inside to fetch the altar cloths we have been working for the Abbey of Alban. I cannot bear that he should leave so soon.

'Is there any news?' I ask.

'All is well with Roger,' he replies. 'But there is grave news from London. The Queen died on the kalends of May.'

'She is dead? Queen Matilda?'

'And buried in the Abbey at Westminster, three days ago.'

Alfwen has returned and hands the precious linen to Ulfwine, wrapped in a clean length of calico.

'Surely the King will return from Normandy now,' I say.

'Pray God he won't,' Alfwen retorts. 'These Norman kings cast a dark shadow.'

I turn to her. 'But he must, or who will rule us? My father says he never sleeps easy when King Henry is away, fighting in France.'

'It's no business of ours,' Alfwen says. 'The Lord Jesus is the only King we need.'

'True, Mother,' answers Ulfwine. 'But he acts through those who have been anointed. The peace must be kept by men. They say that the prince, William Aetheling, will be regent now, till the King returns.'

Alfwen takes Ulfwine's arm. 'We mustn't keep you with our chatter,' she says.

He is about to go and I find myself disappointed to be left alone again with Alfwen. Surely he could stay a little longer.

'I knew you would come today,' I tell him.

He looks down at me, his brown eyes widening in enquiry. He is older than my brother and more gentle, but he is quick-witted like Gregory. I enjoy talking with him.

'How did you know I would come?' he asks. 'It was not in my mind to stop off here until this morning.'

'I saw your face when I was at prayer. I just knew...'

'Come, Christina, it's time for Terce.'

Ulfwine takes no notice of Alfwen's interruption. He looks at me thoughtfully. 'Roger, too, has this gift of seeing, ahead of time. Often the Spirit reveals to him who will visit us and so it turns out.'

I am taken aback to hear Ulfwine speak of me and of Blessed Roger in the same breath. And to liken us, one to the other. I can only watch as Ulfwine crouches to pass under the fence pales and out to his tethered horse.

Alfwen is not yet kneeling to pray when I come back inside. I take the psalter down from its shelf but the air is heavy with what she is waiting to say.

'Christina.'

My heart sinks. When Alfwen has this look on her face, she could be my mother. 'What is it?' I ask. 'Have I displeased you?'

'It is not me you need to please, Child, but your heavenly bridegroom.'

'What have I done wrong? Only last Lord's Day, you said I have grown in obedience and that I bear my trials patiently.'

She is regarding me keenly. 'And so you do. But I must say what I see, when your purity is at stake.'

'My purity?' I cannot think what she means.

'When we expect a visit from Ulfwine, you get restless. Your eyes become bright and you circle about the anchorhold like a ewe in autumn.'

'But… you don't think I…'

'The flesh is weak and the Fiend is cunning.'

My face grows hot. Ulfwine?

'Look to yourself, Christina. If you feed the fire of lust it will flare up and consume you.' Alfwen grasps my hand and forces me to touch her scarred cheek. 'See what earthly fire can do. Let this be a reminder, as it has been these long years to me. The fires of hell will burn far worse.'

129

I pull my hand away, disgusted by the feel of the ridged, webbed skin under my fingertips.

'But Ulfwine is ugly! How can you think I would care for him?'

'Don't raise your voice to me, Child. Don't you have any respect for age and wisdom?'

'You are not wise – didn't you hear what Ulfwine said? He thinks you are stupid.' The words rise up from a well deep inside me and I can't keep them from rolling off my tongue. 'And you are as ugly as he is – so ugly that sometimes I can't bear to look at you!'

Alfwen's eyes are wide with shock and pain. Her hand flies up to her cheek and she opens her mouth to reply but then seems to think better of it. Instead she takes up her beads and kneels on the prayer stool, her back turned to me in stiff reproach. I long to get away but where is there to go except the cupboard I sleep in?

I throw myself down on the mattress, the psalter in my hand, and slam the door behind me. Tears are welling up in my eyes and escaping down my cheeks. Lanky Ulfwine, with his thinning hair and his bulbous brown eyes. How can the woman think that I desire *him*? I was one of the most beautiful women in Huntingdon. My hands and face are hot, as if the very blood in my veins were simmering with rage. Opening the book, I find the psalms appointed for today and try to read but the words are just spider scrawls on the page – so much black ink.

Before long, my anger begins to fade and now comes guilt to take its place. I wince, thinking of what I said to Alfwen, and get up to go and beg her forgiveness. Listening at the door, I hear her intoning the *Ave* and stop short. She will be angry if I interrupt her. I can only wait and suffer my shame till she has finished –it's no more than I deserve.

Back on the mattress, I try to search my heart. Could it be true, what she says? I am on tenterhooks all day when I know Ulfwine will come, and when he leaves I am disappointed. But she is wrong. I think of him as a brother. I would no sooner have him touch me than Gregory.

My shameful, unkind words to Alfwen sound again and again in my head, accusing me. It's no good. I live in poverty and pray and punish my body with fasting but I will never be good and kind, like my sister Margaret. Wickedness is hidden inside every fold of my heart, like the flaw that runs through a bolt of cloth. I hear the taunting voice in my head. *You – a bride of Christ? And what else is there for you now? You have thrown away your chance to be the wife of a man.*

'Aagh!'

The psalter flies up into the air as I thrust it from me. Something was squatting on the open page, staring up at me with big golden eyes. A toad, covered in ugly warts. Now it's on the floor and there is another crawling across the mattress towards me. I jump up with a shriek.

'What is it, Mistress?' Johanna is at the door.

'Toads! Look, there. How did they get in?'

The girl squats down. 'Where?'

'On the floor,' I say, impatient. Johanna is so slow.

But when I look again, there is nothing on the mattress or among the rushes on the floor. 'They must have gone out, under the door.'

Alfwen has come to see what the fuss is about. She sends Johanna into the yard and then turns to me. 'There are no toads here, Christina, leastways no earthly ones.'

131

I stare at her.

'I told you to beware. If you open the door to the devil, you must not be surprised when he walks in.'

## Tenth day of May, AD 1118

Today is the day that Roger comes to the church to hear Alfwen's confession, so she sends me into my cubbyhole to read there. I repeat the words of the psalm but my mind is busy and will not come to rest. A long time passes and I can still hear the low drone of Alfwen's voice. What can she have to confess that it should take so long? We live like peas in a pod and I know better than anyone that her life is above reproach.

I think of Roger, the renowned holy man, standing in the chapel, just a few feet from me. What I wouldn't give to speak with him? Osbert the priest hears my confession after Mass every Sunday, but he never comments, even though I open my heart to him. I blush, thinking that this coming Sunday, I must repeat to him the cruel words I said to Alfwen. The penance he prescribes is always the same: to pray fifty times for the soul of Ralph de Tosny, who built this church here.

Now, at last, I hear the creak of the little window in the chancel wall, as Alfwen closes it. A few footsteps and she opens my door.

'It's all settled. You are to leave me, Theodora.'

*Theodora?* Why is she calling me by my old name? Fear grips me of a sudden.

'What's happened? Have I been discovered?'

'No.' She looks surprised. 'But it's not right - you being here with me,' she says. 'Do you take me for blind? You despise me. I knew it, even before you said so.'

'But I don't despise you, I was only angry...'

She raises her hand for me to stop. 'You think I'm ignorant – no, don't try to deny it.' Her fingers fly up and lightly brush against her cheek. 'But now I know that even my appearance offends you.'

'But, Mother, I am sorry I displeased you. Please forgive me,' I cry, scrambling to my feet. 'Please don't send me away.'

She shakes her head. 'It's all settled,' she says again, then looks me straight in the eyes. I see that she is more sorrowful than angry. 'I may not be a lettered woman, Theodora,' she says, 'but I know what I see. And I tell you again - you should look to your chastity.'

I reach out to Alfwen but she only backs away from me.

'I have put the matter in Roger's hands and he will decide where you are to go.'

She turns from me in her quick way and I understand, at last, that there is no more to be said.

*Thirteenth day of May, AD 1118*

When the time comes to take my leave, I am distraught. Alfwen barely looks at me and she pulls back when I go to embrace her. Along with the pain, I feel a sharp edge of anger. I have confessed to her and begged her forgiveness, yet still I must go. And she is wrong about me and Ulfwine. At the very last moment, Alfwen relents a little.

'I will pray for you,' she says.

An old man with a grizzled grey beard, I suppose another of Roger's companions, has come to accompany me to the hermitage. His name is Acio.

Sometimes at night on my mattress I have dreamed of walking again in the open air, but now that the day has come at last, a cold wind is whistling through the newly hatched beech leaves and I shiver inside my cloak.

'Is it a long way to go?' I ask. My legs ache at the unaccustomed exercise and I feel weak, as if recovering from a fever.

'The hermitage is not far, close to the old road. An angel appeared to Roger on his way home from Jerusalem and showed him the place in the woods where he should make his dwelling.'

'Roger went to Jerusalem?'

'Yes – he went for a pilgrim, many years ago now.'

We reach the old Roman road. Many of the stones are cracked and last night's rain has made pools where some of them are missing altogether. We cross over and into the cover of the trees so as not to be seen. Before we have walked a league, Acio turns to me.

'We are almost there. Soon we will come to the ditch that marks his land.'

I can smell wood smoke and my heart seems to plunge down into my belly. For a moment, it's all I can do to stay upright.

'What is to happen to me? Am I to stay at the hermitage?'

He shakes his head. 'There are no women lodged here. It is only Ulfwine, myself and Leofric and Blessed Roger, and those who come each day to serve us, of course.'

'Then where will I go?'

He hears the fear in my voice and looks at me with pity.

'Perhaps you are to hide with the hermit women who live in Eywood. Roger was there only yesterday - it could be that he has made arrangements.'

'And will I see him when we arrive?'

Acio looks away, embarrassed.

'What is it?'

'You are not to speak with any others of our company. Anything you need, you are to ask me.'

So I am not to be permitted to converse with Ulfwine or with the holy man himself. A wave of humiliation washes over me. No doubt Alfwen has laid bare all my failings to Roger.

We cross the ditch on a plank of wood and soon come out from the cover of beech trees into the clearing. The hermitage is more extensive than I thought. Four small huts and another longer one form a circle around a patch of grass. There is smoke escaping from the roof of the largest building. A woman is standing at the wide doorway, wafting a cloth in front of her red face. Now I see another building, set a little behind the others. It is somewhat larger and more weathered, reinforced partly with stone, and close to it stands what I take to be a dovecote.

'That's the chapel Roger built when he came here,' Acio explains. 'He made it circular, to figure eternity. And next to it is his cell.'

I gaze at the chapel. I have not set foot in a consecrated place these two years and in my dreams I am often back in the priory church of Mary in Huntingdon.

Acio leads me to the doorway of the long hut and I see that

this is where the cooking is done. Steam is rising from a black pot above the fire. A young boy perches on a stool beside a block of stone, and I realize with a jolt that he is milling grain with a handmill. Who owns this land then? Is Roger not obliged to use the lord's miller? It comforts me a little to think that the holy man has such influence.

Acio addresses the woman. 'Do you know where Master Roger is?'

She shakes her head. 'I saw him down by the stream earlier.'

'Stay here, with Nelda,' Acio says to me. 'I will go and find out where I am to take you.'

Nelda is a stout woman, with rough skin, but she seems friendly enough and fetches me a stool to sit on. Her eyes are on my coarse tunic.

'Have you come far?'

'Only from Flamstead,' I answer.

'Take your ease, Mistress,' she says, hearing from the way I speak that I am a person of rank. 'You look done in.'

She brings me a cup of ale, then goes back to her work. Acio does not return and I am left fearful and wondering what will become of me. After a while, the ale revives me and I get up and go to the open doorway. There is no-one to be seen in the clearing between the huts. What harm can there be if I slip into the chapel for a while? If I'm not to meet the holy man, at least I can pray a while in his oratory.

The cold wind at my back, I cross to the chapel and open the door. Inside, all is calm. There are two candles burning on the simple altar and a silver cross but nothing else of any fineness or beauty. The benches set beside the limewashed, curved walls are rude and rough-hewn. Yet the chapel seems to breathe a holy tranquillity and I find my eyes filling with tears.

For the first time since my outburst to Alfwen, the love of God flares inside my soul - a tiny flame of warmth. Throwing myself onto the floor face down, I cry out to Jesus and his mother for help. After a time, I feel the prayer-soaked walls of the chapel enfold me, like the arms of a loving mother. Assurance comes - a place of safety will surely be found for me.

The candle light sways and flickers for an instant and I feel a draught of air at my back as the chapel door opens. Acio has come to take me away but I find I can't move. Nothing in me wants to leave this place of peace. The chapel is small and the old man has to step across my body. He stands in front of the altar, looking taller now than he did when we walked through the wood.

He turns and looks back at me over his shoulder and my eyes meet his, two deep wells in the dim light of the chapel. His hair is grey, like Acio's, but this is not Acio. This is a tall, spare man, with stooped shoulders. At once I am reminded of my old friend, Canon Sueno. I gasp in shock. This can only be the hermit himself. He has about him an invisible mantle of goodness, so pure and hard-edged that it frightens me. I think of Moses coming down from the mountain, radiant with the glory of God. All this I see in the blink of an eye. And something else too, that takes my breath away: for all his holiness and my worthlessness, I see that we belong together, that we are like two garments, cut from the one cloth.

The hermit makes a sign and I get up from the floor and follow him to the bench, where he motions for me to take my place beside him. He peers at me, his eyes piercing my soul. Here, in his chapel, in the shadows cast by the candlelight, everyday behaviour and speech seem to have no place. I tremble under his gaze. Yet the longer he stares, the more certain I am that he feels the same accord between us.

At last, he looks away into the darkness and a long sigh escapes him.

'You are Christina, come from Alfwen,' he says into the space. It's the first time he has spoken and I can tell that he is not used to being contradicted. 'Now I see with my eyes what my companions heard.'

'I don't understand, Father.'

'These last weeks, at their prayers, Acio and Leofric have heard the voice of virgins singing the psalm with them. I knew it to be the betokening of a gift.'

He turns to me, suddenly, as if remembering something. His face is unshaven; the grey stubble on his cheek almost close enough to touch.

'And where were you born, where are you from? Alfwen told me, but I have forgotten.'

'From Huntingdon, Father. I am the daughter of Auti the merchant.'

'From Huntingdon,' he repeats, nodding. A look of wonder has spread across his face. 'Indeed, the Lord never does anything without first revealing his plan to his servants, the prophets.'

I look up at him, a little frightened. What does he mean by quoting the scripture? Perhaps he notices my fear because his voice softens a little.

'All is well. You will stay here with me, at the hermitage. A while back the Lord showed me that I was to expect something from Huntingdon and I have been waiting for it.'

Suddenly he takes my face in his hands. His eyes are wide, an incredulous smile softening his features. 'I had no idea that it was to be a daughter.'

# Chapter 15

*Hermitage de bosco*

*St John's Eve, twenty-third day of June, AD 1119*

I have not yet heard the bell for Terce, but already it is sweltering in the old wood store. The only light comes through the gap under the roof so I cannot gauge how far the sun has climbed. Yesterday, I sat on the bare stone, wedged between the walls of my tiny hiding place and sweated. I tried to remember what it was like here in winter, when the snow blew in through the gap and I longed for enough space to move my arms, at least, to keep warm. These last three days, there is only heat, holding me in its vice. No breeze. No movement in the dust-choked air.

Roger left early for St Albans and I miss the familiar sounds of him moving about on the other side of the wall. Outside, it is strangely silent too. I strain my ears - none of the usual clattering of pots from the kitchen. Where is Nelda's voice, shouting instructions to the boy? Over the months I have learned the rhythm of the hermitage day: the bell summoning Roger and his companions to the chapel, Nelda's little girl banging the pail for the hens' feed, now and then the maddening scent of onions or rosemary wafting across from the kitchen.

My throat is dry and I reach for the cup of ale I brought into the store with me, but then think better of it. There will be no more till Roger returns. Now comes a sound - the crunch of twigs - and I twist around to get a better view of the gap under the roof. Any time now, when he has climbed up the firewood stacked against the outside of the store, the black velvet face of Gyb the tom cat will appear. I love it when he comes, though he doesn't have the courage to jump down to where I sit, perched on my slab of stone. I used to try and coax him. But then I thought of what would happen if he jumped down and could not get back out and his mewling brought attention to my hiding place.

My eyes are fixed on the gap but Gyb does not appear. Instead I hear the door of Roger's cell creak open and footsteps crossing the room. *The Bishop's men - they have discovered that I'm here and have come to take me.* The sinister jumping in my chest starts up again and all feeling drains from my left hand. Already I sense the prickling run up my arm. There are scuffling and dragging sounds, as if the heavy log leant up against the door is being moved away.

'Christina? It's only me.'

I recognize the voice of Ulfwine and feel my breath escaping in relief. He pulls open the door and I practically tumble out into the space and freedom of the room. But why has he left Roger's door open? Anyone could come in and catch sight of me.

'It's all right. I have sent Nelda and Osmund to St Albans for the last day of the fair. They won't come back till tomorrow.'

Breathing a sigh of relief, I venture to the doorway, past Roger's prayer stool and the one luxury he allows himself - his teacher's chair. Laid open on the lectern is his beautiful psalter that was a gift from the Abbey of St Albans. On the other side of the room is a simple pallet bed. No-one coming in would notice the straw mattress tucked underneath that he pulls out for me at night. Not that he allows himself many hours of sleep. More often than not I wake to find that he is in the chapel, keeping vigil till dawn.

By the doorway, there is the gentlest trace of a breeze and Ulfwine comes to stand beside me as my eyes accustom themselves to the bright sunlight. Even in this heat, there is smoke spiralling from the thatched roof of Acio's cell.

'How is Acio? Is he any better?'

'Recovered from the fever, but still weak,' Ulfwine replies. 'Leofric tends him like a son.'

The unaccustomed freedom – to leave my hiding place in the daytime – is like a dream, but I am still anxious in case someone comes from the village. The cooking fire is burning steadily in the empty kitchen and it is so hot that I feel I will faint. I down a cup of ale and then another straight off, and start on a third. Late yesterday, after being shut up in the wood store all day, blood began to drip from my nostrils and I was frightened. When Roger came to let me out at sundown, he told me it is the body's way of begging for water.

Ulfwine walks with me to the stream and here it is blessedly cool under the beeches. I am reminded of walking through the wood with Acio, the day I came here - more than a year ago now.

'Have you been to Flamstead recently?' I ask. 'How is

Alfwen?'

'Alfwen does not welcome our visits, as she used to.' Ulfwine looks away, to where the stream bends out of sight, barely a trickle in this dry weather. 'I think she suspects that Roger is hiding you here.'

I am sorry and wish with all my heart that I was not the cause of dissension between them.

Ulfwine looks pensive but he is not thinking of the rift with Alfwen.

'I'm glad Roger has gone to the Abbey, after all,' he says. 'At first he said he would have nothing to do with the election of the new Abbot.'

'Perhaps,' I suggest, 'now that Abbot Richard is dead, whoever is chosen as his successor will leave Roger in peace to live as he wishes.'

'But he must be careful - for all our sakes.' Ulfwine sounds worried. 'This land here might belong to St Pauls, but on all sides we are hemmed in by St Albans estates. And who's to say that the new abbot will not cosy up to Robert Bloet just as much as the old one did?'

Robert Bloet - the Bishop of Lincoln. I wish Ulfwine wouldn't remind me of my enemy.

'Why does Roger need to be present for the election?' I ask. 'It's not as if he is a monk of the Abbey.'

Ulfwine smiles his dry smile. 'The abbots of St Albans know what is good for them, and their coffers. It does the Abbey no harm to be connected to such a famed man as Roger.' He turns to me, more sober now. 'Christina, you are closer to him than any of us. I know he cannot bear Norman cant and the arrogance of the monks but beg him not to offend the new abbot more than he needs to.'

143

Ulfwine's words disturb me. He doesn't understand. What we share - Roger and I - is nothing to do with appearances, nothing to do with the Abbey or pleasing men. It is something more wondrous than that - something beyond the telling of words.

I cannot think how to answer him, so I stay silent.

He sighs. 'Roger is an old man now and has the old man's lack of regard for his own safety.' Then he looks at me and his face seems to lift. 'But we need not worry over much. He will do nothing to endanger the safety of his Sunday daughter.'

I look at him, puzzled.

'Didn't you know that is his name for you?'

I shake my head. Roger never speaks to me of the bond between us.

Ulfwine laughs but there is no rancour in it. 'We all know that you are dearer to him than all his other sons and daughters, just as Sunday is the most blessed day of the week.'

At late prayers in the chapel, when the sun is getting low, I feel the heat start to loosen its grip. Compline, after the servants have gone back to Caddington, is the only time of day when it is safe for me to join with the others. For the first time in weeks, Acio is feeling strong enough to join us. He sits on the bench by the wall and we sing the psalms as usual but without the hallowed presence of Roger, we are like orphaned children. The daylight still lingers as I stand by the door and watch the others go back to their cells for the night.

Surely Roger must be back soon from St Albans. I picture him riding through the heat-scented dusk, keeping to the old road. Perhaps he is already at Redbourn or even, please God, as close to home as Flamstead. Was it a warm night like this, all those years ago, when he first set eyes on these woods and heard the angel's voice in his ear, telling him that he was home? I wonder what it is like to go on pilgrimage to Jerusalem and to touch the very soil where our Lord walked, and sit at the feet of the monks from Mt Athos.

I walk down to the stream and here, in the lush green shade, I can scarcely see my feet, though the heat of the day still clings in the unmoving air. I kneel on the grass and dip my hand in the cool water, closing my eyes and letting the gentle force of the stream beat against my fingers till they no longer seem to be part of my body.

I get up and walk back towards the clearing but the only sound is the cawing of the rooks high above. Why doesn't he come? Soon it will be truly dark and he is riding alone. I think of the black woods that border the road from Flamstead all the way here. Robbers have been known to wait there, hidden among the trees. I see him, lying in the road, pitched from his horse and beaten, blood trickling through his grey hair. The fear that has been hovering around me seems to enter my belly and ripple up towards my head, leaving my arm tingling and numb. Tonight is the eve of St John; could something more evil even than robbers be riding abroad? The villagers will light a fire to ward off the spirits but Caddington is two miles away or more. My fingers fly to make the sign of the cross. *In the name of the Father and of the Son and of the Holy Spirit, keep your servant from all peril, bodily or ghostly.*

A thought comes to me, as if in answer to my prayer, and I hurry across the clearing. This morning I noticed yellow star-shaped petals amongst the undergrowth behind Ulfwine's cell. I pull a clump of St John's Wort from the ground and run with it into the chapel, placing it on the altar beside the silver cross. The worst weight of fear begins to lift from me but still my arm feels heavy and numb, the fingers cold to the touch. I notice how hungry I am and venture into the kitchen to find some bread. Though I know that Nelda is not here, still my heart beats faster. Concealment has become a part of me, woven into my body like the veins that carry my blood.

Now, at last, I hear the sound I've sat listening for so many times, hidden in the wood store: the unmistakeable rhythm of Gabriel's hooves. Relief washes over me. At the kitchen door, I watch Roger dismount and lead his horse towards the stream to drink. When I run to him, he turns and nods in greeting but he seems wrapped in thought.

'Are you hungry? Shall I fetch something to eat?'

'No,' he replies.

Roger takes his horse to the shelter by the latrine that serves as a stable and tethers him for the night. Even now, the sky retains a tinge of light. We walk back to the cell and I light a candle. He fixes me with his eyes.

'It has been so hot. I was fearful for you, closed in all day.'

'No Father, Ulfwine let me out.' I cannot wait to tell him about my day. 'He sent Nelda and the others to the fair and I have been able to go about freely. I even went into the woods where it was cool. Do you know what I found there? A tiny warbler's nest, tucked under a branch. The chicks must have fledged – it was empty - and I heard the Lord's voice speak to me. He promised me that, one day, I will be free to live openly as his bride.'

He says nothing in reply, only looks down at his feet. The toes showing between the leather straps of his sandals are gnarled with age and covered in dust. 'Christina, I am weary.'

'Of course, Father.' My heart sinks a little. 'Do you need to sleep then? Shall we not pray in the chapel tonight?'

'There is nothing I need more than to be in the presence of God,' he says. 'Come with me.'

Inside the chapel, all is blessed calm. I stand beside him to pray, as always, but tonight my thoughts are bustling and will not consent to rest. I cannot seem to find my balance. Roger turns to me.

'Be still,' he says sternly. 'How many times must I tell you? A still body is the door to oneness with the divine.'

I cannot bear that he should be angry with me, not tonight. My eyes smart with tears and even in the shadows thrown by the candlelight, he sees it and softens a little.

'You are restless. After a day free from restraint it is natural,' he says. Now he looks deep into my face and into my soul. 'You rejoice in your freedom and it has made you happy. But what of tomorrow? Tomorrow, for your own safety, you must hide again. How will you be content then?'

The tears begin to flow freely down my cheeks.

'God has given you the greatest gift he could give. He has shut you up in a small space so that you may more easily discover what I had to go the Greek monks in Jerusalem to learn. They showed me how to be still, and silent, and attend to my heart, where God dwells. The freedom you crave is already within you. Isaac the Syrian said *Enter eagerly into the treasure house that is within you and you will see the things that are in heaven.'*

He turns back to face the little altar and, suddenly, he is striding towards it.

'What is this?' he asks, picking up the St John's Wort. 'Did you put it here?'

He is angry. My fears of earlier appear fanciful to me now.

Worse, they seem to tarnish the radiant purity of what he has been saying. For an instant I think of denying it but I can keep nothing from him and blurt it all out.

'You didn't come - and I thought of you bleeding on the road and I was frightened in case it was a true seeing - and I felt the presence of evil and we have no fire for St John.'

He is still holding the bunch of green, the yellow stars drooping now amidst the leaves. I half expect him to fling it away but instead he replaces it on the altar.

'Enough. There is nothing to fear,' he says, more kindly, and resumes his place beside me.

Calmer now, I stand listening to the sparrows settle in the thatch of the chapel roof.

'Pray the prayer of the breath,' Roger says. 'The one the Greek brothers taught me.'

I take in a slow breath from deep in my belly, as he has instructed me. *Oh God, make speed to save me.* Then I let the breath go slowly. *Oh Lord make haste to help me.* Again and again I breathe: *Oh God, make speed to save me; Oh Lord make haste to help me.* Little by little the enclosed space of the chapel seems to expand, to open out to the balmy night. There are no walls, no constraints, nothing can come between me and the heavens. I feel an intense heat in the air, which seems to be emanating from the old man beside me. I open my eyes and see the flames licking around Roger's chest, though not with my earthly vision. Love is pervading the chapel - pure and clean and sharp - mingling with the scent of the elderflower that grows at the woods' edge. I watch, undismayed, as the flames leap across the space between us. Now, though we are not touching, I can feel the heat in my own heart, an unflinching love that spreads through my body, scalding and

148

healing at the same time.

Without opening his eyes, Roger speaks. 'You feel it too. Take heart. This inner fire is all the protection you need from evil.'

# Chapter 16

*Hermitage de bosco*

*Annunciation of the birth of our Lord, twenty-fifth day of March, AD 1120*

The low hum of voices coming through the wall from Roger's cell has halted and, for a blessed instant, I think they have gone. I shift my buttocks from side to side on the unforgiving stone, trying to lessen the discomfort. The little light that comes through the gap is fading - I can no longer make out the veins on the backs of my hands. Surely Roger's visitors must go soon and he can move the log and let me out.

The high laugh of Goddescalc's wife carries through to me – they are still here! If they stay talking any longer I swear I will not be able to hold my water. A new wave of urgency passes through me and the effort of keeping it in brings a sweat to my forehead. I could not bear the shame of fouling this tiny space that must serve as my oratory.

*Mary, Mother of God, look upon me with mercy. Mary, Mother of God, look upon me with mercy.*

There are footsteps and voices. The door to Roger's cell creaks, then silence. Soon – soon now, he must come. But he doesn't come and I hardly dare breathe for fear of giving way. At last I hear horses' hooves. And now Roger is heaving the log aside and the door bursts open and I am pushing past him.

'Has Nelda gone home?' I call over my shoulder, though heavens knows what I would do if he said no.

'Yes – yes. There is only me and the brothers.'

I run, stumble, then run again, down to the latrine. Banging the door shut behind me, I struggle to reach the wooden seat but already the warm piss is trickling down my legs and I feel myself blushing with shame. The relief is beyond words. I clean myself as best I can and pray that Roger will not notice the dark patch on my tunic. I remember with a shudder how it used to be when I still had a monthly flow of blood. *Thank you, Mother Mary, for sparing me that, at least.* There is very little flesh on me now and I cannot stop shivering.

Inside the cell, Roger is lighting another candle. He looks up and sees my trembling. 'What is it?'

Beneath the blunt words, I feel his care for me and everything comes tumbling out.

'This morning - at prayer - I had such consolation. I thought it was an angel but then he left me and ever since Sext I have felt so strange – I couldn't feel my arm, it was dead to me and all my side too and then my head began to pain me - terrible sharp pains - and I couldn't move to relieve it and, worst of all, I had such need…' I stop – not wanting to speak of the rest.

Roger stands looking at me. He seems more stooped: a little smaller somehow, though his spirit burns as clear as ever.

'Calm yourself,' he says, 'and tell me about the consolation.'

He puts the candle down and directs me to his own chair. It feels wrong for me to sit while he stands but I know better than to argue with him. Tears are forming in my eyes and I cannot keep them from trickling down my cheeks. The psalter is open on the lectern before me and I scrub at my face in case a tear should drop onto the vellum and spoil the colours.

'This morning, I was trying to pray but all I could think of was what Eadwin told you -about the Bishop of Lincoln - that he is still searching for me.'

Roger's mouth twists in the way it does when something disturbs him. 'Go on.'

'And then it seemed as if a man appeared before me, though the door was still shut tight. And he was holding a cross of gold in his right hand. I was frightened - but he said I should not be afraid and that I should take the cross from him. *Hold it firmly*, he said, *pointing straight up, not to the left or the right*. I remember that clearly. And he said something else. *All who wish to travel to Jerusalem must carry this cross*. Then he gave me the cross and said that he would come to take it back again after a short while.'

'And what happened then?' Roger is listening intently.

'He disappeared and I felt so comforted. That was at first, but ...'

I think again of the man's face, the smooth weight of the gold cross in my hand. Roger has warned me many times of setting too much store by my visions.

'But it was not a true seeing,' I say. 'I know that the Devil comes dressed as an angel of light.'

'And how were you made certain of the vision's falseness?' Roger asks.

The tears start up again and I cannot speak for a moment but only gulp them back. 'Because as soon as he went, the numbness came again to my arm and all my side and up into my face and it seemed to me that the world was sullied and full of danger.' I stop to wipe my cheek. 'And then, after the bell rang for Sext, came a terrible pain in my head, over my left eye, and I thought I must be sick. And dreadful thoughts kept coming, of what would happen if the Bishop's men found me.'

I force myself to go on. It is better if I do not keep anything from Roger, even if it angers him.

'And the thought came to me that you are sick and will die and I will be left defenceless.'

To my consternation, Roger smiles grimly. 'There is truth here, at least in part. It is certain that I shall die in the course of time. But these are distractions. What have I taught you to do with distractions?'

'To look over their shoulder, to the truth beyond,' I say.

'And these fearful thoughts - they still whirl about you, biting, like the gnats down by the stream?'

'Yes, but how do I escape them?'

I look down at the book laid open at today's psalm and my eye is caught by the figure of King David within the capital, peering up at God in trust. He has on a blue cloak with lining of vermilion.

'You will never escape them,' he says.

I look up at him quickly. Then there is no hope, only sorrow upon sorrow.

'Not while you are observing them with the eyes of your

mind, your lower reason. St Diadochos tells us to descend from the mind into the heart. It is only from the heart that we can apprehend the truth of God.'

He turns away and walks to the window, looking out into the darkness of the evening. All is still and quiet and, little by little, I find myself calmer. When he returns, I am astonished to see that there are tears on his cheeks. I have only ever seen him weep at prayer, in the chapel, smitten by the arrow of divine love. But this is different. He is smiling now through the tears and seems suddenly less worn. He strides over to me and takes both my hands.

'Benedictus Deus, quia liberavit pauperem a potente et pauperem cui non erat adiutor.'

'What does it mean?' When he speaks so quickly I cannot make out the Latin.

He reverts at once to the Saxon tongue of his mother, the language we share. 'Never mind,' he says. 'It is time to lay down your sadness, my Sunday daughter.'

Now I cannot believe what is happening. He is pulling me to my feet and whirling me round in the cell as if it were the May dance and he is laughing and I cannot help laughing with him. I am dizzy long before our capering comes to a stop and he sinks down onto the chair, breathless. At last, he can speak again.

'Your seeing was a true seeing, Christina. I feel it in my heart. By the grace of God your trials will soon be at an end.'

*Twenty-seventh day of March, AD 1120*

I wake in the morning to find Roger shaking me, his voice full of alarm. 'Get up! Quickly - you must hide.'

I stagger up from the floor, and now he is pushing the mattress back under his pallet bed and flinging my coverlet on top. It is barely light and there is a damp chill in the air where the cell door is half open. I hear horses' hooves in the woods and someone calling.

'Make haste, Christina!'

He picks up the coverlet again and throws it to me. 'Go to the store - I must close you in.'

'What is it? What's wrong?' I am shivering now, with fear as well as cold.

He bundles me into the tiny space. 'Riders,' he says, closing the door between us. 'Osmund found them waiting at the gate.' I hear him panting as he strains to drag the great log into place. 'I am expecting some monks to come from Bermondsey.' He catches his breath. 'But it cannot be them at this hour.'

Now he is gone and I can do nothing but keep quiet and wait. I wrap the wool around me, knocking my elbow painfully against the wall, and listen, hardly daring to breathe. How many horses? More than one for certain, perhaps three or four. The Bishop's men? Fear clutches at my innards as I think of Loric and what happened to him in Lincoln, at the Bishop's house. But he was a peasant - surely they would not dare to harm me.

The horses come to a halt in our yard; I hear boots thudding on the grass as they dismount, and the stamping of hooves.

155

Now Roger's voice, calling in greeting. One of the men replies -I can't hear what he is saying. Perhaps, after all, it is only the brothers from Bermondsey Abbey. Suddenly, I gasp out loud. Burthred! Surely that's his voice. A chasm seems to open up in my chest, as if my very heart had taken fright and fled.

I strain my ears – I hear Roger, Burthred, sometimes a different voice, but it's impossible to make out the words. They talk for such a long time. Perhaps this augurs well - perhaps Burthred will only speak with Roger, then ride away.

But it's not to be. I hear the creak of the cell door, footsteps coming towards my hiding place. My tongue is like a dry bone in my mouth. Every inch of my body tingles with fear. The log is being dragged away. The door falls open, and there is Roger, alone. But where are the men? I haven't heard them ride away. I clutch at Roger in terror.

'It's all right,' he says quietly. 'It is safe to come out.'

'Is it Burthred?' I am too afraid to move. 'What does he want?'

'He has had a change of heart. You will see.'

'But how did he know I was here? I cannot come out. If he sees me, he will go straight to the Bishop.'

Roger takes me by the shoulders. 'Calm down. It is best that you show yourself. I believe what he is telling me and if it is so, it will not be in Burthred's interest to go to Robert Bloet.'

Everything in me screams that I should stay hidden on my stone, wrapped in the blanket. My woollen tunic is stained and I reach up to touch the cap that does not quite cover my greasy hair.

'Christina, trust me,' Roger says.

I look up into his face. Some fragrance of divine peace that

156

lingers about him communicates itself to me. I allow him to help me out of the wood store and into the room.

'Ready?' he asks and I can only nod, though I am far from ready to set eyes on my husband.

Roger goes out to fetch the men and I try to rid myself of the splinters of wood caught in my tunic. My hand catches on my hip bone - how scrawny I have become. I hear voices at the door.

Now that I have made up my mind to face him, I feel the first flicker of a new courage. When Burthred looks at me, he might see these poor clothes, my unkempt hair, my wasted body, but these are nothing to the treasure I have found within, where my Lord dwells. Burthred promised that we could have a chaste marriage and then he betrayed me. But which of us has prevailed? He has had no wife in his bed these years, while I have lived by my vow.

They follow Roger into the cell: first Burthred, then two other men whom I recognize as his brothers. One is a canon by his dress and the other a layman. The cell is suddenly crowded and stools must be produced and a bench.

'As you see, the lady you seek is here, with us,' Roger says.

They bow to me and I return the courtesy - for all the world as if we were in the Guildhall, at a banquet. I cannot take my eyes from Burthred. After four years, his shoulders seem broader and his sandy hair is cut short and bobbed in a new style. He seems nervous and does not meet my gaze but looks instead to Roger, sitting in his own chair.

'Well,' says Roger. 'Perhaps you should address yourself to the one concerned, and tell her what you have told me.'

I see the colour blossoming in Burthred's cheeks as he reluctantly turns to face me.

157

'I can no longer struggle with my conscience,' he says. Even now he will not look into my eyes. 'It has become clear to me that you were, indeed, vowed to Christ from your youth. It is my wish to release you from our marriage and place you under the protection of the Father here.' He looks up at last and his face is crimson against his fair hair. 'I suppose that is still your wish?'

Can he really be setting me free? I can hardly believe my ears.

'Does my father know I'm here? How did you find out?'

'We were sure that the hermits would know of your hiding place.'

Burthred's brother - the one without the tonsure - breaks in, addressing himself to Roger. His cloak is an expensive dark wool and the clasp he wears is finely wrought silver - that of a merchant perhaps.

'My brother came here straight away - the day his wife absconded,' he says, his tone accusing. 'Yet you did not see fit to reveal that she was with you then.'

Roger frowns and I can tell that he's angry, but he keeps his words civil enough. 'My companion, Leofric, spoke the truth when your brother came that day. She was not here.'

It is obvious that the merchant does not believe him and I am indignant. But now Burthred addresses himself to Roger, intent on avoiding a dispute.

'Father, I am eager to mend my life. Perhaps I too might come to you for counsel from time to time. If you will receive Theodora into your protection straight away, I will be happy to release her from her vow, with my brothers as witnesses.'

This is more than I could have hoped! Truly God has touched the heart of my husband.

'You are welcome, Burthred, to any wisdom that I might have to offer you, if you truly wish to mend your life,' Roger replies. He turns to me. 'What your husband has not told you is that he now wants to wed another and his marriage to you is an impediment.'

The townsman in the brown cloak leans forward angrily, suspecting Roger of mockery. Roger puts out a hand to placate him, and turns back to my husband.

'In truth, Burthred, I believe that God would have you free to wed and make children, as any man might wish to do.'

'Then let us shake hands now, in token of my release of Theodora,' Burthred says at once.

I am awash with joy but then Roger replies and I can scarcely believe my ears.

'It would be wise for us to take a few days to consider this matter. And then, if all are decided, you could return with more witnesses. Perhaps Ralph, lord of Flamstead, would be amenable and even the priest who betrothed you - if he could be persuaded.'

I am astonished and Burthred, too, looks disappointed. But now the second brother, the clerk, stands up and speaks for the first time.

'The Blessed Father is right, Burthred,' he says. 'Let us come back with others.'

Burthred frowns at him, then turns reluctantly to Roger. 'If that is your wish, Father. We will come again on Tuesday to make an end of this business.'

Roger nods and gets up from his chair. He goes to the door of his cell and opens it.

Last to leave the room, Burthred looks back at me quickly. He seems to feel as distressed as I do.

159

As soon as Roger returns from seeing them off, I run to him.

'Why did you say that? He would have released me here and now, and it would be over. Now he may think better of it and, who knows, he might even go to the Bishop.'

Roger sinks down into his chair and takes a deep breath. 'We must be wise as serpents, Christina. This is only the start. I think that Burthred means to release you but it would be better if the witnesses were men of higher standing than his brothers. Better for him and for us. That is why I had him return.'

'But what if he goes to Robert Bloet?'

'Trust me, he will not. He cannot wed another without this marriage being annulled and only a bishop, or one higher than a bishop, can perform the annulment. Remember that we are in the Bishop of Lincoln's jurisdiction here. Do you think that he would ever be persuaded to do it?'

I remember standing before the Bishop of Lincoln. That wily face - the sharp eyes, the beaked nose. The glee with which he shattered all my hopes.

'He would sooner see me excommunicated.'

'So, it is in Burthred's interest to have men of power as his witnesses. He may wish to go above the head of the Bishop of Lincoln to try for his annulment.' Roger falls silent, thinking. 'Robert Bloet is an old man, like me. It may be that he will not live much longer and a new bishop will look favourably on your case.'

I hope with all my heart that he is right or that Burthred will come back with greater men and set me free. Roger gets up from the chair and comes over to me.

'Take heart, Christina. Once Burthred has released you

into my care, annulment or no, I think that it might be safe for you to live here openly.'

It takes me time to grasp what he is saying. 'I will not need to hide any longer in the daytime? Might I even go about with you or with Ulfwine when you travel?'

His face breaks into a grin. 'I think it might be possible for you to take your leave of the wood store. If we are careful.'

# Chapter 17

*Hermitage de bosco*

*Holy Monday, fourth day of April, AD 1121*

It is Holy Week. There is nowhere else in the world I would rather be than here in the chapel with my beloved Roger and our companions in Christ. I close my eyes and listen to their familiar voices, singing the psalm. A picture comes to me of the willow catkins I saw in the wood this morning, the purplish-brown fur, so soft on my finger. The day was bright, with a gentle breeze, and quite warm. Even now, as it grows dark, there is still a mildness to the air.

In front of me, Roger seems unsteady on his feet. It's no wonder. He has slept only an hour or two, these last nights, keeping vigil with our Lord as he approaches Jerusalem and the Cross. Now that Compline is over, he sinks down onto the bench by the wall. I wish he would take more rest but when I say so, he just growls at me.

Leofric has already left the chapel and now I hear him

calling. Outside, he is staring up into the night sky.

'Look! The Moon!'

The others have followed me out and now we stand, peering upwards, a knot of humanity floating in the vast sea of the night. What I see makes my scalp tingle. The Moon should be full tonight but instead a monstrous shadow has taken a bite out of it.

'What does it mean?'

Leofric sounds frightened and his fear communicates itself to me. I reach into the pocket of my tunic for my prayer beads.

'Don't be alarmed,' says Ulfwine, who has studied in the schools. 'It's only the movement of the heavenly bodies. Keep watching and you will see the Moon all but disappear.'

My neck is aching but I cannot tear myself away. The Moon becomes a sharper and sharper crescent, and the night grows steadily darker. Acio and Roger, the old men among us, have seen this wonder many times and do not appear troubled. I saw it once before but I was a child then and too young to be fearful.

Leofric is no scholar and has a simple turn of mind. 'But what will happen if the Moon's light goes out?' he asks Acio. 'Will the seas not overflow the land?'

'No, son,' he replies. 'The times and the seasons, the heavenly bodies – they are all in the hands of the Father.'

'See the red?' says Ulfwine. 'The Moon is changing colour!'

He is right. The Moon, now a ball of shadow with just the tiniest sliver of light at its edge, has become a dull earthen red. In the fearful darkness, the stars shine brighter than ever, as if trying to make up the lack. Jacob's Ladder arches up into the heavens, a great band of milky light. The last sliver of brightness disappears, leaving only the ochre-red ball.

My heart is beating fast and Leofric is ill at ease - I know it. 'But what does it mean, when the Moon bleeds? Is it a sign of great bloodshed to come?' he asks.

We turn to Roger, like children to our father, but he says nothing. Ulfwine answers instead.

'There is sure to be a cause – I don't know it but the masters in the university could tell you.' Ulfwine loves knowledge and learning; to him, there is always a reason for everything.

Now, as we watch, it seems to me that the darkness is less intense. The thinnest curved blade of light has reappeared and gradually it fattens to the shape of a Saracen scimitar. The shadow is retreating from the Moon's surface!

'Men look for signification in the movement of the heavens,' Roger says, speaking for the first time. 'They seek to predict what is to come, here on Earth. But they miss the simple lesson God would show them tonight.'

'What is that, Brother?' Acio asks.

'Only that when darkness closes in, even the darkness of death, it is not the end. Light and life come again.'

The sky has lost its murky red hue and the full orb of the Moon is revealed, in her milky whiteness. Full of gratitude and wonder, we stand a while longer, then Ulfwine wishes us good night and Leofric and Acio follow him across the muddy ground to their cells. I find myself shivering - it has grown cold.

Inside the chapel, both candles are still burning. I take up my place before the altar with Roger to my left, and close my eyes to pray. Breaking into the holy silence, I hear Roger's voice beside me, gruff and a little awkward.

'It is my wish to be buried here, beside the chapel.'

My eyes fly open but Roger is looking resolutely ahead at the silver cross. Unease begins to unfurl inside me.

'What do you mean? Why do you say that?'

He speaks into the darkness. 'Because it is in my heart that you should inherit the hermitage when I die.'

His words pierce me like a shower of arrows.

'Don't talk like that! You are not so old – Acio is older than you and he has been ill - but you are strong.'

'Nevertheless,' he says, 'plans should be made.'

He closes his eyes and says no more, as if now we should turn to prayer. I try but I cannot find the silent place of peace inside my soul.

I whisper into the gloom. 'What about the others - Ulfwine and Leofric and Acio?' To dwell here - an unconsecrated woman - to be mistress of men. It is unthinkable.

Roger turns to me, his voice stern. 'Why do you let this distract you from your prayer? Trust yourself to the faithfulness of the Lord.'

A sob is forming in my belly and I turn away from the altar, but then I feel a hand on my shoulder. Roger's voice, more gentle now, comes in my ear.

'The brothers will find another place where they can live before God. But you are in a different position. I must make provision for you.'

I lie on my bed but I can't sleep. My body is warm and tingling with life. I feel as if I could run and jump and sing out loud and not care that anyone should hear. Roger intends me to stay here with him, always. He won't die for a long time yet. He is not so old, after all, and he is never sick.

The hopeful thoughts build, one upon the other, like bricks, forming a solid wall of happiness. Burthred has released me and surely, since such important men came to witness his oath – even Ralph, lord of Flamstead – it is only a matter of time before the Bishop annuls my marriage. I shall live here always, as a bride of Christ.

I am not learned and wise like Roger. I do not deny myself as he does. But he is teaching me and in time I will grow adept in the art of contemplation. I begin to see myself, a woman the age of my mother, seated in Roger's chair, here in this cell. His psalter is open before me and I am reading from it to some young girls, who sit on the floor before me. They listen, rapt, as I explain the deeper meaning of the words to them. I say something that surprises them and their laughter rings out, but I don't rebuke them. I am not strict with them unless they are obstinate or disobedient.

Suddenly it is as if I am being drawn away from the cell and up into the night sky, above the clouds and into the heavens. In the midst of brilliant silver light, a woman sits on a throne. It is Mary, the Queen of Heaven. She is attended by angels on lesser thrones, twinkling like stars. My eyes are drawn to the Queen again and again. I cannot look away though if we were in the realm of Earth my eyes would not be able to endure the light that surrounds her.

As I stare in delight, the Queen turns to an attendant and I hear her words as clearly as if they were spoken to me.

'Ask Christina what she wants, because I will give her whatever she asks.'

Looking down, I see the whole world opening out before me as if it were a great scroll: hill upon hill, plain upon plain, woods and fields, manors and castles, streams and rivers, emptying themselves at last into the ocean. I see all this dimly, as if through the shroud of a thin mist, but there is one place that seems to bask in sunlight. I peer down and the ground comes up to meet my vision. It is a clearing among some trees. The hermitage! There is the vegetable patch and Ulfwine's cell and the kitchen and, most radiantly shining of all, Roger's cell and the chapel.

'I wish to have that place to dwell in,' I hear myself say.

The Queen turns to the angel and, holding her sceptre aloft, makes a pronouncement. 'She shall certainly have it and even more would gladly be given if she wanted it.'

For the space of a breath, there is a towering silence. Then the hermitage pulls away and the twinkling thrones disappear into invisibility, like stars in the morning. I find myself back in the unbroken dark, lying on my mattress, the coverlet scrunched up in my hand. My heart is racing and the whole of my body tingles with joy and wonder.


*Redbourn Manor*

*Twelfth day of May, AD 1121*


It is wonderful to be on the road on such a day. The beeches are newly-green, the maythorn is in blossom and the spring sun has warmed us all through the five-mile ride from the hermitage. Goddescalc is not so young and he keeps his horse at a steady pace, while I sit pillion behind him, chattering in his ear. He has been already to Redbourn at Roger's behest and spoken with the Archbishop and assures me that he is not a man to fear. Now that we have arrived at the manor, though, I begin to be nervous. My mouth feels suddenly dry.

Goddescalc helps me down and speaks to the groom before he leads the horse away. We are shown into the vestibule and told to wait. I look around me, my eyes unaccustomed to new surroundings after so long at the hermitage. The walls are bare, the furniture rough. It does not seem a fitting place for an archbishop.

'Is Archbishop Thurstan staying here long, at Redbourn?' I ask.

'I don't know. The Abbot of St Albans has made the house available to him for as long as he needs it.'

Goddescalc sees that I am anxious and puts his hand on my arm.

'Have no fear, Christina. The Archbishop of York is a godly man and a humble one too. He is eager to meet you.'

Soon I am ushered into the hall, where a stout man of about fifty years sits at table, the remains of his breakfast still strewn on the board before him.

'Welcome, Mistress Christina,' he says, 'come and sit with me, if you will.'

I obey, instantly relieved. Looking into the face of the Archbishop, I see only curiosity and a disposition to be agreeable.

'Roger has approached me, asking that I grant you my patronage,' he begins.

I bow my head in acknowledgment. 'My lord Archbishop.'

'I have known Roger a long time – since we were at St Paul's in London,' he begins. 'If he believes that your vocation is a true one and that this marriage of yours was entered into under duress, then I have no doubt that it is so. But why don't you speak of it in your own words?'

I find that it is not difficult to tell him everything: my

vow at the church in Shillington when I was a girl, how I came to betroth myself to Burthred against my will, the hard treatment I had at the hands of my parents, my escape to Alfwen and from there to the hermitage and Roger. I even tell him about Bishop Ranulf trying to seduce me, though perhaps it isn't wise to do so.

'And now Burthred has vowed before witnesses to release me from my marriage, but the Bishop of Lincoln will never agree to it.'

The Archbishop sits back and regards me. Is it possible that his eyes have become misted with tears?

'I, too, made a vow when I was young. Once the King and the Church no longer require my services, I shall keep that vow and withdraw from the world.'

He stands and takes my hand in his own.

'Go back to Roger now and learn from him all he has to teach you. Have no fear. If it can be managed, I shall make provision for you to stay on at the hermitage.'

I curtsey and try to extract my hand but Thurstan has not finished speaking.

'And these things I promise you as Archbishop. When the time is right, I shall have your marriage annulled, so that this Burthred may marry again. And I shall see to it that your vow is confirmed.'

# Chapter 18

*Hermitage de bosco*

*Twelfth day of September, AD 1121*

In my dream I hear running footsteps - shouting - and I wake to Leofric's face in front of mine.

'Christina! Wake up - it's Roger!'

His face is white. *Oh Mary, Mother of our Lord.*

I scramble up off the mattress and stagger after him to the door but then remember that I am wearing only my shift. I run back for a cloak to cover myself.

The chapel door is open – I can see Ulfwine moving about inside. Old Acio comes up behind me and takes my arm.

'Courage, little one,' he whispers in my ear.

'Where is he?' I cry.

It is dark in the chapel - one of the candles has burnt down – I can't see Roger anywhere. Over by the bench, Ulfwine is bending over something on the floor.

I have to look away – that dear form - slumped, unmoving, on the rushes. I don't remember opening my mouth but there is a dreadful wailing coming from it nonetheless. I cover my ears but the pain in my head only grows louder.

I feel my knees buckle and Acio's hand under my elbow, holding me up.

'God has taken him, Christina,' he says in a broken voice.

'No!' This can't be. 'He is just sick – that's all it is.'

He shakes his head. 'He's cold - the breath has left his body, child.'

'But last night – when we were together, in prayer - he was …'

'The Lord is faithful, Christina. He will not suffer you to be tested beyond what you are able to endure,' he says.

Ulfwine straightens up. His eyes seem to search around and now they find Leofric, his back pressed against the door, eyes wide with horror.

'Tell the boy to bring a trestle and a board,' he says. 'Then you can help me lift him onto it.'

I break away from Acio and run to Ulfwine. 'What are you saying? We should send for the physicker.'

Ulfwine looks past me, to Leofric. 'And tell Nelda to send to the Abbey with word. They should be made aware.'

'Stop it - let me see him!'

Ulfwine seems to notice me for the first time. 'Of course.' He moves to the side and I edge closer to the brown humped shape on the floor. He is lying on his side, knees bent, mouth a little open. The skin of his face is grey. It's all right - his eyes are open!

'Father!' I am on my knees, my face close to his. 'It's me, your daughter.'

But there is no movement - his eyes are unseeing. His face has become that of a young man, the lines of age and care

171

smoothed away. An exquisite pain slices through me. This is not Roger – this is no more than a corpse. I hear Ulfwine's voice in my ear.

'You are his heir, Christina. Shall we lay out his body here in the chapel? We can keep vigil. The villagers will want to come …'

I cannot abide him being so calm, so unfeeling. Anger is writhing inside my chest, threatening to split me apart. I batter his chest with my fists. 'Don't you care that he is gone? Don't you care that I have lost everything?'

I stumble up and run – out of the chapel into the morning light. Nelda is standing at the kitchen door, her baby boy clinging to her skirts. When she sees me, she makes the sign of the cross. Her eyes are red. She runs out to meet me and the child, abandoned, starts wailing. She folds me into her arms and I feel the coarse cloth of her tunic against me, her onion-breath in my face but none of that matters.

'There, there, Mistress,' she says, again and again. 'There, there.'

The day has passed somehow, like a troubled dream, full of pain, and now night has fallen again, for all the world as if nothing grievous had happened. Kneeling in the chapel beside his body, I am chilled to the marrow but I will not leave him, whatever the others say. Outside, the wind is whining in the trees. The mortuary candle flickers in the draught where the door has become warped and no longer fits.

I look for the hundredth time at his face but there is nothing there – no life, no warmth. I cannot bear this blankness. *Why won't you speak to me?* I clench my fists in rage. *Why have you left me?*

I close my eyes and suddenly I am back in my father's house, smelling again the fresh tansy that Wyn has strewn on the floor of my chamber. I am kneeling there too and trying to pray but all I can think of is Father stripping me of my gown and jewels, the hardness in his eyes. Since this morning my thoughts keep straying, as if by themselves – back to that old life. I hear my mother's voice.

*You think only of yourself, Theodora. Why can't you be like your sister?*

It's true. Blessed Roger lies still in death and instead of praying for his soul, I can think only of what will happen to me. It's no wonder that my Saviour has withdrawn the sweetness of his presence from me. I have been kneeling so long that a sharp pain shoots through my back, forcing me to double over. I welcome it - I deserve to suffer. Perhaps Roger been taken from me that I might be purified through suffering.

I hear a click as the latch on the chapel door is lifted. The candle flame gutters. It is Ulfwine. What can he want of me now? He doesn't speak - just stands before the altar a long time, his head bowed. Now he kneels beside me and I see that there are tears coursing down his cheeks. My heart melts and I am pricked by guilt. How could I forget? He and the others will have to find another home now. I reach out to him but he pulls away, scrubbing the tears from his face with his knuckles.

'We must have courage,' he says but his voice is flat with anguish.

It makes me afraid - to see him like a lost child. I shoot a prayer to heaven and feel my fear give way for a moment, like loose scree on a hillside. I am shocked to catch a glimpse of something firm beneath it, untouched by the calamity that

173

has befallen us. I think it is a kind of peace.

'He has not left us without hope,' I hear myself say and, as I speak, I know that it's true. 'Remember what he said on the night of the eclipse – death cannot separate us from the love of God.'

*Next morning*

Nelda hands me the cup. 'Drink it, Mistress, it will do you good.'

She has warmed the wine and infused it with herbs; I smell chamomile and another sharp scent that I don't recognize. Nelda is right - I must try to eat something. The priest will come from Caddington today, to bury Roger's body.

A dog is barking out by the gate – more villagers here to pray for Roger's soul. I reach the kitchen door just in time to see two horses canter into the clearing. The riders are not villagers – they are dressed in Benedictine black.

Ulfwine heard the horses too and has followed me. 'That's the St Albans habit,' he whispers.

'Have they come for the burial, do you suppose?'

He makes no answer, his eyes on the path where more horses are now appearing through the trees - three of them. These are not monks. I see a short sword hanging at the side of the rider nearest me and another has a cudgel.

One of the monks - the elder of the two - reins in his horse and the handsome grey beast circles, his ears pricked. He reminds me of my own Samson. The rider, a man of middle age, remains in the saddle.

'I am Prior Thomas, from the Abbey,' he says, his accent betraying him for a Norman.

Acio has joined us but there is no sign of Leofric. After a cursory scan of our faces, the Prior addresses himself to Ulfwine.

'On behalf of Abbot Geoffrey, I offer you condolences on the death of your Master.'

'Thank you,' Ulfwine answers. He eyes the armed men nervously. 'Can we offer you refreshment? Perhaps you will stay to be present at the burial. The priest is coming at midday.'

The Prior turns to his companion and as they confer quietly, Leofric comes running towards us, along the path. 'They have a cart – at the gate,' he murmurs, when he has reached us.

I see a look pass between Ulfwine and Acio that I don't understand. It fills me with fear.

The Prior speaks again, looking down at us from the height of his horse. 'Unfortunately, this priest will have a wasted journey. Blessed Roger was under the authority of the Abbot of St Albans, and Abbot Geoffrey has determined that he should be buried in the Abbey, as befits his godly life.'

My heart seems to stop. 'But the grave is dug already, in the place that our Master chose, between his cell and the chapel.'

The Prior ignores me, fixing his gaze on Ulfwine. His voice is smooth, untroubled. 'You, his closest companions, were blessed by Roger's presence during his earthly life. No doubt you would wish the many souls who visit the Abbey to benefit from the virtue of his presence in death.'

'But it was his wish…'

The other monk, a younger man with a dark thatch of hair, turns to me. 'Who are you, anyway? His niece? His cousin?'

175

He does not trouble to hide his contempt.

'I am Christina,' I reply, furious, heedless of the danger. 'And Roger named me as his successor here.'

I feel the restraining pressure of Ulfwine's hand on my arm.

'Where does Blessed Roger lie? In the chapel?' The Prior is addressing Ulfwine, his voice even but laced with steel. 'Our orders are to take his body with us now.'

I cry out but the armed men are dismounting. One of them calls for the kitchen boy to hold the reins. Another helps first the Prior, then the other brother, to dismount.

We follow them, helplessly, as they file into the chapel, strangers crowding our sacred place. Acio goes down onto one knee and stretches out his hand. 'Father Prior …'

'Have no fear, old man.' Prior Thomas speaks gently. 'We will treat him with the utmost reverence.'

The soldiers stand back while the Prior approaches the trestle and studies Roger's face, then makes the sign of the cross. 'It is him,' he says.

The Abbot's men go to lift his body from the table on which it rests.

'No!'

I will not let them take him. I throw myself across his body but the young monk seizes me by the shoulders to prise me away. There is a ruckus behind me and the sound of a blow and Leofric's voice, crying out in pain.

The Abbot's men have Roger now - one holding his shoulders, the other two his legs. The torment of it – to see his arms hang down helplessly. I hear more horses outside and the rumble of a cart's wheels. There is nothing we can do.

They move quickly, placing his body in the cart and

covering it over with a heavy cloth. I look up at the sky but there are only high, white clouds in the blue expanse. I could not bear it if rain were to fall on him.

The cart rumbles away, followed closely by the soldiers. We stand watching as the monks mount their horses. Tears are streaming down my face. Acio puts his arm around my shoulder.

'Please do not distress yourselves,' the Prior says. 'You will be informed when the burial is to take place.' He takes up his reins and starts to walk his horse, but then circles and comes back to us again. 'Abbot Geoffrey is consulting with the Bishop and, no doubt, he will visit you soon to discuss the future of the hermitage.'

Now they are gone and we stand, bereft, in the morning sunshine.

'We must send to the Archbishop – he will know what to do. Perhaps he will act on our behalf,' says Acio.

I shake my head. Thurstan is in the north country and by the time we get word to him in York, it will be too late. Roger will be buried at the Abbey.

Ulfwine is standing, staring into the woods, after the riders. At last he turns back to us.

'Acio is right – we will send Leofric to York, with a message for the Archbishop,' he says. 'But meanwhile, you must leave here at once,' he says to me. 'A safe place must be found for you.'

His words make no sense. Surely, it is he and the others who must leave.

'You heard him,' says Ulfwine. 'Abbot Geoffrey is consulting with the Bishop of Lincoln, your enemy. He means to have the hermitage under his own jurisdiction. And now he will have news that you are here and claiming to be Roger's heir...'

His voice trails off into silence. I did not think there could be anything worse than the grief of losing Roger, but perhaps I was wrong.

# Chapter 19

*Pocklinton, East Yorkshire*

*Twenty-ninth day of March, AD 1122*

A sickening shudder passes through my body as I lose my footing on the muddy track. I grab out for something -a bramble branch - to save myself from falling headlong, and feel the thorns bite into the heel of my hand. There are wet patches on my mantle - even my tunic is spattered. I stand still a moment to catch my breath, and look around me. The mud has probably ruined my shoes but it is worth it, to be out in the open air. The lashing winds and rain kept me inside my chamber all through Eastertide.

Clouds speed past, high above me in the blue sky, and suddenly I am a child again, standing with my father on the shore at Wisbech and watching for his ship among the billowing white sails at sea. I swallow away the lump that has formed in my throat. This north country, with its sweeping skies and its wide, flat pastures, has a kind of beauty, I suppose. But what I would not give to wake up to a breeze caressing the leaves of my beloved beech trees. And Leofric ringing the bell by the chapel door.

No-one has passed me on the way today, all these four miles back from the church of St James at Warter. I have taken to going there whenever I can, to hear service and receive the body of my Lord from the priests. They live together before God and have all things in common, just as Sueno and the fathers in Huntingdon do. Father Guillaume asked me this morning why I do not go to the church close by in Pocklinton. I suppose that it might be safe to go out in public, in this country where no-one knows me; Willa, the steward's wife, has put it about that I am her cousin. But still, I don't like to be seen over much in the town.

A weight seems to settle back on my shoulders as I join the lane that leads to the manor house. I remember how it looked the first time I saw it, a large house but shabby, on the edge of the busy wool town. I was tired out after those fearful weeks of hiding here and there, always having to move on under cover of darkness. I should be grateful to Archbishop Thurstan for finding me this place of safety, even if it means being alone in a house of servants, so far from home.

There are more horses tethered in the yard than usual and the stench of dung is stronger than ever. A groom is rubbing down a sturdy-looking black and, as I pass, he looks up at me with curiosity. I have never seen him before. At the door to the hall, I hesitate; there are men's voices coming from inside. Of course - today is the meeting of the court leet. How do I get back to my chamber, without going through the hall? Cynric tells me that as a guest of the Master's I should make free in the house but at the same time he contrives to let me know that my presence is an added burden.

I walk quickly around the house to the back, past the orchard which slopes down to the carp pond, ashamed to meet anyone in my soiled clothes. At the hermitage, we all wore rough clothing for the sake of Christ, but it is different here. I see the derision in the servants' eyes when they look at me.

There is a clattering of pans from the kitchen but I am glad no-one sees me climb the outer steps, like a servant taking firewood to the upper chambers. The door to the little room that serves as a chapel is ajar and, darting past, I think I hear someone moving inside. Without stopping to look, I make for the safety of my own chamber and close the heavy oak door behind me. It is the only place in this house where I remember who I really am. I take off my mantle and hang it on the pole. Once the mud is dry, I will go in search of a brush and I shall have to brave Willa about the shoes too. I don't know why I should feel so timid. As the wife of Athelwulf's steward, she is only a glorified servant after all.

I draw in my breath -someone is knocking at my door. Who could it be? In this busy house, no-one disturbs me from dawn till dusk. If I do not come down for the noon meal, it is not remarked upon. Sometimes I think that if I were to die in the night, no-one would know.

'Who is it?'

'Your host – Athelwulf.'

*Athelwulf?* The lord of this house never comes here. Cynric is in charge of everything.

I smooth down my tunic and push back the hair from my face. My feet are bare! But perhaps that is better than muddy hose. I push the ruined shoes out of sight and unlatch the door.

'May I come in?' he asks.

I stand back and he enters, a tall man with curly chestnut hair, not so different in colour from my own. He walks to the fireplace then turns to face me, but not before I have seen his priest's tonsure. Of course – Cynric makes so much of his Master's being at court with the King that I had forgotten that he is a Prior too, a man in holy orders. He is younger than I thought. Being Archbishop Thurstan's friend, I suppose I had imagined him a man of the same age. He is strong-limbed, his movements assured, but there is an affability about him too.

'Forgive me,' he says, 'for not welcoming you in person before now.'

He is one of us, as his name betokens, not a Norman. There is a northern edge to his English that reminds me of Alfwen, though his speech is refined.

'It is for me to thank you. You gave me succour in my hour of need.'

He shakes his head. 'When Thurstan asked me, I was glad to do it. Has he been to see you? We are close to York here, so no doubt he will look in on you from time to time.'

'Oh, but I shall not need to prevail upon your kindness for much longer,' I say. He makes it sound as if I shall be here forever. 'The Archbishop will ensure my return to the hermitage soon.'

He nods, but is that some doubt I see in his face?

'It is only a matter of time and the Archbishop's convenience in arranging the annulment,' I insist.

He nods again and casts a glance around my chamber, at the bed and the prayer stool, at Roger's psalter that I brought with me when I fled.

'Cynric and Willa – they are looking after you well?' he asks. 'Are you comfortable here?'

'I am free to pray and to fast, that's all I ask.' I look up into his face, trying to gauge what manner of man he is. He meets my gaze frankly: his eyes brown with a hint of gold.

'Cynric is a good man. I trust him with my land and my house – I would trust him with my life. But he has a lot to oversee here – and at the mill, of course. And Willa …' His mouth curls into a smile. 'Let us just say she is a woman of few words.'

I find myself returning his smile, and now it is as if we have a secret between us. Athelwulf's eyes come to rest on my prayer stool.

'Would you like me to have a priest come to say Mass for you in the chapel here?'

'You are very considerate,' I reply, 'but I like to walk to St James.'

'So I see.' He crosses the room and, bending down, retrieves one of my mud-caked shoes from under the bed. He holds it up and now he is really laughing. 'From the look of these, the road to Warter must be one big morass.'

I feel my cheeks becoming hot. 'I fear they are ruined and they are the only pair I have.'

He shakes his head as if this is nothing. 'I will speak to Willa – she will have someone take this to the bootmaker. He can make a new pair.' He puts the shoe down and takes a step closer towards me. 'Tell me about Roger the hermit – you knew him well, I think. His fame spread even to us in the north.'

Perhaps it's his kindness or perhaps it's the mention of Roger's name, but my eyes fill with tears. Athelwulf flinches a little.

'Forgive me my thoughtlessness. It has not been so long since his death. I should leave you, perhaps, to recover yourself.' He edges towards the door.

'No – no.' I don't want him to go. 'It's just that … sometimes, without his guidance, and without the comfort of my companions …'

'I understand,' Athelwulf breaks in, his face animated. 'I feel it, too, when I must leave my brothers.'

'Your brothers at the Priory? How many are you?'

'There are twelve of us – like the disciples of our Lord. There were eleven when I first came to them, just poor men living before God together, and now He has seen fit to make me their Prior. Do you know how it came to be? Perhaps Cynric has told you the story.'

'No. He speaks more of you being at court with King Henry.'

'He would. He loves to brag, even if it is on my behalf.' He looks at me closely. 'Of course, it is an honour to serve the King as his chaplain when he requires me. And I cannot deny that it pleases me to see new places and new faces. But my heart is at Nostell, with my brothers.'

All thoughts of my bare feet and my soiled clothing have fled. He might be lord of this manor and chaplain to the King, but it seems that this man is a true follower of Christ and his way.

'It was two winters since. I was travelling north with the King and we were staying at his castle in Pontefract when I was taken sick – a phlegm of the chest. I was too weak to ride on, so they had to leave me behind. As I grew better, I took to hunting with the Constable of the castle and his men to build up my strength. One day, I lost touch with the others.'

He laughs out loud, remembering. 'I was overcome with a fit of coughing and the palfrey took fright and threw me. It was the most propitious day of my life!'

He looks at me, still grinning. 'No, truly. For the horse threw me near the wood where the hermits were living – the hermits of St James. And they found me and took me back with them - my rib was broken by the fall. They cared for me with such tenderness and generosity – I had never known the like, not even from my own mother.'

I cannot help interrupting. 'Roger, also, was like a father to me. And his companions – they are more truly my brothers …'

I often picture Ulfwine and Leofric and dear old Acio, living on at the hermitage, without me. Though it may be that they have had to leave too.

'And is it true, what they say of him – of Roger? That no man was so forgetful of his own comfort.'

'It's true.' I think of him, standing in the chapel through the long, cold nights, praying. 'And he was so fierce in his fight against sin. At first, I was afraid of him.'

I feel that the picture I am painting is not a true likeness and somehow it seems important that this man should understand.

'But he could be gentle too, when you least expected it. And he didn't shun comfort to punish his body, not only that. It was more that he grew oblivious to everything else but God. Sometimes, when I was with him in the chapel - it was like coming between two lovers.'

Suddenly, I am embarrassed. But Athelwulf is listening, his eyes wide. I think he grasps something of what I am trying to say.

185

'It is said that he knew what would happen before it had come to pass,' he says now. 'Is that true also?'

'Many times, yes, he would see in his spirit things that were happening far from the hermitage.' I know it is my pride but I can't help continuing. 'I, too, have this gift – I would often know if someone was coming, before they had set foot across the ditch.'

After so long alone amongst strangers, it is like the first warmth of the sun in spring to have Athelwulf stand across from me, his eyes never leaving my face. Again, I feel a compulsion to be scrupulous with the truth.

'But Roger would often remind me that this foreknowing is not, in itself, a proof of holiness.'

He is looking at me with something like awe. Perhaps I have spoken too much.

'Tell me, Father, how you came to be chaplain to the King.'

'Oh, that was an accident of fortune, you might say.' Athelwulf moves across to the window, where fine horn panels keep out the wind and rain. Through them, it is still possible to make out the fields, stretching away to the horizon, an expanse of green and brown. 'See this land – it belonged, all of it, to the crown. But then King Henry took Edith, the daughter of Forne fitzSigulf as his mistress. And so, of course, he would visit this country sometimes to see her and the children she bore him. And while he was here once, my father did him some service, such that Henry made over part of his lands to him.'

'What happened to your father?'

'He died in battle in Normandy, fighting for the King's right.'

'So the manor passed to you?'

He nods his assent. 'As the only son, my father would not have had me become a priest.' He laughs again. 'We didn't see eye to eye on that, or on many things. But it turned out that I could not escape the world so easily. King Henry took a liking to me and made me his chaplain.'

It is my turn now to quiz Athelwulf. 'What is the King like? Is he such a hard man as they say?'

He stands by the window and looks out for a moment. My heart sinks; I have overstepped the mark. But when he turns to face me, I see no hint of reproach.

'Since the death of his son, two years back, there has been a change,' he says slowly. 'Perhaps the King is fearful for his own soul as any man - even a king - must be. All I know is that, soon after the drowning, he broke with Edith fitzForne and married her to the Constable of Oxford Castle.'

He takes a few steps towards me. 'And when he returned from Scotland and found me well and full of praise for the hermits at Nostell, he had Robert de Lacy give the brothers the land for their priory and he himself gave twelve pennies a day for their upkeep.'

Athelwulf's face breaks once more into a grin. 'Best of all, he allowed me to become their Prior.' He walks over to the prayer stool and appears to be examining the open page of the psalter, but his thoughts are still with the King. 'I would not wish the death of his son on any man, but sometimes it is only through adversity that God can shape us as he wills.'

There are footsteps on the stairs and in the passage outside.

'My lord! Where are you?' It is Cynric's voice.

Athelwulf goes to the door and opens it. 'I will be down presently.'

The steward sounds flustered. 'The bailiff would have you

see the damage before you go.'

*Before you go?* So is Athelwulf not to stay, even for one night?

He closes the door and turns to face me. I am almost sure it is regret I hear in his voice.

'I must go. It was the violence of the wind on the eve of Good Friday – they tell me the mill needs urgent repair.' Then his mouth curls one last time into a wry smile. 'And the villeins are loath to do it, after so many omens in the sky on the day of the Cross. They are always troubled when Lady Day and Easter come together.'

He comes a step closer to me and reaches out for my hand but I can't decide whether he intends to shake it or to kiss it in farewell so I stand, foolishly, hands clasped to my sides. He backs away, smiling a little.

'I am more than glad that we have been able to talk like this. You are most sincerely welcome in my house.'

To my chagrin, he crosses the room and picks up the muddy shoe again, holding it up like a favour. 'And I shall take this to Willa now. We can't have you unshod and unable to go to St James.'

He is at the door and the only thought in my mind is when he will return, but I do not see a way to ask the question.

He makes the sign of the cross. 'The Lord bless you, Christina,' he says and he is gone.

# Chapter 20

*Athelwulf's manor house, Pocklinton, East Yorkshire*

*Eleventh day of May, AD 1122*

A soft, yellow light fills my chamber: bright spring sunlight filtering through the horn panels at my window. I kneel at my prayer stool, Roger's psalter laid open before me. Though it was uttered so long ago, the prayer of King David could have come straight from my own heart. But then he, too, spent years in the wilderness, hiding from his enemies.

*Show me a token for good: that they who hate me may see, and be confounded.*

A token for good. I feel tears pricking behind my eyes. *Please, dear Jesus, send me a sign, anything, to show you have not abandoned me.*

Drawn by the beauty of the colours, my eyes stray down the page to the opening of the next psalm. There is a bishop with his crozier, standing before a church, as if to bless it. The cope he has about his shoulders is worked in circles of mulberry and pale carnation and suddenly I am back in my

189

father's storeroom, fingering the rich velvets, the figured silks from the East. *The Lord loveth the gates of Sion above all the tabernacles of David. Glorious things are said of thee, O city of God.* The psalm is in praise of Jerusalem, where Roger went on pilgrimage, and where I will never go.

The bishop's tunic is palest celestrine blue and behind him stand other priests in robes of orange tawny and light green. Their hair is painted a shade of tan brown. *Athelwulf.* I am flooded with sudden warmth, reliving for the thousandth time that day after Easter, the knock on my chamber door. I remember every word that passed between us, the way he listened when I spoke, the hair that curled about his ears, his laugh. A thousand times, at my prayers, I have thanked God for giving me this new brother, in the stead of Ulfwine and the others. When will he come again? Surely he must come to Pocklinton soon, to oversee the house.

Rising from prayer, I wrap my mantle around me and go down the stairs to the great hall. The men have long gone out to their work in the fields. Cynric and the bailiff, Rainald, are standing by the great fire, talking, and I pass close by them on my way out to the kitchen. I have taken to listening to their conversation when I can - if they have had word from Athelwulf, surely they will speak about it. This morning, I hear only some complaint about the hedge reeve.

In the kitchen I drink my thin ale and take the small piece of bread that is all I allow myself in the morning. I wander outside with it, into the brightness. The sky is clear and there is no wind to speak of. I look towards the henhouse, hoping that Willa has already fed the birds and I will not come across her in the orchard. Suddenly, I hear a man's voice, calling. I turn back. There, at the door of the hall, stands Athelwulf.

He waves, then comes striding towards me, a riding cloak still around his shoulders. My blood seems to race through my veins and up into my head.

'Where are you going?' he calls, before he has even reached me.

'Nowhere. I just came out to take the air.'

'Let's walk,' he says. 'It's a fine day. I have been up since dawn, riding from Wicston. Shall we make for town?'

He turns to go back through the house but then he sees my reluctance.

'Or we could go along by the river, to Bielby.'

We thread our way between the apple and the pear trees, the branches weighed down with pink and white blossoms, surrounded by the scent of dew-wet grass drying in the warmth of the sun. Happiness rises up inside me like sap, and spreads through my whole being. There comes a loud squawking and I turn back to see Willa fastening the door of the hen run. Athelwulf calls to her but she only turns and stares after us.

The cloak Athelwulf has on is the colour of ripe plums, the fabric finely woven. He catches me looking at it.

'Not a suitable cloak for a Prior, is it?' he smiles wryly. 'The King gave it to me at Oxford – I could not refuse it.'

'Oxford. Is that where you have been?'

'Yes. Henry summoned me there. And now I must get back to Nostell and tell my brothers the good news. Wherever he goes, the King secures more income for our Priory.'

'You must be much loved by him.'

'I am,' he replies, then laughs a little. 'But King Henry does nothing purely out of love. The greater the number of religious houses up here in the north that are obligated to

191

him, the more influence he has. I think he fears the power of the Scots.'

We have left the manor land behind and are following the track that leads to the goose farm. The beck is to our right, flowing fast after the Easter rains, the light dancing on its surface.

Athelwulf turns towards me. 'But enough talk about Nostell. I want to know how you are faring here at the house. Has my friend the Archbishop sent word to you? Is there any news of your annulment?'

I shake my head. 'There's been no word from him. Do you think he could have forgotten his promise? It's hard to wait, with no certainty of the future.'

'Yes,' he says, and touches my arm: a brief gesture of comfort such as a brother might make to his sister. We walk together for a while in an easy silence.

'I shouldn't be afraid,' I say, 'not when the Queen of Heaven herself has promised me I shall return to the hermitage.'

Athelwulf halts and turns to me. 'You have heard the Virgin speak to you?'

'Yes - in a vision. I saw the whole of the earth laid out before me and she asked what it was that I wanted. I chose Roger's hermitage. She said she would have given me more if I'd asked it.'

He seems to pull back a little. Perhaps he does not believe me.

'I know that visions can be false -the enemy can masquerade as an angel of light. But when I saw Christ himself, in the wood store, Roger said it was a true seeing.'

'The wood store?'

'Yes, it was tiny. I had to hide there all day on a stone,

sometimes without food or drink. He gave me a cross of gold, our Saviour I mean, and soon after that my husband came to release me.'

Athelwulf has been staring at me, as if in wonder. He seems discomfited.

'Your husband released you from your marriage? He came to the hermitage?'

'Yes. Burthred came, with his brothers, but Roger made him come back with greater men, to witness to his oath. But it's not enough to annul the marriage - not while the Bishop of Lincoln still opposes me.'

Athelwulf has recovered himself. 'I will pray, Christina, and my brothers at the Priory. You shall return to the hermitage - if the Mother of our Lord has willed it, nothing can prevent it.'

We can hear the honking of the geese now as we near the farm. 'Let's ask for something to drink here,' he says, 'then we must turn back.'

We walk on a little but before we have reached the ditch that surrounds the enclosure, he speaks again. 'I see now how much you have suffered to guard your chastity. Nothing must be allowed to stand in the way of your calling.'

Athelwulf has business at the mill to attend to for the rest of the day. He is to stay here at the house tonight, so we eat our great meal in the evening. When I come down, I am surprised to see that Willa is seated and it is Athelwulf himself who passes round the wine jug. The others look uncomfortable but I understand - he is only seeking to imitate our Saviour. In the hermitage, Roger would often serve the rest of us at table.

The estate workers seem glad to have their master here,

or perhaps it's only the strong ale he has ordered for them from the buttery, in honour of next week's Whit holiday, he says. There are five of us at the top table: Cynric and Willa, Rainald the bailiff, Athelwulf and myself.

'Will you have some wine?' he asks me at the first offering, but I never take anything stronger than the weak ale we drink for thirst's sake.

'Would you dishonour me in my own house by refusing?' he asks.

I look up and see that he is only jesting, but still it seems churlish to insist. He pours red wine into my cup and I offer him the jug in return, as the custom is.

The main dish is carp, baked in the earth oven with leeks and herbs. For the first time in months, I find myself eating with relish. Willa sits beside me but we don't converse and, instead, I content myself with listening to the talk of the men. Athelwulf has his steward on one side and his bailiff on the other and it gives me pleasure to see how they love him. It's no wonder to me that King Henry made Athelwulf his chaplain and often bids him leave the Priory and ride to court.

Cynric seems to come alive when his lord is here. Rainald, the bailiff, is a local man; he has a broad northern manner of speech and becomes more garrulous after his cup has been filled a few times. By the time the fruit is brought in, he has been persuaded to regale us with a tale about the miller's father and the ghostly fox he has seen circling the walls of the mill. When Athelwulf comes to me a second time with the wine jug, I make no protest.

There is a boy lolling against the wall by the door, watching us eat. I don't think I have seen him before.

'Who is that?' I ask Willa.

'That is Rainald's boy,' she replies.

'Why is he not with his mother? He is very young.'

Willa answers in her quiet voice. 'Rainald's wife is dead.'

I could not be expected to know that, but somehow I feel I have been rebuked. A cutting reply comes into my mind but before it leaves my lips, I am struck by a new thought. Willa and Cynric have no children. Perhaps she grieves for the lack of them and that is why she is so sour. I put as much gentleness into my voice as I can muster.

'Would you have liked to have a son?'

Willa lifts her face to look at me. She has large grey eyes – I haven't noticed them before. They are her best feature.

'The Lord has not seen fit to send me a child,' she says.

Once again, I feel as if I have spoken out of turn and am being judged. It's almost like being back at home, with Margaret reproaching me in her quiet way.

I turn away to watch the men and when Athelwulf comes a last time with the jug, I take no notice of those grey eyes of Willa's which I'm sure are watching me. What is wrong with taking another cup? Didn't my heavenly bridegroom turn water into wine at the wedding at Cana?

The meal and the tale-telling over, Rainald goes to his son, while Cynric and Willa help the servants to clear away. I get up from the table to go to my chamber, but Athelwulf follows me to the stairs.

'Christina, I will take my leave of you now,' he says. His face is ruddy from the fire and the food and drink. 'I will be gone early tomorrow.'

The words open up a chasm inside me. 'So soon?'

He nods. 'I must be back at Nostell for Whit Sunday.' He

takes my hand and holds it between his. 'But, when I come next, we will walk again and you will tell me more about your visions.'

His eyes are on my face, travelling up to my hair, my eyes, and then down to my mouth. I can feel the heat coming from his body. But then he smiles and drops my hand as if he had only just noticed he was still holding it.

'And before I go, I will tell Cynric to keep a watch.'

'A watch? For what?'

He laughs, so perhaps he is only jesting in his usual way. 'In case that husband of yours comes seeking you here, in the ungoverned north.'

# Chapter 21

*The river path by Pocklinton beck*

*Twentieth day of September, AD 1122*

I steal a glance at Athelwulf, striding beside me. After so many weeks of waiting, he has returned and we are walking again by the stream, across the sheep roam to Bielby. The ash trees that line the river are in full leaf now, some of them even showing the first hint of autumn yellow. The day is soft and still, though, as it was before, and blue butterflies are flitting between the stems of knapweed and cocksfoot on the bank. Athelwulf hardly seems to notice the beauty. He is talking about the King.

'I have been with Henry in York. We are lodging at St Peter's, at the hospital by the gate.' He pauses. 'I could not be so close and not come to Pocklinton.'

*So he did want to come. But is it only the estate that draws him here?*

'I have never seen York,' I reply. 'We passed by it when I was brought to your house.'

'It's the greatest town in the north -much bigger than Pocklinton - and the Minster is very fine. But it teems with the poor – you should see them, begging at the town gates, a multitude of them. They used to sleep in the streets before the hospital was built. Henry stays there - to show his compassion for the destitute, of course.'

I see by his smile that he is jesting.

'No, but it is a shrewd choice of lodging. Everything the King does has its reason.'

'So, what is his reason for calling you from your duties at the Priory this time?' I ask.

He is quiet for a moment and seems to be reflecting, but then he shrugs his shoulders.

'After Michaelmas he will travel further north – to Durham at least, maybe further. His daughter, Sybil, the one he married to the King of the Scots - she died in the summer, before she could give birth to an heir. I think he fears for his influence with the Scots.'

Athelwulf looks up into the sky. 'Perhaps we should start back. I cannot be absent all day. The King has his birthday feast tonight.'

We turn and start for home.

'He has asked me to join him from time to time, on the journey north,' he says.

When I have nothing to say in reply, he looks at me and smiles. 'That means I shall have opportunity to visit here more often.'

His mood is playful so I match it with my own.

'Do you need, then, to visit your estate so much? I thought you said that you trust Cynric to manage your affairs.'

He laughs, delighted at my subterfuge.

'I find a greater need to check on the manor and the mill than I used to,' he says, 'before you came to be my guest.'

We walk on in silence, my heart overflowing with happiness. The flat pastures on both sides of the river are empty of sheep now, as we approach the great Pocklinton fields. Athelwulf stops in the shade of a knot of ash trees by the water's edge. He turns to face me and now there is no laughter in his face.

'God has brought your friendship into my life,' he says. 'I believe you have much to teach me – as much as anything I might be able to do for you.' He looks away towards the stream. 'You cannot guess what a relief it is to be able to talk openly about the King. To someone who is discreet.'

I look up into his face and see that he is sincere.

'Christina, I wanted to speak with you all through the summer, but I was prevented from coming. The fair for St Oswald lasts for three days and there was much to do to arrange it and to accommodate the traders.'

He takes both my hands in his and peers closely at my face.

'You are thinner,' he says. 'Have you been ill? And all this time, I have been talking about my own affairs.'

'No,' I reply, eager to reassure him. 'I have not been ill. It's only that ...'

'What?'

'Nothing. Just that 'hope deferred makes the heart sick,' as the scripture says.' At once, I fear that he may misread me. 'Hope for my return to the hermitage, I mean. I have heard nothing from the Archbishop.'

My conscience pricks me. If he knew the battle I have waged all through the summer, thinking of him when I should be praying.

'Thurstan will do all he can – I am sure of it,' he says. 'You must be strong and keep faith.'

He kisses me on the cheek, the kiss of a spiritual friend, but the touch of his lips on my skin sends ripples of sensation throughout my body. He takes my chin in his rough man's hand and guides it round so that I am looking straight into his eyes. Now his lips are full on mine and they are warm and wet. I am trembling all over but I manage to pull back from him.

'No,' he mutters, 'no. How can this be wrong? You are God's gift to me.'

He draws me back to him and there is such sweetness in obeying. Through our garments, I can feel his body, taut and strong, yet he is trembling too. I feel he is going to kiss me again but, all at once, he jerks away and I feel the forsaking as a physical pain. I hear shouting – a man calling his dog, perhaps. The caller is not close but here, in this flat country, we can be seen from a long way off.

Athelwulf steps back into the middle of the path to get a better view, shielding his eyes against the sun. In the distance there is a wagon and four or five men walking beside it, with tools for harvesting. In the great field, oats sway gently in the light breeze, tall and ripe. Some of the strips have been cut already.

'We should go, Christina,' he says, and I fall into step beside him.

When the wagon passes us, he greets the men. They are not our workers but from the King's manor. Now, in the fields by us, I see the bent backs of villeins, their scythes sweeping through the yellowing crops.

'They will keep at the harvest till night falls,' Athelwulf says, 'this dry weather can't last.'

He is gone and I am alone in my chamber, more bereft than ever before. Losing Roger was not like this. It was a clean grief, with no sin to sully it. What am I to do? *Look to your chastity.* I can almost hear the words of Alfwen – see her look of reproach. *Do not feed the fire of lust.* My cheeks grow hot with shame. Fear twists in my guts as I think of the eternal flames of hell.

I try to conjure the presence of Roger, bent over the pages of a book, his mouth working in the way it did when there was a thorny question to consider. His dear face, so craggy and lined. I could never hide anything from him and it is no different now that he is gone.

*You would tell me to look past this temptation, but I can't seem to do it. What should I do?*

I wait, but no answer comes. Sometimes Roger would teach me patiently, with tenderness. At other times he was gruff and angry. Now there is nothing – just this tormenting emptiness.

I get up from my prayer stool and cross to the bed. Changing my mind, I lie down to rest on the floor among the rushes, with no covering to warm me. How can I indulge myself when these thoughts of Athelwulf fly again and again, unbidden, into my mind?

Sleep eludes me for a long time. I lie on the unforgiving floor and listen to the screeching of the barn owl from the orchard, welcoming the cold, the aching of my hip, as a penance. At last, I feel myself drifting off. In that weightless place beyond thought, I feel a gentle presence, an embrace, as if the Queen of Heaven were once again resting her head in my lap. There are no words.

When I wake, stiff but strangely comforted, my mind is more at peace. Nothing has passed between us but a kiss. Does St Paul not say 'greet one another with a holy kiss'? My vow is not broken. And the thoughts, the imaginings – they serve to teach me how I must desire union with my heavenly bridegroom.

*Twenty-eighth day of October, AD 1122*

Outside, the sky is clouding, full of rain that must surely fall before night comes. There is no longer enough light to see my stitches. I move closer to the window but soon I will have to stop or go to beg another candle. She never oversteps the mark but still she contrives to make me feel that I have been wasteful. Next time Athelwulf comes, I will speak to him about Willa and her moody insolence.

I put the work down and suddenly a picture comes to my mind. Athelwulf, saddling up his horse, the King's old riding cloak about his shoulders. There are stables and a groom and others - many others – and noise, and behind them a great wall, with a gate. Could he be in York, then, and about to ride to Pocklinton?

In an instant I am on my feet and down the stairs, hunting for Cynric.

'Have you had word – is the Master coming?' I ask, when I find him at the accounts.

He looks up, his face illuminated by the candlelight.

'Now? It's well-nigh dark. I am not expecting him.'

He looks after me curiously as I turn to climb back up to

my chamber, the bitter taste of disappointment in my mouth.

I wake in the morning to a knocking at my door and at once I am on my feet. Elisa stands at my door, breathing hard from climbing the stairs.

'What is it?' I ask. No one attends me in the morning in this house.

'The Master says you are to go to his chamber as soon as you are able.'

'The Prior is here? When did he come?'

'Last night – late. He rode from York, and before that he was in Durham.'

So it was a true seeing! She goes and I ready myself as best I can, heart beating fast, fingers trembling. Why is he asking for me so soon? Perhaps he has news from Archbishop Thurstan.

I knock quietly on the door of his chamber. Silence. Was Elisa mistaken? Is he still in bed after his night ride?

'Who is it?'

'Christina. You sent for me.'

I open the door and then quickly turn my head away. He is still lying on the mattress, his cloak wrapped around him.

'Come to me, Christina,' he says, 'and close the door behind you.'

I waver, then do as he says, coming to a halt a few feet from the bed. His face is flushed, his eyes brighter even than I remember them. His curly hair lies tangled on the bolster.

'I will come back later, when you are dressed,' I say.

'No,' he says, and his speech is thick as though he has been drinking wine, but it is early in the morning. 'Come closer.'

I edge towards the bed, then my heart seems to stop. His eyes are fixed on mine, wild and blacker than I remember them. I see that, under the cloak, he is naked. I give a little cry, sick with shock.

'Come to me,' he demands. 'God knows I have tried but I cannot think about anything else.'

'No.' I back away, appalled. In my sinful imaginings, we are always under the trees, the birds singing above us, his lips on mine. It is never this. This reminds me of when I was a girl. Bishop Ranulf on the bed, slavering, his legs apart.

'No!' My voice is stronger now. 'Cover yourself. What are you doing? Athelwulf, think of your calling.'

But he is shameless. He springs up from the bed and clasps me in his arms before I can stop him. I can feel the heat of his body through my tunic. He whispers my name, again and again, his wet mouth on my forehead, in my hair: his hands pressing my back, my buttocks, drawing me towards him. My whole body tingles with pleasure. Like a disobedient child, it ignores the dictates of my will and moves towards him. He is plucking at my tunic.

'Take off your clothes,' he whispers in my ear, 'or I shall tear them from you.'

He is murmuring lasciviously, not in anger, but his words rouse a sleeping beast. The face of my father, hideous in his rage, stripping me of my gown and my jewellery, ready to throw me out of his house onto the street. The memory is like a dart of ice, piercing my ardour.

I pull away from him and he lets out a howl of frustration. Is he going to strike me? No, but he has grabbed my hand. 'Touch me, Christina, at least you can do that. There is no loss in that. I know you want to touch me.'

I allow him to pull me back and having his arms around me once more is like coming home. My cheek rests against his chest, just below the breastbone. I can feel the tickling of hair, the rapid beating of his heart beneath the skin. We have become like one body rather than two, so close that I can hardly tell if he is touching me or I him. I close my mind to everything but this delectable movement, our bodies kneading together, slow and fraught with tenderness at first, then more clamorous. My breath is coming quick against his neck; he is clasping me to him with one hand, his lips kissing, sucking at my temple, where the hair begins to grow. Sinful pleasure is building, deep and low in my belly, but then his body jerks once, twice. He lets out a grunt and releases my hand, stumbling back from me.

I cannot bear for it to end. The bliss recedes like the tide, leaving a desolate expanse of guilt that frightens me so much I can hardly think. At last I open my eyes. Athelwulf has turned away to the bed, reaching for the cloak to cover himself. I look down, horrified, to see his milky seed on my fingers, the wet patch on my tunic.

Now he is sitting on the bed, pulling a tunic over his head. The curls of hair cling around his ears, damp with sweat. He smiles at me, a little sheepish, but then he sees that my eyes are filling with tears and, straight away, he is on his feet and returning to me.

'Don't fret yourself, Christina.'

I pull away from him, wiping my fingers again and again on my tunic, then hiding my hand under my armpit.

'What have you done? What have you done?'

He enfolds me again with his arms and there is the smell of sin on him, and on me too. My body clings to him but all comfort is draining away like water between my fingers, leaving only a gathering darkness. He seems to divine how I

205

feel and gives a small, impatient shake of his head.

'You have not been swiven,' he says quietly, using the old word. 'There is no harm done.'

I wonder at his blitheness, his lack of shame.

'But surely we have sinned.' My voice drops to a whisper. 'And is it not unnatural?'

'What?'

I cannot frame the words and point, instead, to the wet patch on my dress.

'To spill my seed? Would you rather, then, that I had planted it in the natural place?' he asks.

I look up quickly and cannot believe that he is smiling. How can he make a jest of this? It pains me more than I can say.

He sighs. 'You have nothing to reproach yourself with, Christina.'

Now he is looking around the chamber. He sees his boots by the door and, fetching them, sits down to lace them on.

'Pray God the wind has died down,' he says. 'And the rain. I was soaked through as I rode here.'

I turn my back and walk away from him. I can't stop trembling. Through the window, I can hear the whistle of the wind, blowing the last of the red leaves from the ash tree in the yard. I thought the Prior understood my heart. I thought he was a man of God. I feel the blood rush to my face, remembering how my flesh consented.

He is beside me now and looking out, his thoughts already turning to the day's tasks. More than anything now, I long to be back in my place of prayer.

'I shouldn't be here, in your chamber. What if Cynric comes in or one of the servants?'

'They will suspect nothing. I made sure they all heard me

give Elisa the message to summon you.'

I am left speechless by his deceit. Had he planned this sin, then, in the cold light of reason? Tears of confusion are beginning to trickle down my cheeks. He seems startled.

'Perhaps it would be wise for you to go now,' he says. 'I have to meet with Cynric.'

He takes my arm and guides me towards the door.

'I shall have to put the doctors of the Church right,' he says, teasing me in his usual way. 'We are taught that it was Eve who tempted Adam - that a woman's lust burns hotter than a man's.'

I cannot answer but only wipe my cheek with the back of my hand. He seems so insensible to what has been done, what has been despoiled.

'No, but in truth,' he says, 'you have nothing to reproach yourself with. If it were not for your resolve, who knows what I might have done? You were the one to act from reason, like a man, when I have played the weak woman. Forgive me.'

He opens the door and leads the way down to the hall to break our fast. Cynric is waiting for him. I can hardly touch my bread and I sit in a dream, listening to their talk. Athelwulf speaks of being at Durham with the King and how news came while he was there of the death of Ralph d'Escures, the Archbishop of Canterbury. Cynric listens with interest, then engages his master with questions. No-one would guess in a hundred years what has passed between us.

# Chapter 22

*Athelwulf's manor house, Pocklinton*

*St Cecilia's Day, twenty-second day of November, AD 1122*

I wake, stiff with cold, on the floor of my chamber. The wind has turned sharp these last nights and the mice are scurrying in greater numbers among the rushes. I long to bury myself on my mattress and pull up the coverlet around me, but instead I get up from the floor to dress.

Kneeling at the prayer stool, there is barely enough morning light to read the pages. It is the tenth day before the kalends of December - St Cecilia's Day. As if from nowhere, a sob forms itself within me and breaks like a wave as I remember sitting on the bed, recounting the story of St Cecilia to Burthred. With all my heart, I long to be that young girl again, pure and virginal, full of hope.

Another lonely, empty day stretches ahead, with the memory of Athelwulf, naked on the bed, lying in wait to ambush me. I wash my face but don't dare to touch any part of my body for fear the embers of lust will flare into flame. I cry out loud at the perverseness of it. The thing I yearn for above all - a visit from him – is the very thing that has the power to destroy my soul.

I go down to the hall and, thankfully, no-one is there. When I meet Cynric these days, he looks at me out of the corner of his eye and then turns away. Does he suspect something? Yesterday, at dinner, he pressed me to take some meat, but I can't allow myself. Everyone knows that eating flesh excites the passions. In the kitchen, I drink some water and take a little of the left-over greens.

It comes to me that perhaps, after all, I might go to the canon fathers at Warter to hear Mass, but how can I receive the body of the Lord? Before I have time to think better of it, I run up for my cloak and my outdoor shoes and leave the house through the back way. Willa is coming out of the kitchen and she makes a little bow as I pass, but I do not believe her deference for one instant. Looking back, I see her staring after me, scorn written all over her face. I am sure she knows.

With no shelter in this accursed flat country, the wind whips across the fields without mercy. Soon I am thoroughly chilled. The spire of the church seems to come no closer, however fast I walk. My belly is growling for food and now I find myself yawning, again and again, with no respite. I can hardly feel my hands or my feet.

I try to picture myself at the chancel steps, receiving the Host, but the nearer I come the more I know it for a cruel mirage. *Therefore, whosoever shall eat this bread, or drink the chalice of the Lord unworthily, shall be guilty of the body and of the blood of the Lord.*

Father Guillaume. He is not at all forbidding. I could make confession to him and then, surely, I would be counted worthy.

*Have you been bedded by this man?*

*No, Father.*

*Has your body been penetrated, Child?*

*No, Father.*

*Then your virginity is intact.*

But should I not be obliged to confess the actions of my hand, the spilling of his seed? And what of the nights when I have called it to mind, again and again, my flesh burning with lust? Surely all hope of a virgin's crown is lost forever.

At last I reach the wall that surrounds the house where the fathers live. There is the gate. The canons would receive me, I know, but my feet will not seem to take me any further. I can no longer feel the ground. A bright circle of light, no bigger than the head of a pin, rolls before my eyes again and again, travelling always from left to right. Everything becomes blurred. I hear a din of roaring and now there is an ugly black shape crouching before the gate, wild and unkempt. A bear! It is barring my way to the fathers, to the comfort of the Mass. *Help me, O Lord, take pity on me.* The bear is loping back and forth, growling. Now the path under its paws drops away, sucked down from within. The roaring grows fainter. The bear slips out of sight. Now the sinkhole is growing, spreading, till I feel the ground on which I stand falling away.

When I come to myself, I am lying on the frosty ground with two of the fathers standing over me. I try to speak but my lips are numb and cannot seem to form the words. I do not know their names, only that they wear the robes of St James. They wrap me in something warm and then I must fall asleep because the next thing I know, I am beside the fire in the hall at Pocklinton, laid upon a bench and swathed in covers. The heat from the flames is comforting but my head feels as if it will burst with pain and I find myself retching and spewing onto the floor. Elisa comes then and clears up the mess, tutting and fussing over me, her fingertips gentle on my face. Willa has been standing, watching, and now she comes closer. What she has to say sets my heart singing.

'Cynric sent for the Master. He will be here soon.'

I am warm at last and at peace, after the draught that made me sleep. Athelwulf brought it to me himself and held the cup while I took sips, till it was gone. There was fear in his eyes.

'You must eat,' he says, again and again. He keeps bringing me eggs and soft custards of cream from the kitchen.

It is enough just to rest, knowing that he is in the house. Now I hear his knock at the door. He walks over to the bed and sits on a stool beside me.

'There is more colour in your cheeks, Christina,' he says. 'How are you feeling?'

'Much better. I can't stay idle any longer, keeping you from the brothers at Nostell.'

He says nothing in reply and I am alarmed to see that tears are gathering in his eyes. He takes my hand in his.

'I have been frightened, that God would take you from me.'

Such a sweetness courses through me that I cannot answer him.

His eyes never leave mine as his fingers brush across the back of my hand and up my arm towards my neck. His brown eyes seem to grow larger and I can sense his body become taut, like that of a sinuous leopard, ready to spring.

211

'No,' I whisper. 'We must not sin.'

It can only be the grace of God, but I find that when he is here with me, I am able to withstand temptation.

He drops my hand and stands up, kicking the stool away in his frustration. He walks to the door, then turns to face me.

'I will ride back to Nostell tonight,' he says in a flat voice. 'Cynric will send me news of you.' He is about to go. 'It pleases me to see you looking stronger.'


*Ninth day of December, AD 1122*


The sound of hooves in the yard and I run to my window to watch for a glimpse of the groom. I try to prepare myself for disappointment. It will only be Cynric's horse, or Rainald the reeve's, or a nag belonging to one of the servants. At last there is a clip clopping on the stones and the groom appears, leading a grey horse - Athelwulf's grey!

I kneel and begin to recite the psalm, to steady myself. It is almost noon. Will he come to me before dinner? At last comes a knock at my door, but it's only Elisa.

'The Master bids you know he is here and dinner is brought in.'

I follow her down the stairs. Athelwulf is seated apart with Cynric and they are eating already, their heads close together in conversation. As I pass, he lifts his eyes and nods to me briefly. I sit with Willa and we make a little conversation, though I don't have any appetite. Why didn't he come to me first? Perhaps there has been some misadventure at the mill. Willa leaves the table but I stay, toying with my cake. At last,

Athelwulf beckons me over.

'Come and join us, Christina,' he says. 'I have news that I think you will find of interest.'

Cynric makes space on the bench beside him. Across the table, I see that Athelwulf's hair has grown long and I yearn to reach out and touch the curling tendril beside his ear. Why can we not be alone to talk?

Athelwulf is animated. It seems that he has just come from being with the King at York.

'I am to ride south after Christmas, to Gloucester. King Henry has called a council of all the bishops and the abbots - to choose a new Archbishop of Canterbury. He wants me to advise him.'

Cynric nods gravely, giving careful attention to everything that is said to him, as always. He is proud of his master.

'That's not yet the best news. What I have to tell you now is for your ears alone.'

Athelwulf includes us both in his glance and I am gratified.

'On his journey north, Henry took a detour west to Carlisle. He is having the town walls fortified against an invasion from the Scots.'

Cynric's eyes narrow.

'Don't worry, there is no danger here – we are too far south,' Athelwulf says. 'But the country of Cumbria is under the jurisdiction of the Bishop of Glasgow.'

'Does that affect you, at Nostell?' I ask.

He pauses a moment. 'No. But the King told me something in confidence. He is considering whether to make a new English see in Carlisle. If he does so, he has promised to make me the first Bishop.'

Athelwulf laughs at Cynric, who is staring, wide-eyed.

213

'There's no need to look surprised. Do you not think me capable of such a task?'

'Of course, sir,' replies Cynric. 'I believe that you are capable of anything you put your mind to. There will be a new estate of course, and lands over in the west.'

'Perhaps, but not yet. Just now, this is an idea in the King's mind, nothing more.'

Cynric merely nods but I see the thoughts racing through his mind: a bishop has great lands and even greater income. 'I must get back to work,' he says, rising from the bench.

At last, we can talk alone, though the servants are clearing away the food around us. Athelwulf looks across the table at me.

'I am glad of this opportunity, for I have something to tell you,' he says. 'The Archbishop was with us in York.'

'Thurstan? Did he speak of me?'

'No – well, yes, but I'll come to that.' He looks down at the table. 'My conscience has been troubling me. I made confession to him – of the way I have importuned you.'

The palms of my hands are suddenly hot.

'I hope you can forgive me, Christina, as God has done. From now on I shall keep to the Priory and not trouble you with my presence.'

I am gazing at his face, stricken.

'In any case, I shall be gone in the New Year, in the south.'

At first I am speechless, but then grief and anger loosen my tongue. 'And what of your brothers at Nostell? What about the simple life of prayer and contemplation? I thought that was your calling, not the high life of a bishop.'

He looks away, as if I have struck him, but then turns back, his eyes blazing.

'What is this now? First you upbraid me for my incontinence. Then, when I have repented, you try to shame me afresh.'

He stands up quickly and looks away. I cannot bear it.

'No, don't go like this.'

He relents and turns back. His face has softened, but I see that his mind is made up. 'You were right all along, Christina. It would be folly and worse to throw away my calling, for a brief moment of pleasure.'

# Chapter 23

*Athelwulf's manor house, Pocklinton*

*Twentieth day of April, AD 1123*

To be sitting by the hearth in the great hall, warmed by the fire, the comforting presence of Archbishop Thurstan beside me on the bench, is too much, and I can't hold back the tears.

'Come, come, Child,' he says. 'It is all good news that I have brought. Why do you cry?'

'But you have been so long in coming ...'

'Forgive me,' he says. 'I should have thought of you, sitting alone, waiting for news. I would have come in January, after the death of Robert Bloet, but I have been taken up with other affairs. I was in Rome during Lent.'

'Robert Bloet? The Bishop of Lincoln is dead?' I cannot believe it.

'I thought you knew. Did Prior Athelwulf not tell you?'

Heat rushes to my face. It gives me pain to hear his name on the Archbishop's lips, but an exquisite pleasure too.

'He never comes now. I have not seen him since before

Christmas.'

Thurstan looks at me closely, alerted by something in my voice.

'Of course, of course.' It is as if he is remembering something.

'Well, with the death of the Bishop,' he continues, 'a way has opened up for you. When I was in Rome, I took the opportunity of speaking to His Holiness about your case. As I hoped, he has granted an annulment of your marriage.'

The Archbishop leans back and beams at me. He is not so stout as I remember him; the rigours of the journey to Rome have taken their toll.

'You aren't pleased?' he asks.

I force a smile onto my face but it's true, his words have done little to lift the weight of misery.

'There is more,' he says. 'At Easter, King Henry appointed the new Bishop of Lincoln. It's to be Alexander, the Bishop of Salisbury's nephew. I have spoken with him and he is eager to support the vocations of godly women. Now that you are free, he has agreed that you can return to the hermitage.'

'I am to return?'

It is everything I have longed for, but now I cannot seem to make sense of it.

'Yes, unless you would prefer to go elsewhere. I am making provision for a house of nuns at St Clements in York. Perhaps you would rather lead them?'

'No, no.'

'Then you will be Mistress at Roger's hermitage, as he intended. And I have no doubt that, in time, many maidens will come to live under your direction.'

'But what about St Albans? The Abbot will interfere, as he

did before.' Every time I think of the way Roger's body was torn from us, I am filled with bitterness afresh. 'No doubt Abbot Geoffrey has turned out my old companions. Do you know – is Ulfwine still there?'

'I am not sure,' the Archbishop answers. 'But the hermitage is under the jurisdiction of the Bishop, not the Abbot. Alexander will support you.' He takes my hands in his. 'Christina, this is the answer to your prayers. God has seen fit to reward you for your faithfulness.'

I withdraw my hands and look away. The fire is burning low. A boy comes over to put on more logs and I am grateful for the chance to gather myself. How can I lead others when I myself have failed?

When the boy has gone, Thurstan draws close again, concern showing on his face. Suddenly I am conscious of my own lack of gratitude. In front of me sits the Archbishop of York, who has inconvenienced himself on my behalf. If he were a different man I would tremble just to be in his presence. But he is not a different man.

'What is troubling you, Child? You can tell me.'

I long to tell him everything, but how can I? *It is shameful even to speak of what is done by the evil in secret.* I feel the blood surging to my cheeks.

'I think I can guess the cause of your discomfort,' he says.

I look at him, appalled. Has God revealed to him my sinful imaginings, my secret acts of sin?

'Athelwulf made confession to me. I will not reveal what he said, but I suspect you have been sorely tempted.'

'I have been tempted, Father,' I say, 'and ....' I long to unburden myself but the words are strangled in my throat before I can speak them.

'Peace, peace,' Thurstan says. 'Every soul that would live chaste and forsake the world must suffer temptation. Think of St Anthony in his cave in Egypt, harried by the demons of lust.'

Now he smiles at me and his voice becomes tender. 'I wondered, at first, if I had made a mistake in asking Athelwulf to house you here. But you have overcome, Christina. You have triumphed over everything the enemy has thrown at you.'

I open my mouth to refute what he is saying but all the while a dull certainty is gathering weight in me. I am not going to tell him the truth: not now, not ever. And this deceit only compounds my guilt. The tears are trickling down my face but, good man that he is, he takes them only for tears of relief. He heaps coals upon my burning head.

'Think of all you have endured,' he says. 'The violence of your family, the loss of home and loved ones, the years of hiding. Now you have passed the greatest test of your purity and, in return, God has given you the desire of your heart. To return to the hermitage and to live openly as a bride of Christ.'

He talks on, of the arrangements he will make for my journey, of sources of income for the hermitage that he will pursue. The boards are laid for dinner and the men begin to come in from the fields. He stands up, rubbing his hands together at the prospect of the meal.

I murmur my thanks to him.

'It is my pleasure to advance your vocation in any way I can,' he says. 'For the sake of my friend, Roger. He will be looking down from heaven, Christina, and rejoicing to see this day.'

I shudder. If only the Archbishop knew the pain he inflicts on me by speaking of Roger, when I have betrayed his trust so miserably. The truth is that it was not Roger who had foresight in this matter, it was Alfwen. She saw truly the degradation of my soul.

*Hermitage de bosco*

*Eve of the Assumption of St Mary, Virgin, fourteenth day of August, AD 1123*

The day is menacing with a heat that seems to suck the life from me. Here, in the shade by the stream, there is some relief but even here the one side of my body feels heavy and strange. More and more now it comes to me, this troubling numbness, and with it a sense that the flames of hell are close, licking around my head, waiting to claim me. Then the darkness lifts and in its place comes a pain in my head that I can scarcely endure. Some days, even when there is no pain, I can hardly drag myself from my bed for the early morning prayer. Nelda collects chamomile to make tea for me, but it does precious little good. I was so glad to find her still here, after the long journey from Yorkshire. It was from her I learned about Acio's death and about Ulfwine and Leofric moving away. Her baby is a boy now, running around, and full of chatter. And her girl grows taller with every passing day.

There is an ash tree on the far side of the stream, its leaves like shapely fingers drooping in the heat. Seeing them, I am suddenly taken back to that day with Athelwulf on the sheep roam. His hand cupping my chin, his lips on mine under the ash tree. The lewd memories crowd in now, unbidden - his naked body on the bed, the sweet-sour smell of his sweat. I live again in my thoughts the pleasure we had together and feel my body begin to rock to and fro with sinful movements. I spring up in horror, thrusting all thoughts of the Prior from my mind.

Soon it must be time for None. The more these temptations plague me, the more I am resolved to keep the hours fastidiously. Here is something I can do, though it be only whiting the sepulchre. My prayers seem to me earthbound, mired down in a bog of hopelessness.

I make my way out into the lacerating heat of the sun. The cells of my old friends are empty now. Ulfwine lives in the woods past Caddington, with Leofric. He will come tomorrow, for the Assumption. And, of course, the priest will come too. Thinking of it, my heart sinks lower than ever. I know that I draw down condemnation on myself every time I receive the Host without making full confession.

I pass Roger's cell – my own now – but then the door opens and I hear a woman's voice, calling. I turn and my heart truly stops beating for an instant. Margaret – my sister Margaret – is standing in the doorway, her face pink, her fair hair gleaming in the sun. She smiles at me, a quick, uncertain smile.

Though she is like a shade risen up from the dead, from a life I don't care to remember, I run to Meg and embrace her. For all her scheming with my mother, she is still my sister and she looks so scared, standing there. Her cheek against mine is damp with sweat. She seems older; her face and her body have filled out. There is someone else with her - a young woman, not much more than a girl.

'Go inside, into the cool,' I say, then cross to the kitchen to tell Nelda to bring some ale.

Margaret is still standing when I return, clasping her hands together. I insist that she uses Roger's chair, but she only perches on the edge of the seat. I draw up a stool for her companion and one for myself.

'This is Adelaisa,' my sister says. 'You remember her father, from the Guild? He is dead now.'

I nod to the girl but she is too shy to speak.

'I'm glad you came,' I say to Margaret. 'How long has it been?'

'Seven years,' she answers at once. 'It is seven years.'

I think that she is going to say something else, but no more words come. She looks down at the floor, like a servant before her mistress.

'What news of our father? And our mother?'

'They keep well,' Margaret answers, 'apart from Mother's chest. They ask to be remembered to you.'

She leans forward and now the words start to flow, though it's clear that they are costing her.

'They heard of the annulment. And that you are here, under the authority of the Bishop of Lincoln. They will not see you, Dora, but it is more from shame than from ill will. I know it.'

'Christina is my name now. I have not been known as Theodora for a long time, not since I escaped their clutches.'

I hear the bitterness in my own voice and I see Margaret flinch, but she has never been one to bite back and she does not do so now.

'Father asks if you have enough to live on. He has given me these for you.'

She searches in the purse at her belt and holds out some silver to show me.

'No, tell him no,' I say firmly, 'my needs are few and I prefer that they are met by those who fear God.'

Her face reddens and she puts the money away. Why must I be so unkind? The truth is that I do have need of income - I am not always able to pay Nelda her due.

'How is Gregory?' I ask. 'Does he work with Father?'

'He does, but he has suffered a great loss. Of course, you don't know that he married, four summers ago now.'

'Married? Who?'

'Ursule -the daughter of the Constable at the castle.'

'A French woman.' It disturbs me, somehow, that he has aspired to the household at the castle.

'Yes, but she died this last spring, giving birth. The baby too.'

I am taken aback at how their lives have carried on without me.

'Gregory is distraught,' she continues, 'and now he seeks to mend his life. He is to be a monk.'

'Gregory - a monk.' I cannot help smiling at this, despite the hard news of his bereavement. I look up and, for the first time, Margaret meets my eyes and she is smiling too.

'Yes – he goes to Alban's abbey at Michaelmas.'

'St Albans?' In my mind's eye, I see again the haughty faces of the Norman monks who took away Roger's body.

Margaret clears her throat nervously.

'Dora – I have not only come with news of our parents. I have come to beg that you will forgive us - for standing in the way of your vow.'

I am so surprised that I can only gaze at her. She continues,

223

her words tumbling over each other in her haste.

'If you will have me, I wish to join you here and live under your direction. And Adelaisa, too.'

I glance at the girl. She is small, with eyes that seem too big for her face. 'My mother has given her permission,' she says. 'She has married again and has money to give you.'

I turn back to my sister. 'But how can Mother spare you?' I ask.

When I think of them, they are inseparable, Meg the shadow of my mother.

'You are not the only one who may hear the call of God,' she says, and there it is again, the gentle rebuke that I remember from when I was a child. But she is right, of course. I look at my sister with new eyes.

'And our niece, Agnes, is to come and help Mother, so it is all settled. If you will accept me.'

My eyes are growing full with tears. Margaret, who is humble and useful and does not know how to do wrong. She is willing to place herself under my authority?

My sister gets up and walks over to me. She takes my hands in hers. 'We heard about the woman from Canterbury, the woman with falling sickness. And how you were the instrument of her healing.' Her eyes are shining.

I turn away, trying to shut out the remembrance of it. St John's Eve, soon after I returned from the north country. The woman came to the hermitage, saying that the martyr, Margaret, had appeared to her in a vision and that I was to pray and she would be healed. I remember that week, the agony of uncertainty. Yet I did pray and she did seem to recover. The day of her affliction dawned – a Tuesday, when always before she would have a seizure - but no seizure came.

She went home rejoicing.

'The news of the healing will travel and others will come,' Margaret says. 'There will be much to do to feed them and make them welcome.'

'No – no!' I take her by the shoulders. 'Margaret, you must not speak of it to anyone.' She is taken aback by the force of my words. 'Promise me.'

'If you wish it.' She backs away but I can see she is puzzled.

Perhaps I should try to explain to her: the terrible doubt I endured all the time that woman was here, with no assurance of her healing. And my own maladies – that seem to afflict me in new ways with every passing month. How can I pray for the healing of others? No – I can't tell her.

'What news of Matilda, our sister?'

'She is married to Tostyn the wool dealer, and living in the town. And she has a boy – they named him Henry after the King.'

So there is more. My little sister has endured childbed and I am now an aunt.

'Is he a good man, this Tostyn?'

Margaret nods. 'Father was pleased with the match. I think Tilda is happy.' She takes a deep breath. 'But I don't want to marry. I wish to live godly – here at the hermitage. And Adelaisa is set on doing the same. Will you accept us?'

Perhaps it is seeing my sister perched on Roger's chair, but all at once I feel something of his calm presence. I close my eyes. For the first time in many months, I am able to rest in the quiet place inside myself where God dwells, as he taught me. Perhaps all is not lost. Perhaps I can still be of some use.

I open my eyes and there is Meg's placid face, waiting for an answer. I know that she will try my patience, with her quiet

225

endurance. She will be a gentle thorn in my side, making me seem impatient and changeable, even to myself. Perhaps that is God's purpose in sending her to me.

'You are both welcome,' I say, 'and it may be that the Lord will send others to join us.' Even as I say the words, I feel the truth of them.

Adelaisa kneels down in front of me for my blessing. Then, to my horror, Margaret joins her. My own sister. But as I mark them with the Cross, a conviction that this is fitting settles over me, a cloak of peace that is capacious enough in this moment to cover everything. They get up from their knees and I embrace them both. It is a comfort not to be alone.

# Chapter 24

*Hermitage de bosco*

*Twenty-third day of October, AD 1124*

Terce is over and I lead the way out into the fresh morning: a shock of cold after the stale air of the chapel. Rain fell during the night but I am pleased to see the ground is not too wet. Margaret follows me out, then Adelaisa and Emmy. Because I'm watching they make an effort to walk with dignity, as I keep telling them, like the graceful nuns in the Abbey of Alban. Perhaps I might afford now to have those new tunics made for them. In my mind's eye they are a dove grey, simple of course and modest, but the material must be fine enough that it hangs well.

Nelda's girl comes running to tell me that my visitor has arrived and is waiting in my cell. It is only Ulfwine, but I find myself nervous as I hurry to him. It is not certain that I will be able to persuade him of the errand I have in mind.

'God bless you, Christina,' he says, and I return the greeting. It's good to see him, but I am a little taken aback by his informality. My companions address me as 'my lady' and I have become accustomed to it.

'How is Leofric?' I ask.

'He has gone to Haselbury, in the west country, to consult with Wulfric. He will not be back for a week or more.'

I nod, hoping that this will not make Ulfwine refuse my request. It will mean leaving their enclosure untended, but only for a short time. Suddenly I remember that he has not heard my good news.

'Our prayers are answered, Ulfwine! The Lord has provided.'

He looks up at me.

'Lady Eva, the wife of Osbert de Arden, came to visit us a few weeks ago, all the way from Warwickshire. She is a faithful woman - she would live religious if she could, but she has children to care for.'

'What did she want here?'

'She prayed with us in the chapel, and then she stayed a long time, asking me questions about the hermitage. Now her husband has sent word that he is to grant the church at Kingsbury to us, for income!'

Ulfwine grasps my hand. 'That's wonderful, Christina.'

'It will not cover all our costs, but it's a beginning.'

I know I should ask after him – he and Leofric have precious little to cover their own needs – but I am anxious about the time passing.

'Ulfwine, will you do something for me?'

'Of course,' he answers, 'if it's in my power.'

'I would not ask you but this is something I cannot do.'

I can see that he is growing impatient.

'Will you go to St Albans for me and speak to the Abbot? It

must be the Abbot himself, no-one else.'

Ulfwine looks at me, puzzled. 'Abbot Geoffrey? What can you want with him?'

He's right; I have no love for the Abbot. How many times have we talked about that terrible day when the monks came and stole Roger's body? It still fills me with indignation. And since my dream, the thought of the Abbot's arrogance comes again and again into my mind. I feel my blood boil even now.

'Ulfwine, you know what they say about him - he stole land from the Abbey to build a hall for his sister when she was married. Half the monks are murmuring against him.'

'Yes, that's what I heard. Blatant disregard for the law, even for a Norman.'

'But that's not all. Two nights ago I had a dream.'

He draws up a stool and one for me. Ulfwine is no stranger to my dreams and visions and he knows how much Roger took store by them.

'Do you remember Alvered?'

'Of course,' Ulfwine replies. 'He was the holiest man in this district, next to Roger. If he had still been alive, he would have spoken out against this Abbot's worldliness.'

Ulfwine's words are the confirmation I have prayed for and I feel a tingling spread from the top of my head, all down my spine.

'That's just it! Alvered came to me in a dream. He was holding a candle and he spoke to me – he was very fierce, just like always. He said that Abbot Geoffrey is planning more wickedness in secret and he must be stopped. Then yesterday, I chanced to hear from someone in the village that the Abbot's brother is coming from France with his wife and children. Don't you see? He must be planning to defraud the Abbey

229

again, as he did before.'

Ulfwine seems troubled.

'You are going to rebuke him?' He sounds incredulous.

'That's what Alvered told me, in the dream – that he should be called to account.'

'But can you be sure, Christina? Perhaps the dream was revealing some other corruption in his heart.'

I feel like shaking him. It's as clear as day – why else would I learn of his brother's arrival, just the day after the dream? But Ulfwine must be left to come to the truth in his own time.

He leans back against the wall, breathing out slowly through pursed lips. I can see that he is considering the matter, looking at it from all angles.

'Christina, think back carefully. In your dream, did Alvered say anything about the Abbot's brother?'

I close my eyes and there, again, is Alvered, with his silver tonsured hair, the candle in his hand. I try to recall every word he spoke, but my mind is a blank. Nothing will come. Then, suddenly, as if written in letters on a manuscript, the name Guillaume appears before my closed eyes. William, but in the French. The brother is to come from Normandy. That must be his name!

'I see it now, Ulfwine! His brother's name is Guillaume.'

Ulfwine is staring at me with awe in his eyes. He is not like me. He seldom hears the voice of the Spirit whispering to him.

'Are you certain?'

'Yes. I am certain.' Suddenly I do not feel so sure. 'I believe it is a true seeing – I dare not ignore it.'

I look up at my friend. This is the moment I have been dreading but it must be done.

'Ulfwine, you know I would never be granted an audience with the Abbot. Will you go and take this message for me?'

He shakes his head. 'He won't listen, he is a proud man. These Normans don't look for wisdom from the holy poor, as we English do.'

I begin to be desperate. How can I convince him?

'The Abbot may not listen, but if the dream is from God and I do not obey, what will become of me?'

Ulfwine is silent for a while, then he gets to his feet. 'I will go. The Abbot must learn that, here in England, the hermits of Christ do not fear to confront wickedness, wherever they see it. I will go today.'

'Today?'

'Why not? If it must be done.'

Weak with relief, I fetch him something to drink from the kitchen and some bread. He blesses me and turns to go.

'God will reward you, Ulfwine. I will fast and pray while you are gone,' I say.

'He may not see me today. If not, I'll stay the night at the Abbey and wait for an audience.'

I watch him as he rides away between the beech trees, my heart full of gratitude for my friend. I call for the others to come but, even as I charge them to pray, a cloud of unease settles over me. What if I am wrong and the Abbot has formed no such plan? If this arrogant man rides roughshod over his own monks, what will he do to me?

After evening prayer is over, Margaret and the others join me in my cell. They are excited but fearful too. It is no small thing to send word to the Abbot of St Albans with a rebuke from God.

Adelaisa is sitting on the floor, her arms hugging her hunched up knees.

'What will the Abbot do? Won't he be angry?'

It is odd to think how shy Adelaisa was that first day, when Margaret brought her here; now she is the chatterbox amongst us. I smile at her.

'If he fears God, he will listen and change his mind. In any case, what can he do? It is Bishop Alexander who has jurisdiction over us here, not the Abbot.'

After a day without food, I feel unsteady on my feet, but there is joy in my heart.

'Don't be afraid,' I tell them. 'This evening, when I was praying for his ears to be unstopped, I felt the movement of the Holy Spirit.'

The younger girls are looking up at me, listening intently. Emmy's eyes are shining. She joined us only in the summer, but already I know that she has the gift of seeing, if I can draw it from her, as Roger did from me.

'Tell us what it's like,' Emmy says, 'to feel the Holy Spirit.'

'It is like a gentle fluttering in my breast, like the wings of a bird. Or sometimes, I feel a tender brushing of fingertips on my face – as if someone holy, like the hermit Evisandus, is blessing me. When I feel these things, I have assurance that my prayers have been answered.'

A divine peace seems to settle in the room. Outside, the wind rustles the beech leaves but we are rapt, held together in the hollow of God's hand. Until Margaret speaks up.

'Will Ulfwine return tonight, do you think?' she asks.

It is always my sister who spoils the moment with her talk of practical things.

'He may have to wait to see the Abbot. He won't return

until tomorrow at the least.' It is getting late and I stand up. 'Let us go to our beds.'

I watch my charges disperse, then close the door and start my preparations for sleep. Before I have undressed, the stillness of the evening is disturbed by the thump of hooves out on the track by the ditch. I go to the door and see Nelda running from the kitchen, where she and the children have their beds.

'Who's there?' she calls. 'Are you expecting anyone, Mistress?'

'No – unless it's Ulfwine back already. Surely, it can't be.'

The galloping hooves have slowed to a walk and now Ulfwine's horse appears through the trees. I let out my breath in relief.

'All is well,' I call to the girls, who have come out to see what is happening. 'Go to bed.' They linger, eager to know the news, and I am obliged to be firm with them.

Ulfwine jumps down and leads his horse to the stable. It is too dark to see his face. Back in my cell, he throws off his cloak. Margaret is waiting by the door, uncertain. I tell her to join us. I have a sinking feeling but perhaps it is just faintness from fasting.

'What news, Ulfwine? I didn't expect you back tonight.'

He looks straight at me for the first time and I notice a smudge of dried dust on his left cheek. There is no life in his eyes.

'I didn't have to wait. He saw me straight away.'

'Tell me - what did he say?'

Ulfwine scrapes with his finger nail at a blob of hardened wax on the small table. 'He was angry, Christina. No, worse than angry - condescending. As if we were foolish and ignorant of the things of God.' Ulfwine's voice is low, with an edge of bitterness. 'He advises you, and me, not to put our trust in dreams.'

I can only stand and stare at him. The room begins to spin around me and I sink down onto Roger's chair. Was I deceived? Yes, it must be that - I have fallen prey to pride and presumption. My hatred of the Abbot has blinded me. Margaret takes a step forward, into the pool of candle light and I'm sure I detect a look of reproof on her face.

*Twelfth day of November, AD 1124*

The latch of my door clicks open and Margaret appears, holding a cup of ale. She comes over to my bed and places it on the stool beside me.

'Are you any better this morning?'

I lift my head from the bolster carefully and move it gently from side to side. The mysterious prickling remains, running in waves from my head to my feet, but the nausea has left me and the pain in my head is less. In truth, it began to ease a few days ago, on the feast of St Leonard and the day of my birth. But the thought of getting up from my bed to fulfil my duties seemed intolerable. What would be the purpose?

'Can you eat? I could bring you something - Nelda has made a posset.'

I shake my head.

My sister's forehead is set in a frown. She looks a little afraid. 'The others keep asking me when you will be better.'

I turn my head to the wall. Why does she torture me with

these questions when I am so downcast? I sometimes forget that Margaret doesn't know the truth; she thinks I am chaste and holy, just as the others do. And then they wonder why I was deceived by a false dream and why the remedies they give me do nothing to help. But perhaps my sister does suspect something - I think I see it in her eyes sometimes.

Now she is reaching out to take my hand and, all at once, I want to cry.

'Come to the chapel, Sister, if you are able,' she pleads. I cannot deny the love in her voice. 'It may be that saying the psalms will ease your pain.'

Perhaps she is right, though it is absolution I crave, not healing. I allow her to help me dress and we walk slowly to the chapel. When Emmy and Adelaisa greet me with tears of joy, like a long-lost mother, I find I am comforted.

It is raining heavily as we file out of the chapel. The squeak of cartwheels carries to us from down the track and Margaret calls for Nelda to see to it. But when the wagon comes into view, it is not the miller's boy with the sack of flour after all. The wood of the wagon frame is smooth and polished and it is drawn by a hackney, not a packhorse.

The driver calls the horse to a halt in the mud and the door of the wagon opens. A man dressed in Benedictine black climbs down. He has his cowl up.

'I am looking for the Lady Christina,' he announces in English, with a marked Norman accent.

I step forward, weak and trembling from lying sick in bed.

'I am the Lady Christina. Come into the chapel, Father, out of the rain, I pray you.'

He follows me inside and I direct him to the bench that follows the contour of the wall, but he will not sit. The monk pushes back the hood and his head is revealed. He is a man of middle age, perhaps ten years older than I am, with straight, dark hair. His features are clearly defined, the nose sharp, the eyes black. They scan the interior of the chapel quickly: intelligent, appraising. I get the impression that nothing would escape his notice.

'You have come far?' I ask, not liking to ask his purpose outright. The man has an air of authority.

'Only from St Albans. I am Abbot there, by the grace of God.'

*The Abbot?* For an instant I think I will lose my balance and fall to the floor. I search around for something to say but he takes pity on me.

'I am come to thank you,' he says.

'To thank me?'

'Was it not you who sent word to me, nearly three weeks ago?'

Everything inside me shrinks from answering him. 'It was. I felt sure that my dream was from God, or I would not have …'

He interrupts. 'Tell me, how did you know that my brother, Guillaume, is to come from Normandy? Who told you his name?'

I look at him coldly; his rudeness has given me new courage. 'I know only what has been revealed to me by God.'

I blush, remembering that it was from the village that I heard of his brother's coming. But the name – Guillaume – that was from above.

'Who was he, this man who appeared in your dream?' he asks.

'He was one of your monks - Alvered.'

'Alvered. But he passed from this life last winter – he lies buried in the Abbey churchyard.'

'I know. He appeared to me from heaven and warned me of your intention.' I am loath to say more but the Abbot gestures to me to continue. 'It came to me that you planned to build a house for your brother, Guillaume.'

'You know his name, yet I have told no-one this, here in England. Nor of my plans.'

He is looking at me with incredulity. Now he smiles for the first time – and I notice how both his eye teeth are sharp, giving him something of the look of a wolf.

'You will be gratified to know that I have changed my plans,' he says. 'No doubt that will please some of those who oppose me at the Abbey. I have decided to build elsewhere for my brother, not on St Albans land.'

The walls seem to close in on me, then to open out again, as if I were being held within a beating heart. Though it is impolite to sit while my visitor is standing, I sink down onto the bench, glad to feel solid wood under me.

'Are you ill?' he asks, coming to stand over me.

'I have not been well,' I reply, 'but I am recovered now.'

'I will take my leave,' the Abbot says. Then he turns back and offers me his hand. 'My name is Geoffrey. It was I who had the body of the Blessed Roger brought to the Abbey.'

I refuse his hand. 'It was against his wishes and ours. He was to be buried here in the hermitage.'

The Abbot feigns not to notice my discourtesy. 'You will be pleased to know that pilgrims come from far and wide to venerate his remains.'

He pauses and it dawns on me that he is expecting gratitude. I cannot trust myself to reply.

'However that may be,' he goes on. 'It is clear that you are one to whom God reveals his secrets. If you are agreeable, I will visit here from time to time, to ask for your prayers. In return, I could perhaps lend my aid to your community.'

He is a man who is used to being obeyed and he does not wait for me to answer, but only walks to the door of the chapel, opens it and leaves.

# Chapter 25

*Hermitage de bosco*

*Feast of St Anthony, seventeenth day of January, AD 1127*

It is so cold that Nelda has warmed the wine and Ulfwine clasps the cup in his hands as we talk. Coming out of the chapel after Matins, the sky looked leaden with snow, waiting to fall.

'How is she settling in – Matilda?' he asks.

I think about the new French girl. She has dark hair that curls in screws about her pale face unless she pushes it back into a wimple. Her eyes, too, are unusual: a pale blue, with dark lashes.

'She has a sweet disposition. I think she will do well. Though I have had to speak to some of the others.'

'Why?'

'You know how girls can be. They don't understand her accent. And she is very pretty.'

Ulfwine smiles. 'You will look after her, Christina.'

He drains the cup and I fetch his warm cloak from the

bench. He is on foot but it isn't far to his house in the woods.

'Send Leofric my love in Christ,' I say, opening the door, only to be greeted by the stamping of hooves. A horse is circling on the grass, its hot breath making clouds in the freezing air. The rider, dressed in black, dismounts by the kitchen and leads his horse over to the stable.

'Who is it?' asks Ulfwine, pulling his hood up against the wind.

'It's the Abbot,' I answer, feeling awkward. I brush away a crumb of cake from the edge of my mouth. 'He graces us with his presence from time to time though he has not been here for a while.'

'Abbot Geoffrey? Then I will take my leave of you straight away.'

Ulfwine blesses me quickly and strides out into the morning. The two men pass one another but the Abbot does not acknowledge him and I find myself irritated.

'My lord Abbot,' I say. 'As you see, my companion Ulfwine has just left.'

Geoffrey turns to look after him as if only just registering his presence.

'Is that the hermit who lived with Roger? I am surprised that he still comes here.'

I offer him the chair and go to the door to call for another cup. It dawns on me that Geoffrey has no recollection of Ulfwine. Is he so full of his own importance?

'You may have wondered at my absence,' he says, when I return. 'I was at Windsor after Christmas. The King summoned his nobles, and all the bishops and abbots. He had news that may bode ill.'

I am still angry and choose not to reply. Does he think I

240

sit waiting for him to visit? He flicks back his hair with that quick movement and fixes me with his dark Norman eyes. 'Tell me, my lady, did I appear in your dreams? Has the Lord revealed anything to you?'

I turn away and walk toward the small window of the cell, doing battle with myself.

I cannot deny that I have wondered about his absence, and whether he no longer wishes to consult me. Though why this should concern me I don't know, when his presence is often a burden.

'I have felt discomfited,' I say at last. It is true that when I pray for his soul, I have only a sense of unease.

The Abbot rises quickly from Roger's chair and comes to stand beside me.

'This unease - is it about the King, do you think? He made us swear to put his daughter on the throne, after his death but how can this be natural? I fear there will be unrest.'

I keep quiet. He thinks only of worldly dangers, of court and battles and allegiances, not of the health of his soul. But perhaps that is why God has brought him to me.

'I will pray for you, as always,' I say. 'And if I receive any message, have no doubt that I will relay it to you.'

'Merci.' He seems reassured. Now he glances around the room as if appraising it. 'Are you warm enough here in this weather, with such a meagre hearth?'

I give him a scornful look. 'When Roger lived here, he had no fire at all. He did not allow himself any comfort.' I think of the nights that we stood side by side in the chapel, oblivious to the cold, warmed only by the fire of the Holy Spirit.

'We live simply,' I continue, 'those of us who have chosen the way of the hermits and anchorites. Like the first disciples

241

of Christ.'

The Abbot twists his mouth in annoyance, though I have been careful not to decry the wealth of the Abbey and the comfort in which he lives. This is a matter we have spoken of before.

'Is there not anything I can do for you?' he asks.

I go to refuse but then my conscience pricks me. It was he who arranged with Matilda's parents for her to come from Mezeaux, and she came with a generous gift of money.

'Let me send one of the monks to say Mass for you,' he says. 'You would like Old Thomas – he was at Paris in his youth and he is the soul of humility. He could be your confessor too.'

I would much prefer to keep a distance between us and the Abbey, but I suppose it would do no harm to let him have his way in this. The priest who comes from Caddington to say Mass is not a learned man.

'Thank you. We would be pleased for Father Thomas to visit.'

He looks at me closely, as if I might be tricking him in some way, but then he puts down the empty cup and wraps his cloak around him.

'I will send him, Christina.' He walks to the door and turns to take his leave. Standing tall there, in his fur-trimmed cloak, he looks every inch the Abbot of a great monastery. 'And I beg you to consider again when you are to be professed,' he says. 'As you know, some of the Chapter look for any pretext to oppose me. They whisper about my visits here – to a woman who has not been consecrated a virgin by the Church.'

When I do not choose to answer he opens the door, letting in a cold blast of air, and strides towards the stable.

*Twenty-eighth day of March, AD 1127*

Father Thomas refuses to sit but stands before me, short and stout, wringing his hands. He is a regular visitor to the hermitage now but I have never seen him so distraught.

'It is Abbot Geoffrey, my lady,' he says. 'He has been taken with a sickness. I implore you to come to him.'

'What kind of sickness? Is it a fever?'

'No – but he has been struck down with it twice before. All his joints are swollen - his knees won't take his weight. And he can't get his breath - he daren't even sleep because he wakes, gasping for air. He fears that the end is near.'

Father Thomas is a good man but he does exaggerate and he is prone to believe the worst. 'Wait a little,' I say, 'I have learned that one should not carry lilies without reason.'

'Lilies?' he asks. 'Oh … lilies. I take your meaning, my lady. But there is good reason to fear - the doctors can do nothing. Will you come? If you don't, he will insist on being brought to you and he should not travel.'

I take a deep breath. What if the Abbot truly is close to death? Yet still I find myself reluctant to leave the hermitage.

'I will pray, Father Thomas, and seek guidance. Perhaps I shall come in a day or two. I don't like to leave the girls.'

'But – your sister. Can't they be left in her charge?'

'Margaret is away. She has gone with Adelaisa, to see her mother at Westminster. I expect them back soon.'

The Father is not content but he takes his leave. 'Don't neglect to intercede for the Abbot,' he says. 'I shall assure him of your prayers. And we shall see you tomorrow or the next day.'

The day has passed in a haze of indecision and now I lie sleepless on my bed. Must I go? The arrogance of the Abbot maddens me and there is little understanding between us. Yet he craves my prayers and perhaps to intercede for him is my penance.

I get up and wrapping myself in my warm cloak and pulling on my shoes, I leave the cell and walk across the frosty ground to the chapel. The owl which roosts out beyond the stable is disturbed and sets up his screeching. Inside the chapel, I light a new candle and drop to my knees before the altar table. I think of Abbot Geoffrey, waiting for me to come, certain that my prayers will save him. Suddenly, panic grips my shoulders in a chill vice.

*What if he dies? Show me, Lord, I beg you. Is he going to die?*

The silence of the chapel is unbroken; there is little wind to find its way between the cracks and worry the candle flame, but I feel no peace – only the old doubts rising. If the Abbot knew the unconfessed lust I carry in my soul, he would never come to me for advice. I try to calm myself, to rekindle the tranquillity that flowed in this very place, when Roger was alive. But all that is gone; the chapel is no more than a hollow shell. At last, I get up from my knees and blow out the candle. Perhaps, back in the warmth of my bed, sleep will come.

I stumble across the rutted mud, hardened to rock by the unseasonable frost, and feel myself begin to fall. The everyday world recedes and it seems that I am caught up to safety, transported up and away from the hermitage, away from the wood. Below me, pale grey in the moonlight, is the wall around the monastery of St Albans. I am being carried over it and now below me are the Abbey grounds, the tiled rooves. One of them peels away to reveal the interior of the Abbot's parlour. I see Geoffrey, sitting in the corner. He has a staff between his knees and he is leaning his head against it, as if the weight is too much for his neck to bear. It is a pitiable sight but I feel nothing, only curiosity.

There are monks, three of them, standing close by. Now I notice the two women, seated in the parlour. My sister Margaret and young Ada, in their travelling clothes! At once I understand that they must have stopped by at the monastery on their way home from Westminster. A servant opens the door, carrying a tray with wine cups and some kind of sweetmeat.

The Abbot raises his head with some effort.

'I am glad that you came,' he says, addressing Meg. 'If only the lady Christina knew that we were sitting here together.'

'I am certain that her prayers are with you,' says one of the monks, 'though she cannot be here in person.'

Margaret nods in agreement. 'Yes indeed, Father Abbot.'

I feel myself being drawn away. My sister and Adelaisa and the Abbot grow smaller and more indistinct, then they are gone altogether and I am back to myself, standing shivering in the cold night, between the chapel and my cell.

All through Matins, though my lips are forming the words, inwardly I am marvelling at what I have seen. And at the certainty that has been growing within me ever since. The Abbot will recover.

*Thirtieth day of March, AD 1127*

All through yesterday I went about my duties with a serenity that nothing could shake. After Vespers, I told Nelda to bake more bread.

'Margaret and Ada will be back soon.'

Emmy heard me and looked up with those liquid eyes of hers. 'Have they sent word?' she asked.

I smiled at her but kept my peace.

We have sung Prime and now fingers of sunlight are feeling between the beech trees, as I return to my cell. Soon I will be able to blow out the candle. I sit in Roger's chair and take up my sewing but then comes a knock at the door and I open it to find Margaret, still in her travelling cloak, her cheeks pink. She is breathing fast, her face full of good news.

'Benedicite,' I say, giving her the kiss of peace. 'Welcome home. I have been waiting for you.'

'Christina ...'

I put my finger to her lips to silence the words that are starting to tumble from her mouth. 'Wait. I have something to say first.'

I tell her what happened when I left the chapel on Monday night. Everything that I saw in the Spirit: the Abbot's parlour, where each one was seated, what they were wearing, the words that were spoken.

My sister's cheeks lose their colour and she stares at me, her mouth open.

'It was early yesterday morning,' she says. 'During Matins. He said he felt his strength start to return.'

'He will recover,' I say. 'I am sure of it.'

Meg takes my hands in hers, excited. 'He has recovered already. The swelling in his joints has gone – he no longer needs the staff. And his breathing is steady. He would have come here yesterday but the Infirmarian prevailed on him to rest a little longer.'

'God be praised!' I say.

My sister goes to greet the others and I am left to wonder and rejoice over the news. I am gratified but why is there some misgiving woven in with the joy? For good or ill, I sense the invisible tie that binds us to the Abbey growing stronger.

# Chapter 26

*Hermitage de bosco*

*Last day of Marymass, twenty-first day of August, AD 1131*

Something wakes me and I sit up in bed, in the dark. The strident sound comes again: the cockerel crowing from his perch above the henhouse. I push the cover away, anger quickening my movements. It's nearly dawn and well past the hour for singing the nocturns. Why didn't they rouse me?

I go to the door of my cell and throw it open. The air is still and musky with the scent of lavender from Nelda's garden. The squat huts where the maidens sleep, the beehive chapel, the long kitchen block, all just denser grey shapes in the grey morning. No-one is stirring and now even the cockerel has fallen silent. The world seems to be resting under a heavy coverlet of sleep and my irritation fades, folded into the embrace of an unearthly calm.

I feel a soft touch on my left shoulder, then the lightest brushing against my right elbow, my knee, my back. I seem to be surrounded yet somehow there is no fear, only wonder. I turn to see that my room is full of shadowy figures. They weave about the chamber, passing one another, touching, yet the peace is undisturbed by their movement. As the first daylight begins to seep in through the open door, I see that they are youths: lithe, perfectly formed, unmarked by filth or disease. One of them has something in his hand; it gleams brightly, casting a glow all around him. He draws nearer and holds it up towards me. It's a crown, but not wrought from any metal I have ever seen. It radiates a white light that is so pure, my eyes can scarcely bear to look at it. Now I see that two strips of cloth hang down from the back of the crown, like the fillets of a bishop's mitre. I draw in my breath. The fillets are worked in a delicate pattern of the palest robin's egg blue and white, with fringes of silver. The youth lifts the crown and places it on my head.

'You marvel at this but you would not marvel if you knew the art of the craftsman,' he says. His words make no dent in the stillness. 'This has been sent to you by the son of the Most High King.'

Slowly it becomes clear to me that the youths are not moving at random but instead are dancing in my honour: a stately progress of steps, such as I could never have imagined, and all performed in perfect silence. The crown rests on my head, as easy and light as if it were made of reed, bathing me in its soft light. Full of wonder, I stand and watch the youths until they fade away, one by one, in the waxing sunlight. I put my hands to my head but the crown is gone.

It is growing late in the day as I walk down to the stream in search of some shade. My head is not paining me as it sometimes does and there is no numbness; every part of my body seems to course with life. The tranquil beauty of the vision has stayed with me, my scalp still tingling with the imprint of the crown. Surely, it can mean only one thing. Over and over again, I give thanks that I have been deemed pure. Could it be that my vow is unbroken, after all?

I think of what Margaret said to me after None. *Surely the Abbot will not ride here now, the day is too advanced.* She is wrong. He is, this very minute, on his horse, on the road from the Abbey. I know it as certainly as I know when he loses his temper with the Prior or when he is troubled about his father back in Normandy. And besides, I told him that I would give him a final answer at Marymass and today is the last day of the Feast. He will not care to wait any longer than he needs to.

Sitting on the log under the great beech, I hear the sound of his horse's hooves on the path. I walk out from the cover of the trees in time to see him dismount. The sun is descending but the heat of the day is still in the air.

'Greetings, my lady!' Geoffrey calls, as the kitchen boy leads his horse to the stable.

'Let me not disturb your walk.'

'I was not walking, just resting.'

'Then I will join you.'

By the stream, I perch once again on the log, while he leans back against the trunk of the beech. The flies are attracted by the sweat on his neck and he has to brush them away.

'I have never seen a murrain the like,' he says. 'Cattle lying dead in the pastures all the way here. And with so few oxen at ploughtime, the harvest will be scant.'

'It's no longer only cattle and swine,' I reply. 'The hens have it too. Nelda says we have lost five of them this last week.'

'Pray God it will dissipate once the summer is over.'

For a while he watches the trickle of water in the riverbed and then a sly smile creeps across his face. 'I rode here late on purpose, to test you. Tell me truly. This time, you cannot have foreseen that I was coming to visit. How could you expect me to come at this hour?'

'But nevertheless, I did know. It was revealed to me.'

Strands of dark hair are sticking to his temples. He tilts his head and looks at me through narrowed eyes. Does he think that I lie to him – that I am a fraud and no true visionary? Yet at the same time he begs for my prayers. For the thousandth time I wonder how such a man can be father to his monks. He seems to have so little faith, in man or in God.

At last, he comes to the reason for his visit. 'The Feast is over, my lady.' He gazes down at me.

I take a deep breath. 'Yes. And with it has come the certainty I have been craving.'

Now I have the Abbot's full attention. 'You have decided? You will be consecrated at the Abbey?'

'I will.'

He leans his head back against the trunk and closes his eyes. 'It is none too soon.' He laughs a small, mean laugh, revealing his neat, pointed teeth. 'This will silence the Prior. Once you are professed before the Bishop, he cannot object to me consulting you.'

He looks at me curiously. 'Tell me, I still do not understand why you have prevaricated so long. Is it not what you wanted, all these years, to be consecrated a bride of Christ?'

I look down at the log beside me. A woodlouse is making its slow progress across the fissured surface. How can I begin to tell him of my agony of guilt, this Norman abbot, with his

251

cunning, worldly ways?

I look up to see that his eyes are still on me, waiting for an answer. The thought of standing before the Bishop at the consecration– answering his questions - has been keeping me awake in fear. Now, on the very day of the Virgin's Feast, this vision has reassured me. But I can tell the Abbot none of this.

'It's only now that I find a freedom in my soul to agree to what you ask.' I speak coldly and look away so that he will not ask any more.

He shakes his head, as if my thoughts are a riddle he will never solve.

'Still. You have given consent and that is why I came.'

He turns to go and now I remember the demands of courtesy. 'Won't you at least take some refreshment before you ride back?'

'No,' he replies. 'Thank you. I only ask that you continue to pray for me. The Pope has called a council for the autumn, to be held in Rheims. No-one knows if Henry will go himself or send a deputy; pray God he does not choose me. It is a thankless and a dangerous task to represent the King.'

As we walk to the stable, Geoffrey is silent, his mind busy with possibilities.

'A service of consecration should be held on a Feast Day. St Matthew's Feast would be fitting - he was the first to consecrate holy virgins. I shall speak to Bishop Alexander tomorrow. And there are invitations to be sent.'

I can see the Abbey Church in my mind's eye, crowded with priests and monks and townspeople. Perhaps the Abbot will even ask his relations at court. There should be flowers. And I must wear a white tunic. My mind begins to dart here and there. Perhaps something new for Margaret, too, and the others. Would silk be thought too opulent? Perhaps not.'

The sun is dropping below the treetops as he mounts his horse. He takes his leave and heads towards the path, then turns back.

'Christina – I noticed on my last visit that the binding of your psalter is coming loose. Let me take it to the Abbey to be repaired.'

I look at him in surprise. 'I don't like to let it leave the hermitage. The psalter belonged to Roger.'

'Yes – but it was made in our scriptorium. Richard, my predecessor, gave it to him as a gift. '

A jolt of anger passes through me. He took Roger's body to the Abbey. Must he take the psalter from me too?

'It will not be gone long,' he says, seeing my reluctance. 'And I will send another tomorrow, for you to use in the meantime.'

I tell myself that it would be churlish to refuse his offer. Churlish and perhaps unwise. Without the Abbot's efforts on our behalf, we would not have many of the grants that provide us with our income. I murmur my thanks and ask him to wait, while I fetch the psalter.


*Abbey church of St Alban,*

*Feast of St Matthew, twenty-first day of September, AD 1131*

Abbot Geoffrey is reading the gospel, his voice echoing around the walls, unrecognizable in this vast space. Here at the Abbey, he seems like a stranger: a daunting figure, vested all in white, flanked by the endless line of arches. I look up to the painted stars on the ceiling and long to be standing by the chapel, looking through the branches at the real night sky. Stealing a backward glance, I gasp at the size of the congregation that has gathered and search for familiar faces among the crowd. Ulfwine and Leofric are there and some of the other hermits from the district - dear old Evisandus and Avicia from Eywood. And can that be my sister Matilda, bending over a child? It is her. I turn back, my heart beating fast. Is my father here, then?

Now that the gospel is over, my candle is lit by an attendant. My hands are shaking so much that the flame flickers wildly. The congregation falls into silence as I walk towards the altar. The leather soles of my new shoes are stiff and they scuff loudly against the stone floor. Half-hidden by the rood screen, Bishop Alexander himself appears, seated on the Abbot's chair. My candle is taken and placed between two others in a tree of three, to symbolize the Trinity. The Bishop stands. He is a big man, with broad shoulders, his face very smooth. I cannot see any hair under the rim of his magnificent mitre – white, like his cope, and decorated with gold thread.

'Are you the virgin who is to be consecrated this day?' His voice is refined and unexpectedly light for such a leviathan of a man.

I clear my throat. 'I am.'

Bishop Alexander starts to address me, but I hardly hear what he is saying. My senses are besieged by everything before me in this great church: the opulence of his clothing, the altar cloth of whitework, so delicate it makes my heart ache, the sweet, spicy scent of the incense. I hear him say something about a crown.

'Christ. Christ will be your joy and your crown, not only in heaven but here on earth. Christ, the Son of the Virgin and the Bridegroom of virgins.'

I feel a warmth in my breast – like the fire I felt with Roger, when we waited together before God. I think of my vision of the angels and the crown with its white light. The Bishop continues to speak and now the words seem to me like a promise.

'He will call you into his presence and into his kingdom, where you will sing a new song as you follow the Lamb of God wherever he leads you.'

The Bishop beckons me closer, till I am only a few feet away from him. It is time for the questions, but all my doubts and fears have flown. Alexander raises his voice so that all the congregation can hear.

'Christina, will you attest before God's holy people that you are chaste in body, mind and soul?'

I hear my voice answer, as strong as his own. 'I will.'

'Will you persevere to the end of your days in the holy state of virginity?'

'I will.'

'Are you resolved to accept solemn consecration as a bride of our Lord Jesus Christ?'

'I am.'

The Bishop is grasping the crozier in his left hand and now he raises his right hand and prays for me, a prayer of protection from the Devil.

'Defend her from the cunning and deceit of the enemy. Keep her vigilant and on her guard. May nothing tarnish the glory of her perfect virginity.'

He sits and indicates that I should kneel before him. The heavy white silk of my tunic rustles as I drop to my knees. The stone is unyielding and cold through the fabric. There is a flash of sapphire blue and Alexander, Bishop of Lincoln, takes hold of my trembling hands and enfolds them between his great ones. The skin of his palms is smooth and warm. I notice his fingernails; they are clean and well-tended.

A server approaches, holding a small velvet cushion. The Bishop releases my hands and takes something from it.

'Receive the ring that marks you as a bride of Christ,' he says, placing it on the third finger of my left hand. The ring has a spur of silver set at right angles to the band, forming the shape of the cross.

The sound of singing voices swells to fill the space. I listen in awe to the words of the antiphon. *I am espoused to him whom the angels serve. Sun and moon stand in wonder at his glory.*

The congregation is dispersing as I stand talking to Ulfwine. I see the stooped figure of Evisandus across the nave and he comes to join us, his lined face abeam with joy. He has walked all the way from Cheshunt, from his hermitage by the river Lea, to witness this day. He greets me with a holy kiss and takes my hand. There are tears on his bristly cheeks.

'Bless you, my daughter. My old friend, Roger, is rejoicing from heaven to see this day.' I feel the tears start to form in my own eyes. 'It's good to know you are carrying on his work in the hermitage, among the maidens God has sent you.'

Ulfwine is looking over my shoulder and some subtle change in his face alerts me. I turn to see Abbot Geoffrey approaching.

He barely nods to my companions. 'Come with me,' he says, imperious. 'I have something to show you.' He moves off towards the west door and, gesturing farewell to my friends, I have no choice but to follow him as he threads his way between the remnants of the congregation, stopping now and then to acknowledge some great personage. He leads me out into the daylight and along the path to the Abbot's lodging.

'I must ride back to the hermitage,' I say. 'Margaret has left already, with the others.'

Geoffrey takes me into his parlour and removes the heavy cope he wore for the ceremony. He calls for refreshment and then leads me to the table. A sheet of vellum is laid out on it, with what look like plans for a building.

'The Bishop is to be my guest for a few days, before he returns to Lincoln,' he says. 'I will arrange for you to converse with him before he leaves.'

He looks at me closely. 'So, at long last, you are a bride of Christ and have the blessing of the Church.'

I meet his gaze but do not return the smile. Surrounded by his own kind, Geoffrey seems more foreign than ever to me. Sometimes I think he will never understand me and my friends, however often he comes to visit the hermitage.

'The ceremony was beautiful,' I reply. 'But nothing has changed. I entered into marriage with Christ twenty years ago, in this very place, before any soul knew of it. '

Geoffrey's dark eyes, quick and sharp as a bird's, flit quickly away, then back to my face. He has nothing to say to this. Instead he indicates the parchment on the table.

'Can you guess what this is?'

'Do you plan to enlarge the Abbey buildings?'

'Not the Abbey,' he says, and his lips curl in a smile. 'Look closer.'

I try but I can make no sense of what the papers refer to.

'This is the new house I will build for you and your nuns.'

When I am unable to do more than stare at him, he laughs. 'I have a plot of land in mind on one of the Abbey estates. It will be more convenient.'

The world seems to stop turning. 'But I have no wish to leave the hermitage! Roger left it to me – it is the only place I have known peace.'

Geoffrey looks at me, surprise turning to displeasure. 'I have talked it over with Bishop Alexander and he agrees that it is not expedient for you to reside on land belonging to the canons of St Pauls.'

I feel a weight of anger building inside me, whetting my tongue. 'No doubt you and the Bishop have your own thoughts. But the hermitage in the woods was given to me by the Mother of God and I will not leave it while I live.'

The Abbot's face is losing its colour. 'You do well to remember,' he says sharply, 'that now you have been consecrated, Bishop Alexander of Lincoln is your father in Christ.'

He turns his back on me and walks towards the fireplace but I am not frightened of Geoffrey, whatever he says. Instead, I feel the first faint pricks of remorse for what must seem to him like ingratitude.

'Forgive me,' I say. 'You have gone to great trouble on my

behalf.'

He is silent for a while, then he turns back to face me. 'I suppose it is not of such consequence. My builder can alter the plans, to build in the woods.' He looks down at the floor, then back up again. 'We will make a start after the winter.'

What can I say? I have no great need nor desire for anything more elaborate than the simple buildings we have. But the Abbot is a man of wealth who thinks only of worldly things. I am sure he has reasons of his own for wanting to help me. Behind his generosity lurks some fear I don't understand.

He rolls up the plans and takes them over to a tall cupboard that stands against the wall. He turns back. 'I forgot to tell you – your prayers for me have borne fruit.'

'I am glad, but in what regard?'

'The Pope's council at Rheims. Bishop Alexander tells me that the King is to send his adviser, Prior Athelwulf, on his behalf. So I am spared.'

He unlatches the cupboard, secures the plans and starts to search inside for something else, totally unaware of the impact of his words. *Prior Athelwulf.* Just at the sound of his name, I am undone. I stand by the table in my bridal white, the token of virginity on my finger, licentious thoughts flooding into my mind.

Geoffrey has something in his hand - my psalter. He hands it to me but all I can think of is getting away, back to my chapel in the woods.

'Turn to the hundred and fifth psalm,' he says.

I look at him, uncomprehending. A pressure is building around my head, like a tight vice. I feel unsteady on my feet.

He takes the psalter from me and finds the page himself, then lays it open on the table. 'Look,' he says, pointing to the initial.

The C of *Confitemini* has been painted in gold – a thick enclosing arc of gold- and inside it is a picture I have never seen before, worked in rich hues of red and green and aquamarine. I gaze at it dumbly and, at last, I see that the old initial has been cut out and a new one pasted over the hole. There is no doubt that the work is beautifully done. On the right half of the picture stands Christ, resplendent in a cloak bordered with gold against a ground of blue like the heavens. In the left half stands a woman against the green of earth, reaching out across the divide towards Christ. Her left hand has penetrated heaven and is touching his fingers.

'See?' Abbot Geoffrey says. 'That is you. And this figure is me.'

I see now that the woman stands at the head of a small group of monks and Geoffrey is pointing to the monk just behind her. He is touching her shoulder.'

'I had it made, as a gift. To celebrate your consecration,' he says, his eyes watching for my response. I do not know what to say.

'See – I had them inscribe this. Does it please you?'

Some new words have been added to Roger's psalter, above the initial. *Spare your monks, I beseech you, O merciful kindness of Jesus.*

'It gives me great comfort to know that you are interceding for me and for the brothers at St Albans,' says Geoffrey.

The Abbot is so happy with himself and his gift that he hasn't noticed my discomfort. All I can think of is getting away from here so I can be alone.

'It's beautiful, and I thank you, but I am not feeling well.' I pick up the psalter. 'I must go home.'

# Chapter 27

*Hermitage de bosco*

*Twelfth day of July, AD 1133*

Most days, when I stand to deliver an exhortation after Terce, it gives me pleasure to see the faces of the maidens looking up at me. The French girl, Matilda, with her pretty dark curls and blue eyes; no wonder the others were mean to her at first. Adelaisa is a woman now, though she is still the smallest of them all, and still quick to laugh and play. My eyes love to rest on Emmy, when she is praying. Jesus loves her as I do and shares his secrets with her. It was Emmy who saw the Virgin Mother give me a lozenge, that time I was so sick, and afterwards I was cured. I pass quickly over the tawny head of Godit for she tries me with her gauche, ugly movements and her loud voice. And of course, there is Margaret. How I envy her calmness, her virtue. Her very manner is a rebuke to me.

Most days, it gives me pleasure to be mistress here, but not today. The maidens file out of the chapel and separate, some to their chores and some to their solitary devotions.

Everything in me longs to run to the woods – to be away – but I can't. I stand by the door and force myself to look out at the blackened heap of burnt wood and rubble that, only a few days ago, was the new kitchen.

Nelda is bent over a makeshift hearth on the grass, where a cooking pot rests over the fire. She straightens up and looks across at me. The fire was not her fault - it was one of the kitchen girls who had been left to tend to the cooking - but she blames herself. And, to be truthful, I too am frightened of what the Abbot will say. Buildings, grants, titles, income; these are the things that are important to him. Every day I hold him in the presence of God and pray for his soul and perhaps he is closer to grace than before but still he comes to me, boasting that he has bested this lord or that bishop. Perhaps I should never have let him build here, on the holy ground Roger was shown by the angel. Is that why the new kitchen has gone up in flames?

Suddenly I feel a craving to see something of beauty. Turning my back on the sorry ruin, I cross the clearing and open the gate into Nelda's garden, where she grows flowers in amongst the onions and the beans. Gatekeeper butterflies are flitting amongst the borage plants in the morning sunshine. One of them alights on a stem of feverfew, its flame-coloured wings at rest. I marvel at the round dots, like eyes, one at the tip of each wing.

At my request, Nelda has trained some roses along the fence and, yesterday, I noticed a tight new bud - a deep brazilwood pink. Perhaps its petals will have started to unfurl- the palest pink, almost white. But before I reach the fence, my eyes are drawn to something much more humble, growing at the edge of the path. Gold of Pleasure, my mother used to call it. I bend to touch a spray of tiny flowers at the top of the swaying stem. Each one has four petals the colour of butter; together they form a mass like a blaze of yellow stars. Touching the spray, something strange happens. I feel a stirring of the love of God within my soul, as if dear old Evisandus were greeting me, brushing his fingers across my cheek. All at once, it seems possible that Abbot Geoffrey will not be so very angry. After all, a fire in a kitchen is a common thing. And if I am careful with the money that comes to us, in time there will be enough to replace what was lost. Plucking a couple of the sprays of yellow flowers to have in my chamber, I leave the garden, being careful to close the gate behind me.

I have been expecting Geoffrey ever since we sent news of the fire but it is not till after Sext that I hear the sound of his horse. I run to fetch Meg and together we stand on the dry grass and watch as he dismounts and the horse is led to the stable. The Abbot's face is dark, his features pinched and tight. I approach him, my heart beating fast, but he gives only a cursory glance towards the ruined kitchen.

'I must speak with you,' he says.

I catch my sister's eye, willing her to follow me, but he sees it. 'Alone. This is a personal matter.' He strides towards my cell.

In my chamber, I close the door behind me, a broiling of fear in the pit of my belly.

'It was the fault of the new girl and I have dismissed her,' I say quickly.

'What?' he asks.

'The fire – in the kitchen.'

'Oh, that.' He shakes his head impatiently. 'That is of little consequence.'

263

I stare at him, uncomprehending, this man with his dark, darting eyes and his quick movements.

'Have you been deceiving me?' His features are taut with suspicion. 'Tell me it is not true.'

'Deceiving you? I don't understand.'

'Word has reached me that you are not chaste.'

My heart seems to stop beating. 'What do you mean? What have you heard?'

'It doesn't matter how I know. Is it true?'

He comes closer. He is only inches away and I flinch from the anger in his eyes. There is dread in his face, too, or perhaps it is only my own terror. What has he heard? Surely Athelwulf has never spoken of what passed between us.

Before I can begin to frame any sort of answer, the door of my cell opens a little and Margaret's head appears.

'Master Evisandus is come,' she says.

Without waiting to be invited, the old hermit brushes past her and walks into the room. He is leaning on his staff for support but his eyes are bright and full of life. With his coming, it is as if fresh morning air had entered a fetid stable.

'Greetings, Christina,' he says, 'and Father Abbot. I am glad to find you here.' He blesses us both. 'I saw you, Geoffrey, in my prayers this morning.'

'Have you come far, Evisandus?' I ask, stepping away from the Abbot. 'Have you had refreshment?'

He doesn't answer, just peers at us, his glance resting first on me, then on Geoffrey.

'There is unrest here. I feel it.'

It is the Abbot who speaks, his tone sharp and indignant. 'You are right, Father. Word has reached me that the lady here is not what she seems. I have put all my trust in her - to intercede for me and for my abbey. As God is my witness, I have repaid her handsomely all these last years. Now perhaps I should demand my money back.'

Evisandus turns to the Abbot. 'God is indeed your witness, Father. And do you give credence to this report that has reached you?'

My left hand is cold and now all the feeling leaves it and the room begins to sway around me. I stagger to the fireplace and drop down onto a stool. Geoffrey takes no heed.

'I do not know whether I can trust it – that's the point. One of the servants had it from his cousin that there was impropriety when she was hidden in Prior Athelwulf's house in Yorkshire.' Geoffrey glances down at me and then away again. His voice becomes more strident. 'It may be only false rumour but I must have an answer.'

I can scarcely breathe for the dark weight of shame pressing down on me.

Evisandus says nothing in reply, only leans on his staff and looks around the cell, indifferent to the Abbot's urgency. The yellow flowers I picked this morning lie on the bench by the door. The hermit walks over and picks them up.

'Camelina,' he says.

'Gold of Pleasure, we call it,' I say, my tongue loosened at last.

Geoffrey moves closer to me, impatient. 'Christina – was it one of the Prior's servants? Did he accost you? Give me your answer.'

The old hermit intervenes, turning to me for all the world as if the Abbot had not spoken. 'Tell me, my daughter, what made you pick this flower and bring it in? It is not celebrated for its beauty.'

'I don't know, Father. I was drawn to it.' I hear the tremor in my voice but then I remember Nelda's garden in the morning air, the sun's rays warming me, the sweetness of God's love.

Evisandus nods his head slowly. 'Perhaps there is some meaning in this choice of yours that God would have us read.' He peers at the tiny butter-yellow petals. 'Oil of camelina is known to ward off maladies.' He turns to Abbot Geoffrey. 'This is a matter of some significance to you, Father Abbot, I think.'

Colour rises to Geoffrey's neck and up into his face.

The hermit continues, his voice gentle. 'You have special reason to fear sickness, perhaps?'

'From time to time, I suffer with a malady,' Geoffrey says. He looks down. 'It comes upon me suddenly and I fear one day it will steal my life.'

'So you seek protection in the prayers of this holy virgin?' Evisandus asks.

Geoffrey raises his eyes, his reply quick and bitter. 'If she is indeed chaste and holy, as she claims.'

A tear blurs my eye, then breaks and starts to trickle down my face. I look to my old friend, Evisandus. 'Father...' No more words will come.

The old hermit does not seem to have heard me. He throws down his staff and limps across to Geoffrey, the sprays of camelina still in his gnarled hand. I watch, puzzled, as he takes one of the sprays and crushes the flowers roughly in his fist. He opens his hand and holds the palm out to the Abbot.

'See? My hand is dry. There is no oil.'

I get up and edge closer to see what he is doing. Geoffrey is gazing at Evisandus as if he were crazed.

'This herb is the lady Christina,' the old man says, 'and the flower is the honour of her virginity.'

He takes the other sprig of Gold of Pleasure and presses the tiny blooms gently and delicately between his fingers.

'Look!' He holds out his hand to me, then to Geoffrey. The tip of his finger glistens with oil.

'You would do well, Father Abbot,' says Evisandus, 'to approach Christina with kindness and with gentleness, not rashly and on impulse, if you wish to benefit from the healing balm of her purity.'

Geoffrey is still staring but his look has changed to one of wonder. Now Evisandus seems to lose his balance and he stumbles backward. Geoffrey reaches out to steady him but once the old hermit has righted himself, he retains the Abbot's hand. He looks into his eyes.

'I see your fear, Geoffrey.' His voice is kind. 'But be assured. You have not misplaced your trust.'

After None, I leave the cool of the chapel and come out into the dusty heat of the afternoon. Margaret falls into step beside me.

'What did the Abbot say? Is he angry about the kitchen?'

'No – he's not angry.' I turn to wait for Geoffrey. He said Mass for us at Sext and has stayed on longer than usual, in order to talk with Evisandus.

'What is to happen about the kitchen? How will we manage?' Margaret asks.

Sometimes she is like one of the tormenting flies down by the stream. I give her a cold look. 'That is not your concern.'

She looks at me as if I have struck her, but says nothing in reply, just turns and walks away.

Evisandus is tired and I take him to the guest chamber so that he can rest. Outside, Geoffrey is waiting for me, hopefully to take his leave. Instead, he suggests that we walk to the stream and my heart sinks. The sun is still high and there is no breeze. As we pass across the worn, yellowing grass between the cells, I see my sister standing by the open cooking fire. I feel her eyes following us as we disappear under the trees.

It is uncomfortably warm, even here by the stream. I smell the Abbot's sour sweat. My heart is beating fast. Will he question me again? Or perhaps the words of Evisandus have reassured him.

'Forgive me. I should have known it was just another slander,' he says.

I let out a long breath but then look away, troubled. There has been no opportunity to be alone, to tease apart the threads of all that has happened: his accusation, the fright it gave me. No time to savour the comforting words of Evisandus, for that matter. Surely, if God deemed me impure, the hermit would perceive it and would not defend me.

Geoffrey's mouth twists in a wry smile. 'God knows there is enough calumny spoken about our friendship.'

It's true. I know what the wagging tongues of Caddington say about the Abbot's visits. Little do they know that it's not the Abbot who appears, naked, in my dreams.

'I suffer no lack of opposition from within the Chapter. Prior Alchinus and his confreres try to block me at every turn.' He looks at me. 'They don't think so much of you, either. It is said that you are no more than a shrewd woman of business with an eye to further your house and that is why you are my friend.'

This allegation is not one I have heard before, and it stings me, being so far from the truth. I sigh. 'Those of us who

268

would live like the disciples are promised suffering,' I reply. 'My mother beat me because I would not marry. And the recluse who first housed me – she threw me out on a false accusation.' I say nothing about the worst abandonment of all. My father, who loved me best, tearing the clothes from me, his eyes hard as adamant.

Geoffrey is watching me. Often, I find that he misreads me, his mind full of his own fears. But, for once, he seems to divine my true thoughts.

'The world is full of those who would do us harm,' he says. 'We must trust one another, Christina.'

He makes as if to go and as I follow him back out of the cover of the trees, we are confronted by the ruins of the kitchen.

'I will send my workmen,' he says, 'it won't take long to rebuild. And if they come to my own steward for their pay, not to the Abbey Sacrist, that should silence any objection from the Prior.'

# Chapter 28

*Hermitage de bosco*

*Christmas Eve, AD 1135*

A knock on my parlour door. I put down my work but find myself reluctant to leave the warmth of the fire. These days my bones seem to ache in the cold weather.

'Who is it?'

'Lady Christina, a visitor has come for you.'

The Norman French and the hesitant voice tells me that it's Lettice who has brought the news. I rise from my chair and go to the door. Ulfwine stands behind the new girl, his dark travelling cloak flecked with flakes of white.

'I have come to wish you joy of our Saviour's birth,' he says, blessing me. 'And I bring greetings from Leofric, and the hermit Ailward. He is with us for the Feast.' He removes his cloak and places it on the bench. The snowflakes are disappearing, one by one, in the warmth of the room. 'Oh, and Alfwen sends her greetings too.'

'Alfwen? I thought she had left the anchorhold.'

'She has – there was no longer income enough for her support. She is to move to the west country.'

I pour Ulfwine some ale and hand it to him, anxious to speak of other things than Alfwen. Lettice has been hovering at the door and now she comes right in, closing it behind her.

'What do you want?' I ask. Perhaps she has misunderstood her duties; her English is not fluent yet. 'You can leave us now.'

The face of the young woman begins to colour and she seems flustered. 'Oh, I beg your pardon. I thought… At my last house…' She does not tell us what she thought but, instead, makes a little bow and leaves. She doesn't even close the door behind her and I have to do that myself.

'Who is she?' asks Ulfwine. 'I haven't seen her before.'

'She's a cousin of Abbot Geoffrey's, not long come from a convent in the Mayenne. She will do well once she is used to my ways.'

Ulfwine smiles a wry smile. 'Perhaps the mistress of her last house didn't receive male visitors alone.'

I hadn't thought of that. It would explain her strange behaviour.

'It's the Benedictine way,' Ulfwine continues. 'They would have us all safely sequestered, men and women apart, and unable to travel freely. But how can we then live in the manner of the apostles?'

Ulfwine looks around the room with interest. He has not seen my new parlour since it was completed. I see his eyes take in the new hanging, the glass in the windows, the carved wooden shelf above the fireplace. Suddenly these things seem unnecessarily lavish.

'I'm glad to see you have kept Roger's chair, at least,' he says.

'Abbot Geoffrey has been very generous,' I say. 'But it's not only to us here. He gives far more to the poor than most people know. And I believe he has plans to build a hospital for lepers in St Albans.'

'Well, you should know, if anyone does.'

'What do you mean by that?' I am angry at his insinuation.

Ulfwine raises his hand, as if to avert conflict. 'I mean nothing more than that it's clear you have his ear, and must know his secrets.'

'And is it not a good thing that he comes to me? It shows that he wishes to conform his thinking to the will of God.'

'Of course.' Ulfwine's tone is conciliatory. 'If that is the case. But I counsel you to be careful. If you recall, Roger always kept his distance from the Abbey. And he succeeded.' He looks away but I still hear the murmured words. 'While he lived, at least.'

I move closer to the fire, as if to warm myself, but in truth I don't want Ulfwine to see how much his words have discomfited me. I try to forget that it was Geoffrey who sent the soldiers to take Roger's body.

Ulfwine breaks the awkward silence. 'How is your brother, Gregory?'

'He is well, thank you. The Abbot gives him leave to visit us here often.'

'And your parents? Have they been here to see the new buildings?' His eyes take in the spacious parlour. 'You always used to say how much they loved finery. They would approve the changes.'

I don't like his tone.

'They would not be welcome, if they did come,' I reply, coldly. 'I have not forgotten how they opposed the will of

272

God.'

*Why must he harp on about the improvements here?*

Ulfwine sits down on a stool near to the fire, nursing his drink. His long nose is still red from the cold and now it has started to drip. He wipes it with the back of his sleeve.

'I do not mean to cause offence,' he says. 'We should be taking joy in the Saviour's birth, not quarrelling.' He takes a draught of ale, then looks up at me. 'Christina, did you have any visitors yesterday?'

'No.' The day was wet and cold, like this one.

'Then you will not have heard the news,' he says. 'Stephen of Blois, the old king's nephew, was crowned on Sunday, at Westminster.'

'Crowned, already? But what about Henry's daughter? The nobles all swore to make Matilda queen after her father died.'

'Yes, but they think better of it now – many of them. And Henry's steward swears that the old king changed his mind on his death bed, naming Stephen instead of Matilda.'

'Could that be true?' I ask.

'Perhaps. The Archbishop of Winchester says so. But then, he is Stephen's brother.'

I catch Ulfwine's eye and we share a smile. This news of the coronation is troubling, though. I have no doubt it will make Geoffrey anxious.

'Does Stephen have the support of the Church?'

'Well, he has promised the Church great liberties, so it is said. But he will have to act quickly against the Scots. They have marched south and look to take Carlisle if they can.'

Talking with Ulfwine like this, I feel the warmth of our friendship rekindle and a part of me curls up in comfort, like a cat basking in the sun. It reminds me of the old days when he and I were companions, living together in simple poverty like the first disciples. Suddenly, the face of Roger comes into my mind; he is standing beside me in the chapel, rapt in silent prayer, tears of joy running down his cheeks.

Ulfwine seems to sense something of what is in my thoughts. He puts down his ale and comes over to me.

'Forgive me, Christina,' he says, 'for questioning your conduct. No doubt the Abbot's involvement here is God's provision – for you and for all the maidens.' His brown eyes look intently into mine. 'Just don't forget about the rest of us who are your friends too - Leofric and Ailward and the other hermits and recluses. We miss you.'

He steps back and turns to pick up his cloak.

'Wait, Ulfwine!' I follow him, brushing a tear from my cheek. 'Won't you stay and sing Sext with us?'

*Early hours of Christmas morning*

It is so cold in the chapel that I have allowed a brazier to be brought, to warm us while we sing Matins. Now that we are finished, I move along the line of maidens, greeting each one with a kiss and wishing them joy of Christ's birth. Their faces are raised to me, their eyes shining in the candle light, and I am filled with love for them all, even Godit. They file out, smiling and whispering, to return to their beds and I am left with Margaret. She embraces me.

'Happy Christmas,' she says. 'Shall I sit vigil with you?'

Meg knows that I will not leave the chapel till morning brings the birth of the Saviour. Perhaps I should let her stay, but her presence distracts me.

'You get some sleep,' I tell her. She will be up early enough as it is, managing preparations for the Christmas feast.

It is peaceful in the chapel: only the gentle hiss of burning wax and, from time to time, the ticking of the coals in the brazier as they cool. I wrap my cloak closely about me.

I think of the Virgin in that dark stable, long ago, waiting and yearning for the coming of her Son. I close my eyes and sense her desire, feeling it in my body. A longing for the end of pain and the coming of joy. For the morning, and the birth of a Saviour. Now the face of Abbot Geoffrey imposes itself into the darkness behind my eyelids and, at once, the peace of the chapel is spoilt. In its place the familiar, stale anxiety bears down upon me like a yoke. The task of protecting him is the burden I must carry, the penance for my sin. But how can I be sure that his heart is truly converted? *Dear Jesus, turn his heart to you. Keep him from sin. Keep him from sickness.*

It was snowy like this when he was taken sick last time –almost a year ago, in the Octave of Epiphany. I think of that afternoon, a Sunday: the lowering grey sky, the messenger come in haste from Oxford, where he was. *The Abbot is stricken down again. He is close to death, my lady. He begs your aid.* There was a great fever with it that time and the same terrible weakness and loss of breath. Remembering it, I feel again the tremor of fear. And then the tears as I lay on the chapel floor, pleading for his life, all the prayer within me coming to a point, a keen knife-tip, ready to pierce through anything the Enemy would erect against him. What would become of me if the Devil were to take him before his salvation is assured?

I remember the relief when a glowing orb of light appeared

275

at the corner of my vision, then a second and a third, just like it. It sometimes happens that way when my prayers are being answered. At last I could rise from the floor and go to find the messenger and tell him that all would be well. I think of his face when I told him. *Your master will recover. He will stand in this very place five days from now.* He looked at me as if I were mad. *He is close to death, my lady.* I only smiled at him, certain of the Spirit's witness within me.

A change in the light awakens me from my reverie and I open my eyes to find that one of the altar candles has burnt down to nothing. My back aches and I can no longer feel my feet, so I get up from my knees and sit on the bench, resolved to keep vigil till morning comes.

Thinking of Ulfwine's visit and his words, I shift uneasily against the wall. Perhaps he is right and Roger would disapprove of my new comforts. Would he rebuke me for being so reliant on the Abbey, on Geoffrey? I shake my head, as if to erase the troubling thought, and think instead of Ulfwine's news about the new king – Stephen. Perhaps he will replace the Abbot with a man of his own choosing. I bring to mind the Abbey, the great church with its tower. At this very moment, the choir monks will be seated in their stalls, the air full of incense for the Nativity. A voice sounds in my thoughts.

*Would you like to see him for whom you are anxious, to see how he fares?*

I hold my breath, waiting, though for what I am not certain. I am filled with a longing for reassurance and now, before my eyes, Geoffrey appears, standing with his back to the altar, arms stretched out in welcome. I shiver, though whether from cold or from awe at the clarity of this seeing, I can't tell.

I peer at his face but all is well. His cheeks are ruddy with health, matching the magnificent red of his cope.

The vision fades and I lean my head back against the wall and rest. When I wake, it is morning and the Christ child is born.

*Twenty-seventh day of December*

Last night, the wind changed to a westerly direction and the snow began to melt, so I am not surprised when a visitor comes from the Abbey, though it is not Geoffrey but only the sub-Prior, Alexander. Alexander is Geoffrey's man and does not sing to the tune of the Prior, as some of the Chapter do. I lead him into my parlour, a little disquieted. Is there bad news from the Abbey?

It would seem not. Alexander is in good spirits and eagerly devours the cake Nelda has made for the feast. He has come with money to pay the workmen who are deepening the ditch around the hermitage. Geoffrey wants to erect a more secure fence.

'How is the Abbot's health in this cold weather?' I ask.

'He is well, thank you. There are visitors at the Abbey that he cannot neglect, but he asks me to say he will ride down to you when the Feast is over.'

I remember my vision and itch to test its veracity. 'The snow prevented me coming to Mass, on the eve of Christ's Day. Tell me, which cope did he wear?'

Alexander is warming his hands before the fire and he straightens up, his brow furrowed in an effort to recall.

'It was the white one, I think, that he usually wears.'

I am taken aback. But Alexander is not a man to take note of these things. He wears the same soiled riding cloak every time he comes here.

'Think carefully, again, if it was the white one,' I say. 'I saw him vested in red.'

He looks at me, eyes widening in the fleshy folds of his face. 'It was the red cope – I remember now – the one the Abbot of St Ouen sent him. But I thought you said you were not able to come to Mass on Christmas Eve.'

'I was not able. Nevertheless, I saw him,' I reply.

The sub-Prior is confused for an instant but then the meaning of my words dawns on him. It pleases me to watch the colour leave his face and a look of awe come into his eyes.

# Chapter 29

*Sixth day of April, AD 1136*

Waiting at the rail, I gaze at the familiar shape of Gregory's back, the left shoulder sloping a little, just like my father's. There is grey beginning to show now in the band of hair encircling his shaved head. Yet again it seems a wonder to me: my worldly brother a monk, and now a priest too. From time to time Abbot Geoffrey sends him to say Mass for us; he knows how much I love my brother.

When Gregory turns and holds the Body of Christ aloft, I glance along the line of faces beside me. Each woman dutifully makes the sign of the cross, her eyes raised to the Host. Gregory approaches me and I open my mouth, shooting an anxious prayer heavenward, as always. *May I not be found unworthy.*

I feel the Host on my tongue and a thrill passes down my spine. No longer merely a scrap of unleavened bread – baked yesterday by Nelda in our own kitchen – it has transmuted

279

into the body of my Bridegroom.

'Corpus Christi, corpus Christi, corpus Christi.' I hear Gregory repeat the words again and again as he passes down the line of women. He is my brother but he is also a priest, the vicar of God.

It is an unseasonably cold day. Having fasted in preparation for Communion, I am grateful for the soup at dinner. Supping in my parlour, just the three of us, it is almost like being back at home in Huntingdon when we were children; Gregory and I prattling while Margaret watches and listens. I am impatient for news of Geoffrey. A feeling of dread has been with me ever since he was summoned to the King.

'How long has he been gone?' I ask.

'Two nights,' Gregory replies. 'The Prior said nothing in Chapter about when he will return.'

'It troubles me,' I say. 'The Abbot was with the King at Easter. Why should he summon him to Westminster again? Why could Stephen not have spoken with him then?'

Gregory shrugs his shoulders. He is not in the Abbot's confidence, but still I find myself pressing him for information he cannot give me.

'There's no need to trouble yourself, Christina,' he says. 'Geoffrey is one of the highest abbots in the land. It is no surprise that Stephen should call him.'

I look from my brother to my sister. Gregory is making light of my worry and Margaret has that blank look on her face. Who knows what misdeed she is judging me for now?

'Surely it can only mean trouble,' I insist, 'if the Abbot is forced to show support for the new king. Everyone says the barons will rise up against him. Where will Geoffrey be then?'

Even I can hear how shrill my voice has become.

Gregory pushes away his bowl and leans back on his stool, resting his head against the wall. 'It's not your concern, Christina. The Bishop will advise him.' The warm food has made him sleepy and he yawns. 'Or is it the hermitage you fear for? I'm sure the Bishop will let you stay, whatever happens.'

'It's not myself I am thinking of.'

Though I love him dearly, Gregory doesn't understand anything – he never did. He seems bemused by my sharp tone.

'The Abbot is here more and more often.'

In unison, my brother and I look across the table, to Margaret. It is a shock to hear her speak.

'Of course the Abbot visits here,' I reply. 'Gregory knows that.' What is she implying?

'He comes to inspect the new building work, of course,' my brother says.

'Yes, but that isn't the only reason.' Margaret looks straight at me and continues, her voice quiet and steady. 'You talk about nothing but the Abbot. You seem to pray only for him.'

I don't understand it; Margaret never questions me. 'What are you trying to say?'

My sister's eyes drop to her plate and I only just catch her words. 'People are saying already that …'

'That what?' I am trembling with indignation, my conscience completely clear. 'There is nothing in our discourse that is not pure.'

Gregory reaches out his hand to me. 'I am sure Meg is not accusing you of anything,' he says. He has never had to play peacemaker between us before.

I turn to him, eager that he should not be misled. 'The

Abbot comes to beg my prayers, and my advice too. That is all.' I glance towards Margaret, then back to my brother. 'He has complete faith in what God reveals to me. He is loath to do anything without my blessing.' There – it is the truth and why shouldn't they know it?

Gregory laughs. 'Oh come now, little sister. You always did make much of your own importance.'

I feel my cheeks grow warm with the rush of blood. 'How can you say that? All this neighbourhood knows that God shares his secrets with me – the Abbot believes it, he knows it is true.'

Gregory is regarding me with surprise.

'We know that you are shown many things,' Margaret says quietly. I wait but she says nothing more. Her unspoken thoughts hang in the air, polluting it.

'You must be circumspect, sister,' Gregory says to me at last. He sounds worried. 'If what you say is true, you must be careful to advise the Abbot well.'

I push my plate away from me, impatient with this talk. Why does no-one understand? I have no choice in how I advise Geoffrey. I speak only of what I know and what is shown to me. And nothing has been shown me about this summons to court. What does it mean?

*Seventh day of April, AD 1136*

The sun is low in the sky when, at last, Adelaisa comes running to tell me that he is here. I wrap my cloak around me and go out into the chill air. He jumps down from his horse but keeps hold of the reins, dismissing Nelda's boy with a wave of his hand.

'You are returned from Westminster, then. What news?'

Geoffrey pulls back the hood of the riding cloak to reveal his face, pale with fatigue, his dark eyes blacker than ever by contrast.

'I cannot stay.'

'What is it? What did the King say?'

'He wishes to send me to Rome - to the Pope,' he replies.

I see that he is frightened. 'Will you not come inside and tell me all?'

He shakes his head. 'I must ride back to the Abbey. Thomas must be dispatched to the Archbishop - perhaps he can suggest another to take my place.'

'But why are you to go? What does the King want?'

'First he seizes the throne, and now he wants the blessing of Pope Innocent for his reign. It seems to me like putting the cart before the horse.' Geoffrey's voice has a bitter edge.

'And who is to say that Stephen will prevail, in any case?' I say. 'You told me that some of the barons have petitioned Matilda to return and challenge him for the throne.'

He nods but says nothing. He is absentmindedly stroking his horse's back, just at the base of her neck. She luxuriates in his touch, turning her face towards him again and again.

Like wine spilt on the rushes, the full meaning of this news is beginning to soak into my mind. If he goes as the King's embassy, he will be thought the King's man, and it is too soon to see whether Stephen will keep the throne. Suddenly, the world outside seems full of uncertainty and the malice of others. At times like this, all Geoffrey's vexing ways seem of no account and I feel as if we truly stand together.

A shiver passes through me as I think of how far away Rome is: the rigours of the voyage, the mountainous roads, outlaws. It appears that Geoffrey's thoughts are running on the same track.

'The journey will take weeks – I will be gone, perhaps, for months.'

We both know that it's not the length of time away that is at the root of his fear. More than once before, the privations of travel have brought on his dreaded sickness.

'Intercede for me, Christina,' he begs. 'It may be that the King will change his mind, or that others can be found to go.'

Geoffrey makes as if to mount his horse but then stops and turns back to me. He looks discomfited.

'One last request.' His lips draw back from his teeth in an awkward smile. 'Will you do something for me? Will you sew me two chainses for the journey?'

The more uncertain he is, the more he reverts to his French words. I have noticed this before.

'You want me to make your undershirts?'

I am insulted. Am I to be his wardrobe maid now? Then another thought, more shaming still, comes to me. A wife might sew undergarments for her husband. Margaret's insinuations rush into my mind.

'What would people think?'

'No-one would know,' he replies. 'And surely it would ward off the sickness - to have next to my body something sewn by pure hands.'

He sees my disquiet. 'I beg you, Christina.' There are tears in his eyes. 'When the fever came last and the time before, you were near at hand, to pray. But if I am in Rome or on the ocean ...'

The setting sun is casting a golden light on the new-cut stones of the wall encircling the well. I turn away from his pleas, despising him. And troubled too. I am not chaste in the way he thinks me. What if he were to know how these hands of mine were once employed in sin?

Yet it is this very trust he has in me - like the trust of a little child for his mother – that binds me to him. And is the burden of protecting him not my penance?

'I will sew them. And with every stitch I will pray for your safety,' I say.

He nods briefly, with something like his usual arrogance and calls for the boy to help him mount.


*Hermitage de bosco*

*Twenty-seventh day of April, AD 1136*


There has been no word from the Abbey but even Geoffrey's absence can do nothing to counter the happy certainty that abides in my heart. Abides and grows only stronger with time. Margaret is puzzled by my gaiety and keeps asking if I have heard news of him.

*Yes*, I reply, because it's true. But then she looks even more confused when I say nothing more.

The beeches are in leaf – tender yellow-green, with a soft fuzz of hair at their edges - and I love to walk among them now. Every day, there are fresh signs that summer is on its way. More and more often, I take Emmy with me and we talk of seeing in the Spirit and of the knowing that is beyond reason. She is growing in God. When we are together, I am reminded of Roger and how he was able to uncover the divine within me. If I can do the same for Emmy then perhaps, after all, I have not failed in every task. The others are jealous, of course and see nothing special in her, but I say that a prophet is never lauded in his own country. My family could never see the hand of God upon me.

It is while we are in the woods that Lettice comes to tell me I have a visitor: Father Thomas - returned from his mission on Geoffrey's behalf. I hurry back to the hermitage. It cannot be other than good news – I am sure of it. There is such lightness in my heart when I think of Geoffrey: as if there is no more need of my prayers, for they have been answered already.

Father Thomas has been shown into my parlour and I find him seated, his head dropping with exhaustion. He looks up when I come in.

'Oh, my dear child,' he says. 'I am getting too old for these long rides. And all to no avail. The Bishops, the Abbots – all agree that Geoffrey must be part of the Papal embassy.'

I stare at him. His words should fill me with despair but nothing can dislodge the certainty in my heart. Geoffrey is safe. This proposed journey will come to nothing.

'Have you seen him?' I ask. 'Geoffrey?'

He shakes his head. 'I stopped by at court but he had left – perhaps he is already at Dover. May I stay here tonight and ride on in the morning? He will be waiting for my report.'

'Yes, of course, Father.'

I am searching within myself for any disruption his words have brought to my inner peace, but there is no change. It seems stubbornly clear to me that Geoffrey will not make this journey to Rome. The ship may sail, even with Geoffrey on it, but something will prevent it. He will be recalled. Something will intervene.

'And I am to take a parcel to him,' Thomas is saying. 'You have something for him, he said.'

'I have?' Then I remember - the undershirts. 'Never mind that now, Father. You rest.'

I call Godit and tell her to bring ale and biscuits for the priest. Then I draw up a stool next to him.

'Thomas, I have been interceding for the Abbot. I have fasted and prayed and wept tears on his behalf. Then, last Thursday, I was in the chapel and I heard a voice from above.'

He looks at me, his eyes widening. Father Thomas knows my secrets – all except those that may never be spoken. He has faith in my visions, just as the Abbot does.

'What did the voice say?' he asks.

'It said *Behold the wall*. So I opened my eyes and looked at the chapel wall and I saw the Abbot fixed there, as if he had been cemented into it, alive. I saw him as clear as I see you now.'

Father Thomas draws in his breath. 'What do you think this means?'

'That was not all. I heard the voice again. *As long as he remains firmly fixed in the wall, the protection of God will never desert him.* Those were the words. I wrote them down to remember.'

I take the priest's hand. 'Father Thomas. Every day, every hour since then, I have looked inward with the eyes of my spirit and each time I see Abbot Geoffrey, safely enclosed in the wall of God's protection.'

Thomas signs himself with the cross. 'May it be even as

you say,' he breathes. 'This journey will be full of dangers.'

I close my eyes and quiet my thoughts, the better to perceive the truth.

'Father, I cannot say how, but I am sure that he will not leave these shores. You need have no further fears.'

He closes his eyes and takes a deep breath. 'Pray God you are right. The Abbey is not a happy place for me, with the Prior in charge.'

Thomas seems revived and now he gets to his feet.

'I will set off at once to Dover and tell him what you have said.'

His excitement makes me smile. 'You are tired and there is no need. I would not be surprised to learn that he has already been relieved of his task and is on his way home. Why not go back to the Abbey and wait for him there?'

'Perhaps that is best,' he says, 'if you are certain.' He looks relieved. Going to the door, he recalls something and turns back.

'The parcel. He said you have something for him, that I am to take.'

I think of the fine linen undershirts, carefully folded and wrapped in calico. 'Oh – that. I do not think he will need that now.'

'Are you sure? He was quite insistent that I should not forget.'

'I am sure.' I deliberately add a note of ice to my voice. It would not do for him to ask any more about the parcel.

## Whit Sunday, tenth day of May, AD 1136

Adelaisa's mother is sick again and I have granted her leave for another visit to her mother at Westminster. Margaret is to accompany her, as she did before. The wagon is packed and the horses are eager to start, when a thought comes to me.

'Wait!' I call, and return to my parlour.

Unlocking the chest, I feel inside for the calico packet, hidden beneath winter bed furs. Its presence there has been troubling me. I take it back out to where Meg and Adelaisa are waiting.

'Farewell,' I say to them both, 'pray God you will find your mother improved, Ada.'

'I slip the packet into my sister's hand.

'What's this?' Margaret asks.

'Just some clothing for the poor. You can give it to the almoner at Westminster, to distribute.'

My sister looks at me. 'Do we not have enough poor of our own, here in Caddington?'

I can't suppress my irritation. 'Why must you question everything I do?'

'Forgive me,' Meg murmurs. 'Of course I will take it to the almoner.'

I embrace both women and the wagoner clicks his tongue to start the horses. Walking back to my parlour, I feel pleased. If I had given away such fine shirts close to home, awkward questions would be asked. And besides, I have been waiting for an opportunity to give a thank offering, ever since the King changed his mind and recalled Geoffrey from Dover.

Now, on the Feast of Pentecost, it has presented itself. What more fitting day could there be to give away something so costly? Though I confess it irks me a little to think of such fine linen on the back of a London beggar.

# Chapter 30

*The road to St Albans*

*Eleventh day of February, AD 1137*

Mercifully, it has not rained for a week but still the horses must swerve to avoid the frosted ruts in the road and then they fall out of step with one another and the litter sways alarmingly. Margaret sits opposite, so close that our knees are touching, but however small I am grateful to Geoffrey for the shelter of this conveyance.

We sit in silence, broken only by the little gulping noises my sister makes as she weeps. I turn away and give myself over to the bubbling ferment of grief. Geoffrey would not have sent for us if Gregory's sickness was not a mortal one. My brother is dying. I speak the words silently, feeling around them with my mind, as a tongue explores a rotting tooth. There is pain, yes, and the sour taste of death. But the sadness is sweetened a little when I think of how I woke in the night, praying for Gregory, and how the words came to me, so clearly, so gently. *You may be sure his Lady loves him.* I knew then that the time would not be long.

The litter lurches to one side. Though the morning is advancing, it is dark behind the curtain and I feel Meg's fingers on my wrist. I sense her care but she says nothing and, for once, my sister's restraint is a blessing. I close my eyes and savour again the reassuring words. The Virgin Mother is enclosing Gregory around with her protection, in preparation for the journey he must make. A memory comes to me – a dream, from long ago; I am resting on velvet cushions, a gracious lady reclining beside me, her head in my lap. She turns her face so that I can see the love that shines in her eyes. *I have chosen you from your father's house. And not only you, but your brother Gregory also.* I feel fresh tears beginning to form in my eyes. So it has proved to be. Me and my brother, and Margaret too; we have each of us been snatched to safety from the godless abode that is my father's house. Wasn't it earlier that very day that I stood cowering in the passageway, fending off my mother's blows?

Hastily I return to thoughts of Gregory on his sick bed. *You may be sure his Lady loves him.* The words come again, audible only to the ears of my soul, but this time there is more. *And she loves you also.* My heart begins to beat faster. A sense of forewarning drapes itself over me gently, like a pall of dark velvet. Is my own death, then, approaching? I open my eyes to find that Margaret has nodded off to sleep. I am glad of the solitude while these new words find a home in my soul. Am I to enter eternity hard on the heels of my brother?

I lift the curtain and peer through the aperture: bare winter branches, a patch of dove-grey sky. Will I never again see the burgeoning green of spring, watch the swaying kittentails on the willow by the stream? I am overtaken by a delicious melancholy. For surely the words mean that I am to be counted worthy, after all. And who can receive the summons of the Queen of queens and not be content?

## Abbey of St Alban

Brother Odo, the Guestmaster, is at the Orchard Gate, waiting, when we arrive. The litter is lifted down from the shafts and he helps us out.

'Come quickly,' he says. 'I fear your brother's condition is worsening.'

Not being permitted in the cloister, we follow the Guestmaster along the Orchard Path, past rows of lichen-blotched apple trees. They seem to retract their clawed branches against the bitter wind.

The door is opened by the Infirmarian himself, his face grave. He bows to Brother Odo and to me. When he looks up, I catch the pity in his eyes.

'Father Ralph will show you to your brother,' the Guestmaster says. 'I will go to prepare your lodging at the guesthouse.'

It is gloomy inside the Infirmary, its small windows set high up in the brick wall, but there are fires burning in every grate and the sudden warmth is welcome. From somewhere above, where stairs lead to another floor, comes the sound of wailing. I follow the broad back of Father Ralph past empty beds and now we turn a corner and some of the beds are inhabited. A young monk looks up from the bowl set beside him to collect blood from his opened vein.

Meg is walking beside me now. 'Where is Gregory?' She

sounds close to tears.

Father Ralph turns round. 'I have made him as comfortable as I can, Mistress. His bed is next to my apothecarium.'

He indicates a chamber abutting the Infirmary wall, an open doorway and, beside it, a bed against the wall. A man lies in it, his head on a bolster. My brother! I want to run to him but an aged monk stands in the way, bent over his stick. He lifts his head and seems to look in my direction but his eyes are cloudy and unseeing.

Father Ralph takes the old man's arm and leads him away and now we are at Gregory's bedside and the sour stench of urine from the wooden bucket is overpowering. A boy appears at the doorway and, seeing us, he runs off. I stand and stare at the wasted face on the pillow, the skin a fearful yellow, the eyes closed. There is a clattering coming from the Infirmary kitchen, at the far end of the hall. I want to scream for it to stop.

Meg has taken Gregory's hand and now the boy comes back with stools for us and, at the same moment, my brother opens his eyes. He tries to heave himself up against the bolster. The sight of his thin arm on the coverlet is a shock.

'You've come.' Gregory screws up his eyes, searching for Margaret. Now he turns his head to me. 'I prayed that you would come.'

He is so weak and there is a rattle to his breathing but it is still my brother's voice, his mind. He has not left us yet. I feel tears forming at the corners of my eyes.

'How bad is the pain?' Margaret asks, her voice close to breaking.

'Not so bad. It is this itching ....' He does indeed seem to be restless, moving about under the bedcovers, and now he tears with his finger nails at the skin of his neck.

'Try to keep still, Gregory.'

The Infirmarian has returned and he stands watching, hands hidden in the sleeves of his habit. Now he walks past me to the head of the bed and holds the back of his hand against Gregory's forehead.

'He has a fever. This has come on only in the last day or two.' Father Ralph goes to the foot of the bed and holds up three fingers. 'How many fingers do you see, Father?'

With a great effort, Gregory pulls himself forward. Why is he squinting like that – my hawk-eyed brother?

'Is it two?'

I feel a sick, lurching sensation in my belly. 'Can nothing be done?'

Father Ralph moves away from the bed and beckons to me. It pains me to leave Gregory's side but I go to him, my mind full of dread.

'I have conferred with the apothecary at Ely - he has seen this before. Your brother has an excess of black bile that has caused a tumour in the abdomen, and the yellowing of the skin that you see. It comes on very quickly and there is no cure. I was warned to look out for any changes to his vision - they portend the end.'

I close my eyes for a moment and then open them again. 'In my heart, I knew as much. And there is no benefit in bleeding him?'

'It has been done, my lady, but to no effect.' Father Ralph puts his hand on my arm, and looks straight into my eyes. 'He has already confessed his sins to the Abbot, and received pardon.'

I return to the bed. Margaret is holding Gregory's hand

and he is struggling to speak.

'Three times,' he is saying. 'Three times she has come to me.'

A thrill passes down my spine. I take his other hand and the skin is hot and tight.

'You have seen the Virgin? I too had a showing. And, Gregory, I was given a message for you. You are to know your Lady loves you.'

Gregory leans forward, his movements suddenly stronger. 'She said that?'

Margaret cuts in, her forehead creased in a frown. 'Gregory is talking of Ursule, his wife. It is she who appeared to him.'

'Ursule?'

'She has come – three times - with the child,' Gregory says. He sounds distraught. 'Why does she come? I have renounced the world.'

A tide of pity and love engulfs me. I reach across the bed to him. Heat seems to emanate from his face and his body as if he were on fire.

'I beg you, don't be troubled. It is the Queen of Heaven who is your Mistress now and I have been assured of her love for you.'

He pulls his hand away from mine and claws at his arm, the scratch marks white against his yellowed skin. There is a tear running down my cheek now.

'Gregory, I believe that she is summoning you to her presence. It is time to prepare yourself.'

He leans back against the bolster and closes his eyes. Each time he takes a breath, the rattling noise comes again, from deep in his chest. Margaret has turned away to pray; I see the movement of her elbow as she signs herself with the cross. I probe my own soul, casting about for the calm that surrounded me in the litter but here, in the Infirmary, death seems only a thing of horror, coarse and ugly. Gregory is quiet for a time - not so restless now. I wonder if the end has come already, but then he opens his eyes and speaks again.

'Father Ralph,' he says, quite clearly, though his voice is weak. I turn and see that the Infirmarian has been standing there, all this time, with us. 'Send to the Abbot. I wish to be anointed with oil.'

Father Ralph nods and I sense his agreement that it is time. 'You will have to leave now,' he says, looking from me to Margaret.

Meg kisses Gregory's hand and gets to her feet.

'I want to speak with my brother alone,' I say, and gaze steadily at the Infirmarian, ignoring his frown.

My sister pauses for a moment and then turns to go. I know her feelings are hurt but no matter. I am protecting her if she but knew it. When they have both gone, I draw close to Gregory. His breath is foul – it smells of old eggs.

'There is one more thing, Gregory, before I bid you farewell. I hope it may bring you comfort. I truly believe that where you go, I shall soon follow.'

His eyes open wide and he draws in his breath. 'You are sick?' he asks.

'No. But the same words were spoken to me as to you. I was told that my Lady loves me also.'

Gregory stares at me and then his lips begin to twitch and I wonder if it is a new spasm of pain but then I see that he is trying to smile. Suddenly, he is no longer a monk and a priest, about to depart this world, but the brother who teased me all through my childhood.

'You never did like it,' he says.

'What?'

I miss his whispered answer and have to move closer still to hear. The sulphurous stench is all but unbearable.

'I never did like what?'

'To be left out of anything.'

It takes a moment for me to grasp his meaning and, when I do, blood rushes to my face in humiliation. But then Gregory clutches at my hand with his jaundiced fingers.

'Bless me, Theodora,' he whispers, 'I would have your blessing before I die.'

Hearing him say my childhood name, my heart feels that it will break and I begin to sob in earnest. I place my hand on his forehead and pray, but now Father Ralph is here and he is gently pulling me away and I will not go. Gregory opens his eyes and, looking at me all the while, he smiles and I know that it is time.

The boy leads me away, past more beds and to the door of the Infirmary kitchen. Looking back, I see a procession of monks approaching Gregory's bedside. Geoffrey is at their head in his alb and stole, a cross in his hands. I glimpse candles and sacred vessels but then the Infirmary kitchen door is closed and I am hurried away.

*The Abbey guesthouse*

*Twelfth day of February, AD 1137*

I must have slept after all, because I am awoken by an insistent banging in the distance. What is it – is there a fire? My eyes fly to the window, high up. The patch of sky is no longer pitch black but neither is it lurid with flame. I sit up and see that Meg is awake too, kneeling beside her bed in the guestchamber we have been given. She turns to me and there is fear in her eyes. The din – it is like slate striking stone, again and again -seems to be coming from the far side of the cloister. Now there are other sounds: running feet, low calls, a door thudding shut.

I rise and, wrapping my cloak around me, I go to the door. The maid who takes care of guests is disappearing down the passageway and I call to her.

'What is happening? Ask the Guestmaster to attend us.'

She comes back and makes a curtsey. 'Brother Odo cannot come,' she says. 'The brothers are summoned to the Infirmary. They must all go.'

Margaret is at the door now. 'The Infirmary? Is it our brother – Gregory?'

The maid's eyes are wide in alarm. She shakes her head but it is clear to me that she knows nothing.

'We will get dressed and come at once,' I say.

'Oh no, Mistress,' she blurts out. 'It is only the brothers and the fathers who are summoned.' She is fearful of giving offence but more frightened that we will override her. Her voice trails away. 'It would not be seemly.'

Back in the chamber, Meg pours water from the pitcher into the bowl and we hastily wash our faces and our hands, and pull on our clothes. The fire in the chamber fireplace is not lit but I hardly notice the cold.

'Where is the Abbot?' I ask my sister, though it is a question she cannot answer. 'Why doesn't he come and speak with us?'

The banging has stopped and now the guesthouse seems unnaturally quiet. We venture down to the hall, where there is a fire at least. There is no-one to be seen until a tall, lean young man enters, letting in the cold, early morning air. He is not dressed in the habit of a monk but, pulling back his hood, he greets us with deference. He does not speak like an unlettered villein.

'Lady Christina, Mistress Margaret,' he says and gives a bow. 'I am the Guestmaster's assistant. Brother Odo regrets that he cannot attend you at present. But I am to make you as comfortable as possible in his absence. Would you like to break your fast?'

I give an impatient shake of my head at this. 'Why have the brothers been called to the Infirmary? We are anxious for news of Father Gregory – he is our brother. Where is Abbot Geoffrey?'

The young man seems taken aback, then increasingly discomfited.

'What is it?'

'No doubt you heard the summons,' he says, at last. 'The Infirmarian calls the brothers to come when one of their number is about to leave this world.'

Beside me, I feel Margaret shudder.

I have to be certain. 'Is it Gregory?'

The Guestmaster's assistant nods his head. 'I thought you had been told,' he says quietly, his face twisted in anguish.

'No. We have been told nothing.' I cannot keep the bitterness from my voice. 'I suppose the Abbot is not to be disturbed.'

'He is leading the brothers in the litany of saints,' he replies. He studies the floor, as if something of great interest might appear at any moment from amongst the rushes. The fire crackles in the hearth. At last, he looks up at us.

'If you need no refreshment, perhaps you would wish to keep vigil in the Church. I can have seats brought for you.'

Margaret takes my hand and clasps it tight.

'Yes,' I reply.

The young man leads us out of the guesthall and into the great court. It is fully light now – a leaden, icy morning. A fine rain, just short of sleet, is falling. A cart is being loaded with empty wine barrels, as if it were just any other day.

We enter the Abbey Church by the Great Western Door, passing close to the Abbot's lodging. Inside is Geoffrey's parlour, where I have been received before, once or twice. But there has been no invitation and he is not there.

Seats are brought for us and set up in the nave, close to the quire, and there we sit when our knees are chilled from praying on the stone floor. People pass close by from time to time– townspeople come to their church– but no one speaks to us. As ever, my sister keeps her own counsel. I suppose she must grieve in her own way.

I try to keep Gregory's face in my thoughts, repeating the *Ave Maria* over and over, imagining the Queen of heaven enfolding him in her arms. But, try as I might, my thoughts slip away. Why has Geoffrey not come? Surely he could send word, at least. Here, in the Abbey, it's as if I am merely a woman like any other, to be kept safely away.

301

It must be past noon when, at last, there comes the sound of a heavy door latch being lifted, some distance off in the transept, and at once the sound of voices chanting. The singing grows steadily louder. Has the end come then? Are we soon to see my brother's body? But now it seems that the procession has halted, perhaps at the Lady Altar, and still we have no view of the monks, though the psalms continue unchecked.

'What is happening?' Margaret asks, but I have no answer to give her.

Time passes with an agonizing slowness and still the brothers chant. Are they going to proceed through the whole of the psalter? I can no longer feel feet or hands and, despite myself, hunger is beginning to growl in my belly.

Then the voices seem to falter and to straggle and, all at once, there is a thunderous clanging of bells from way up in the tower and now, in between the peals, the ringing of lesser bells further off, in the cloister, and by the great gate.

At the shock, I reach out for my sister's cold hand.

'Surely ...' Meg begins, 'surely this means ...'

'Hush!' I say, not wanting to hear her say the words.

I stand and look around, but the great height of the nave reduces me to a creature crawling on the surface of the earth, forgotten or overlooked. Why does no-one come to us?

At last, I spy the Guestmaster's servant at the Western Door. He walks over to us with his head bowed.

'Brother Odo has sent me to tell you that Father Gregory has breathed his last. He has entered eternity.'

Margaret's hand flies to her forehead, as mine does, and we sign ourselves with the Cross. Her tears come immediately and course silently down her cheeks.

'Now, at last, we will we go to him,' I say to the servant, making sure to speak with hauteur so that he will not dare to object.

But he shakes his head. 'Forgive me, Lady Christina. Father Gregory's body must be prepared and he can only be attended by those of his brothers who are priested. In due time, he will be brought to the chancel and you may attend his Mass and be present at the burial.'

He bows and leaves us and I cannot contain my anguish. Every part of my body thrums with grief and with rage.

'Surely, now, Geoffrey could come to me. But no, it is the Guestmaster who sends word, and he does not even come himself – just sends his boy!'

I am shocked to see that Margaret has covered her ears with her hands.

'No – no more,' she says, her voice tight and strange. Her eyes are open and full of pain and blame. 'The Abbot – always the Abbot! I will hear no more about the Abbot. I have just lost my brother.'

She drops her hands from her face, turns and runs across the nave from me, towards the great door.

I stare after her in disbelief. But soon the shock is swallowed up in a flood of misery such as I have not known for many years. I am unable to move but only sit, alone and abandoned by all. I think of all the nights I have spent sleepless, interceding to keep Geoffrey safe. Of all his visits, begging for my prayers, my protection. Where is he now, the man who would have me sew shirts for him? And now the old accusing voices are in my ears. The contemptuous face of my mother appears, the cold, righteous eyes of Alfwen. She knew me better than I knew myself. And how foolish to think that

I could mend the tear of my secret sin. These years of high regard, of comfort, of dedication to the Abbot's salvation, now these seem to me no more than the ugly darning of an unskilful needle.

I sit alone, the old numbness creeping up from my left hand, along my arm and into my face. I try to pray but nothing relieves it. Nor is anything able to lift the pall of wretchedness as, much later, when the congregation has assembled, I witness the procession pass by. The cross comes first, then the boys of the Abbey, followed by the monks, then Gregory behind them, carried upon a bier. I catch a glimpse of his covered body and strain to see, but the hood of the cowl has been stitched together over his face. Last of all, Abbot Geoffrey comes, walking slowly under the weight of his cope of darkest indigo blue. He passes within three feet of where I stand but under the ornate constraint of his mitre his eyes gaze implacably ahead.

*The Abbey guesthall*

*Thirteenth day of February, AD 1137*

There are other guests at table, when we break our fast: some brothers from Ely are visiting the Abbey. After greeting us with a blessing, they keep to the far end of the bench. I look across the board at Margaret. Since her outburst, there has been strain between us. Her eyes are red from weeping. She could not contain herself at Prime, knowing that the office was to be sung for Gregory. It is as if she is the only one to have lost a brother, when I was always closer to him.

The Guestmaster has been absent but now he appears at the door of the hall. He takes the serving man aside and speaks a few words with him, then walks across to us.

'I bid you good morning. I'm sure it will please you to know that all left-over food and wine in the Abbey today will be given to the poor, on behalf of your brother.'

I should be gratified by this but I am not. It only serves to make Gregory's death more real.

Brother Odo continues. 'I have a message for you, from my lord Abbot.'

At last. I have had no converse with Geoffrey all the time we have been at the Abbey. Is it only two days? It seems like a world ago.

'He may be able to speak with you after Vespers this evening. That is unless you have returned to the hermitage by then.'

I stare at him. 'After Vespers?'

Can he not spare a moment for me before that? I turn my head away so that the Guestmaster should not see my humiliation.

'Please tell him that we shall be leaving before noon,' I say firmly, ignoring Margaret's look of surprise. 'My companions are awaiting my return. Perhaps you can arrange for a litter to take us back.'

Brother Odo seems uncertain. 'I will speak to the Prior. It may be possible.'

I can hardly believe the evidence of my ears.

'The Abbot sent a litter to bring us here. I am certain that he would want us to be transported in comfort.'

'The Abbot – of course.' He seems relieved. 'I will see to it.'

Back in our bedchamber, Margaret collects together the

few things we had time to bring with us, while I try to calm my fearful thoughts. I must have offended the Abbot in some way. How dare he treat me with such indifference? I am wary of speaking to Margaret after her eruption yesterday but I cannot help it – she seems so unconcerned.

'Are you not scandalized at how we have been treated?'

She shrugs her shoulders. 'Geoffrey may be the Abbot but there are powerful men here who do not see eye to eye with him – so you have said many times. Remember, it is from his own means that he supports us at the hermitage.'

Her answer is true enough but it disquiets me. Am I despised at the Abbey, then? Can some of them really suspect that Geoffrey makes of me a paramour?

Climbing onto the mattress to look through the window, I see a litter being carried across the courtyard.

'Come – we will leave. We are not wanted in this place.'

Margaret follows me out of our chamber and along the passageway, then down the stairs into the guesthall. The monks from Ely are gone but Brother Odo and another monk are there, talking with an old couple. The monk holds some dark cloth in his hand that looks familiar – surely it is Gregory's cloak, his good one. Now they move closer to the candle, to examine it better. The old man walks with a limp.

'Father!' Margaret is pushing past me now and running to them.

My blood seems to freeze in my veins. This man is not my father – he has white hair for one thing. My eyes jump to the old woman. She is too short to be my mother and round like a barrel, and yet I remember that hood, with its border of marten fur, drab now and faded.

He turns, the old man, and puts out his arms to Meg, and it

*is* my father. Seeing my sister in his embrace, a heavy weight of envy seems to land on me like a cat and come crawling down my head, scratching and scraping with its claws, filling my vision, weighing me down. Father looks past Margaret to me and our eyes meet, just for an instant. I wrestle with the beast till I have mastered myself and shaken it off. And now I am calm.

Turning my head away from the troubling sight, I wrap my travelling cloak around me and walk towards the door of the hall. Out in the courtyard, the litter is waiting on the ground. A groom helps me inside, saying he will fetch the horses.

'I thought there were two ladies,' he says.

'My companion will be here shortly,' I say, pulling down the curtain.

I wait in the darkness, trembling, till I hear Margaret's footsteps. The litter is in the shafts now and the horses are harnessed and ready. My sister's face appears.

'You have managed to drag yourself away from them at last?'

'Christina,' she says. 'Won't you come inside and speak to them?'

I turn my head away from her.

'Life has been hard for them,' she goes on, 'since the old king died. They say that Stephen's enemies hold the castle now and trade has fallen off. They have had to rent out the house.'

'So that is why they have come to the Abbey – to get their hands on Gregory's cloak.'

She winces at the contempt in my voice and I half expect a tart reply, but she only climbs in with a sigh.

'Not only so – they have lost their son, remember.'

I knock on the wooden frame of the litter and the groom commands the horses to walk on. Their hooves begin to clatter on the stones and, even in the dim interior, I catch the look in my sister's eyes. Behind the reproach I think I see something else that fills me with fury. Who is she to pity me?

# Chapter 31

*Hermitage de bosco*

*Second day of January, AD 1139*

It is three times, now, that Lettice has not been in chapel for Matins. This morning, I sent Matilda to rouse her and she came at last, tousle-haired and red-faced. But now that she is kneeling before me in my parlour, waiting for a reprimand, I have to compose my face and try not to smile. Lettice is a pliable girl and her heart is pure but she was born to a soft life. I see something of myself in her.

'This will not do,' I begin. 'Does your Saviour deserve less devotion from you, just because the mornings are dark and cold?'

'No, Mistress,' she murmurs, wiping a tear from her cheek. 'Well then …'

A knock on the parlour door spoils the moment of intimacy, and I find myself irritated. 'I said that I was not to be disturbed.'

To my surprise, the door is opened anyway and there stands

Margaret. No-one else would have dared to defy me. I can tell from her face that it is important.

'He is here,' she says, 'the Abbot.'

At last. It has been so long since he came.

I motion to Lettice to stand up. 'You are to refrain from meat until I tell you,' I say quickly. She looks stricken and then I remember the season. 'Until Epiphany. You may end your fast then.'

She curtseys and moves towards the door. As she does so, Geoffrey strides into the room, followed by a stranger: younger than Geoffrey and half a head taller, with broad shoulders and a mat of brown, wiry hair cut close to his head.

To my astonishment, the stranger takes Lettice's hand, greeting her fulsomely in Norman French. Her face lights up and she replies, speaking too quickly for me to follow her meaning. Now Geoffrey is joining in – his French taking on the same unfamiliar accent.

'You may go, Lettice.' I have to speak loudly to be heard above the gabble. 'But look to yourself. I have been lenient this time.'

She looks flustered, exchanges a few more words with the stranger and then she is gone.

Not before time, Geoffrey remembers his manners.

'Christina, I don't think you have met my kinsman Walter, from the Abbey at Lonlay, near my home in Domfront.'

So that is it. Lettice came to us from a baronial family in the Mayenne. Perhaps she and this Walter are related. Geoffrey presents his relative, looking at me as if to emphasize his words. 'Walter *de Luci*.'

De Luci. Richard de Luci is one of the most powerful courtiers in the realm. Is this man, then, of the same family?

The stranger bows, revealing his monk's tonsure, and takes my hand in a firm grip.

'I trust that you are treating my little cousin Laetitia well,' he says. His brown eyes meet mine frankly but is that a trace of warning I see in them?

'She is happy here with us, I think. Have you been in England long?'

'Since last summer,' he replies. 'The Abbot has been kind enough to extend me hospitality for some months now.'

I don't know which surprises me more: his command of English or the fact that he has been at the Abbey so long, without my knowing of it. But then Geoffrey's visits have been so few and fleeting lately.

The Abbot sits on the stool I offer him but Walter prefers to stand in front of the fire, warming his hands, his bulky figure blocking the heat from the flames. Why has Geoffrey brought him here?

I move closer to the Abbot, so that we can speak more privately. 'Is all well at the Abbey? I thought you might have come before Christmas.'

'All is as well as usual,' Geoffrey replies, getting up to join his kinsman by the hearth. 'We were at Westminster most of December.'

Walter turns to face me. 'At the Church Council called by the papal legate. Then at court.'

The parlour door opens and Margaret appears, carrying a tray with cups and a jug of wine. There is a plate of fig biscuits too and Walter eats with relish, taking one after the other without a pause.

'Abbot Geoffrey was representing St Albans at the Council, of course, and you …?' My eyes stray to his head. He seems very presumptuous, for a mere visiting monk.

'It has not yet been officially announced but Walter is to be made the new Abbot of Battle,' Geoffrey says. 'Warner, the last Abbot, resigned his office at the Council.'

The two men exchange looks and Walter laughs. Clearly there is more to this than they are prepared to divulge to me.

'May I offer my congratulations on your preferment,' I say, with a bow of my head, before addressing Geoffrey. 'How did you find Archbishop Thurstan at the Council? I hear that he has been ill.' I turn towards Walter to explain. 'The Archbishop was my patron and protector, long before your kinsman took an interest in our hermitage here.'

'Thurstan sent his apologies,' replies Geoffrey. 'I gather he is so weak that he has to be carried by litter these days. I fear his days on earth are numbered.'

This news grieves me and not just because of my affection for Thurstan. With the Archbishop dead and Geoffrey distancing himself, how would we be placed?

Walter de Luci's commanding voice breaks through my thoughts. 'But the Abbot has news of an honour of his own.'

'Yes? What honour is this?' I scrutinize Geoffrey's face, but cannot read what I see there.

'While we were at the Council, an emissary arrived from the Pope. He has called a great Council of all the Church, to be held in Rome – in April. It was not thought wise for all the bishops and abbots to go – not with the country at war and the Empress Matilda expected from France any time to further her claim.'

Walter breaks in. 'The Abbot is being modest. A small group is to go and Abbot Geoffrey was the first to be chosen.'

'To Rome?' I search out Geoffrey's eyes but he avoids my

gaze. 'You are asked to cross the Alps at the coldest time of the year?'

'It will be a pleasure to be at the papal court,' he replies, with spirit. 'I have many friends there. And there is talk that the Empress will try to submit her case before Pope Innocent, even though he has settled firmly on King Stephen. I would not miss that for the world.'

Walter laughs, launching again into the French dialect that is so hard to make out. Geoffrey answers in kind and they carry on an animated debate – I catch the name of Robert of Gloucester but little else.

I busy myself with the cups and the tray. Time when Geoffrey would have ridden down to me at the first opportunity to beg my prayers and my blessing, for much smaller enterprises than this. Another trip to Rome, and in the winter months. What if his fever were to flare up?

The debate ends and I sense that it is Walter who has pressed home his point. He takes up his cloak, as if they are about to go. Geoffrey steps towards me.

'We must make haste, Christina. The King's Christmas court is still in session and we have only returned to the Abbey so that Walter can make arrangements about his possessions. We are both expected at Canterbury in a few days, for the consecration of the new Archbishop.'

So Geoffrey has not come for advice then - only to crow.

'I am honoured that you found time to ride here, in that case.'

Geoffrey bows his head in acknowledgement. 'I'm sure that Walter would be grateful for your prayers and the prayers of your maidens on his election as abbot, as I would on this journey to Rome.'

'Indeed,' says Walter, who is now clad and ready.

They are waiting for a response but I am not inclined to be hurried. I look steadily into Geoffrey's face. 'And will you be requiring undershirts for the journey this time?'

Walter laughs. 'Undershirts? What is this, cousin?'

'It's nothing - just a jest.' I watch the colour rise from Geoffrey's neck and bloom on his cheeks.

'Farewell, Christina.'

Geoffrey turns on his heel and Walter proffers me his hand. 'Farewell, my lady.'

I wait till they are at the door before speaking again.

'I will continue to intercede for you, as always.' Geoffrey turns and I continue. 'The will of God will be fulfilled, whether you go or stay.'

Now that they have ridden away, I put another log on the fire and stare into the flames, my thoughts tumbling over one another. The noon meal must be over but I am too disturbed to eat, in any case. Another knock comes on the door of my parlour. Is it time for None already? Why has no-one rung the bell?

The door opens and there stands Geoffrey on the threshold, his face a mask of anger. I peer past him.

'Walter is waiting on the road,' he says. 'I came back for my gloves.'

I look behind me and, sure enough, his leather gloves are on the floor beside the stool where he sat. I fetch them and hand them to him. He makes no move to come into the room.

'What did you mean, to shame me before my kinsman?' His voice has an edge as sharp as a knife.

I am not cowed. 'How can the truth be shaming? You did once beg for my protection, did you not?'

He sidesteps this. 'And you made no promise to pray for Walter – you were barely polite to him.'

I know that I should hold my tongue, but I cannot. 'Why is this Walter so important? It has always been my counsel you have sought in secret, above that of all others. And now you say you wish to go to Rome - when before you were desperate to be excused. What if the fever returns on the journey?'

The chapel bell is sounding now for None and I usher him into the chamber and close the door, in case one of the girls passes by and hears our raised voices.

'I have no choice but to go.' He is pulling the gloves through his hands again and again, impatiently. 'And anyway, you don't understand. This time, it is different. The Pope has confirmed Stephen's right to the throne. Stephen has given concessions to the Church. There is no danger in the mission.'

He makes as if to go but then turns back and his face has softened, though now there is a shadow of fear in his eyes.

'Christina, I crave to know that this journey is in the will of God.'

I gaze at him and, suddenly, a thought comes to me. 'You left your gloves behind deliberately.' It is a statement, not a question, and he does not deny it.

'Will you not give me your blessing, and promise to intercede for me?'

Hearing his words, my heart begins to swell with a peace I have not tasted for a time.

'You may have forgotten me, these last months,' I say quietly, 'but I have not forgotten you. I have been interceding for you faithfully. And last week when I was at prayer, I saw a kind of enclosure surrounded by high fences. It was like a cloister but it was round and the grass in the centre was greener than

315

any earthly grass. You were there, Geoffrey, standing within the enclosure. I wondered how you would get out, for there were no doors, but then an answer came to me. *This enclosure that you see has but one doorkeeper, God, and that man cannot come out except by divine intervention.*

The Abbot is staring at me: his gaze, for once, steady and focused.

'I am looking now, with the eyes of my spirit and I see you there on the grass still, safe and happy. So, you see, I do not believe that you will be going to Rome.'

I smile, feeling the gentle flutter in my breast that tells me the Holy Spirit is hovering near. But Geoffrey catches me by the wrist, his grip punishingly tight. He raises his other hand and I think, for a moment, that he is going to whip my face with the leather gloves.

'No! It is not God who keeps me enclosed but you.' His eyes seem to bulge – dark and glittering even here, away from the firelight. I can't tell if he is enraged or terrified. 'I will go to the Council, whatever you say.'

He releases me and strides towards the door. He does not look back.

# Chapter 32

*Hermitage de bosco*

*Sixth day of February, AD 1141*

A sudden yowling tears through the night and I am instantly awake. The unearthly screeching comes again and now I know the sound for what it is - only the kitchen cats brawling. I turn on the narrow mattress to relieve the ache in my hip and pull the fur more closely around my neck. The air is bitterly cold.

The last shreds of sleep fall away, leaving the dread that stalks me, these winter nights: as if the Enemy himself were standing beside me, jeering in my ear. Intimations of death seem to crowd into my chamber, like so many impatient creditors, not to be denied their due. It was Candlemas, and cold like this, when Gregory first fell ill. And only last year, around this time, that news came to us of Thurstan's passing.

I lie shivering, fear grabbing me by the throat. Abbot Geoffrey has not ridden here since the autumn, and he came precious few times over the summer. It seems he has lost

317

faith in my seeing. How long before he withdraws all his support? There are many at the Abbey who think ill of me. And with Archbishop Thurstan gone, what will happen to us then?

I close my eyes, my lips moving as if by themselves. *Mary, Queen of Heaven, defend me from all perils and dangers of this night, for the love of your Son. Mary, Queen of Heaven, defend me from all perils and dangers of this night, for the love of your Son.*

But the words are empty, a mockery. Even as I try to pray, my thoughts are not looking to heaven for comfort. Instead they are taking their old, shameful shape and are flying back to the north country, long ago, to Athelwulf's house in Pocklinton. To his chamber and that delicious, sinful embrace. The Enemy at my side is laughing but I take no heed, intent now on pleasure, since it seems that all else is lost. I remember Athelwulf's breath on my face, his hair, his hand guiding mine. Every movement of his body against mine is as clear as if it were yesterday, not twenty years ago. I feel the fire of lust quickening and taking hold in my aging body.

But now someone is ringing the bell for Matins and I hear footsteps outside, as the maidens make their way to the chapel. A terrible, bitter weariness descends upon me as I think of the day ahead. I turn to face the wall and close my eyes, waiting for the knock on my door.

When it comes at last, my sister does not wait for an answer but enters. Seeing me still in my bed, she hurries across, all concern. 'What is it, Christina? Are you sick? Is it your old malady?'

I cannot suppress a sigh. Now that she says it, I notice that my left arm and leg are cold and numb. Perhaps she is right.

318

Margaret is waiting for an answer but the effort of opening my mouth seems too much.

'You take my place, Margaret,' I say at last. She is peering at me closely, trying to see into my soul.

'What shall I tell the others?'

'Tell them I am sick.' Still she stands there, so I turn my face to the wall. 'For pity's sake, leave me.'

At last, I hear my sister's footsteps and the door closing behind her.


I wake to the gentle touch of a hand on my shoulder. Opening my eyes, I see they have sent Emmy to me. They know her peaceful presence comforts me when I am mired in the pit of despair. But just now she has an urgent look in her eyes.

'The Abbot has come, Mistress. Are you well enough to see him?'

Geoffrey? After all this time. Why today of all days? I drag myself off the bed, taking the tunic that Emmy holds out to me.

'Show him to my parlour. I will join him there.' She hurries to the door. 'And make sure the fire is lit and he has been offered refreshment.'

My heart beat thuds in my ears as I dress, but walking along the passage to the parlour the feeling starts to return to my leg - as if the blood is beginning to flow once again.

Geoffrey is standing in front of the fire, still in his riding cloak, warming his hands by the feeble flames. Hearing me come in, he turns and quickly signs a blessing. Before I have had time to respond, he launches into speech.

'I bring news,' he says 'Perhaps you have heard already –Robert of Gloucester rode against Stephen at Lincoln. The

319

King has been captured.'

'Captured?' It is hard to take this in. 'By the forces of the Empress? Are they spread so far north?'

'Stephen gave the castle at Lincoln to Ranulf of Chester – only last year. But now he has come out for Matilda.'

Geoffrey's dark eyes are darting about the room in his agitation.

'Lincoln is laid waste – the citizens have fled or been taken, along with the King.'

'Where is the King? What will they do with him?'

'No-one knows. Bishop Alexander has heard nothing. But they say the King surrendered to Robert himself - perhaps he will take him to Gloucester. The Empress is there.'

I am trying to make sense of what this means. Geoffrey is intimate with the Bishop of Lincoln. What does this mean for him? And who will rule the land if Stephen is in captivity? Surely the Empress can't become Queen while the King still lives.

These questions pass through my mind but they seem to belong to a distant sphere and I can't quite keep hold of them. It's a matter much closer to home that burns in my heart.

'It is many months since you were here,' I venture.

'What?' The Abbot looks at me, his brow furrowed in surprise.

I can't keep the bitterness from my voice. 'Did you not think to visit all this time?'

He seems astonished by my censure. 'Lady Christina, surely you are not so hidden here in the woods that news has not reached you? The whole country is in flux. Cornwall, Devon, Somerset – they're all in the hands of the Empress. There is fighting everywhere – the earls and barons take whatever they want. I have been obliged to travel all this last year to secure the Abbey's holdings.'

I cannot think how to reply and cross to the little table to pour some wine. I hand him a cup.

'Will you not take off your cloak? Perhaps you might stay to say Mass for us.'

'I can't delay, Christina - there is much to do. I have to go to the Bishop. We need to decide how to place ourselves, now that the King is taken. Matilda will pursue her claim to the throne now and seek the blessing of the Church. We mustn't be found on the wrong side.'

He puts his cup down and moves closer to me, staring into my face as if to read there what he needs to know. 'Tell me, has God revealed anything to you? What does your spirit tell you – will the Empress prevail or should we remain loyal to the King? It's still possible he will escape.'

All these cold months of winter I have waited for him to come. To seek my advice, to ask for my prayers. And now he has come and I have nothing to offer him. I search my soul but there is no knowing, no certainty, nothing but an abyss of guilt and dejection.

'Well? Can you not at least answer me?'

I venture a glance upward and there are his eyes – glittering with anger. I know him well enough to know that his anger is born of fear, but still I can't conjure words from emptiness.

'If you will not speak, then I shall return to the Abbey,' he says, reaching for his riding crop. 'But there is no knowing when I shall return.'

At the door he hears the odd, choking cry that has escaped from my mouth and turns back. I have started sobbing, for all the world as if I were a girl again. Tears are rolling down my cheeks. He stares at me, aghast, then walks back. He is uneasy, his movements awkward.

'What is it? Don't upset yourself,' he says. 'Let me call for someone.'

I can only shake my head, amidst the tears. He fetches a stool and helps me down onto it, then stands over me, frowning. At last he speaks.

'Forgive me – perhaps I was too hasty. I am thinking now of old Evisandus and what he said that day. Do you remember?'

I think of the wise old man of God and at once I feel calmer. I remember him gently rubbing the Gold of Pleasure between his fingers, to extract the oil.

'He said that I should approach you with kindness.' Geoffrey smiles ruefully. 'And not hastily, as I have done today.'

I am undone by the change in him, by the gentleness in his voice. All at once, I long for him to be undeceived – to know the whole truth of what I am.

'Geoffrey, I cannot give you the answers you need. I …'

'No, of course,' he breaks in. 'Forgive my impatience. I must give you time to pray.'

'But that is not all!' The need to unburden myself is like a flame, taking hold amidst tinder, growing stronger with every moment. 'I am not worthy of your trust. God cannot reveal his secrets to one such as me – one so unholy.'

He sighs. 'Those who are the purest always protest their imperfection. Was it not St Paul who called himself the chief of sinners?'

He fetches another stool from the hearth and sits down beside me.

'Do you think I would risk censure by coming here if I did not have every confidence in your sanctity?'

'But you don't know...

He cuts me off before I can finish. 'I know well enough. I know that when the fever came upon me, those two times, you prayed and I recovered. And when Stephen chose me to go to Rome, you were shown that it would come to nothing.' His lips twist in a wry smile. 'Even when I was determined to go to the papal court.'

I listen to his words and there is no denying the truth of them. Despair begins to loosen its grip on my thoughts.

'Christina. I ask you only to intercede for me and the Abbey in these perilous times. I will return before I meet with the Bishop, to see if God has shown you anything.'

He gets up to leave now, less agitated than when he came in: as if his own words have reassured him. He glances around the room.

'You know if there is anything you need, you have only to send to me.' His eyes alight on my face once again. 'It would be easier for me to help you if the hermitage were to come under the Benedictine Rule. How would you like to be made Prioress?'

I can only stare at him.

'Well, that is not a matter for now,' he says, opening the door. 'But be sure to pray and I will come again soon.'

*Later that day, at table*

Margaret turns to me. 'It's good to see you looking better.'

I smile back at her. 'I feel my strength returning.'

It's true and perhaps that is why I have ordered honey to

323

be brought as a treat, for us to have with our bread at supper. Further down the bench, there is laughter. It sounds as if Adelaisa is in good spirits too.

Matilda sits across the table from me, chewing her bread daintily. You would not need to hear her speak to know that she comes of noble stock. Everything she does has a French nicety to it. I know that the others feel a little in awe of her, even now. My eyes stray to Godit, next to her. They are like chalk and cheese. Whatever Godit does, there is an awkwardness to it, a rashness that is tiresome to see. That is why I insist that she sits beside Matilda at meals, to learn from her.

Godit has wolfed her bread, as usual, and is frowning down at her lap, lost in thought. Margaret starts to say something but I don't hear the words. Instead it is as if God has opened a door for me into Godit's mind and suddenly I am privy to her thoughts and what I see is not to my liking.

'Do not do it, Godit!' I say sharply.

The others fall into silence and she looks up at me in shock. 'What, Mistress?'

'What you were thinking of just then.' All eyes at the table are on us.

'But I was not thinking of anything that is forbidden,' she says. Even now she seems to have no shame.

'Come here to me,' I say, and she climbs out from the bench and walks around to me, forgetting to curtsey in her nervousness. I am minded to speak out in front of the others to teach her a lesson but I decide to spare her.

'Come closer,' I say, 'and let me speak privily.'

She bends down and I whisper in her ear.

'You were thinking of the ivory comb that Matilda has in

324

her cell. And how you might be able to steal it from her. I am right, am I not?'

The young woman's flaming cheeks give me all the answer I need. She drops to her knees beside me.

'Lady Christina, I beg you,' she whispers, 'not to tell the others. I did not do it - I would never have done it. I only thought about it.'

The others are all staring. 'Get on with your supper,' I say to them, before turning back to Godit. I speak quietly.

'This time, I will say nothing. But remember, God does not see only our actions. He sees the desires of our hearts.'

# Chapter 33

*Hermitage de bosco*

*Twenty-sixth day of January, AD 1145*

I let Father Thomas sit in Roger's chair because it is more comfortable for his back, and he needs the slope for writing down what I tell him. After all our times together, I think he still baulks at taking the chair while I sit on a stool, but it's good for him to take the pre-eminent place. And good for me, perhaps, to take the lower place. The side of my body away from the flames is chilled, despite the good fire crackling in the hearth. Father Thomas answers my question.

'The composition is going well,' he says. 'I have written about your childhood and the years when you were in hiding. And how you first came to know Abbot Geoffrey. All that is complete.'

I imagine him in the scriptorium at St Albans, bent over his writing table. It still seems strange to me that all the richness of my life can be rendered into something that lies inert, at the Abbey, on a piece of vellum.

He looks across at me. 'What I need now – I think I said it last time – is to show something more of your sanctity. Your visions and how you receive them.'

Thomas has always been awed by my seeings. But he seems less interested in what I am shown and more in how it is given to me, though this is of little concern to me.

He takes up an old, used piece of parchment and turns it over to the back, then picks up his quill pen, ready to take notes.

'For instance,' he suggests, 'have you ever been privileged to see our Lord himself, in a vision?'

I can't control the little smile that escapes my lips. 'I have, and perhaps not only in a vision.'

As the import of my words dawns on him, Father Thomas's eyes widen in surprise.

'Tell me, Mistress Christina,' he says, his pen poised above the parchment.

I rest my back against the wall to ease the aching in my hip, and think back to the first time the man came, last autumn, as the beeches were turning russet brown.

'A pilgrim came to the hermitage last year. He was not from any of the houses we know – nor a hermit I think - and yet such goodness shone from him.'

'How old was he? What did he look like?'

I try to picture him. 'He was not young but not old either. His features were pleasing and he had a beard, still dark, I remember that. There was no grey.'

'Did he stay long?' Thomas asks.

'Not the first time. But then he came again, some weeks later. He prayed with me and we talked together. I tell you truly, Thomas, listening to him speak of the scriptures, I felt quickened somehow, filled with the zeal of God.'

Thomas is scratching away at the parchment. He looks up and I continue.

'Margaret was there with me that time. We asked him to stay and eat so that he could speak with me again.'

'And with your sister?'

'No. She was busy - overseeing the preparation of the meal.'

'Just like Jesus at the house of Mary and Martha,' says Thomas, triumphantly.

I look at him and feel a prickling along the length of my neck. I had not thought of that, but he is right.

'We talked all the way through the meal. Our converse was so full of God and his works and his ways - I think we hardly touched the food. I remember there was fish sitting on his plate and I encouraged him to eat it, but he refused. He said that he ate only enough to keep body and soul together.'

Father Thomas is looking at me closely. 'What happened then?'

'He blessed us and took his leave. We talked about him often then, my sister and I, wishing he would return. But he didn't come again. Then, do you remember, I was taken sick just before Christmas?'

'I heard something about it.'

'Of course, you did not visit us here during the Feast – your leg was troubling you so you couldn't ride. Father Gervase came to say Mass in your place.'

Thomas looks a little embarrassed; he does not like to be reminded that he is getting old. 'Go on,' he says.

'I was lying sick in my bed on Christmas Eve, too weak to attend the vigil. Some brothers had come to say the hour with me and I was dozing on and off but then I heard them say the words: *Today ye shall know that the Lord will come and tomorrow ye shall see his glory.* As soon as I heard that, I was wide awake. I knew that God had spoken to me.'

Thomas puts down his pen. 'Can you explain, Christina? How did you know it was God?'

He looks at me intently. There is no challenge in his question, only curiosity. I try to think how I can best describe it. 'It was as if the words had an extra depth and roundness - as if they were giving off a kind of warmth that I could feel. Anyhow, I knew with certainty that I would see the glory of the Lord on the morrow. All that night, I tossed and turned, wondering how it was to happen. Then, early in the morning – I had asked that the doors of the church should be kept open for me to hear the maidens singing at Matins – I heard the anthem *Christ is born*. And at that very moment, the pain went and I knew I was well.'

I see that Thomas's eyes are shining, his soft, fleshy face radiating reverence and fellow feeling. He is easily moved to tears.

'But that was only the beginning. It was as they sang the *Te Deum* - I felt myself borne away to the church at St Albans and it was as if I were standing on the steps of the lectern, you know, where the lessons are read at Matins. I looked down and there, in the midst of the quire, was a man. He was watching the monks around him at their singing. I don't know how I knew but it was clear to me that he was pleased with them. And, Thomas, he was such a man! He wore a golden crown, encrusted with jewels. It had a cross on the top and fillets hanging down on either side, worked with such skill and delicacy.'

Tears are pricking at the corners of my own eyes as I think

of it. 'I remember. The vision was so clear that I could see something - what seemed like drops of dew - on the surface of the emeralds.'

Thomas is wide-eyed. 'Were you in the body or out of it?' His voice is quiet with awe.

'I don't know. I have thought about it many times since. It was so vivid. But then a vision can be very distinct, can't it?'

He only shakes his head in wonder. I walk over to the little table to pour us each a cup of wine and to warm myself by the fire. Then I return to my stool.

'I got up from my bed when it was light and told Margaret that I was well. Then, Adelaisa brought news that the pilgrim had returned and wished to celebrate Christmas with us! It was as if my cup of joy had been filled to overflowing. I led the maidens in the procession - our first Christmas in the new church – and all the villagers who joined us were following on behind, and the pilgrim too. He was there all through the Mass – I watched him.'

'After it was over, I led the procession out and waited at the door to speak to him but he didn't come. Someone said he had stayed to pray in the church so I sent Matilda in to invite him to break the fast with us.' I feel the goose bumps rising on my skin, even in the retelling. 'She couldn't find him anywhere.'

Thomas is leaning forward in his chair. 'Could he have left through another door?'

I shake my head. 'The side door is not yet in use – the masons have boarded up the opening until the door is made and fitted. The only door is the great one and Margaret herself locked it once we were inside and only opened it when the service was over.'

Thomas draws in his breath and a stillness falls in my parlour, as if gentle hands had draped a coverlet of fur over us both. The crackle of flames in the hearth has died down to a hissing and whispering. Outside, from over by the duckpen, I hear the rasping call of the drake.

Father Thomas looks at me, then begins to speak in the voice he uses when he gives a sermon at Mass.

'Lady Christina, there can be no doubt. The pilgrim was either an angel or...' He pauses to sign himself with the cross. 'Or our Lord himself. You may recall how in the gospel, the disciples encountered Christ as a stranger on the road to Emmaus and as he talked, their hearts burned within them. And then when they asked him to stay and eat, he blessed the food and gave them to eat but would not eat himself, just like your pilgrim. I believe that our Lord Jesus chose to reveal himself to you, first in a vision, and then in the guise of a mortal man, as he did to the disciples. You are indeed a privileged soul.'

I see that Thomas's hand is shaking as he takes up the pen once more.

*Hermitage de bosco*

*Twentieth day of February, AD 1145*

I cannot bear the love and pity in Emmy's eyes: how they follow me everywhere. All through the funeral service when I stood in front of them, adamant, lifeless as a statue. Emmy and the others think it is simple grief - they do not see the

331

fear. I feel Death circling above me, a carrion crow, waiting to pounce and carry me into the next life, unshriven. Not in all the years of hiding, when I was in danger, did I feel terror such as this. As if my skin has been flayed from me and I am left cowering and defenceless. There is only one thought in my mind, now that Margaret has been laid to rest in the ground. I must make my confession. Nothing must be kept back to fester and poison me from within. Father Thomas should know what I am and Geoffrey, too. Oh why must the Abbot be away at court, when my sister has died?

I run from the weeping maidens, from the pile of freshly-turned earth, and escape to my parlour. I give the servant instructions that no-one is to be let in except Father Thomas. At last he finishes his priestly duties and comes to me. The sight of his kindly, round face is more of a blessing than any words could be.

'Father, I wish to make confession,' I say, my voice tight and strained. 'Now, if you please.'

He takes both my hands in his. 'My lady, you are exhausted with grief. I see it in your eyes. Your confession can wait.'

He leads me to Roger's chair and helps me into it. I notice how old he looks today, the skin around his eyes wrinkled and red as if he, too, has been crying.

'She was righteous – my sister – truly righteous. Why has God taken her? She was not yet an old woman.'

Thomas brings a stool and sits close by me.

'Would it help to tell me how it happened? I know only that there was an accident.'

I recoil from thinking of these last two days of nightmare, but I must not hide any longer from pain.

'I told her it was too wet to go to Sopwell – I knew the track

332

would be a sea of mud.'

'Margaret went to visit Avicia?'

'She took some provisions because the women there have nothing compared with us. That's why she took the cart. If only she had gone on horseback!'

'Was it the cart that turned over?'

'It was the mud. I told her not to go till the ground was dry. But she would go.'

A sob twists itself in my chest. 'Even then, if it had been just a fall … but the ox …'

I cannot bear to think of the heavy beast, wild with confusion, its powerful hindleg, the hoof crushing down against my sister's fragile ribs.

Father Thomas is wiping the tears from his eyes. 'And Matilda told me that she breathed her last here, at the hermitage?' His voice is as gentle as a child's.

'Yes – they brought her back to me. I sent for Father Ralph but there was nothing to be done. How can I go on?'

It is not only the loss. My heart is racing, driven along by fear. Death could take me at any moment, just as it did my poor sister. She had no reason to fear; her soul was blameless. I know that she has been welcomed straight into the presence of God and I am glad for it.

I become aware of Thomas speaking.

'Your parents?' he is asking. 'No doubt they will be here soon to comfort you. Are they able still to ride?'

I stare at him, a fresh wave of horror rising inside me, catching in my throat, stealing my breath. I had not thought of them. Not once.

'I cannot see them,' I blurt out at last and see at once the shock written on Thomas's face. 'They came before – when

Gregory died. I will not see them.'

I am back there, in the hall of the Abbey guesthouse, the day after my brother was buried. The ugly, bent couple. My mother and father.

'She told me I should speak to them – she said so.'

'She?' Thomas seems at a loss.

'Margaret. She knew it was fitting – but I closed my heart to them.'

The old priest takes my hand again, as if to offer comfort that I do not deserve. I shake it free.

'She always knew, my sister. She was the one who was pure in heart, and I was too proud to listen to her.'

That look she would give me, her eyes clear and untroubled. Then the humble turning away, the silence. Sometimes, she would even speak out – especially if it concerned Godit. She always defended the girl.

'Once, at dinner, I reproved Godit in front of the guests. I knew – I saw it in the spirit – that she had defied me and picked the purslane where I told her not to. And afterwards, my sister came to me and said I had been wrong.'

'I remember it. I ate dinner with you that day.'

I look up at Thomas sharply. 'You were there? Then you know how I treated Godit. I was not so harsh with her, was I? She was disobedient. I had told them all to accept nothing from that village woman's garden. She denied me a sprig of chervil, once, when I asked for it.'

To my consternation, I see that Thomas is smiling.

'Godit was in the wrong. I had to reprove her, didn't I?'

Thomas will not meet my gaze. He deliberately looks away, for all the world as if he had become my sister.

'Well? Answer me, Thomas.'

He speaks quietly and I can hear how much care he is taking with his words. 'Perhaps it was not necessary to point out her fault in front of us all.'

An unbearable weight seems to press down upon me.

'But I am the one charged with the souls of the women here – not you, not Margaret. If I do not reprove them, how will they learn? And her fault was shown to me by God. What was I to do?'

The priest's face is changing: its usual ruddy colour fading. I give him no time to reply.

'You always did take Margaret's part. I saw you – whispering with her in the passage. You think I didn't notice? She was always asking, 'when is he coming, when is Father Thomas coming?' I think she loved you more than she loved me, her own sister.'

Thomas has recovered himself a little. He places a hand on my arm, all gentleness and solicitude, but I am angry now and sore at heart.

'Lady Christina, why do you not take a rest? These last terrible days have taken their toll. Perhaps, after that, I can hear your confession.'

'No.' I rise to my feet and walk across to the shelf, turning the page of the psalter over, to today's psalm. I will not humble myself before this man.

'Father Thomas, I will not detain you here any longer. You will be wanting to return to the Abbey. As you say, I need to rest.'

# Chapter 34

*New church*

*Priory of the Holy Trinity de bosco*

*Twelfth day of May, AD 1145*

The service of consecration is nearly over. My companions stand tall in a row beside me, a line of grey in their new habits, their familiar features tempered by awe. How could I not be proud of them? Behind us, a great congregation fills the new church. The air, usually so cool, feels stuffy and thick with the presence of so many bodies. I look down to where my carmine cowl drapes in folds at my collar bone and, once again, I trace with my finger the ornamental stitching along the edge of the hood. It is so fine that no-one but me can see it. The cowl is heavy for such an unseasonably warm day. Under the layers of fabric I feel a fierce heat begin to gather beneath my sagging breasts and spread out across my body and up to my neck and my face. This sudden warming comes to me often now. It is not till the end of the *Deo gratias* that the heat begins to dissipate, leaving me cool and even shivering a little.

Bishop Alexander stands in front of the altar, magnificent in his cope of lapis lazuli and elder green. He pronounces the blessing but does not dismiss the congregation. Instead he proceeds across to the table that has been placed to the side of the nave. Behind me, there is the shuffling of feet on the stone floor. A murmur of talk begins to rise. Now a clerk comes forward, carrying some documents and a quill and ink, and places them on the table.

At a sign from the Bishop, those who are to witness the charter start to gather around the table. I reach up to my forehead to check for any stray hairs. The lustrous copper hair of my youth is faded but it is not quite grey, not yet. I walk forward to join them, the only woman amongst this group of eminent churchmen, but I hold my head high. If it were not for me, these great men would not have gathered here today.

Bishop Alexander has brought his Dean from Lincoln, and there are two, no three, Archdeacons. Robert, the Prior of Merton, has come and now I see that he has brought Father Rainald with him – how I wish Margaret could be here to witness this! She used to love it when Rainald would visit and entertain us with his stories. I have never known anyone who could make her laugh like him.

Dean Ralph of St Pauls nods gravely to me. He had one of his canons lay their gift upon the altar before the consecration. I bow my head in acknowledgement, grateful beyond words that these woods I love have been granted to our community in perpetuity. I look across the table; some of the priests' faces I do not recognize. Then I see Abbot Geoffrey, the one

337

representative of St Albans.

We stand, grouped around the table, as Bishop Alexander takes up the quill pen to make his mark on the foundation charter. I had thought that we might each have to sign it but instead the clerk is taking note of the names of the witnesses. One by one, we are called forward to have sight of the parchment. It states that the Bishop confirms the agreement made between us and the canons of St Pauls, saving the rights of his own bishopric of Lincoln. And that he has this day consecrated our new church, dedicated to the Holy Trinity. I feel a prickling behind my nose but I will not weep, not in front of all these people.

Now, as if from nowhere, a knot of unease pulls me up short, like a snag in the thread when I am sewing. Roger. Is he looking down from heaven and watching us? I can see his weathered face, the eyes burning with purity. *Where is the rough chapel I built with my own hands, a circle with no end and no beginning, like the love of God? What has happened to my simple dwelling, hidden away from the snares of the world and the Church?*

I look around at this church, built in the Norman style, the richly-clad Churchmen. Disturbed, I glance across to where Geoffrey stands, splendid in his Abbot's mitre. I remind myself of that long debate we had, back in the winter, and try to comfort myself. I did not concede on the most important point, at least. The Abbey will have no power over who joins our community. As Prioress, I and those who come after me will have the final word. He was reluctant but he surrendered at the last. It's a blessing that we are beholden to St Paul's for the land, not St Albans, for St Paul's is far away in London. My eyes search the congregation for Avicia and her nuns from

Sopwell. They have not been so fortunate. Abbot Geoffrey means to have strict control of the house he is founding for them.

It is gratifying to see so many friends in the congregation. Emmy catches my eye and smiles, more diffident than usual among this great throng. It gladdens my heart whenever I see her. She is so patient with the new girls and such a pure vessel for the Holy Spirit. She is a daughter to me – as they all are, my daughters in Christ. I straighten my neck and adopt a calm pose: no longer merely their mistress, but Prioress of Holy Trinity de bosco.

The signing over, Bishop Alexander dismisses the congregation. The doors are thrown open and there is a hubbub as people begin to make their way towards them. The warm, dry weather means that the servants can lay the victuals out in the open air. This morning, they erected a trestle on the grass and I instructed them to fasten a great piece of canvas from the branches at the edge of the clearing, to provide shade. Watching them do it, an old memory came to me: standing with my father at Wisbech and watching the billowing sails of his ships, as they left harbour.

We cannot all leave the church at once and, waiting in the blocked aisle, Geoffrey makes his way over to me. I bow my head in greeting but he does not seem quite himself; he is distracted. His breathing seems laboured too.

'You will have many guests to host tonight at the Abbey,' I say, to make conversation. 'I take it Dean Ralph and the others from London will be staying. And I saw the Archdeacon of Buckingham and the Bishop of Limerick – surely they must lodge at the Abbey.'

A spasm of disquiet passes across Geoffrey's face. 'Not at

the Abbey,' he replies. 'I will be hosting them at Westwick.'

'Westwick? Your brother-in-law's house?'

The Abbot nods, then looks up at me with a sardonic smile. He keeps his voice low.

'He cannot gainsay me in this matter, but I would rather not rile him any more than is necessary.'

It takes me a moment to understand whom he is referring to. 'The Prior?'

'Him and all his faction. They are angered by my gift to you and this house.'

Tendrils of guilt wrap themselves around me. Geoffrey has been very generous, diverting the tithes from Cashio and from Watford for our support. I know that there are those at the Abbey who seek to discredit him wherever they can.

Geoffrey is looking around at the congregation – so many hermits and recluses who have come from near and far to be with us for the consecration. The sour note in his voice becomes more marked.

'Perhaps my gift was not so much needed after all,' he says.

I am filled with soft feeling. 'My beloved Abbot, where would we be without your support? You know that my nuns and I will always be indebted to you.'

He dismisses my words with a haughty look but I can tell that he is mollified, nonetheless.

*Christina's cell*

*Priory of the Holy Trinity de bosco*

## Fourteenth day of May, AD 1145

The spell of dry weather has broken and a spring rain is pattering against the window of my cell. One of the monks will come from the Abbey today to say Mass. I miss Father Thomas and our times together but until he returns from Paris we must make do with whomever we are sent. Geoffrey tells me that the work on our book can be completed when he returns.

I kneel at the prie dieu and pick up my beads, my soul recognizing these familiar actions of the body and settling itself for prayer. My hands reach for the psalter and all at once I remember that Geoffrey has had new pages written and inserted, to mark the founding of the Priory. Carefully turning over the leaves that contain my beloved pictures, I come to the last one, of King David playing his viol. I lift the square of velvet that protects it and admire, for the hundredth time, the intricate design on the lining of his cloak. The new pages have been inserted here. Geoffrey told me that he copied them himself, in the scriptorium. I am eager to see what he has chosen as his gift to me.

The first new page is illustrated; there is a man, a woman, a ship, but who is depicted here? I read the titles: *Blessed Alexis, chosen youth ... Behold blessed Alexis received onto the ship.* It is the story of St Alexis. The text begins, the lines alternating between red and blue ink. Geoffrey writes with a fair hand - but it's in French! I feel a spasm of irritation. He knows that French does not come easily to me. He could just as well have written it in Latin. And why has he given me the story of the virginal St Alexis, when St Cecilia is much dearer to my heart? I know why - Alexis is venerated at St Albans. I remember standing in the chapel at the Abbey, and Geoffrey telling me that it was Bishop Ranulf Flambard who paid for it and dedicated it to the chaste saint, back in the time of King Henry. I think of the lewd bishop, laid out on the bed at my aunt's house, trying to trap me into wickedness, and cannot help a wry smile.

I turn the pages, so many of them covered in writing. How did Geoffrey find time to copy this out? I suppose I must show him the appropriate gratitude. Now at last comes something I can readily understand. It's a letter of Pope Gregory to Secundinus the hermit – and then more French lettering below. There are exquisite red and green curlicues in the capitals. But why has Geoffrey copied all this in French? To make me learn it, perhaps, as if he were the schoolmaster again and I were one of his pupils.

I turn the leaves, and at last come to another picture. It is the two disciples on the road to Emmaus after the resurrection, and there is Christ, walking with them. I peer at it closely and now, with delight, I see why Geoffrey had this painted. Our Lord is dressed as a pilgrim. He has the hat and the bag and the staff of a pilgrim, just as when he appeared to me and to Margaret. How apt! Turning over the page, I see Jesus at supper with the two disciples and then his body disappearing as he ascends into heaven. The indigos, the greens, the rose madder reds shine out from the vellum. A fish with blue stripes on its skin lies in a bowl on the supper table. How has the painter got that colour for the bowl? It is pale but a true yellow, not like the birch bark dye I use for my threads. I love the picture. But why did he not have Jesus depicted at the house at Bethany, with Mary sitting at his feet? That would have been a gift indeed.

There is more to see over the page but now comes a tap on the door of my cell. Perhaps the priest has arrived early from the Abbey.

'What is it?' I ask. The women know not to disturb me when I am at prayer.

Adelaisa answers. 'Your sister is here, my lady.'

A shiver runs through me. Meg is dead and buried in her plot under the plum tree. It comes to me that she must mean my younger sister, Matilda.

'Show her into the parlour, Ada. I will see her there.'

Rising from the prayer stool, I walk up and down a little in the cell till my knees have lost their stiffness. I don't want to appear like an old woman to my sister, though she is no longer young herself. Last time she visited me at the hermitage, I spied a few grey hairs among her dark curls and her children are all grown and married.

When I open the door to my parlour, I see that Matilda has taken off her wet riding cloak and thrown it across Roger's chair, where it will drip on the embroidered seat. She always did act without thinking but I love her none the less.

She comes forward to greet me and I sign her with a blessing. 'It has been too long, Sister,' she says, 'since we saw each other last.'

'You are always welcome here, Tilda. You know that,' I reply.

'And now there are only the two of us left,' she says.

So she heard about Margaret's death. Why didn't she come before? Though they make their living in the world, my sister and her husband are devout. They hoped their younger son might enter a monastery but he would not.

343

'I hope my nephews are well and my niece. How are things in Huntingdon? Is there still enough call for the dying of wool?'

Matilda looks grave. 'Tostig has had to let his men go, all except for two. Business is bad. You would not know the town if you came there now.'

My sister looks around the parlour, her eyes drawn to the hanging on the wall by the door.

'Did you make that, Christina? It's beautiful.'

It is the Queen of Heaven on a throne, her robe worked in thread of blue woad. It still gives me pleasure, though I hung it at least a year ago, maybe two. Is it that long since Matilda was last here?

'Would you like to see the new church?' I ask. 'It was consecrated by the Bishop just two days ago.'

She nods her head. 'We heard that the hermitage was to become a Priory and you a Prioress.'

I move towards the door but she does not follow.

'I'll show you the church first and then send for some refreshment.'

Matilda looks down at the floor and I sense the difficulty between us rise up and start to fill the room. I know what is on her mind, but I will not ask. She must speak of them first.

'The news of Father is not good,' she says. 'He cannot walk any more to the market, or to church.'

To my surprise, I discover some small relief to hear news of them. When no-one came from Huntingdon after Margaret died, I thought they might be dead. I take a deep breath.

'Can the physicker do nothing for him?' I ask.

She shakes her head. 'Nor the surgeon neither. They say it is his great age that brings on the pain.'

Matilda grasps my hand in her impulsive way.

'They are in trouble, Christina,' she says. 'Will you not help them, now that you have risen so high? Surely you have land settled upon the Priory that brings a good income?'

Inside my chest, it feels as if there are wires being drawn tight. 'Does Father not have the rent from our old house to live on?'

'Didn't you know? He had to sell it, to pay off his debts. The money is almost gone.'

I do not want to hear this. The house where I was happy as a child, lived in by strangers. I feel a surge of anger.

'So why do you and your husband not help them? Can't they live with you?'

'They do. They have been with us this twelvemonth, but since the troubles we have little enough to spare.'

I look directly into Matilda's face, which is reddening with shame at having to beg. But is she telling me the truth? I cannot conceive of Auti of Huntingdon, the great merchant, being reduced to poverty.

'What about Father's ships – the imports from the Lowlands?'

My sister releases my hand and turns away. 'You don't understand, Dora. Our brother sold off the ships long ago. He sells cloth now for another man, and makes precious little for himself.'

Our half-brother, Simon. He was kind to me that terrible night when Father would have thrown me out into the street. After all they did to me, how do my parents presume to send Matilda now, asking for help?

Matilda turns back. 'I wanted to come,' she says quietly.

I look at her, uncomprehending.

'When we heard about Meg and the accident. But Alice was birthing again and I promised to be with her.'

'Alice? She has had another child?' My niece already has a brood of children.

'He was born breech and lived only a few days.' Matilda's eyes are brimming with tears.

'I'm sorry to hear of it, truly. Give my condolences to Alice.'

'Thank you, I will.' She looks at me and her voice drops still further. 'Tell me, about Meg - did she suffer?'

I close my eyes, wanting to erase the memory of those few days. 'She never spoke from when they brought her back, until the time she died. But she was in great pain.'

Matilda reaches out to embrace me. There are no words spoken but her care is like a healing balm being rubbed into my skin. My little sister! I cling to her.

'I will see what can be done to help our parents,' I say at last, pulling away.

I cannot mistake the relief that spreads across Tilda's face.

'But only because the scriptures tell us to honour our father and mother. I cannot forget how cruelly they treated me.'

'They are truly sorry for it now,' she replies, 'we all are.'

I look at her carefully. She seems to be sincere but I cannot be sure. I lead the way to the door. 'I will arrange for some relief and send word soon. Come now, and let me show you our new church.'

# Chapter 35

*Hospital of St Julian for leprous men*

*Kingesho, near St Albans*

*Twenty-sixth day of February, AD 1146*

Abbot Geoffrey opens the garden gate and ushers me through, onto the path. The beds are mostly bare, of course, but for the rows of leek and the colewort.

'Master Ilbert plans to have more ground dug this spring,' Geoffrey explains. 'The brothers must have wholesome food.'

I wrap my cloak more closely round me and look up. A cold wind is sending clouds scudding across a wan winter sky. The sun comes out and for the first time I sense spring, biding her time at the margins, ready to come in like a flood.

Geoffrey takes my arm and, walking beside him, I hear his breath coming fast and uneven. He is growing old. We have crossed into the herbarium now and I pluck a tip of rosemary and rub the pungent leaves between my fingers.

'Is there any remedy for the men's sores?'

Since the Abbot had this hospital built, I have thought often of the afflicted men who live here and their holy suffering.

'The Infirmarian makes them a tincture of pennyroyal but it doesn't have much effect, only on the open wounds. There is nothing to be done but to provide shelter and to tend their souls.'

'How many men are housed here at present?'

'A score. A new man took the oath only last week. He leaves a wife behind in the world, and children.'

I pause, trying to compass in my mind the torment they must suffer.

'Here he will be fed and clothed. The Abbey is generous – even today I have money to give Master Ilbert, for shoes for the men. A great deal of leather is needed.'

I look at him, puzzled.

'They must wear long boots to protect their feet.' He looks away. 'Though some of them have little enough flesh left to protect.'

I wince at his words.

'The hospital is a costly venture, all around. We have had to hire women from the town - the men's clothes must be washed twice weekly. And, of course, the lepers cannot work with their hands. The gardens must be tended and the ale brewed and bread baked, all at cost of wages.'

Geoffrey is proud of what he has built but this long speech has left him struggling to catch his breath.

'Are you unwell?'

The Abbot shakes his head. 'It's nothing. I seem to tire more quickly - just the long winter.' He smiles at me. 'You don't need to be concerned. I have no fever.'

We leave the garden, shutting the gate behind us.

'You are not permitted to enter the sleeping huts, or the chapel,' Geoffrey says, 'but Master Ilbert says he will show you the bakehouse.'

I have been curious to visit the hospital for a long time. It took a time to persuade Geoffrey to countermand the rule and allow a woman to enter the precincts. Now that I am here, he seems glad to show me what has been achieved.

We walk towards a building that must be newly completed, the soil here streaked with stone dust. I look around, hoping to catch sight of one of the leprous brothers. But there is no-one to be seen save for a priest dressed in black, hurrying along the path towards the chapel, just visible in the distance.

As soon as we enter, I am hit by a wave of heat and the enticing smell of baking bread. Master Ilbert is waiting. He is a tall, lean man with a bulbous head that seems too big for his frame.

'Welcome, Prioress,' he says, and bows to Geoffrey in the customary way.

He leads us through the bakehouse, past a couple of trestles laden with wooden troughs.

'This is where the dough is kneaded,' Master Ilbert explains, 'but the bread for today is already baked.'

He moves on to the two dome-shaped brick ovens. A young lad wielding a long peel turns from his task of depositing loaves on the floor of the oven. He is red-faced from the heat, his apron smeared with dough. We move on to another trestle, covered with bread, cooling on iron racks. I am struck by how many of the loaves are white.

'Are these for the priests?' I ask.

Geoffrey shakes his head. 'Each leper is allowed seven loaves a week: two coarse maslin and five white. The

349

manchet flour is thought to be better for their weak constitution.'

One of the bakers, a man with a pot belly, tests the temperature of the cooling bread. He carries the rack over to the door, emptying the white loaves into a great basket which stands beside it.

'I am glad the brothers are treated with such generosity,' I say.

Geoffrey is gratified but I am struck by how pale he looks, even in the heat of the bakehouse. He stumbles a little as we follow Master Ilbert towards the door.

'You should leave now, my lady,' Ilbert says. 'It will soon be time for Mass.'

'Do the afflicted brothers hear Mass?'

'Yes. They will be leaving their cells soon to walk to chapel.'

The door of the bakehouse opens and a figure appears in the threshold, dressed in a tunic and cowl made of coarse reddish-brown cloth, his hood up. My heart gives a jump – this must be one of the lepers if he is wearing russet. My eyes dart to his hands but they are covered by the long sleeves of his tunic. The man seems dismayed at finding me here and averts his head.

Master Ilbert steps forward. 'This is Brother John, come to fetch the bread for the brothers. He is not permitted to enter but only to take the basket and return it empty.' He turns to me to explain. 'A leprous man may not touch anything used to make food for the undefiled. Bread is baked here for all the community, for the priests and such.'

The brother keeps his silence. How can he endure to be spoken about in this way? Before he turned his head, I caught sight of a nose, misshapen and pockmarked. Yet there is something about his bearing that tells me he is a man of some breeding. Geoffrey greets Brother John with the Abbot's blessing, but he keeps well back.

The leper bends to heave the basket onto his shoulder and though his sleeves are fastened at the wrist, they fall back a little to reveal his hands. Some of his fingers are missing. A thrill of pity and of awe passes through me. Lepers are to be envied, for they suffer the pains of purgatory here on earth and go straight to heaven when they die. If I could only have that surety.

On impulse, I step forward and catch hold of his tunic with my hand. 'You are truly blessed, Brother John.'

He shudders and pulls away from me with a desperate force. At the same moment, Master Ilbert steps between us. 'He is not permitted contact with a woman, my lady.'

Without a word, the afflicted man turns his back and leaves the bakehouse, the heavy basket of bread on his shoulder.

Abbot Geoffrey came to fetch me in the covered wagon this morning and now he is to accompany me as I return to the Priory. The road is tolerably dry and we trundle along it at a good pace. I can think of nothing but the lepers and Master Ilbert.

'It must be a joy to care for those whose suffering is so holy. And to share in that suffering.'

'To share in it?' Geoffrey asks.

'It must be a burden to be surrounded by such ugliness, day after day.'

Geoffrey smiles grimly. 'Ilbert knows that he is doing the will of God, and doing the Abbey a great service. The prayers of a leper have especial efficacy. I have commanded that they pray every day for the Abbey, without fail.'

351

I am disappointed. Why must everything boil down to a cold calculation? Can nothing be done only for beauty or for love?

'I thought you had acted from pure compassion for your fellow men.'

He sighs and the old arrogance creeps back into his voice. 'You are responsible only for a handful of women. You do not understand my position.' He leans forward, his eyes darker than ever against the pallor of his skin. 'I have also commanded that they pray for my own health. It eases my fear.'

His words sting, like a rebuke. 'Why so fearful for your health, my lord Abbot? You know that I hold you always before God, and my maidens with me. As you say, the fever has not returned these many years.'

He does not reply but only leans back against the wooden frame of the wagon and closes his eyes, as if I were no longer worthy of his notice. His manner incenses me and I cannot hold my tongue.

'And why, too, are the lepers so circumscribed? Don't they have tender human feelings, as we do? Master Ilbert spoke about that poor man as if he were a beast, deaf and dumb. And you couldn't bring yourself to speak to him at all.'

Geoffrey jumps to the bait. 'How dare you take me to task?' He is having trouble catching his breath. 'I pay Ilbert from my own purse to shelter them and feed them and bind up their wounds.'

'You do, Abbot, you do. But the Good Samaritan tended the afflicted man in the gutter with his own hands first. You seem unwilling to touch the brothers.'

Anger has brought the colour back into Geoffrey's face and

now, when he searches for a retort, the words will not come, but only a spluttering sound. He has started to tremble and I watch him, appalled. I see panic begin to gather in his eyes.

I reach for his hand. 'What is it? I was wrong to rile you – forgive me.'

The red is fading from his face and droplets of sweat are breaking out on his forehead.

'I can't breathe,' he gasps. His hand is on his chest. 'Here… a pressing…'

Frightened, I call out for the man driving the wagon to stop. 'Turn around and take us back to the hospital, quick as you can.'

Geoffrey shakes his head. 'No – no! The Abbey.'

Why, oh why does it take so long? The distance is not far. The horses seems agonizingly slow and all I can do is watch him, slumped forward, grimly silent in his struggle for each breath. If only I had not angered him. *Mary, Mother of God, have mercy. Mary, Mother of God, have mercy.* We cross the river on the new bridge and at last the tower of the Abbey comes into view.

'The Great Gate, my lord?' the driver calls out.

Geoffrey shakes his head.

'The Orchard Gate, for the Infirmary,' I shout back.

As the wagon rattles along the rutted road between rows of bare apple trees, I sense a lessening in his pain. We draw up at the door of the Infirmary and now the words seem to come more easily to him.

'Help me out, Christina.'

'Can you walk, my lord?'

'I think so, it is passing.'

When the Infirmarian's boy sees the Abbot leaning on my

arm, so pale, the sweat on his forehead, he looks aghast.

'Go and fetch your master, now.'

Father Ralph makes as much haste as he can, though he is not so steady on his feet these days. He takes one look at Geoffrey and turns to me, without any proper greeting.

'Does he have chest pain?'

'Yes, and he cannot get his breath.'

The Infirmarian calls for the assistant and together they help the Abbot onto the nearest bed, rather against his will.

'It's nothing,' he protests. 'The tightness has all but left me.'

Father Ralph doesn't answer. He has his thumb on Geoffrey's wrist. 'You need to make water for me,' he says to the Abbot, and sends his assistant for a flask. He instructs the boy to fetch the Prior.

'There is no need to call him,' Geoffrey complains.

The flask is brought and only now Father Ralph remembers my presence.

'I must ask you to go.'

The Abbot pushes himself up on his elbows. 'I wish her to stay close by. You will not gainsay me.'

Father Ralph holds the back of his hand against Geoffrey's forehead.

'You see? I have no fever,' says Geoffrey.

'Perhaps you would wait in the chapel, Prioress.' Father Ralph's voice is cold.

I bow my head in agreement and take one more look at the Abbot. His face is regaining a good colour. He looks almost his usual self again, just a little puffiness perhaps, in his cheeks.

'There is no call to be anxious,' he says. 'When the sickness comes, it gives me pain in my knees and my ankles but, see,

I was able to walk. Now go and pray. The Lord may reveal something to you.'

A troubling thought has been hovering about my mind ever since Geoffrey was taken ill. The Infirmarian has shown me precious little in way of welcome but I pluck up the courage to speak.

'Father Ralph, the Abbot has just now come from the hospital – from the lepers …. But he did not touch them.'

He purses his lips. 'This is no defilement, Lady Christina, but rather a weakness ….' He seems about to go on but then refrains. 'Go now to the chapel, I pray you.'

The Infirmary chapel is empty and the weak winter daylight filtering through the narrow windows does little to dispel the darkness. The candles on the altar table give off a sweet honey smell that seems at odds with the terror in my heart. It was one of these dark days of winter when I was summoned to the Abbey, to my ailing brother. Since Gregory's death, the Abbey Infirmary cannot be anything but a place of dread for me.

I drop to my knees on the cold stone of the floor and try to lift the Abbot up in prayer but guilt is jabbing, pricking at my thoughts without mercy. I have brought this sickness on him. Why did I see fit to anger him? Uncushioned against the hard floor, my knees are flaming with pain, fitting penance for one whose soul is eternally stained. The old sense of shame gathers around me in the dim light of the chapel, a pernicious miasma. And now the shame seems to spiral downwards to become a quagmire, slowly but surely sucking the life from me.

Icy damp is creeping up from the floor into my knees and spreading through my body. I wrap my cloak around me but there is no warmth in the material, no comfort that can melt away this despair. I am growing old and have no more strength. All at once, I feel that I can't run any more from the fearsome phantom that has stalked me through the years. Deep in my heart, I feel a movement, a turning to face my pursuer, to surrender. A fierce desire is overtaking me - to declare my sin at last, even if it spells the end of everything.

There is no-one in the chapel, no confessor to hear me, but I can't keep the truth inside any longer. I whisper the words out to God himself, as the psalmist did, and my voice sounds alien to me, and terrible.

*Lord, in my youth I sinned with a man. All these years, I have treasured the memory of it and sinned again and again, in my thoughts. Even now, my heart and my body stir when I remember him. I have made a mockery of everything.*

I think of the years of privation and contempt, all endured for nothing. My beloved Roger – who taught me so faithfully. He saw God in me but he was mistaken.

*I have kept my sin close to me, loving it and petting it like a lap dog. I should rather have flung it from me like a loathsome serpent.*

The tears are flowing now as I think of my companions, of Abbot Geoffrey. They think me pure and beyond reproach. They do not know what I am.

*In your mercy, you gave me a task – to watch out for the soul of this abbot and protect him with my prayers. Why else would you reveal your secrets to me again and again? But I have failed, even in this. Instead of saving him from sickness, I have brought it upon him.*

I drink the wine of degradation to the dregs. The cup is empty. And I find that in the emptiness, there is a kind of peace. Deep within me, I feel the old, gentle stirring that I have not felt for so long, as it were the wings of the Spirit of God, fluttering.

I have opened my heart to God and now answering words form on my lips without thought, as if they have not come from my mind but from a truer place in my soul.

*Have no fear. Your anguish will soon be over.*

I kneel upright, my back straight, scarcely daring to breathe for fear the words and the stillness that gave birth to them will vanish. But the air in the chapel seems to have undergone a change. Now it seems infused with hope, the honey scent of the beeswax no longer a cruel taunt but a blessing.

Perhaps the Abbot is not going to die, despite the grave face of the Infirmarian. Geoffrey was right – he has no fever, no aching in his joints. This is not the old sickness he fears. Only a weakness, as Father Ralph said.

*Mary, Mother of God, protect him and give him strength. Raise him up to full health once again. May he not die, Lord. In your mercy, may he wax strong and live.*

I wait, searching my soul for assurance. There are no words, no thoughts, but the calm presence and benediction remain and seem to grow stronger, moment by moment.

Behind me, the door opens and a servant comes in. He goes to the altar and sets about trimming the wicks of the candles, which have begun to smoke. I struggle to my feet and leave him to his task.

Father Ralph is sitting beside the Abbot's bed. I am relieved to see that Geoffrey is sleeping, but perhaps he is just resting for he hears my footsteps and opens his eyes. I see the question in them. He sits up in bed.

I sign myself with the cross. 'When I pray, I have an

assurance that all will be well,' I say.

Geoffrey lets out his breath in a sigh and I see his shoulders relax back against the bolster. He turns to the Infirmarian.

'I will rest a little longer and then I'll get up from my bed.' He puts his hand up to stop the protest that Father Ralph is beginning to make. 'You heard the Prioress.'

'I think it would be wise to wait, my lord Abbot,' the Infirmarian says. 'You are feeling stronger now, but …'

'I am,' Geoffrey replies. 'And don't you remember when I was taken sick before? Both times, it was revealed to Lady Christina that I would recover, and I did so. Now, Father Ralph, I bid you take the Prioress to the chamber I had built for Henry's queen. I want her to stay at the Abbey for the time being. And have someone ride to the Priory to tell them.'

Father Ralph seems discomfited at this. Nevertheless, he calls for his assistant to make the necessary arrangements.

I bow to Geoffrey but, in front of the Infirmarian and his assistant, I do not take his hand as I would wish to.

'I will return before Vespers to see how you are,' I say, 'if you permit it.'

He nods. 'Of course.'

The Queen's chamber, as they call it, is well-appointed. And once a fire has been lit in the hearth, the chill in the air begins to dissipate. I find myself tired and lie down on the bed, wrapping the fur around me.

I wake to a knocking on the chamber door. Outside, the light is fading.

'Come in.'

It is Father Thomas and I am overjoyed to see the face of a friend in this Abbey that holds out a cold face to me. I push back the cover and swing my feet to the ground. Father Thomas approaches and now I see that he is agitated. More than that, he is shaking.

'Prioress, you must leave, now. I have arranged a litter. Come quickly.'

I stare at him, uncomprehending. 'Abbot Geoffrey wishes me to stay.'

Thomas bites his lip. 'The Abbot has suffered an apoplexy, my lady. He cannot speak. The Prior has charge of the Abbey now and he wants you to leave. I am sorry.'

A surge of bitter fluid rises from my throat into my mouth. *An apoplexy.* What does it mean? Why has the Prior taken charge?

Father Thomas helps me up. 'There is nothing to be done. You must go now.'

I wrap my cloak around me and he leads me down the staircase, along the passage and out into the courtyard by the Great Gate. The clouds are grey and heavy, weighing down on us as I climb into the litter.

Dear Father Thomas blesses me. 'Take heart, my lady, you can intercede for him as well from the Priory as from here. Perhaps his speech may return – it is wont to do so in these cases.'

My eyes fill with tears at his kindness.

The riders before and aft the litter mount, but they have not yet commanded the horses to walk when a boy comes running across the courtyard, crying something. I cannot make out the words.

Monks are running from every corner. Now comes a strident clanging from the bell tower above. Bells further in the distance begin to ring.

'The Abbot,' Father Thomas whispers. 'The Abbot is dead.'

# Chapter 36

*Priory of Holy Trinity de bosco*

*Thirteenth day of March, AD 1146*

Kneeling on the earth floor, I hear footsteps outside my cell. My body, already tender and aching, twitches with fear. Now I hear the whispering – it's only the women. I close my eyes and forget them but they do not go away: instead comes a knocking on the door. I dragged myself to the church for Sext earlier. Can't they leave me alone now to do battle?

'What is it?'

'My lady, we would speak with you.'

Adelaisa. And someone else with her. Grasping the wooden bed frame for support, I pull myself up and walk unsteadily to the door. Tiny stars seem to burst in all directions in the space behind my eyes. I open the door to a gust of wind: the Fiend himself confounding me with his icy breath.

Emmy is holding back, a step behind Adelaisa. They enter and I close the door quickly behind them, then drop once more to my knees, my face to the wall. Don't they know that I must be at prayer? It is Lent, the time of darkness, of looming death. I may be overtaken at any moment, as the Abbot was.

'My lady.' It is Adela's voice, behind me. 'You didn't come to dinner again. Won't you take some nourishment?'

I do not trouble myself to answer. What is food to me now? There is a rustle of wool and Emmy stands by the bed, her brown eyes wide and glistening.

'We are concerned for your health, my lady. When my mother died, you said I should not let grief overwhelm me.'

I look up into her face. Grief? Do they think what troubles me is only grief?

Now Adela accosts me from the other side. 'Prioress, you are not strong and we are afraid that your old maladies will return. It has become known in the village that you are refusing food since Abbot Geoffrey died.' She pauses to swallow. 'Evil tongues are beginning to wag …'

I look down to the floor, wearied. Doesn't she know that it's the Abbey that counts, not Caddington? And what do I care for either when the spectre of an unshriven death stalks me without mercy?

Before I can summon the words to answer them, there comes a fresh knocking at the door, more urgent this time. Irritation invigorates me and I pull myself up once again. Lettice is at the door. She looks past Adela and makes her curtsey to me.

'I beg your pardon, my lady.' She is out of breath. 'A messenger has come from the Abbey, from Father Thomas.'

'Father Thomas?' *Praise be to God!* I feel the blood begin to surge again in my veins. To have him hear my confession – and be rid of this burden, at long last. A lantern of hope in this valley of the shadow of death.

Adela instructs Lettice. 'Have him shown to my lady's parlour.'

'No!' I smooth down my tunic. 'I will see him here – now.'

The women exchange a look but etiquette is no longer of any consequence to me. When Lettice returns, she shows the messenger into my cell. It is the boy who does Father Thomas's bidding, Wulf, his untrimmed red hair straggled by the wind. He bows to the others, then to me.

'Father Thomas is to come today?' I ask. 'Or tomorrow, perhaps?'

He shakes his head. Reaching inside his riding cloak, he takes out a letter and hands it to me, the figure of St Alban on the seal. I am puzzled; Father Thomas has never written to me before. Wulf glances uncertainly at Ada and Emmy. He keeps his voice low.

'My master asks that you tell no-one he has sent it.'

I break open the seal there and then, my fingers trembling, and begin to unfold the parchment.

As if from some far-away place, I hear Adela telling the boy to go to the kitchen and wait there. The letter is written in an unsteady hand – clearly in haste, with no regard for the niceties.

*Father Thomas to Prioress Christina*

*I may no longer come to you to say Mass – no brother is to visit from the Abbey. The*

*Prior has forbidden it. A priest will be sent from Caddington. Believe me that this*

*grieves me deeply.*

*Ever your humble servant in Christ,*

*Thomas*

*Alas, the book of your life is to be abandoned*

Blackness seems to close in. I feel my legs buckle under me and now Emmy is helping me onto the bed.

'Run and fetch some wine, quickly.'

A burst of cold air and Adelaisa is gone. Pushing against the fog in my head, I try to grasp what this means. The Prior has no love or regard for us here – is he to be Abbot now? What will become of us? There are no answers, only the one cold truth. *Thomas is not coming.*

Emmy is beside me on the bed. She reaches out for my hand and there is such devotion in the way she looks at me, it pierces my soul. I cling to the love in her eyes and, as I gaze, their chestnut colour seems to fade to a dove grey. At the same time, to my inner vision the grey of her habit gathers colour till it becomes the blue of a summer sky. Perhaps I have fainted away, for now it seems to me that she lays her head in my lap, as the great Lady did in my vision, so long ago. She lies there, still as a sleeping child, and a deep peace falls upon me. So deep that when the knowledge of what I must do comes to me, as unwelcome as the cautering iron to close a wound, I do not shrink back but receive it and bear the pain.

Adela returns and holds the cup to my lips. I drink a little and revive. I must act now before pride gets the better of me.

'Fetch the boy – I want him to take a message.'

'Wulf is in the kitchen – I'll go and get him,' says Emmy.

'No! Not Wulf. He can return to the Abbey.'

Adelaisa looks at me as if I have lost my senses again. 'Do you not wish to give him a message for Father Thomas, my lady?'

'No. Wulf may return. But someone must ride to Leofric, now, this moment. Leofric will know where to find her.'

Another of those looks between my companions.

'Who do you mean, my lady?' Emmy asks. 'What is the message?'

'Ask him where Alfwen is. He must take me to her.'

'Alfwen?'

I could strike Adelaisa – she is being so obtuse. And then I remember that these women never knew the anchoress. A terrible thought comes to me. Perhaps she is dead - she must certainly be very old.

'Leofric will know. Have the message sent, now.' I struggle to my feet and begin to search for my shoes. 'I am hungry. Fetch me some bread and whey.'

*The road to Wilden*

*Palm Sunday, twenty-fourth day of March, AD 1146*

We rode through a village before noon and saw people carrying willow branches to the church. It made me think of my nuns, back at the Priory. The priest will come from Caddington today to bless the branches and to say Mass. I remember Adelaisa's face when I told her that I must make this journey – now, even with Easter approaching. *You will go on horseback? What about your hip?* There was horror on her face when she saw the rough tunic and cloak I had put on for travelling. She doesn't understand.

Leofric rides ahead when the track narrows under the trees and I notice how little hair he has left. He has grown wiry and strong over the years but he is still the innocent man I knew in those days with Roger; there is no guile in him. It pains me that he keeps a respectful distance between us. I see in his eyes that he feels a Prioress to be above him, in rank and in holiness. If only he knew the reason for my journey, he would think differently.

I am grateful that he agreed to take me to Wilden, where it seems that Alfwen is living out her dotage, cared for by another recluse. The journey was too long for me to ride in a day, so we stayed at Moddry last night, at Ralph's hermitage. I sat amongst them - simple friends of God such as those who hid me in my youth and cared for me – and I couldn't hold back the tears. In his unschooled way, Leofric made me as comfortable as he could in Ralph's rough dwelling and it put me in mind of his devotion to Acio, in those years before the old man died.

God has been merciful to us - there has been no rain for the last week - so Leofric is able to lead the horses across the river at Tamiseford, while the ferryman takes me in his boat. I let my hand fall over the side, thinking how this very water under my fingers will flow, in time, under the bridge at Huntingdon. Riding today in the flat valley of the Great Ouse, its fields yellowed with early cowslips, listening to the whistle of the redshanks, I could have been a child again, playing with Matilda in the hay meadows.

As the day wears on, the sun comes out from behind the clouds. I remember the heat on my head that other day, so long ago, when I rode through the wilderness with another unlettered man. How did that pure child become a Prioress - a gilded vessel, esteemed but full of corruption?

'Only a mile or two now, my lady.'

We have passed through yet another tiny hamlet and now

I ride abreast of Leofric. Our track runs close to a brook, lined with black poplars, the crimson catkins hanging like tassels from the bare branches. My hip is aching cruelly and my back too, but as we come close to Wilden, the prospect of humbling myself before Alfwen crowds out everything else. How will she receive me, after all these years? I try to picture her face: the scar on her cheek where she fell in the fire as a child, those eyes that pierced my soul. She saw my weakness when Roger did not. If he had known the corruption that was to stain my soul, he would never have left the hermitage to me.

I try to divert my thoughts from the encounter to come.

'Who does Alfwen bide with?'

'A recluse named Gytha,' Leofric replies. 'She tries to keep the crowds away.'

'Crowds?'

'Since Alfwen came back from Wulfric, people come all the time to consult with her.'

I draw in my breath. 'She was with the hermit - with Wulfric? They say that King Stephen rides to Haselbury to be advised by him.'

'And the last king before him. It was Wulfric who foretold Henry's death.'

We ride on without more speech, but I am disturbed by Leofric's words. The Alfwen I remember was not esteemed: just a simple, unlettered woman living as an anchoress. With every thud of the horses' hooves, my discomfort grows.

Scattered dwellings begin to appear and now a little wooden bridge over the brook. A young lad stands on the bridge, a pail of water in either hand, staring after us. The church appears, a way off, but when we come alongside it, I see no sign of an anchorhold.

Leofric points to a small dwelling, set in the burial ground close by. 'That is where they live, my lady. They pray for the souls of the dead.'

He dismounts and helps me to do the same, then taking the reins of both horses, he walks them towards the cottage. I follow him stiffly, my thighs aflame with pain. Sheep are cropping the grass in between the crosses and stones.

There is a hitching post in the yard outside the house and Leofric ties the horses with a long tether, so that they can graze. Then he goes to the door and calls out to announce our presence. I stand beside him, my knees trembling. A woman emerges and Leofric greets her with a blessing. She is of middle height, and the hair framing her pale face is lank and greasy. She is perhaps the age of Adelaisa but I can tell from her hands that she is low-born. Leofric indicates me with his hand.

'This is Prioress Christina. She is from St Albans way and wishes to consult with Alfwen.'

The woman's eyes take in my rough travelling cloak. Drying her hands on the cloth she is holding, she makes her curtsey to me. 'You have brought a gift?' she asks.

I am mortified. I did not think to bring anything with me. But Leofric seems discomfited as well. 'The Prioress knew Alfwen many years ago, Gytha. They lodged together at Flamstead.'

A blush of colour rises up the woman's neck and she nods to me. 'You are welcome. I will tell Alfwen you have come.'

She goes in and Leofric squats down on the ground, leaning back against the door of the cow-byre. He seems quite at ease until he notices my look. It is many years since I have been left standing, unattended.

'She won't be long,' he says. 'No doubt we will be offered a place to rest and refreshment.'

He is right. Gytha comes out to us shortly and we follow her into a simple room with a hearth in the middle, in the peasant way. The smoke catches in my throat but I am glad to sit on the stool that is offered and take a drink of ale. There are oat cakes on a griddle above the fire and Gytha unwraps a muslin of soft cheese. Leofric sets to with pleasure but I cannot eat anything. My whole body feels tight and there is a lump in my throat. Why have I come here? It is nigh on a score and ten years since I saw Alfwen. She will not remember me – or the insufferable things I said to her. I think of her steady gaze, her calm, that day when she told me I must leave.

The door to the inner room opens and there she stands, leaning on a stick, so small and bent that I would have to stoop to look into her face. I get to my feet, uncertain how to greet her. She blesses Leofric, then turns to me and lifts her head, with difficulty, to meet my eyes. The same Alfwen: the livid scar a little smoother or perhaps it is just that age has wrinkled her other cheek so that it shows the less. Yet she is not the same. A light seems to shine through her, as if her body were merely a lantern made of parchment. Her movements are slow now but the eyes still glint and shift in the firelight with the fleetness of a bird. The good half of her mouth breaks open in a welcoming smile and I see that her teeth are almost all gone.

'Theodora -you have come at last! Blessings on you.'

'Christina,' I murmur, but it seems that Alfwen's hearing is as sharp as ever.

369

'Nay,' she laughs, delighted. 'You are Theodora to me - God's gift. Come in and bide with me a while,' she says in her northern way.

I glance back at Leofric, then follow her into the inner room. It is very small, space for a bed, a chair and little else. Though not so smoke-filled, the air is tainted with the smell of unwashed flesh.

She points under the bed and I fetch out a stool. The only place to sit is close beside her chair. I take a deep breath.

'Mother, it is many years and perhaps you do not know how things have changed with me. I was with Roger until he died ...'

Alfwen waves her hand for me to stop and, instead, reaches out and takes me by the chin, bringing my face closer to the candle so that she can scan me. She seems intent, animated.

'God be praised!' she says at last. 'I have prayed every day that you would come. Now he has brought you, I can make my confession.'

I can only gape at her. She takes both my hands in hers, her fingers cold against mine. 'He made everything clear to me. I did not see it but he made it clear.'

Hope begins to die in me. She is crazed, perhaps. 'What are you saying, Mother? I don't understand you.'

'Blessed Wulfric showed me my own soul,' she says. 'I saw sin in all around me because I would not see it in myself. Remember our Lord's saying about the log and the splinter? I was wrong about you and Roger's companion – what was his name?'

'Ulfwine,' I murmur.

'That was it. Ulfwine. I judged you, when all the time your heart was pure. Can you forgive me?'

370

'No!' I cry, not caring that the others will hear through the flimsy wall. 'You don't know – you don't understand. It is I who have come to you ….'

I drop onto my knees beside Alfwen's chair. 'Mother, hear my confession, I beg you.'

She says nothing, just peers down at me in surprise: a simple, childlike waiting.

The years seem to roll back and I am no longer Prioress but the young girl she knew, with no position in the world: eager to please and not be found wanting.

'I have sinned grievously and I have hidden it in my heart and I have taken of the body of our Saviour unworthily.'

I unburden myself, spewing out the poison, though sometimes I have to tear the words from inside me, such is the shame of it. I keep nothing back: Athelwulf - the sinful touching, every fond memory of it over the years, every longing and vile imagination, each time I have kept the truth from a priest, from Abbot Geoffrey.

'The Abbot trusted me, Mother, and I deceived him – that's why my prayers for him were in vain. I took pride in my seeing - I was sure he would live, but he died, and the fault is mine.'

Alfwen says nothing, just fixes me with that look of unwavering clarity.

'You knew - you saw truly the corruption in my heart. You were the only one.'

My cheeks are wet and I wipe them with the back of my hand but still the tears flow. 'It was all I ever wanted – to wear the crown of chastity - and now everything is lost.'

I reach out and grasp the old woman by her sleeve. What do I care if she is not a priest? 'Mother, give me a penance, I

371

beg you. Tell me this stain can be washed away.'

Alfwen sighs and places her hand on my head in blessing. I wait and wait, holding my breath, but nothing comes. It seems she has no answer for me. She is hunched over in her chair. Her eyes are open but I do not think she sees me or the hovel that shelters us. More than ever, the body of the old woman appears insubstantial, a delicate shell housing the vital life within. I get up from the floor, uncertain of what to do but she stirs and calls me back. I sit down beside her once more on the stool and she takes my hand.

'Tell me about your sister,' she says.

I stare at her. 'Matilda? She has a husband and children, in Huntingdon.'

Alfwen gazes at me, as if waiting for me to continue.

'You mean Margaret? My sister Margaret is dead,' I say, and something in my chest twists in pain. 'She was truly pure.'

'Is that so, child?'

'Yes – you never met her. There was nothing but goodness in her. If only I could be as she was.'

She fixes me with those birdlike eyes. 'Truly I say to you, you are your sister's sister.'

I peer back at the old woman. What is she saying? She looks away, her eyes closed, as if straining to hear something. I listen but there is nothing - only the sound of Gytha moving about in the outer room. She turns back to me.

'And your mother and your father? What of them?'

I look down into my lap. Why is she asking me these things?

'I don't waste my time on those who oppose God. We are enjoined not to cast our pearls before swine,' I answer. 'You know how my parents misused me. Don't you remember? I had to run from their cruelty.'

The old woman's shoulders begin to move and, to my astonishment, I realize that she is chuckling.

'Truly I say to you, you are your parents' daughter.'

I gasp at her words then feel myself bristling at what seems to be their meaning. But Alfwen shakes her head as if to silence any rejoinder. She strokes my hand with her cold fingers, again and again, as one might soothe a fractious child.

She says no more and closes her eyes once again but her words from before seem to fill the tiny, sour-smelling room. *I saw sin in all those around me, because I would not see it in myself.*

Is she saying that I am unyielding like my father? Cruel, like my mother? I wince, thinking of how I exposed Godit's sin before all the others at table. Of that day at the Abbey, after Gregory died, when I would not comfort my parents in their grief. A wave of self-pity overwhelms me. I have come to lighten the burden of my great sin, and all she does is add weight to it.

As if the workings of my heart are laid bare to Alfwen, she opens her eyes and speaks.

'You long to be pure, Christina?'

'More than anything, Mother,' I reply. 'But it's too late. The crown is lost to me, now and forever.'

'Nay, Child,' she says, and again she begins to chuckle. 'You and your high-flown talk. You are mistaken. How can the crown be lost when it's within you? It's all within you. The darkness and the light, the sin and the holiness, growing up together like the wheat and the tares.'

She sighs a great sigh and leans back in her chair.

'Gytha will soon dig a hole here for my body, but I'm not afraid. The Lord has already shown me my soul and I see that there is good in it and there is evil. Like all of his creatures – leastways those born of Adam and Eve. The evil will be burnt away by the light of his presence and he will harvest me to himself in love.'

Gazing at Alfwen, it seems to me that what she says is true – that she already has one foot in the kingdom of heaven. But then she has lived a blameless life since she was a child.

'Everything I touch becomes defiled.' The words burst out of me, sour and full of pain, like the bitterness of vomit. 'The Abbey has abandoned me - I withheld the truth from the Abbot and now he has died and it is because of me.'

Alfwen's head is resting against the back of her chair, her eyes fixed on the door with its simple wooden latch.

'Is that so?' she asks. 'All our times are in the merciful hands of the Lord. They were written long before the world was made.'

She looks at me now, with a wry smile. 'Long before Theodora of Huntingdon was born.'

I hear the rebuke. But when she goes on there is concern in her voice.

'Are you fearful for your house? Do you depend on the Abbey for your living?'

For the first time since Geoffrey died, I feel able to think calmly, not confounded by waves of shame and sadness.

'Perhaps we might get by. The land belongs to St Pauls, not to the Abbey. We have other benefactors.'

Alfwen nods, satisfied, then cocks her head again, as if listening. Whatever it is she is hearing has come as a surprise.

'It seems to me that your friendship with the Abbey is not lost forever. You must be patient.'

'But I can't go on, Mother. All my life I have longed to be

worthy.' The abyss inside me seems to open up once more, threatening to pull me down, down to oblivion. My strength is failing - I can only whisper. 'I am not like my sister. There is no good in me.'

'Is that so?' she asks again. 'You are a Prioress. You have souls in your charge. Don't they love you?'

Emmy's face comes to my mind, her eyes shining with recognition as I speak of the things of the Spirit. I remember all the times I sat with Matilda when she came from France, her heart breaking with sickness for her home.

Again, Alfwen seems to know what I am thinking. 'So – return and serve them. All will be well. Now, help me up, child. I must go to piss.'

I stand up and give her my arm to grasp. It is a long time since I felt laughter rising like this, unencumbered. She may have sat at the feet of Wulfric of Haselbury but she is the same Alfwen.

'What? Does a Prioress not have to piss?' she asks.

Gytha is bending over the fire in the outer room, stirring a pot, and the sweet smell of onions makes me realize how hungry I am. She straightens up.

'You and Leofric will sup with us? And I can make up two more cots.' She looks embarrassed. 'It is not what you are used to.'

Alfwen has returned from the privy and stands in the doorway. 'Don't fuss, Gytha. She knows what it is to sleep with the crawlers.'

I smile. 'Yes. I remember.'

## Next morning

The sun has been up some time and Leofric has returned from the brook with a pail and he is watering the horses. Gytha is busying herself with the fire. I know that if we stayed a few days longer I could make her trust me, but as it is she says very little. Alfwen did not eat bread with us at dawn and I don't like to disturb her at her prayers; she never could abide that. Still, I cannot bear to leave without wishing her farewell. In truth, I do not want to go at all, but I must.

Leofric is ready now and I hover uncertainly. It is strange how, in this simple cottage, I feel myself once again a young girl. It is a relief when we hear Alfwen calling from the inner room.

'Gytha? Has she gone?'

I go to the door and open it. Again, the stale air hits me. She is kneeling by her bed.

'Come here, Child, help me up,' she says, and I am astonished to find that there are tears on her cheeks. I never saw her weep in all the time we were together. Once settled in her chair, she takes my hand.

'You have suffered - I felt it in my prayers and I feel it now. Ever since you were a bairn, you have been pining for something, something you don't have. The Lord says it's time to stop pining. What you long for is already here - it's inside you. Didn't Roger teach you that?'

As if too tired to speak any more, she waves me away. I bend and kiss the top of her head.

Outside, Leofric helps me mount my horse and waving goodbye to Gytha, we ride back to the track. All through the woods, I can think of nothing but standing in the old chapel beside Roger, deep in contemplation. Could it be that he was seeing clearly when he saw holiness in me? For the first time in many years, the words that Roger used to quote come back into my mind. *Enter eagerly into the treasure house that is within you and you will see the things that are in heaven.*

Leofric is riding ahead and at the fork in the road he turns his horse's head for home. I call to him and he comes trotting back.

'I've changed my mind. There is somewhere else I must go before we journey back to the Priory.'

He looks at me, puzzled.

'That is, if you are willing to take me. I would like to visit my parents in Huntingdon.'

# Epilogue

'And how were you received by our new Pope Adrian?' I ask.

'Very well, I'm relieved to say.'

Abbot Robert smiles and I am struck, once again, by how much he resembles his uncle at the same age. I think of that first time Abbot Geoffrey came to the hermitage and pulled back his hood: the curtain of dark hair, the piked eye teeth. Robert has the same hair and eyes – almost black – but he is more fleshy and different in his character: softer somehow, without the constant watchfulness.

'He has granted privileges to St Albans and promises of more to come.'

I nod, gratified on his behalf. 'No doubt the Pope has fond memories of his time at the Abbey school when he was a child.'

Robert purses his lips in a wry smile. 'But not of being refused entry to the Abbey to train as a priest. Abbot Paul must have had his reasons – he was not to know Nicholas would rise to become the first English Pope.'

The Abbot leans back with a sigh. 'Rome is a wonderful place but it is good to be home and to ride in the shady English woods.'

He looks tired and weatherbeaten, and I ask after his health.

'I am recovered now, Christina, but I was taken with the flux on the way back, while we were at court in Rouen.'

'You should not have troubled yourself to come here so soon.'

Now his face lights up. 'Ah, but I could not wait to tell you something.'

I look at him, with interest.

'King Henry sent gifts with us, for the Pope - a great chest of money, and gold and silver, and three precious copes. But he would accept none of it. He would receive only a few of the things we offered him.'

I can feel my cheeks become hot.

'Yes. It was your beautiful work that pleased him: the mitres and, especially, the sandals.'

His words are like sweet spiced wine; they fill me with a quiet pleasure. I think of the long days of last summer, when I broidered those sandals – for the Abbot to wear on high feast days, or so I planned. The design came to me in a dream and it was satisfying to see how the verdulet and the gallant red complimented one another perfectly. When Robert asked if he could take them to Rome, it seemed fitting.

He sits there now, his face alight, glad that he has pleased me, and I think how if I had a son, this is what it would be like between us. Sometimes he even calls me Mother. He gets to his feet, yawning and stretching. It is good that, with me, he can put down the heavy yoke of authority he carries.

'I should go.'

'So soon? But I won't keep you from your duty. I am glad to see you returned safe and sound. I prayed for you.'

Robert knows how difficult it is to rise from my chair so he comes to me and takes my hand in farewell.

'Do you have any more news for me?' I ask. 'What kind of court does this new king keep? I remember the first Henry, his grandfather.'

The Abbot straightens up and starts to put on his riding gloves.

'He is not a man for pomp and show - I think he would rather be hunting than holding court. But he is vigorous and has accomplished much already, with his chancellor, Thomas. He has a foul temper so we are learning to tread softly around him.'

Robert turns to go, then remembers something. 'Henry has a soft heart, though. I was with him when news came of the death of his confessor - the Bishop of Carlisle. I could swear there were tears in the King's eyes.'

*The Bishop of Carlisle.* 'Athelwulf is dead?' I ask, my heart beating fast.

'Yes – he has been sick for some time.'

The Abbot sees my face. 'You knew him, I think?'

'Yes,' I reply. 'He was once very dear to me.'

It seems to me as if Robert is going to ask more but then he changes his mind and just nods.

'Farewell, my lady. No - don't get up. I will try to come again soon.'

It is a warm day. The sun's rays filter through the window of my parlour and it is delightful to sit and remember the man I loved, the tears rolling silently down my cheeks. We could not belong to one another but every moment we shared has become a precious jewel, reflecting the light of God.

When Godit comes to tell me that my niece is here with her daughter, she sees that I have been crying and hurries across.

'Is it the pain again, my lady? I can fetch some more of the tincture of rue.'

'Oh no. I don't know which is worse – the pain in my hip or the remedy.'

She looks blank for an instant but then sees that I am jesting. Godit never was fleet of thought. I wonder, though, at how she has grown in God over the years. Of all my nuns Godit is still the most irritating but it is she who rushes to help me into chapel.

'Shall I say you cannot see your niece and her daughter?'

I wipe my face with the back of my hand. 'No – no. I look forward so much to their visits.'

Averil is a winsome young girl, full of laughter, but with a wilful streak. She reminds me of her grandmother, my sister Tilda, when she was young. It is a mystery why she likes to ride down with her mother to see me when she could be playing with her friends.

'But you are in pain, my lady. I see it in your face.'

I shift a little in my chair. 'No, Godit. The hip is quiet and, God be praised, I have much to be thankful for. The arthetica has spared my fingers at least. Tell Alice and Averil to come in.'

She turns to go but I call her back.

'What is it?' she asks.

I cannot resist the urge to crow. 'Here is something wonderful for you, Godit. The Head of all the Church in

Rome wears sandals that I embroidered here, in this very room. Think of that!'

Her eyes are incredulous but then a smile spreads across her plain face. 'I have never seen needlework so fine as yours, my lady.'

I take her hand and plant a kiss on the back of it.

# Afterword

Almost all of what is known about Christina comes from the incomplete Latin *vita* or saint's life composed about her during her lifetime. It was written by a monk of St Albans, possibly at the request of Geoffrey de Gorron, Abbot of St Albans from 1119 to 1146, and seems to have been abandoned around the time of his death. A fourteenth-century version of this text was edited and translated into English in 1959, under the name *The Life of Christina of Markyate: A Twelfth-Century Recluse*. The village of Markyate is not mentioned in the novel because it grew up after Christina's time, along the great Roman road, Watling Street, close to the woods where Roger had built his hermitage. In Christina's time, the hermitage was situated some three miles from the nearest village, Caddington. When the Priory was built on its site, it was dedicated to the Holy Trinity and was usually referred to as the Priory of the Holy Trinity in the woods (*de bosco*).

The account of Christina's life conforms, in part, to the formulaic style known as hagiography, designed to present the subject as a candidate for sainthood and therefore not always accurate in a historical sense. However, the *Life of Christina* is unusual in that it was composed during her own lifetime and contains a wealth of personal detail that could only have come from Christina herself and perhaps members of her family and community.

Certainly, many of the characters who play a part in the *Life* and also in the novel are historical figures and, in the case of some, their involvement with Christina is independently verified. Christina's father, Auti, appears in records as a wealthy Anglo-Saxon merchant. Her sister, Margaret, and her brother, Gregory, appear in the records as nun and monk, respectively, of the Priory in the Woods and St Albans Abbey. Their aunt, Alveva, was known to have been a mistress of Ranulf Flambard, the Bishop of Durham, and to have borne him children. Roger of Markyate is described in contemporary documents as a hermit with a reputation for great sanctity, whose body was buried at St Albans Abbey after his death and from that point on, Archbishop Thurstan of York is known to have helped Christina at several points in her life.

Abbot Geoffrey did steer an uneasy political course during the period of civil war known as the Anarchy (1135 to 1153), supporting first Matilda, then Stephen in their bids to succeed to the English throne after the death of Henry I. He is also known to have founded a leper hospital, dedicated to St Julian, just outside St Albans. Geoffrey's close relationship with Christina is noted in the records of St Albans Abbey, together with the ambivalent reactions it caused within the monastic community. It appears that there was a faction within St Albans which resented the attention lavished by the Abbot on the Priory in the Woods. There was probably also gossip about exactly what sort of relationship Geoffrey enjoyed with Christina. There is some suggestion in the monastic records that some of Geoffrey's actions as Abbot were deliberately reversed following his death.

Whatever occurred with regard to the Priory following Abbot Geoffrey's death in 1146, it appears that by 1155, when Geoffrey's nephew Robert became Abbot, Christina was once again on good terms with St Albans. Items embroidered by her were among gifts presented to Pope Adrian IV by a delegation from St Albans.

We know that Christina lived on until at least 1155 but the account of her life breaks off while describing her situation during the 1140s, so events in the novel from that time onward are imagined. There is no historical evidence that the anchoress Alfwen spent time with Wulfric of Haselbury in Somerset, though he was a contemporary anchorite priest with a significant reputation for holiness. He was consulted by King Stephen and correctly prophesied the unexpected death of Henry 1 just before it occurred. There is also no evidence that Christina and Alfwen met in later life and were reconciled, as described in the novel.

Earlier parts of the novel, informed by the *Life* of Christina, have also been imaginatively interpreted. There is no evidence that the body of Roger of Markyate was forcibly taken to St Albans to be buried there against the will of his community, but it was not unknown for monastic communities in the Middle Ages to steal the remains of saintly figures in order to have them interred in their own churches, thereby attracting pilgrims and the revenue that went with them.

The St Albans Psalter was probably produced in the scriptorium at St Albans Abbey. Although it is not known exactly when the different elements of the beautifully illustrated manuscript were composed and how it came to be associated with Christina, there seems no doubt that it did come into her possession. A calendar attached to the psalter has the birth and death dates of Roger, as well as those of some of Christina's relations and friends, marked on it. In the novel, the psalter comes into Christina's hands from Roger, who was renowned enough to have been gifted such a beautiful book. The later additions could well have been commissioned by Abbot Geoffrey to mark significant moments in Christina's life and that of the Priory.

There is no reference in the *Life* to tension in the relationship between Christina and her sister Margaret but the writer does suggest that Christina could be imperious and difficult. It seems to have been understood by those who knew her that, like the false flax plant known as gold of pleasure, she required careful handling. Again, there are hints in the text that Christina's relocation from Alfwen's cell to Roger's hermitage may have been caused by a rift between Alfwen and Christina, though the reason for the move is never specified.

The Latin account of Christina's life withholds the name of the man in whose house Christina was hidden after the death of Roger, though the writer stipulates that he was a close friend of Archbishop Thurstan and was a cleric who also held a position of secular power. In the *Life*, this man is described as becoming infatuated with Christina, even appearing before her naked in an attempt to seduce her. The text makes no bones about recording that Christina returned his passion, although appropriately for a book designed to suggest the sanctity of its subject, she battles successfully against the temptation to succumb to his advances. In the world of the novel, the unnamed cleric is based on the historical character of Athelwulf, or Athelwold, a protégé of Archbishop Thurstan who was both a Prior and the confessor and adviser of Henry 1, but there is absolutely no evidence to support the idea that he was, in fact, the man who excited such feelings in Christina.

There are still subtle physical traces left of the life of Christina of Markyate and those to whom she was close. The Priory in the Woods, where Christina was probably buried, was suppressed in 1537 as part of Henry VIII's dissolution of the monasteries. A manor house named Markyate Cell was built around 1539 on grounds which had belonged to the Priory and the house, now known as Cell Park, was remodelled and extended in subsequent centuries. Part of Roger of Markyate's tomb is still visible in the south wall of the nave aisle in what is now St Albans Cathedral. The psalter Christina used has been preserved. It was taken by fugitive English Benedictine monks to Lower Saxony in the 1640s, when they were granted permission to rebuild a monastery at Lamspringe. From there it was transferred to Hildesheim in 1803 and is now owned by the parish of St Godehard and kept in the Cathedral Library. The Psalter, one of the most important examples of English Romanesque book production, was digitised and made available to view online free of charge in 2003 (https://www.abdn.ac.uk/stalbanspsalter/) as part of a project funded by the Arts and Humanities Research Board and Aberdeen University.

For Talbot's English translation of the medieval biography of Christina, edited by Samuel Fanous and Henrietta Leyser, see *The Life of Christina of Markyate* (2009). For more in-depth discussion of Christina, her life and context, see Joanna Royle's PhD thesis, *Transitional holiness in the twelfth century : the social and spiritual identity of Domina Christina of Markyate*

(2008), available here http://theses.gla.ac.uk/id/eprint/891 and *Christina of Markyate: a twelfth-century holy woman* (2004), edited by Fanous and Leyser.

# About the Author

Ruth Smith, writing fiction under her birth name – Ruth Mohrman - has a PhD in Medieval English and lives in the Welsh countryside close to the border with England. She has always been drawn to mysticism and has a lifelong fascination with the past, so it is perhaps not surprising that the two come together in her writing. *Gold of Pleasure* is the second novel she has written. The first, *On the Nose of the Antelope*, tells the story of Ansa, a young woman destined to play an important role in the band of Paleolithic people among whom she lives. It will be published in 2022. Ruth's articles on literature and spirituality can be found on Medium.

**You can connect with me on:**
🅵 https://fb.me/ruthmohrman
🔗 https://medium.com/@ruthsmith453

Lightning Source UK Ltd.
Milton Keynes UK
UKHW041353290321
381184UK00005B/1527

9 781838 196509